D0031489

OUT THERE

INTO THE QUEER NEW YONDER

Books edited by Saundra Mitchell
available from Inkyard Press

All Out: The No-Longer-Secret Stories of Queer Teens throughout the Ages
Out Now: Queer We Go Again!
Out There: Into the Queer New Yonder

OUT THERE

EDITED BY
SAUNDRA MITCHELL

FEATURING STORIES FROM:

UGOCHI M. AGOAWIKE

K. ANCRUM

KALYNN BAYRON

Z BREWER

MASON DEAVER

ALECHIA DOW

Z.R. ELLOR

LEAH JOHNSON

NAOMI KANAKIA

CLAIRE KANN

ALEX LONDON

JIM McCARTHY

ABDI NAZEMIAN

EMMA K. OHLAND

ADAM SASS

MATO J. STEGER

NITA TYNDALL

inkyard PRESS

Recycling programs
for this product may
not exist in your area.

ISBN-13: 978-1-335-42589-8

Inkyard Press
22 Adelaide St. West, 41st Floor
Toronto, Ontario M5H 4E3, Canada
www.InkyardPress.com

Printed in U.S.A.

CONTENTS

THIS ANTHOLOGY IS FOR

Ugochi M. Agoawike, Dahlia Adler, K. Ancrum,
Kalynn Bayron, Fox Benwell, Tanya Boteju, Z Brewer, Mason Deaver,
Alechia Dow, Z.R. Ellor, Sara Farizan, Tessa Gratton, Kate Hart,
Shaun David Hutchinson, Kosoko Jackson, Leah Johnson,
Naomi Kanakia, Claire Kann, Kody Keplinger, Will Kostakis, CB Lee,
Mackenzi Lee, Malinda Lo, Katherine Locke, Alex London,
Nilah Magruder, Jim McCarthy, Anna-Marie McLemore,
Tehlor Kay Mejia, Hillary Monahan, Cam Montgomery,
Abdi Nazemian, Emma K. Ohland, Mark Oshiro, Natalie C. Parker,
Caleb Roehrig, Meredith Russo, Alex Sanchez, Adam Sass,
Kate Scelsa, Eliot Schrefer, Tess Sharpe, Tara Sim, Mato J. Steger,
Robin Talley, Scott Tracey, Nita Tyndall, Jessica Verdi, Elliot Wake,
and Julian Winters.

Thank you for going all out with me.

DOUBLERS

Alex London

I DIDN'T SEND MY CONSCIOUSNESS TO BE reborn on Mars because I thought you would fall in love with me again. I think you should know that. Whatever we do next, I want you to know that. I did a lot of things because I thought you would fall in love with me, but not this.

Remember in soccer, when I twisted my ankle slide-tackling you, even though I had no clue how to slide tackle? That wasn't because of my deep commitment to my team's defense. That was so that you'd notice me. So that our limbs could tangle as our bodies fell; so we'd taste the same cut grass in our mouths and our sweat might mix across our skin.

So, yeah. Joining the school soccer league? Totally about you falling for me and, literally, on me. Beaming my disembodied consciousness to another planet? That was something else.

I didn't send my consciousness to be reborn on Mars because I thought you would fall in love with me again, but when I open my eyes in the regeneration room, there you are, sitting by the slab, and I think you're holding my hand. My muscles are stiff, but I look down, and sure enough, that feeling in my hand is your hand holding it.

Except, of course, it is not your hand and it is not my hand, at least, not that I recognize them. They're both bigger and there's a silvery tint to the skin, undertones of copper and gold, with crackly lines running through like on old pottery. The feeling's unfamiliar too, duller but also clearer, like my nerves work differently than they did on Earth.

You squeeze and the signal fires up my arm, through my shoulder and into my brain. I actually feel it happen and there is a moment where I know I can decide *how* to feel the squeeze. Is it affection? Does it hurt? Do I choose to feel it at all?

This is super strange.

"It's super strange, right?" you say, your thoughts echoing mine. For a moment, I think *holy shit, you're psychic now?* But I know that's not how the process works; that's just how *we* work. You always knew what I was thinking at the same time I knew. It's why we were such a good couple…until we weren't. "The rebuilt nervous system is slow to wake up," you tell me. "And it's designed to give you more control over it than you had on Earth. Helps manage some of what we have to do here. We're all assigned pretty physical jobs."

I remember something about this from the orientation video they made me watch before the Upload procedure. Our consciousness would be converted into data and broadcast on a tight beam to a server on Mars. There, it would then be downloaded into a body grown on Mars by our contract holder, to specifications for thriving in an environment that is hostile to human bodies.

The lungs work differently because of the atmosphere; the eyes, skin, and bones too. Everything that Earth biology spent millennia evolving had been redeveloped and repurposed for life on humanity's new home. If indeed we are still humanity and not just, like, human-adjacent beings.

Sort of how our phones stopped really being phones eighty years ago, but we just kept calling them that. Most of them are rings or watches or implants now and nobody actually "calls" each other.

So yeah, I guess we're still human. We're just an expanded definition of it.

I realize now, this isn't my own idea. It's something you once told me, and it came from an essay you read for class. I never read a single one of the essays we were assigned. Probably why my grades were crap.

Though, if I'm being honest, my grades were crap because I spent more time staring at the back of your neck than I did listening to the lesson modules.

"What are you doing here?" I ask you, and my voice comes out weird. I suppose it's the first time these vocal cords have been used. How long had this body been in storage before I was downloaded into it? How long ago had my signal been broadcast from Earth? Was I already dead down there?

I didn't send my consciousness to be reborn on Mars because I thought you would fall in love with me again. I know that's impossible after how we broke up, after the things you said to me and I said back, but when you see me walking through the vacant lot behind the southeast solar farm, I take a grim satisfaction in how you shoot up to your feet like you're gonna run, then go network error still, like a game frozen midsequence.

"What are you doing here?" you ask me, your voice coming out strained.

And you thought I couldn't surprise you anymore. I believe that's one of the last things you said to me when we broke up, remember?

Nothing surprises me anymore, you told me. *Not school, or work, or games, or even you. Everything's like a tram on a track, moving along the same route, over and over and over. I need something new.* Someone *new. Maybe a lot of someones.*

I remember that pretty clearly. You basically dumped me to sleep around, which, sure, I get it. We're young and discovering all the different things our bodies can feel and make someone else feel and yeah, okay, I'm shy about that stuff, but our relationship was more than our bodies. It hurt me a lot more that you wanted to be with other people romantically, to have real relationships with people who weren't me. I'd have liked it better if you just cheated on me in secret.

Except no, I wouldn't have. I wanted you to still want me, but I also didn't want to change.

I remember that you told me: "You're too cynical."

You were crying. That was rich. I was getting my heart broken, but you were the one crying.

"Sorry," you said, wiping your eyes. "Lacrimae rerum."

You always did that, dropped in quotes and sayings, and sometimes they weren't even in English. People thought it made you deep and intellectual. I used to. I was so impressed by how impressed everyone else was. Dating you made me feel smarter, so being dumped by you felt like failing an exam.

I didn't realize that remembering trivia is not a personality. At the time, it seemed like one, at least, one that was better than mine. I guess I was using how people saw you as a way to like myself more. Obviously, it didn't work.

"It's Latin," you told me, though I hadn't asked. "It's from Virgil. A brokenhearted Aeneas tells the sad tale of the fall of Troy and weeps for the world and its suffering."

"So I'm a city in ruins and you're the noble survivor?" I scoffed. I had the urge to punch you. I admit it. I wanted to hit you but also to let you throw me down and ravage me like barbarians sacking an ancient city. Or was it the Greeks? I don't know history. I just knew I wanted your hands on me, one more time, hard. Like with the slide tackle. Something about making you hurt me turned me on.

I probably need therapy. You always said I did. Of course, my mental health is no longer your problem. You don't get to have an opinion or your hands on me anymore. Not in this life.

But you still weren't done dumping me. Remember?

"Disliking things isn't a personality," you said, mirroring my own thoughts about you, though the mirror had a jagged edge. "I'm sad for you"

"I dislike things that suck," I explained. "Ocean acidification. Water speculation. The *Star Wars*-Dickens Crossover Universe."

"That's what I mean!" you told me. "The SWDU isn't even out yet and you've decided it sucks. I'm tired of it. I want to be excited about things. I want the thrill of potential. I need optimism in my life."

"I'm optimistic about us," I told you.

You snorted, like a laugh and snort at the same time. Is that a chortle? You *chortled* at me. "That's one thing you *shouldn't* be optimistic about," you said. "We're done."

And then you walked away. You even left me with the bill for two teas and an untouched scone, even though your family is loaded and mine's on public income. I used to think it was nice how you didn't let your family's money be a thing between us, but acting like it didn't matter was actually bullshit. I understood I had to pay for the scone—I'd ordered before I realized what our conversation was going to be—but you didn't need to make me buy your rosemary pepper tea. That was just cruel.

Also, who orders rosemary pepper tea?

Still, I shouldn't have done what I did next, outing you to the marketing software like that. I apologize. The technology makes destroying each other too easy. I updated one little link on my profile, one little status change, and boom, suddenly all the ads that popped up in *your* life were gay, gay gay.

It was only a matter of hours before your grandma turned on the TV with you in the room and saw what the system was selling you. She knew that the marketing never made mistakes. She probably knew about you before then, but it's one thing to suspect, and another to see it right there on the screen in half-naked rainbow-lit discount prices.

Obviously, I knew how she would feel about it. She was one of the last people on the planet who ate those chicken sandwiches. I'd been offended by the ads the algorithm showed her for as long as we were together. I guess it was time to return the favor, give her a taste of her own marketing.

Did you know I did it on purpose? Of course you did.

I'm curious, is that why you decided to do the Upload? Was it to get away from your family's judgment, to find freedom someplace they couldn't follow? Or did they push you to do it, thinking it'd be better if you had a new life on Mars, away from them? Away from me?

I ask, but to be honest, I don't care about the answer. You made your choice. You dumped me; I hurt you; you signed up.

We were never supposed to see each other again.

Except here you are, standing stunned in the firelight below a bridge past the shantytown, looking as gorgeous as ever.

I admit, for a moment, I don't want to hurt you. I want to take your hand gently in mine and run away with you, both of us on the road, always moving, from haven to haven, hiding out from the scanners and the hunters, and looking up at the night sky together, daydreaming about what the two of us might be up to on Mars.

But the moment passes.

"You know why I'm here," I tell you, because that old trick still works. You know me as well as I know myself.

"You're here to kill me," you say.

I shake my head and remind you, "You're already dead."

I didn't send my consciousness to be reborn on Mars because I thought you would fall in love with me again, but you help me sit up on the slab and find my footing in the lower gravity.

Our new bodies have more mass, so we still stick down to

the ground like on Earth, but it takes a bit to recalibrate the brain. We're in no rush.

"Of all the gin joints…" you say, quoting a movie neither of us has actually seen, but I laugh, because you're not really referencing an old movie; you're referencing us, all the other times you said that to me. "It's not a coincidence you're here, huh?"

"No," I tell you.

I look out the open window onto the rocky fields of Mars. The clouds are low, yellowy-pink and grey. They remind me of the sickly storm that was drifting in the day I went for the Upload.

My ears buzzed, I was so nervous. No one ever talked about the procedure hurting, but I still worried. I never liked needles and didn't have any tattoos. I remember them warning me that yes, there would be some pain.

"Pain is a part of life," they said. "We need to record your responses to it. Pleasure too."

They showed me pictures of us together from public surveillance. They showed images that were real and deep fakes of us together, of you with other people, of me with other people. Of me as a child. Of my parents. Bits of movies I like. Bits of movies I hate. "The process is content-agnostic," they explained. "We measure physiological response and synaptic connections. Your memories and emotions are the by-product of those reactions. We record and transmit the phenomena, not the by-product."

Can you believe that? The technology to transfer human consciousness to bodies on Mars treats human consciousness as a by-product, like toxic sludge from a refinery. I'm shocked it works.

When my dads were teenagers, it took eight months to get to Mars from Earth. A massive amount of energy was burned just to get out of Earth's orbit, and they had to haul everything they needed with them. Once on Mars, the people had to live and work in sealed pods and could only go outside in intense spacesuits that carried their own atmosphere inside them. A puncture in the suit could be fatal. A puncture in one of the habitats was catastrophic.

The Upload solved that problem by converting us into data and transmitting in minutes more settlers than they could've previously done in generations.

Those first settlers established labs to engineer the new bodies in, set up receiving stations, built a whole system of competing settlement corporations to download humanity's settlers and put them to work on labor contracts.

Genetic engineered and biohacking made life on Mars possible. Contract capitalism made it thrive. Now there are open windows.

The view of the red dust mountains and gleaming new buildings makes me think of sci-fi novels I read in middle school. Humanity builds its daydreams, and we marvel when they become real, as if there was any other source for reality. At some point, all this was a fantasy. It was never *my* fantasy. Not until you.

"So it's not a coincidence you're here," you say. "You signed a contract?"

"I did," I tell you.

These better bodies have a cost.

Of course you chose one of the most expensive Upload services. Your new body is stunning and strange, and I suppose mine is too, now. You wouldn't believe what I had to agree to in order to pay for this Upload. Then again, what I had to agree to was the whole point of doing it. I could've chosen any service. I chose the one you used.

I need your help crossing the room. You support me as you lead me to the supply locker like you once led me to the toilet at Safaa Nargasian's party. Remember that?

I'd had one too many hits from two too many vape pens, and turned a seriously awful color. You know when you feel your face changing color and don't need a mirror to tell? Shame does that, and so does puking. I had both about to burst out, and you took me by the arm and led me to the toilet, and rested your hand on my back while I hurled.

"It's okay," you told me. "Our bodies teach us what we need to know. They don't want to hurt us."

I loved that, the tenderness of it. Yes, it was a lie; our bodies hurt us all the time, but as far as lies go, it was a nice one.

So I gave up vaping because of you. That wasn't the last thing you taught me about my body. Even right then, that night, you taught me more. You handed me a towel to wipe my face, gave me a little spritz of the mouthwash you always had on you, and then, after a far-too-brief interim since I puked, you kissed me. Even with the mouthwash, it was a bold choice. Once you decided on something, you did tend to go all the way with it.

Safaa's bathroom was still decorated like when they were little and loved Disney. Characters from *Fro10* and *Toy Story 22* stared down at me when I went down on you. It was super awkward—I'd never done that before—and we both started laughing. We never actually finished the dirty deed (thankfully... I was still totally inexperienced and didn't want you to know). We just laid on the floor and looked up at the characters and talked about Disney trivia until Safaa pounded on the door to make us go home.

Until the day I went for the Upload, people thought we'd had sex in Safaa's bathroom. I never told them otherwise. I assume they still think it now.

I can't believe I feel like myself, remember things that I remember. I'm me and you're you, and we're here. On Mars. But if I remember everything, then so do you. So I ask you now, "What are *you* doing here to meet me? It's not a coincidence either."

You laugh, a real one, not a chortle. "You gave me the push I needed to Upload," you say. "And it's the best choice I ever made. When I heard you were coming, I volunteered to greet you. They were going to send a stranger, but you deserve better than that."

"No, I don't," I admit, surprised that I don't feel my color changing. Do these bodies not blush or do I just not know how it feels when they do? Shame still exists here, I notice. It hitched a ride with me, a parasite of memory, and it'll settle in the universe wherever people like me settle, people who keep secrets.

"We're on a new world!" You grin as you guide me to the door. "Try to relax. Let's leave our old baggage in the old orbits."

I realize I can just do that. I can just let my shame go. I don't *have* to feel it. I don't have to feel anything. I can decide.

Yeah, these new brains are pretty cool.

It's a fine line between forgiveness and amnesia. The cynic in me thinks you've crossed too far into forgetting instead of forgiving, but it's starting to feel really nice to have your hands guiding me, even though they are not the hands I remember. Your voice isn't even the voice you had on Earth, and yet it is undeniably yours. I take it as a good sign that we still know each other in our new forms, a sign that life here isn't so much a break with the past, as a fork in it. All we had to do was say goodbye to our families, give up our bodies, and agree our lives on Earth were over.

Not everyone agrees so easily. Some people can't let go, can't achieve escape velocity from their old orbits. I'm counting on that, in fact.

"I'm still sorry for what happened with your family," I tell you. "For what I did."

"I owe you some tea," you tell me, and just like that, we have our first date on Mars.

"You're paying," I reply, enjoying a real, genuine laugh with you.

"So, why did you come?" you ask. "You'd always been opposed to the Upload."

I wish I didn't have to lie to you on our very first date on a new world.

I didn't send my consciousness to be reborn on Mars because I thought you would fall in love with me again, though I admit, I did do it to find you. It wasn't that hard. There were only so many places a teenage fugitive could hide, and we'd been here before. I expected surprise and maybe some fear, but you regain your cool so quick it startles me.

"Come have a tea with me," you suggest, like we're on one of our dates. Always tea with you. I guess I can admit now that I don't really like tea. It's basically just thin soup people use as an excuse for conversation. I only ever drank it to spend time with you.

"Sure," I say. "We've got time."

There are others around; they eye me suspiciously. Everyone has face tattoos, wild patterns of lines and waves, barcode and QR grids and nonsense squiggles. It's all to trick the face-scanning software. Your face is unmarked, and you're wearing a floppy hat that doesn't suit you. I can't help but notice the lean-to beside you—a tattoo pen rests on a steel barrel. In the shadow, someone grunts. They're getting work done.

"It's not my turn yet," you say. "Anyway, it's nice to see you."

You sound glad I'm here, which throws me. You shouldn't be glad, right? I shouldn't have been able to find you. I shouldn't even know you're alive. If you're upset, you don't show it.

Back when we were together, I loved how you had this adaptability, like any crap that came your way was just an unplanned delight. You can twist your attitude like a blade. Are you doing that now, turning that invisible blade just in case I've come with a real one?

I have, of course. I don't go anywhere without a blade, and haven't for a while.

Remember when we took that long walk by this solar farm and those three jackers rolled up on us with their home-print guns? I never had anything worth stealing, but they took your phone and made you unlock the password by putting a gun to my head. I'd been jumped before, so I knew they probably wouldn't kill me, but you were so sincere in your worry, you didn't just unlock your phone for them, you told them about the credit in each of your gaming apps, and when you saw one had a MageScroll Ultra tattoo, you told him about a great side-quest hack. By the end of the mugging, they gave you your phone back (after draining the accounts), and apologized for "the whole gun to the head thing." You had that way with people. Disarming charm, literally.

"Be careful out here," they told you. "Bad sorts around. Doublers and the like. They'll kill pretty boys like you two for sport."

They left you grinning.

"What?" I asked. "What are you smiling about?"

"They called my boyfriend *pretty*," you said, wrapping your arm around me, pulling me to you. You smelled like dryer sheets and a little bit of sweat. Your breath had a tang of rosemary on it. You kissed my forehead and added, "I couldn't agree more."

I tended to stay the realist, and I suggested we get out of there, back to more populated areas. "I don't think they were lying about the Doublers."

"Of course they weren't lying," you said. "Why would they lie?"

"So let's go!" I urged. I'd never seen a Doubler outside the news or the movies, and I didn't care to.

"They can't be all that bad," you told me. "They're just people. Aren't you curious?"

"About Doublers?" I shook my head. "No."

You looked disappointed in me, like my lack of curiosity was an attack on you. We'd just been mugged, and I still had the metallic adrenaline taste in the back of my mouth and wanted to sit in some air-conditioning and calm down, but I hated disappointing you. You never understood how your beauty combined with your endless optimism was a kind of an aggression. It made people want to please you, even against their own better judgment. At least, that's what it did to me. It overrode my will, rewrote the code that ran my life. You were a hacker, without touching a screen.

"I mean, I'm more curious about how pretty you think I am," I tried, hoping a little flirting would deflect the moment, but you were undeterred.

"Let's go see," you suggested, and started walking below the solar arrays, whistling some song, trying to make yourself conspicuous.

You assumed they'd come out and find you, right? You'd always been rich and smart and handsome, so you assumed people always wanted to meet you. You were the center of any room you entered, even when you weren't. There was no world you could imagine where a bunch of Doublers hiding out in a solar field would not want to meet you.

After forty minutes, when no one showed themselves, you took me up on my offer to go back to the shopping center and make out in the tea shop. I could tell the whole time that you blamed me, like the Doublers didn't reveal themselves because of my doubts. I felt like the kid who ruins Christmas by not believing in Santa Claus.

But the Doublers didn't stay in hiding because of me. They

stayed in hiding because they are criminals, and we were, at that point, still living citizens with a duty to report them.

You thought they were *so* romantic.

I thought they were idiots.

Doublers are legally non-people. Anyone who Uploads but avoids termination of their Earth body is a double consciousness fugitive. They're marked for summary execution. The system doesn't allow for two of the same person, one on Earth, one on Mars. The whole point is to ease the burden on Earth's resources while populating Mars. Most Upload centers eliminate the Earth body the moment the data upload is complete, but it's a privatized system; there are always flaws. Mistakes, escapees, filing errors, bribery. Any system that people can create, other people can find a way to game. It's a law of the world as constant as gravity. Maybe more constant.

There are always news stories about Doublers who become rapists and serial killers, Doublers who steal or spread disease, Doublers who, quite simply, become monsters. Books and movies too.

One, about a woman who stays with her husband after he turns Doubler, was banned, but everyone saw it anyway. They say the book was better than the movie, but the concept didn't feel realistic to me. How could you love someone who abandoned you on a decaying planet and was, at that moment, living a brand-new, prosperous life on Mars?

You loved the movie. I should've known.

"It's only unrealistic because the stories we choose to believe create our reality," you said. "We are what we pretend to be."

"Okay, that's Vonnegut," I told you. I'd found your quoting endearing when we'd first started dating, but over time, I felt like it became my duty to keep you honest or maybe just to remind myself that you weren't smarter than me; you just had more time to read. I had a job.

"True things belong to all humanity," you said.

"So do lies," I answered. It was one of our dumber arguments, for being totally philosophical. Also, as far as I knew, neither of us had ever read Vonnegut. I bet you picked up that quote up from your grandma. She loved all those dead white authors, even the ones who probably would find her worldviews abhorrent. My dads weren't really readers, unless you counted star charts.

I'm sidetracked. Memory's like that. Open one door and find a dozen others to walk through. I guess that's how the Upload works too. With the right equipment, once someone's talking, feeling, their synapses light up. Scientists can clone a body from the tiniest bit of DNA, as long as they have the right cells. I guess they can reproduce a mind from a memory, as long as they find the right one.

We take a seat on some old crates, acting like it's just another date at the tea house, though I can feel the watchful eyes of a dozen Doublers from this little encampment on us, wondering about me. They're right to be wary of strangers, but I'm not here for any of them. I'm only here for you.

"I just have peppermint," you apologize, which is a relief to me. "And no cookies to go with it."

"Well then I'm out of here," I joke. I feel a moment of vertigo; the crate spins under me, and I fear I might topple off it. I smell something sour, and my vision goes white for a fraction of second, like I'm looking directly at the sun. Then

I see double, my own hands echoed in front of my face, my tongue circling two sets of my own chapped lips.

"Relax," you say. "Take a breath. That happens sometimes. It passes."

I regain myself.

Some people say that Doublers dream their double lives and it drives them mad, but I'd been a Doubler for a few days now and all I've dreamed about was finding you. I try not to think about the other me up on Mars, because he wasn't why I did the Upload. Wondering about another life was enough to make you crazy in this one, but I still couldn't help imagining him up there, Reborn Red, as they say, with a new sense of optimism, making new memories and having new experiences that I'd never know about down here. The moment the Upload finished, our paths diverged. For all I knew, he hadn't even been put into a body yet. For all I knew, he wouldn't be for another hundred years. It didn't matter. His life was not my life and mine was not his.

Though mine wasn't mine anymore either.

Down here, I couldn't visit my parents, or see old friends. I had a new ID and a tracking device under my skin. That was the price of the Upload. I couldn't pay the fee, but I could work it off. Up there, I'd be assigned a job as they saw fit, and down here, I would be trained and unleashed as a Disposal Agent.

My job was to track and destroy Doublers, and as long as I did the work, I got to keep going. If anything happened to me in the process, so be it. According to the law, I was already dead anyway. And the moment I strayed from my work, I'd be just another Doubler myself, and another Disposal Agent would eventually take me down. It was an elegant system; I had been recycled and put to new use.

You, on the other hand, had simply run.

I watch your eyes in the flame light while you watch the pot and wait for water to boil.

Contrary to the saying, it doesn't take that long.

"You didn't tell me why you're here," you say as the tea steeps.

"You guessed it though," I say.

"No, I guessed *what* you're doing here. Disposing of me. But you didn't tell me *why*."

It annoys me how observant you are. I also love it. I see you see me chewing my lip and I stop.

"Do you want me to forgive you?" you ask. "You should know that I didn't Upload because of what you did. You need to know that. Or even because of how my family reacted."

"So why'd you do it?"

You smile at me. "I told you when we broke up."

"You wanted something new."

"Everything," you reply. "I wanted *everything* new. A new life, here and there. I wanted to feel things I hadn't felt before and see things I hadn't seen and be someone I hadn't been."

"Are you?"

"Someone I hadn't been?"

I nod.

"Not down here." You shake your head. "Turns out, we always are what we always were."

"That's a Sondheim lyric," I tell you. "*Company.* 1970."

"I love how you never let me get away with my bullshit." You're leaning into me so we're practically sharing a breath, and we look up at the sky together while the tea steeps. I can just make out the gleam of the Red Planet up there, nestled in a sea of white stars.

"You think we found each other up there too?" you ask.

"You think we're looking?" I reply.

You shrug. "If you need my forgiveness, you've got it," you say. "For what you did and for what you're doing now."

"I didn't come here for forgiveness," I tell you. "And I don't actually want any tea."

It felt good to tell the truth one last time.

The tea on Mars is synthetic, just like our bodies, made from little pods and superheated elements, also, I suppose, just like our bodies. It tastes like rust, but I find I love the flavor. I drink it too fast and order another from the little screen at our outdoor cafe.

It's wild to be sitting outdoors on Mars, breathing the air or whatever it is, and feeling the different way the sun hits our skin. I try to look back at Earth from the sky, but I've no idea where it is. I wonder if I've done what I set out to do down there. I hope so. I really do.

"I have to know why you came," you tell me.

"After you left, I thought about everything you'd said to me," I tell you, which is true enough. The lie comes next. "I realized that I hadn't been excited about something for a long time, and maybe, coming here, I could find that excitement again."

"So I was your inspiration?" you ask with a pleased sideways smile that is so unmistakably you, I forget for a moment that I'm not looking at your old face. You don't look like you and yet you look one hundred percent like yourself. I guess our consciousness can transform our bodies the way a house is transformed by the ghosts that haunt it.

What do you see when you look at me? Do you see what's haunting me?

"I was your inspiration too," I reply, "so I guess it's fitting. But I didn't expect to actually find you up here."

"Didn't expect to, or didn't think about it at all?" you ask, and my new skin feels like a window; you're looking right through me, like always. I could deny it or I could laugh it off or I could say something cruel. I suppose those are options in any conversation anywhere in the universe. I go with honesty. Something about drinking tea with the re-bodied consciousness of my ex-boyfriend on Mars calls me toward truthfulness.

"I didn't think about it," I confirm. "I didn't think about what anything would be like up here, in fact."

"It's not up anymore," you tell me. "In fact, right now, Earth is up." You point toward the sky, but I don't see much through the gas clouds.

"Whatever." I shrug off your correction. I decide to be charmed by it, the way I used to be charmed by everything you did. Funny how that's a choice. I like making it. I make it some more. "The thing is, I didn't Upload to come to Mars and start a new life. This is just a by-product."

You raise your eyebrows and cock your head. It's a performance of curiosity, deliberate and contrived, but it gives me permission to go on without waiting for you to ask me anything.

"You went Doubler," I tell you. "Did you know you were gonna do that when you had the Upload?"

You set your teacup down slowly, and your hand shakes a little so that the thin metal cup rattles against its saucer. No bone china up here. The sound of metal on metal is grating.

You knew. I can see that.

The thing about the Upload is that the last memories our new selves have are from the Upload interview itself, before we're unhooked from the machines. No memories after that go to Mars. You won't remember the exit counseling, or your execution, or if you escaped. If you planned to get away, you won't even know if it was successful. For all you know, you've been dead on Earth for ages.

Me, I know where I am, because I decided ahead of time.

I know where you are too. I know you bribed your way out and ran. That's why I did the Upload in the first place. I wanted to be sent after you. I wanted to be the one to hunt for you.

"You're down there hunting for me, aren't you?"

Damn, you know me well.

"It's not down anymore," I remind you and take a sip of tea.

"I didn't send my consciousness to be reborn on Mars because I thought you would fall in love with me again," I tell you. "Or so that you could absolve me."

"So it's revenge?" you ask, as calmly as if you were asking whether or not it was going to rain next week. "You gave away your life here just to get revenge for getting dumped?"

"Wrong again," I say, thrilled that for once you don't know what's driving me, and you don't know what I'm going to do. It's exhilarating and, I realize, totally new. It turns out, even in this same old rotten world, I can feel something new.

"Okay, I'm lost," you add, to my total joy. I can't help smiling.

"We were really great together when we were great together," I remind you, and you nod, because, as you say, the truth belongs to all of us. "I think someone else should get that chance. I was jealous, but I'm not anymore. Loving you and being loved by you was a gift, and I think it needs to be shared."

You frown, absolutely confused, as I reach over the boiling teapot and grab your hand to hold it gently. I squeeze your fingers and you squeeze mine back, puzzled.

You're even more puzzled when I jab your index finger with a needle to collect your blood.

"For the DNA match," I say. "I'm going to report that you have been disposed. They'll figure out it's a lie, but you'll have more time to get away." I glance at the dark lean-to behind us. "Get some of those face tattoos. Maybe you'll find someone to share whatever time you carve out with. Maybe it'll be like that movie you loved so much."

"You loved it too," you say, squeezing your finger to stop the little bead of blood from dripping. "I saw you cry."

"Lacrimae rerum," I quote you quoting Virgil as I pop the needle into my phone's attachment. There's a delay while the app confirms. We've got some time. They'll send a team to collect me, debrief me, and then, once they've realized I lied and let you go, dispose of me. It doesn't much matter what happens to me here. I accept that.

I assume I'm alive in some new body on Mars, or that I

will be soon, working in a water reclamation plant or whatever the corporation up there needs me to do. To be honest, I wasn't paying much attention during the orientation video. I was too focused on this moment, on finding you, hunting you down before someone else did, and then…surprising you.

That's the thing you never understood about me. Sure, I was cynical, but I loved you for real, and I knew you were better than me. I thought you'd bring out the best in me, and I was right. You did. This is the best of me. This is the most generous version of me. Whatever happens, I get to do this, give you this gift. More life. Double life.

And, I honestly think you'll like being hunted. It'll be a thrill for you never to know what tomorrow will bring, all while you can daydream about yourself on Mars, thriving, just like the brochures promise.

If I'm being honest, I believe the brochures too. The truth is, I *have* thought about life up there, a lot. I'd like to thrive under a different sky. I'd like to find you on Mars, if I can. Maybe things can go better for us there than they did here. That's the idea, right? Nothing has to be the same if everything is different. Maybe we'll be different. Maybe the best me is the one waking up there. Can the same people have a different life on a new world?

I hope so.

"So you didn't send your consciousness to be reborn on Mars because you thought I'd fall in love with you again," you tell me. "You sent it so you could help me escape death on Earth?"

I nod and grin. Selflessness is pretty rewarding, especially because I'll never know if I succeeded or failed, and I won't feel any of the consequences. Either way, I'm here now. I don't know if I'll even find you on Earth, or what I'll do if I manage to. What if I do kill you instead of letting you go? Is it still selflessness if it isn't exactly you doing it and you'll never know if you've done it?

"Any idea where you'll be hiding out down there?" I joke.

"Up," you correct me again. Again, I decide not to let it annoy me.

"I think I'm heading to that that solar farm," I say.

"That's likely," you agree.

"Who'd have thought *we'd* be the future of humanity?" I ask, and I can feel that old cynicism sneaking back. "Two predictable teenagers nursing old grudges."

I notice your expression tighten.

"I'm not nursing any grudges," you say. "Anyway, they want young people because our brains are more elastic, which makes the adaptation easier. Also, we're less risk-averse than our parents." You're in full-on expert mode, one of your favorites.

"*And* we aren't the ones who wrecked the Earth," I add. "This is all kind of their repayment to us." I gesture around at the grey-and-pink sky, the red hills and distant ice. "Sorry we wrecked your world, kids; here, have a new one."

"The meek shall inherit the Earth," you say.

"But the kids shall beam the fuck out of there," I finish. You laugh, and it's genuine. I forgot how funny you thought I was when you didn't think I was being a dick. I'm glad you think I'm funny again.

We sit in some extra-gravity silence. We could so easily

become what we were. You the expert at everything, me the darkly comic grouch. We know our parts, and all we have to do to play them is let ourselves.

"Why did you really decide to go Doubler?" I ask, to trade the silence for your story.

You take a deep breath, swirl your tea in its cup on its saucer. The metal-on-metal sound isn't as grating this time. Maybe my ears have adjusted. Or it's like the pain and shame thing. I get to decide how to feel about it. Pretty impressive design, I have to admit. Whoever built these bodies gave us much better features than our Earth prototypes had.

"It was during the Upload, actually," you tell me, and you get a distant daydreaming look. I know that look. It's the look that you used to give when we'd make eye contact in gym class. We were checking each other out in those embarrassing shorts, imagining what was possible with each other. This was your possibility face.

"I remember sitting in that comfortable leather chair they have," you say. "And they showed me arguing with my grandma, and they showed our breakup, and they showed me our first kiss, and I realized I wasn't ready to leave you, but I also knew I had to leave."

"So you bribed them?"

"The technician noticed my thought pattern," you say. "And noticed my account was paid in full. He made the offer to let me slip away, for a price. I accepted. I wanted to experience being a Doubler, but I also..." You clear your throat. "I knew you'd look for me. I knew you'd find me."

It's my turn to set my cup on my saucer with shaking fingers.

"I didn't just happen to see that you'd arrived here," you tell me. "I scanned the arrival logs every day, waiting for you to come. I knew if you came here, it'd mean you also came for me on Earth. And I suppose I liked that daydream. I imagined, if you were hunting for me, I could convince you to run with me. We could try again. I mean, who gets two chances like that?"

"Anyone who goes Doubler," I suggest.

"Maybe everyone should," you say, which I'm pretty sure is as illegal a thing to say on Mars as it is on Earth.

"Your optimism is limitless, isn't it?" I ask.

You sigh and reach across the table to take my luminescent hand in yours. "A double life, here and there," you tell me. "I wonder if we can make it work in one of them?"

I didn't send my consciousness to be reborn on Mars because I thought you would fall in love with me again, but it's really gonna be something to try anyway.

★ ★ ★ ★ ★

AESTHETICALLY HUNGRY

Mato J. Steger

DAYLIGHT CITY IS A SUNLESS HOLE IN THE ground. Neon colors the skyscrapers like candy. We get a dusting of those lights here in the slums, just enough cast-off glow to see.

Rainwater splashes beneath my boots as I turn down the alleyway. I can't believe this is the address. The flyer crumples in my fist. Change your appearance. Be Someone New. Become the true you. Try SOPHISTICATE-X with a free three-day trial! Never go aesthetically hungry again! I feel sparks as the LEDs snap inside the flyer.

Nearby, a man passes a baggie under his palm to a woman with braids made of wires. I exhale. Shove my hood over my ratty, unwashed hair. My binder's tighter than usual. Breathing's like sucking shards of glass through a straw.

SOPHISTCATE-X will change that. Change everything.

Up against a burning trash can, there's some guys passing an old phone around, something solid, unlike the screen attached to my forearm. They're laughing about some girl from their old high school. They are way too old for high school, probably twice my age. The words *fat* and *ugly* are the loudest. I wanna puke. Guys like that don't deserve anyone.

I shrug and roll my shoulders. Pull myself together. The asphalt here is littered with old parts. I swerve to avoid tripping over a hubcap. Conscious not to look back over my shoulder. I don't need anyone looking at me sideways 'cause I look a little too girly for their taste.

My hand flicks to the knife in my pocket. I know better than to carry anything with a chip. Acute awareness that if I gotta stab somebody, then I gotta. I don't want to, but I know what happens to trans people caught by the wrong hands.

A sharp buzz fills the air around me. Cops. At least, their drone. Means they're nearby. I'm not supposed to be out this late as it is. I'm only seventeen, and there are curfew laws.

Worse, I am definitely not of legal age to sign for SOPHIS-TICATE-X. I search the alleyway. The guys huddled by the fire are the only ones left besides me. I should've run like the drug dealer. Within seconds that drone's light blinds my eyes.

"Chip," the drone demands.

I stumble back.

"Identification." The drone's voice isn't robotic. Nah. The cop car would be somewhere nearby, no doubt. They have those little mics on them. Robots doing their dirty work. Dad says not to go near them. Any cops. Too late, I guess.

A long arm extends from the drone. It's all metal and wires with a pincher claw.

If I run, I'm screwed. If I stay, I might be worse than screwed. I cough. The back of my neck prickles. Those dudes are watching me. I feel their stares. The claw snatches my wrist. The blue light scans the chip in my wrist, and I watch in wide-eyed horror.

Name: [REDACTED] [REDACTED]
ALIAS: Wrench
GENDER: Female

The screen keeps going. The dumpster fire of dudebros shouts a slur I haven't heard since yesterday. My stomach hurts. The dudebros keep screaming. I could puke.

"Identification verified. You're free to go." The drone spins off down the alley. My wrist is sore where its clamp held me.

The drone didn't even look at the dudebros. Of course it didn't. I don't know why I even care. I'm almost to the clinic anyway. I rub my wrist. The cold metal claw left a red mark. Even with the drone gone, it isn't. Not really. Not in the residue of embarrassment left inside every atom of my body.

"Hey," a voice comes up behind me. I tighten my hoodie cords. Don't look at me. Don't even acknowledge me. Go away. My skin crawls.

"Hey!" A hand grabs my shoulder and yanks me around. "I'm talking to you."

It's one of the dudebros. I say nothing. Saliva sits in the back of my throat. I think about spitting in his face.

An engine revs nearby. Echoes bombard my less-than-great hearing.

"What?" The dudebro pushes me. His hands are dirty. His face is covered in soot. One of the high school dropouts. I bet he joined the Mechanics' Guild. That's what most guys from school did. Probably thinks he'll get into back-alley augmentation. "You too good for me? Is that it?"

Wheels screech. I turn on my heels. I can't stay here. The dudebro tries for my shoulder again, but we're both stuck in a singular blue headlight barreling toward us.

Dudebro dives to the side as the wheels splash rainwater in different directions. I can barely breathe. My binder is going to get me killed. Perfect. Just how I always wanted to die.

The biker's brakes slam down. My breaths come in rapid succession. The all-black leather-clad biker shimmers in what little neon there is in this dark alley. Like some kind of modern knight, the rider drops a heeled boot to the wet ground.

I'm going to pass out. I suck in another breath, but it's not enough. Light-headedness holds me to the spot. I drop to my knees. Hitting asphalt sends shocks up my spine, banging around in my skull.

"Hey." The rider pulls off their sleek helmet. "Don't die!" Their hand reaches out to me. The dudebro looks ready to give the rider a piece of his mind. Another taps a lead pipe in his hand.

"I'm Ace," the rider says. "Hurry up. Let's get out of here."

"What makes you think I need help?" I gasp, wiping spittle from my lips.

Ace looks to the dudebros coming closer.

"Yeah," I say. "Never mind. Gotta point."

Better dead with this stranger than beaten to death in a back alley. I'll take my chances.

I grab their hand. With a yank, I'm out of the puddles and onto the back of Ace's motorcycle.

"I'm Wrench!" I shout as the wind pushes my hood back off my head.

"Let's save our introductions for after."

Ace revs the engine. Spins water out across the guys. In a flash, we're down the other side of the alley, and a siren picks up behind us.

Red and blue lights flash across the darkened windows and overfilled dumpsters.

Cops.

I wrap my arms around Ace's waist. Out of the fire and right into whatever big-ass frying pan this is. Speeding is one ticket. Being out past curfew is another. But running...well... cops don't like that.

Ace hits the corner hard. The wheels leave black streaks across the road as we meet open air.

The curved edges of the cops' armored rover, with top-of-the-line hover capability instead of wheels, illuminate under the streetlights as they follow us.

Suddenly, I'm way too aware that my hoodie and binder aren't bulletproof. I squeeze Ace hard as they swerve between cars.

Dad would wake up to the news of my death, popcorn covering him, and warm beer staining the carpets. I hope he remembers to feed my goldfish. Stacey didn't do anything to anyone. It isn't her fault her owner makes terrible life choices.

Cars honk, loud enough to make my head hurt. Raindrops splatter off the fake palm trees scattered around the city. The cops stay a few cars back. Traffic's too backed up, and no one likes the police enough to split the way. Ace takes the opportunity. We cut through a red light. My heart beats into my mouth as we narrowly miss a Hummer.

"Woo!" Ace shouts as we slow down. They turn into a garage. A metal door closes tight behind us. "Hot damn! That was amazing."

"Was it?" I try to laugh. "We could've died."

"Why were you in a back alley in this city if you're afraid of a little death?" Ace pulls their helmet off, and this time, with the overhead fluorescents, I can see their, his, teeth shine and the way the light accents the sharp cheekbones of his smile. He runs a gloved hand across his thick, straight black hair. Two long braids come down on each side of his head. The part right down the middle. I recognize him now. Ace.

"I know you." I'm chewing on my lip because I know I'm right. I'm definitely right.

"Yeah," he says. "We met at a Powwow last summer. Spent the whole weekend together. But you refused to give me your connect code. You said Wrench, right? I like that more than the other name. Fits better."

I shove my hoodie back on over my head again, trying my best to hide these ridiculously femme features. I don't want him to see me like this. That's why I didn't give him my number. I remember it all too clearly now. As I adjust, I realize my hands are empty. The flyer's gone now. Dammit.

"Yeah." That's all I can say because I'm biting my tongue now to keep from crying.

"You were in the wrong alley, by the way." He puts his helmet under his arm. "SOPHISTICATE-X trials are up-stairs." He looks at the concrete ceiling. "The entrance is two streets over."

"What?" I spit out. I can't even be mad that he knows what I want. I know I read that flyer correctly. "How?"

"Because Daylight City is twisty and turny? I don't know,

man. Come on. I interned at one of the places next to their clinic. Just answering phones for extra credits. Trying to graduate a year early."

"Then what? Enter the workforce a whole year earlier?"

Ace laughs. "Nah, man. I'm going to get into street racing. You felt that wind, right? Man, I could live that way forever. Come on. Wonder if the X will make me look older, ya know? I could ditch school altogether. Street racers don't need a diploma. But lookin' older would definitely make people take me more serious."

"Street racing?" I say it like I'm questioning him, but I want to know more, and I hope he'll keep talking. Plus, he's really nice to look at.

I remember what he looked like at the Powwow in full regalia. The color of feathers and intricacy of beadwork. I was shocked no one fought me over him. Especially since we met because we were paired together during a dance. My breath catches just thinking about the way his body moved, like a thundering drum calling to our ancestors. The look in his eyes says he remembers that moment too, but isn't saying anything.

"Yeah, man. Lots of money, wind in my braids." He sighs.

"Lots of women?" I ask.

"Nah. I'm not into women." Ace leads me to an elevator. Smacks the button a hundred times.

"Oh," I say. "Yeah, me either."

"So, what's X gonna do for you?" He's nosy, but attractive. I wanna tell him to shut up. If I were more confident, maybe I'd ask him out. But that'd be ridiculous. Because he doesn't like women and that's all I see when I look at myself.

"Hey, you okay?" Ace touches my shoulder. Unlike that jackass from before, this is gentle, inviting.

"Yeah, sorry. I'm shook up. Jerks and cops all in one night. Ya know?"

He nods. "Floor six. Here it is."

"Don't I need the flyer?" I could have sworn it said on it to bring it.

"Yeah, but look." The elevator doors slide open and there are stacks of flyers just sitting on tables. I grab one. It's crisper than the one that'd been shoved under my apartment door.

Ace grins again. "Eh, I'll try it too, huh? Maybe not to be older. What should I do? Purple hair? Oh, man! I know! I should totally make my eyes neon green!"

I sigh. Honestly, I don't think I've ever been so grateful to have someone drop a conversation so easily.

"Hello." A woman who looks too perfect, like a preened Barbie, comes out with a clipboard. "Are you here for the trial, gentlemen?"

Gentlemen. I heard her. She said *gentlemen*. I can't breathe again. This time it ain't my binder. I've never *not* been misgendered before. The whole office seems brighter. Green plants in the corner seem to thrive.

"Yes," Ace says, "we wanna do this trial. How's it work?"

"Well," she says. "One of you at a time." She points to me. "Please take a seat, sir. We'll be back for you after this young man is finished."

"Do you need me to sign any paperwork?" I force myself to lower my voice. I want it to sound deeper. I squeak anyway.

"Everything will be fine." She waves me off. I guess they'll just scan our chips. I pop down into one of their chairs. Hard.

Plastic. They don't want people waiting long. That's fine. I want to be done as fast as possible. I hope this augments my voice too. My nerves tingle as I watch Ace head back with the clipboard woman.

I tap my boots on the linoleum. Every aspect of this clinic is so fresh-looking. Maybe they just threw it together, or cleaned really well. Or something. All I know is the white walls balanced with greenery everywhere feels clean. Somehow trustworthy. I hope I'm right.

Dad said to throw that flyer away. No good comes from augmentations or chip alters. It only took three beers before he passed out in front of the flat-screen watching some bullshit dramatic reality TV show. His usual since Mom took off.

Yeah. I know. There are other ways to transition. After I'm eighteen. 'Least by state laws. But I'm tired of being this way. Tired of my body being…nothing I want it to be. Wires run between the linoleum cuts on the floor. They buzz audibly. Lights flicker off them. I hear a shout from the back room. Ace?

Ace comes back out. His hair is bubblegum pink. He rubs his wrist.

"Shocks," he said. "Like just a little."

"Okay, sir." Clipboard woman winks at me. "Come on back."

"Should I?" I look up at Ace.

He shrugs. "Do you, man."

Why am I asking? We barely know each other. One weekend last summer does not make a close friend. We don't even go to the same school. Yet as the whitewashed walls turn into a room filled with wires and tubes, my stomach churns. I can hear the rev of Ace's engine in the back of my head. Him whisking me away from a certain death to a possible death. And here I am.

Clipboard woman sits me down in a dentist-like chair.

"Relax," she says. "The doctor will be right in."

I tug my binder back down. It rolls up on my stomach even worse though. Digs into my sides. My hips hurt. Blinking lights illuminate the room. Everything. Even the ground is primarily layered black wire covers. All of those wires lead to one centerpiece. Right above my head. It's shiny. Chromatic.

"Ah," a man says. "Two tonight already." He smiles when I look at him. He doesn't have a lab coat on. He's bald, though, wearing goggles. Is this the doctor? I wish I could see the whites of his eyes.

"So." He sits on a stool that has wheels but can't roll on all these wires. "What is your aesthetic hunger, m'dear?"

"I…" I press my wrist into my side. Maybe I won't. Maybe I can just go home.

He grabs my arm, shoves my sleeve up. His hands are like ice. He taps the chip inside my wrist. Same chip we all have.

"Let me guess." He smiles even wider. He's got fangs, like vampire fangs. He's augmented himself. "You desire to be the man you feel you already are."

I gulp and nod.

"Simple procedure. Hold still."

By *hold still*, he means, I don't have a choice. A clamp comes from the sides of the armrest and over my arm. Metal colder than his hands. The chrome wire lowers down. The doctor clicks a series of buttons.

The tip touches my wrist. I gasp. My chest tightens. The metal plunges into my wrist. Black wires like tentacles wriggle beneath my skin. The little pieces dig into my chip. The shocks trickle up my arm. Burn in my bones. Hot acid. A scream retches from my mouth. A deep one. Not some horror movie victim playing it up.

As the black lines latch to my chip, it looks like a tattoo made of cybernetics. And my arm hairs darken. The chromatic needle pulls above me again. My skin seals back, solid, as if never punctured.

"Missy," the doctor calls. "Let's bring this young man a mirror."

They wheel a full-body mirror out. The sound is a bunch of thunks on the uneven floor.

Clipboard woman helps me stand. I pull my hood down. The first thing I do is touch my face. I can feel it. Each coarse little beard hair. No matter how small the goatee is, it's actually there.

"Can I?" I grab the bottom of my shirt.

"Yes," the doctor says. "With SOPHISTICATE-X running through your chip, your body is now just as you desired. So, go ahead."

I do. I yank my shirt and hoodie off. Wriggle out of my binder. And my chest is flat. Not just flat. It's perfect. Scarless. Dime-shaped oval nipples. Little hairs on them.

"Oh, my god," I say. And my voice sounds like my dad's when he's sober. "Oh, my god!" I shout.

"In three days," the doctor says, grabbing my wrist, "this will wear off. If you come back, we can install it for you. The updates will transfer every month after payment is processed after that. Payment is only six-hundred and ninety-nine a month." He winks. "We take credit."

I nod. I can't pay that. Dad has a credit card somewhere. I'd just have to find a job. Fast.

Clipboard woman hands me my shirt back, and I shove it on. But I don't stop rubbing my pecs.

"Whoa," Ace says when I'm back in the lobby. "That's extreme, man, but if you're happy."

"Definitely," I say. "Definitely happy." My face feels tight from grinning so hard.

"Where to?" Ace holds his helmet at his side again, and I officially want to kiss him. I'm so excited. He asks, "You want a ride home?"

"No way," I say. "Take me to one of your street races."

"Hell, yeah!" Ace nods. "If you've never been to a Daylight City street race, you have yet to live. Let's go."

My short hair flutters in the wind. Ace is warm enough to cut the night's chill. We whip through traffic and into the brightest part of the city.

Light here radiates from every corner. Especially the gentlemen's club, with the massive pulsating heart on top of it.

A billboard for SOPHISTICATE-X flashes above us as we speed under an overpass. I press my bearded face against Ace's leather jacket. My laugh blurs with the speeding cars.

Cars and bikes rev louder as Ace takes a sharp corner. People crowd the sidewalks. A guy backs his sports car up and lets Ace slip us through into the street. Music pours from someone's trunk, popped open with a couple of nearby women passing out beers to each other. The vibe here's so different. Freer. People wearing clothes too tight, too small. Skin exposed to the elements. Body paint, tattoos, hair in any color you can think of. Ace's pink doesn't even stand out.

When people look at me, I don't turn away. Look at me. Please. See me.

"You excited or what?" Ace parks us beside some other bikers. When he gets up, he ties his helmet to the dash. He leans close to me. Touches me. Once the helmet is tied, he's still lingering, just next to me. Heat radiates. I'm still sitting on his bike. I'm enjoying being so close to him. Now that I'm not thinking about my body. Binder. Chest. Any of that.

"This is wild," I say.

"Ace, you want to race?" A burly dude with a handlebar mustache walks up to us. He cracks open a beer with his teeth.

"You got a second helmet?" Ace asks. "I want to take Wrench with me. He's never even seen a street race."

"Oh, yeah?" The man turns to me. "You not from Daylight City, I guess?"

"I am. From the South side. Born and raised."

"Slum kid like you, Ace. Yeah, I'll get you a second helmet. What's your bet?"

"Put me down for four hundred," Ace says. "Anyone drop their pink slip in?"

"Not tonight, but you've got three bikes already. Greedy bastard." He laughs. "I'll be right back. Hang tight."

"You own three other bikes?" I cross my arms against my chest, trying not to relish too much how flat it feels. How this shit works, I'm scared to consider. If Ace hadn't reacted to it, I might have thought the whole thing a trick of the mind. But his hair is pink. I can see it. I swallow my worry when Ace turns to me with that full-tooth smile.

"Won't I slow you down?" I reach out. Grab the pocket on the front of his jacket. Pull him even closer to me. He doesn't flinch.

"Nothing slows me down." He says it like a whisper. I can almost taste his lips. His face inches from my own. This is why I spent a whole weekend with him last summer. But this time I'm going to be brave enough to kiss him.

"Here you go!" The burly guy is back. The helmet is sleek black. Shiny visor. Just like Ace's. "We're about to get the next race lined up. Better get going. Be careful out there. I'm not reporting this kid's death just because you're reckless."

"Calm down. No one's dyin' tonight." Ace pulls his helmet on and tightens it. When he turns to me and helps me put mine on, his fingers trace my jawline. My pants tighten and my heart races. I hadn't even thought to check that. I bite my lip. Think of my dad drunk. Things settle back down.

Ace straddles the bike. He pushes us backward. I slide my arms around him, tuck my fingers into his pockets. His body's so firm. So am I. Like a bad habit. Dad drunk on the couch. Think. My heart throbs but my body softens. I sigh.

"For real, this is safe?" I ask.

"Wrench, we've done more dangerous things in the last hour than a race." Ace laughs. "Hang on tight, king."

The engine roars between our thighs, and I can feel myself pressed hard against Ace's lower back. My cheeks burn. He doesn't say anything. We're lined up beside four other people. I can't tell what they look like. The city lights glint off our visors. A man in a sleeveless vest with no shirt underneath and shorts cut midthigh stands in front of us and waves. The flag in his hands dances a little with the breeze. I breathe in deep. Ace smells sweet, like a mini bakery tucked in a busy shopping street.

"All right, you scoundrels!" the vest guy shouts. "Rev your engines!"

They do. The scent of gasoline smothers everything else.

"Ready!" he yells. "Set!" The flag is high above his head. "GO!"

I don't see the rest. Everything blurs. The night air pushes the tails of pink braids into my visor. I giggle, but it's gone in the wind. Like razor-sharp darts, the bikes seem to fly. Ace's right. This is amazing. I feel so free.

People cheer at the sidelines. Ace jams the gas, and we're in front. I look over my shoulder to see someone flip us off. Ace leans his head back and shouts. "You havin' fun yet, man?"

I laugh. Hold him tighter. I could get used to this. I want to get used to this. With X, I can.

Flags swing as we skid through the finish line.

Everyone's shouting, screaming, howling. I hand my helmet off. Once we're both off the bike, Ace has me by the waist in a way that tells me his heart's speeding as fast as mine is.

"Come with me?" He breathes against my neck, kissing it. His teeth graze my flesh.

"Let's celebrate," I say. His mouth is on mine in a second. He leads me past the crowd and through a half-opened doorway. We're in a stairwell that smells like piss beer. But his hands are up my shirt. His teeth dig into my throat. A moan drops from my lips.

I'm hard. So is he. Pressed against me. His leather pants stretched taut across him. My god. His lips fall onto mine again. I bite him, gently tugging. He presses between my thighs.

"Holy f—," I gasp as he kisses my jawline.

"Is this okay?" Ace pulls up, looking into my eyes. His have a little line of green in them, wrapping the brown.

"Very okay," I breathe. "Don't stop."

My hoodie's off. His jacket hits the stairwell. Someone opens the door but closes it quickly, before I can catch a glimpse of them.

A sharp pain hits my wrist. "Ow." I cough.

"Shit," Ace stops again. "You okay?"

The shock goes up my arm again. No. My wrist is writhing with the black tentacles again. It's shorting out. A light pops up from my chip.

Attention. Error. Data Corrupted.

"No," I whisper. My hand jumps to my jaw. The beard is gone. "Oh, my god. Don't look at me." I nearly toss Ace into a wall. I don't have my binder. I left it at the clinic and didn't even notice. Dammit.

"Wrench!" Ace yells after me. But I'm up the stairs and rushing down the hallway. Some half-abandoned apartment complex. I can hear business going above. Slot machines. We're beneath a casino.

Tears burn down my cheeks. I slam into the wall and I careen around a corner. I can't believe it's corrupted. I smack my wrist. Tears drip off my bare chin. "Work, damn you!" I sob.

The ragged carpet underneath me catches my boot. I trip. My face plants on the hard floor. Along with tears, the hot stream of blood from my nose runs down the hills of my lips. Lips that just had Ace's on them. That never would again.

Because Ace doesn't like women. And as I stand up, there in a hall mirror, that's all I can see.

A shadowy figure comes up. A hand touches my shoulder. Ace.

"You okay, man?" He says the words so softly I want to cry even more.

"No," I say. "I'll never be okay. Not like this. No one wants me like this."

"*I* want you," Ace whispers. "I've thought about you all year. I kept hoping I'd see you at the Powwow again this year."

"What?" I turn to him. Holding my arms across my chest.

His hands are bare. His gloves somewhere on the stairs. With a soft brush of his fingers, he wipes tears from my cheek. "I don't care that you're trans. That stuff doesn't matter. You're Wrench. You're a man. And the same man I've been crushing on for a while now. When I saw you in the alley…man, luck of mine. Right?"

"You…" I wipe blood off on my shirt. "You like me how I am?"

"Yeah, man, and I'm still going to like you when you go through medical treatment. If you want to. SOPHISTICATE-X or not. I like you for you."

I crumple into myself. Dropping onto the floor, back sliding down the wall.

"Whoa." Ace kneels down. "Do I need to get you home? To a doctor? What happened when your chip corrupted? Did it hurt you?"

"Like being stabbed," I say. "It's gone now."

"We can wait." Ace sits beside me. "Physical stuff. It can wait. Whenever you're ready."

"Can we…go to my apartment and get a binder?"

Ace smiles. "The nurse lady from the clinic handed me this." He pulls a folded black binder from inside his jacket. "Wasn't sure if you had another, so didn't want to leave it behind."

"Close your eyes." I stand, and as soon as his eyes are shut, and I squeeze back into my binder.

"You can open them now." I sit back down next to him.

"Better?" he asks. I nod. Wiping my face dry with my shirt. My nose has stopped bleeding. Ace squeezes closer to me. With one hand, I grab his jaw and kiss him.

I can wait a little longer. I don't need to be perfectly cis. Ace is right. I'm me. I'm Wrench no matter what I do. With that, I know.

I'll never go aesthetically hungry again.

★ ★ ★ ★ ★

THE RIFT

Claire Kann

LISTENING TO GIRLS CRYING INSIDE AN EMPTY school bathroom always lights a special kind of fire in Kiara's heart.

It burns in pulses, in muted greens that fade into transcendent blues, searing her lungs and filling her rib cage with flames—making her want to do things she normally wouldn't. Offer herself up in ways she shouldn't. With steady steps and breaths, she walks toward the last stall on the right.

"Everything okay?" Kiara asks. She knows who's inside.

Gianna, who tries so hard to be the invisible girl, never in anyone's way.

Gianna, who's bullied in plain sight anyway because they think it's fun to watch her cry.

Gianna, who's too sensitive and too soft for a world designed to hate her.

The sniffling stops. She clears her throat once before answering. "Yes, I'm fine." She pauses. "Thank you."

No one else could be that polite in their time of hurt—only her.

"All right."

Kiara walks away, heading for the door. She opens it, closes it, and leans against the wall, waiting. The bathroom absorbs the silence with its dingy walls and plastic mirrors—everything coated in an oppressive pine-like scent that tries so hard to make the space bearable. Ten seconds later, the stall door opens.

Gianna shuffles to the sink, wiping her eyes. Their school doesn't require uniforms, but she always wears a long pleated skirt, a button-up top, and a nice sweater—all in muted pastel colors. Her dark braids cover her face from the side, but her warped reflection shows her rich brown skin and watery dark brown eyes that haven't lost the will to smile just yet.

You can't buy that kind of inherent hope, but you sure can break it.

Kiara steps forward, startling Gianna, and she pulls a couple of paper towels from the dispenser. Turning the tap on cold, she wets the paper and folds it into a rectangle. "Here. It won't do anything for your eyes, but it'll cool your forehead."

Gianna takes it, frowning the tiniest bit as she does, eyebrows drawing together. "Why are you being nice to me?" The words sound so strange coming from her. Terrible things have happened to Gianna at school, but she's the kind of person who takes things in stride, clinging to optimism when the bright side is determined to shake her loose.

It's…hard not to feel for Gianna. Parts of Kiara's heart that she thought had been closed off and locked away years ago somehow always flare back to life every time she looks at that face.

"Should I be like everyone else, then?"

"Um, no? It's just you usually aren't nice," Gianna says, unguarded before the horror sets in. "I'm sorry. That was rude."

She has more to say—Kiara can feel it needling between them like thread through the eye.

When Gianna finally speaks, her voice is soft as she says, "I don't have money to pay you."

"Did I ask for money?"

"But you don't do anything for free, right? That's what I heard."

Word of mouth is the most powerful advertising tool in existence. No one ever admits to using Kiara's services. She's discreet, respecting her clients' confidentiality, but everyone knows a friend of a friend who's gone to her to make their problems disappear. They create her legend and spread her name, and she becomes more infamous by the hour.

Kiara, a former chosen one without a world to save and almost nothing to live for.

Kiara, a Savior with godlike abilities masquerading as a mere Dimensionist.

Kiara, a mercenary with a cracked moral compass.

No one ever gets it quite right. Not yet. But they will soon enough.

"Right. I also can't help if you don't ask, which you haven't." Kiara pulls a black card from her pocket. One side has a matte finish with her initials, K.D., in gold, and the other looks blank until held up to the light. "Take it."

Gianna obeys with trembling fingers, bringing the card close to her face. She must have taken her contacts out. Kiara remembers the exact day Gianna stopped wearing her purple-framed glasses. Rich Larson threw a basketball at her face during gym, hard enough to snap them clean in half.

"Call me when you're ready."

Kiara is halfway to the door when Gianna says, "I'm fine."

Gianna wears her hurt like a punch in the chest. She cradles it there, protects it with hunched shoulders and a shuddering rib cage like she's afraid it will leak out and inconvenience someone else.

"Everything's fine," she repeats with a nod. After a deep breath, her tender, friendly smile returns—the one held together with It'll Get Better stitches.

What a sweet, careful liar she is.

The bell is close to ringing, but everyone lingers instead of rushing off to class. Kiara walks to her fifth-period class alone, deeply resenting having to be there at all. Not even a former chosen one can escape the hell of the American school system.

When The Dimensional Rifts of 2020 opened, they altered six percent of the entire human population, giving them inexplicable extrasensory abilities—telepathy and telekinesis being the most common. An unexpected side-effect, because the actual purpose of The Rifts was to steal nine-year-old children. Thirty-four of them, to be exact. They were chosen ones, whisked away to train for five years in an alternate reality to become Saviors capable of stopping an apocalypse in that world. Over There.

The altered left behind had been dubbed Dimensionists by the media. They were reviled and then celebrated after three of The Missing 34 returned to stop a similar apocalypse in this world in 2027.

Bea, who died in the process.

Kiara, who saved the world. Both of them.

And Steven, who got all the credit.

Kiara's and Steven's abilities as Saviors far exceed what a Dimensionist could do. They agreed to pretend otherwise, agreed to keep how powerful they truly are a secret from the general population by pretending to be Dimensionist. But while in Over There, they learned how to warp reality itself, among other equally fascinating things. But while he's worshipped as a messiah, inundated with followers and holding public speaking gigs around the world, she trades miracles for future favors in a small town called Spectrum.

"Hey, Kiara!" a voice shouts from her left.

Kiara salutes him—Brian Johnson, a former client—without breaking her stride. Everyone knows her name, but that doesn't mean she has friends. She doesn't need them. They would only distract her from keeping an eye on her debtors, from gaining insight into future clients. At best, she's a people watcher. At worst...well. She's what this world made her. After rounding one last corner, she reaches her class and walks in.

"Hello," she says.

"Good afternoon," Mrs. Esther MacDonald says. She's a vibrant and caring Korean woman with a discerning eye for detail that Kiara admires and has dressed in nothing but black for the past year.

Esther also happens to be a former client. She had called the number on the black card, beaten, broken, and desperate with no idea one of her students would answer. Kiara didn't get propositioned by teachers often—one of the reasons she couldn't wait for college. There, she'd have access to a more diverse range of potential clients with more money and treacherous hearts.

Making Mr. MacDonald disappear for Esther was no small feat. Kiara had to do it without leaving a trace and giving the police probable cause to declare him dead. She treated her abilities like an art, not a one-stop remedy. She would never just snap her fingers, transfer him to the bottom of the ocean, have the paperwork magically land on the chief of police's desk. It had to be organic—a plot of plausible deniability built from the ground up.

It took two weeks of planning and a subtle twist in time to execute her plan. Of course, she did snap her fingers to send him to the depth of the Mariana Trench, but only after all the pieces were in place, ready to cascade down like a row of falling dominos. All for the low, low price of two future favors and one third of the life insurance payout for Mr. MacDonald's untimely death.

"Is it good, though?" Kiara asks.

Esther, ever amused, raises one eyebrow. "And how are you?"

Kiara sits in her assigned seat in the back of the room. "Oh, you know, the same forever and ever amen."

"Stability can be a blessing," she says, attention returning to the stack of papers on her desk. "Your essay was passable but nowhere near your best. I know you can do so much better than a C-plus."

Kiara thought she'd at least be able to get away with not doing any homework after she executed their deal, but no such luck. Esther's exact words were, "Our personal business has no bearing on your education. I'm your teacher, and it's my duty to ensure you receive adequate instruction while in my class."

"Well, that requires caring, and we both know I don't do that." Kiara grins.

There's a quote from an old movie that Kiara loves: "If you were going to take over the world, would you blow up the White House, or sneak through the back door?"

Spectrum is like that—a microscopic, backdoor kind of town. Small enough that everyone knows everyone's business, and the air is always ripe with gossip. Perfect for invasion. Perfect for the evils of the world to swoop in and make it their home base. A perfect place to stash a chosen one, the Savior nobody cares about.

"I'm home," Kiara calls out, taking off her shoes.

Her foster mom, Judy, peeks her head out of the kitchen. "Oh good! I made you a snack."

"How domestic of you."

Judy, a Parallel Realities Monitoring Agency agent, always wanted kids. When her supervisor came knocking with an orphaned chosen one specifically in need of a Black guardian, she jumped at the chance to play house. There aren't many Black families in Spectrum. Kiara has a feeling her hospitable-to-a-point neighbors prefer it that way.

"How was school?" she asks, standing beside the kitchen counter. Her skin is several shades lighter than Kiara's. She wears the same "mom" uniform every day—fitted jeans and a white shirt with her thick curly hair pulled back into a PRMA-approved bun.

Kiara glares, face scrunching in distaste. "How do you think? It's hell. I don't want to go. Stop making me."

Their entire model home with picture-perfect furnishings is bugged and continuously monitored. That morning, she decided to play the role of a moody teenager for the listeners at headquarters. Tomorrow, she might be a Disney Princess and sing her way through the day.

"I don't make you do anything." Judy laughs. "Did you at least go to your classes today?"

"There's an equal chance that I both did and did not."

Judy hands her a plate of apple slices, carrots, and string cheese. "If I have to sit through one more parent-teacher conference—"

"Relax. Everything is eternally under control," Kiara says with a wink. "I'm going to my room. Don't bother me—I'll be pretending to do my homework."

Homework being the code word for research. Judy knows all about Kiara's plan because Kiara genuinely likes Judy. Not as a mom, but as an older sister-type. She keeps her promises, makes good food, and pretends to care well enough that it almost feels real.

Surprisingly, it didn't take much to convince Judy to become a double agent—or to recruit some of her close friends to follow suit. Thanks to her, Kiara has a few more agents in her pocket within the PRMA and even more scattered across various federal agencies.

"Dinner in an hour," Judy says.

If the PRMA has a problem with Kiara frequenting conspiracy forums about The Dimensional Rifts or The Missing 34, they've never said. She isn't looking for anything special, but it's the easiest way to keep an eye on Steven and the general vibe for how the public feels about Dimensionists.

Rarely, if ever, does the press mention Kiara.

One single picture circulates the internet—Kiara standing in front of the apocalyptic vortex proved she was there, but not that she saved the world. The PRMA decided that Steven would be a better poster child. He's the Captain America lookalike this world needs to accept the increasingly ostracized Dimensionists.

No, Kiara, with her dark skin and neon-blue hair courtesy of traveling through the rift, would be too controversial. This world would never unite behind her. This world would never accept her as a Savior. They thanked Kiara for her service, gave her an expensive house, and deposited enough hush money into her bank account to make her life easy on paper.

And now this world believes the lie, showering Steven with fame and flowers.

Before being pulled through the rift, Kiara's parents began teaching her about racism and how to navigate this world, but she forgot those lessons because Over There is different, a true meritocracy. They don't have or even understand illogical concepts like racism. Kiara was gifted an elevated station because of her potential to become a Savior, every inch of her humanity embraced by humanoid aliens.

Kiara's phone rings—her stomach drops, and her heart skips a beat. Her mind buzzes around the thought of Gianna.

"Um, hi. Is this K.D.? I got your card from my cousin, Becky."

"Speaking," Kiara drawls in disappointment. Not Gianna, but a call she's been waiting on for weeks.

"I have a problem. Becky told me what you did. At first, I didn't believe it, but—"

"And how can I help you?"

She hesitates—Kiara can hear her chewing on her nails. "This is legit?"

"I'll be right there."

Kiara hangs up and grabs a pair of house shoes from her closet to put on. She shouts down the hall. "Stepping out for a bit!"

Judy shouts back, "Dinner in forty-five minutes. I mean it!"

Kiara laughs as she closes her eyes, homes in on the calling card signature, and jumps to her left.

"WHO THE HELL ARE YOU?" A girl scrambles to the other side of her enormous room. Her long brown hair reaches her waist, and she's tall, long-limbed with pale skin.

"You called me," Kiara says with a shrug.

"K.D.? Did you teleport? Shit, you are a Dimensionist."

"I'm much more than that." Teleporting is literally as easy as blinking for her.

Back pressed against the headboard, she asks, "This is happening? I'm not hallucinating?"

"Yes, and I don't know your mental state well enough to answer that." A massive vanity is behind Kiara, full of makeup and nail polish. She swivels the chair around and sits.

"I wasn't expecting you to be—"

"Black?"

"No," she says, but her face turns red. "I was going to say *young*. You look my age."

"Right." Kiara snorts. "Your racism won't stop me from

doing my job. At the end of the day, you're all the same to me."

"I'm not racist!"

"Let me guess: You have a Black friend?"

"Several, including my boyfriend." She bristles, chin raised in defiance.

"Anyway. How can I help you?" Kiara squints at her. "Ashleigh Forrest."

She flinches back in surprise. "How do you know my name? I wasn't thinking it. The PRMA says Dimensionists can't read minds like that."

That's true. Dimensionist telepathy isn't a deep, all-encompassing mind probe. They can only read and occasionally influence thoughts as they happen.

Names have the power to attach themselves to beings, wrapping around them like metaphysical ivy. The more they're used, the easier they are to see. All Kiara did was tap into that. She says, "I know everyone's name."

Ashleigh stands up. "I need help for my brother. I messed up pretty badly and asked him to take the fall for me. He's a minor, so I thought it wouldn't be a big deal, but apparently, it's like super against the law to have certain drugs in your possession."

The entire time she speaks, she paces the length of the room, wringing her hands. She cares about her brother, that much is true, but it's clear she doesn't understand the severity of what's she's done. "My dad should have been able to convince some of his friends to help my brother get away with a warning or something. Except the judge is a super-bitch who wants to make an example out of him. So, I need you to convince the jury that he's not guilty. Money's no object."

Kiara manages to suppress an irritated sigh. "So, you want me to get your brother a not guilty ruling for drug possession?"

Ashleigh hesitates, then repeats her ask slowly. "I need you to convince the jury he's not guilty."

"Of the murder charge? Which you conveniently forgot to mention."

She takes a nervous step back toward the door, eyes wide with panic. Her voice is a startled whisper, laden with fear. "How do you know about that?"

"You can't mask your thoughts as well as you think you can." Kiara smiles, all teeth and ready to snap. "Tread very carefully. It'd be a…mistake to lie to me again. I won't give you another chance." To prove her point, she crooks her index finger toward the nightstand. Her little black card flies across the room and into her palm. She slides it back into her pocket. "Now, why don't you tell me what actually happened?"

"Okay." Ashleigh sits back on the bed, spine erect and hands clasped tightly in her lap. "There was an accident. Someone got killed. But it was her fault." Kiara almost falls asleep during her long, rambling explanation. She finishes, "Is there any way you could make it like it never happened?"

Kiara winces for show. "Time travel and resurrection? That's messy with potentially serious ramifications. And expensive."

"I can pay."

She looks her up and down. "You couldn't afford it."

Ashleigh scoffs, entitlement briefly overriding her fear. "Do you know how much my family is worth?"

"Do you know how much ripping a soul from heaven will cost? Or the price for taking one away from hell? Your victim? Missy Winthrop? Her death was most definitely not her fault, and your soul has been promised."

"But it was an accident!"

"There's a lot of parallel worlds, and their ruling inhabitants don't care about 'accidents' when it's clear you haven't learned anything from it." Kiara sits back and props her feet up on the vanity. "But really, that's too expensive. Ask for something else."

"What about pinning it on someone else? Like plant evidence that points to a child molester?"

Kiara sucks in air through her teeth and shakes her head. "Child molesters deserve to be condemned, but by that logic, so do you. You killed a teenage girl and asked your brother to make a false confession to save yourself."

Kiara closes her eyes to concentrate. Viewing possible time lines becomes tricky once their potential moment has passed. Missy died months ago. Time already moved on without her, but Kiara manages to latch on to what could've been—Missy's remaining wisps of fate that are rapidly assimilating into the fog of the forgotten.

Kiara continues, softly and with reverence, "She would've had a beautiful life, but you destroyed it—her family and her future family with three daughters, by the way. All the good she would've done in the world as a pediatrician is gone now, snuffed out like candlelight. Allowing one bad egg to take the fall for another would still be costly."

Ashleigh, unmoved, asks, "Then what can you do?"

"I can do all of it," Kiara snaps, anger getting the best of her. She exhales and forces herself to relax, to remember her plan. The work is the most important thing. She lives to serve that goal, not lose control over individual offenses. "The question is, what can you afford? The help I give you must be equal to the payment you give me. What you're asking for isn't impossible, but it's too much. Try again." She stares at Ashleigh, eyes glittering with promise. Almost there, you're almost free. "Think. Strip it all away to the thing you want the most. What is your truth?"

The truth in question bubbles inside of Ashleigh with a stench like rotten eggs. She's not even ashamed that she's not ashamed. Privilege is the most intoxicating drug in existence. "I don't want my brother to pay for my mistake, and—" she pauses, biting her lip "—I don't want to be punished for it either."

"Now we're talking." Kiara closes her eyes again, envisioning a scale in her mind. She places Ashleigh's truth on one plate and payment on the other, adding until they're equal. "I will ensure your brother gets a not guilty verdict, eliminate all evidence connecting you to the crime, and the case will remain unsolved forever."

Always root the miracle in reality. Ashleigh's brother must go to trial. A pretense of justice must happen—he is innocent after all. And once he's found not guilty, it becomes less likely that anyone present for Missy's murder will be accused either.

She continues, "In return, you will pay me $100,000 and seventeen future favors."

Ashleigh considers this and asks, "Favors? What's that?"

"At some point, I'm going to ask you to do something for me seventeen times. You won't be able to say no." Kiara plans to save the best for last.

"What are you going to ask for?"

"Whatever I'd like. Usually, it's something as small as passing my card to the right person. Becky owes me fifty and has already fulfilled fifteen of them."

"I was one of Becky's favors? You knew I would call you?"

"I had a feeling. It's incredible how many people she knows and the trouble they get into." Kiara raises her hand. "Oh, and more thing. Every day for one hour, you will feel the excruciating pain of Missy Winthrop's mother's grief, in its prime. Every day until the day you die. It will never fade, never lessen. Do we have a deal?"

"Oh." Ashleigh seems unbothered. "That doesn't sound too bad. Just an hour?"

"You sure about that?" Kiara arches an eyebrow and wiggles her fingers. "Would you like to try before you buy?"

"No, I can handle it," she says confidently. "I'll need a day or two to get the money."

"Excellent." And then, Kiara is in front of Ashleigh, gripping her wrist to burn her symbol into the skin. "Consider that your down payment. Renege on our deal, and it combusts, immolating you. Be sure to call me before the jury finishes deliberating. If I have to use time travel, even for a few minutes, the price goes up."

Ashleigh rubs her wrist, tracing her new tattoo.

Kiara doesn't need to close her eyes to picture her room.

She holds it in her mind and says, "Oh, one last thing, I promise. Your first hour of grief begins now."

Ashleigh gasps in pain, eyes rolling back in her head as Kiara jumps to the right.

At school the next day, Kiara watches Gianna from her table in the back of the cafeteria. The room is small but manages to fit half the student body comfortably for Lunch A, including Gianna and the bulk of her tormentors.

The Queen Bee and her workers. The Rooster and his cockerels.

Malinda Tames accosts Gianna, linking arms with her and steering her towards a table. Gianna shakes her head, not wanting to go, but Felicia Graves takes her other arm, trapping her.

Kiara doesn't see what happens next, only the aftermath. Gianna is on her knees, scooping the remains of her lunch off the ground and back on her tray. She knows why—Gianna doesn't want the janitor to clean up her mess. That stitched-together smile makes her cheeks rise, but it doesn't quite make it to her eyes.

The Queen rises from her table. Lucy Cabot.

She's a beautiful girl, average height, and a natural sun-kissed skin tone courtesy of her nonwhite mom. Boys would throw themselves headfirst into a fire to get her attention, and girls would line up for a chance to love her to death. Unfortunately, Spectrum isn't the most tolerant of towns—a bisexual teen attempting to date in the wild wouldn't stay secret for long.

Not even someone as popular and beautiful as Lucy would

survive the backlash. When she heard about Kiara from a friend of a friend, she called and asked for help—granted in exchange for $500 and five future favors.

Lucy's voice rises above the whispers that demand for someone else to help Gianna. "Stop being so clumsy, Mali," she says, sneering as she kneels.

Gianna flinches, blinking at her nearness.

"It's okay. Don't cry." Lucy picks up the bottle of water.

Giana hesitates before reaching for it.

At the last second, Lucy moves it away, opens it, and turns it upside down over Gianna's head. "Now you can cry."

A twitter of nervous laughter spreads through the cafeteria. Condemning eyes glare but don't dare speak a word. Lucy and her friends grin all the way back to their table.

That's happened before, and it'll happen again as long as Gianna continues to take it. If Kiara swoops in to save her, what will Gianna learn? That there are kind people in this world? She already knows that, and this lesson is much bigger than kindness.

It's about respect.

It's about revenge.

"What is going on here?" the lunch monitor asks, arriving two minutes too late.

"Everything is fine," Gianna tells him. "I tripped." She wipes the floor with a few napkins before standing. Tray in her hands, she walks to the nearest receptacle, disposes of her ruined lunch, and walks out of the cafeteria.

Later, Kiara finds her exactly where she thought she would: on the girl's locker room's back steps, wearing her gym clothes. Her regular clothes are inside a plastic bag next to her. Folded in on herself, she's wrapped her arms around her legs, shoulders shaking. Her sobs are delicate hiccups, never meant to be heard.

"Hey," Kiara says, sitting next to her.

"Oh!" She uncurls her body, hands wiping under her eyes and across her cheeks. "I'm sorry," she says.

"For what? Crying isn't offensive. It's human."

Giana nods, smiling and squinting to keep her tears in.

"I'm curious," Kiara says, tracing her index finger across Gianna's wrist. "Why do you let them do that?"

Gianna takes a deep breath, eyes unfocused and frowning slightly. "Because they're hurting too."

She retraces the path. "What do you mean?"

"They're upset, so they focus on me to make themselves forget. It helps them feel better."

Kiara narrows her eyes before tracing one last time. "Why is it your job to make them feel better?"

"It's not. It could be anyone, but they picked me. I'm helping them, and it's not forever."

"You don't believe that?" Kiara scoffs. "No one is that selfless."

"It's better to be kind," is all she says.

"Kindness is not a finite resource. What will you do when you run out? When they take too much? Don't move." She places her index finger right between Gianna's eyes and pushes a quick shot of calm to ease her pain. "Feel better?"

"My headache is gone." Gianna touches her temples. "I didn't know a Dimensionist could do that."

"Because they can't." Kiara grins, leaning toward Gianna. "Can you keep a secret?" Gianna leans in closer, too, nodding eagerly. The faint smell of sugar and blue raspberry candy invades Kiara's senses as she says, "I'm Number Ten."

After The Missing 34 vanished through the rainbow-colored portals that suddenly punched through reality, the media broadcast their faces and real names everywhere. Back then, Number Ten had a gap-toothed smile, black hair parted into pigtails with colorful barrettes, and the name Aisha.

"No way," Gianna hush-whispers. "Of 34? *The* 34? Like Steven?"

"Not exactly." She grins. "I'm stronger. He's my second-in-command."

Gianna gasps, mouth hanging open. She's so cute with her wide, trusting eyes, long thick lashes, and perfect eyebrows. Her face is slender with high cheekbones and a rounded chin—just enough baby fat left to make her adorable without trying.

"Top Secret." Kiara presses a finger to her lips. "I'm technically in the witness protection program. They didn't have anywhere else to put me. Anyway, I can't help you unless you ask."

Gianna continues to whisper, "How would you help me?" She's a good person, a truly good soul, finally pushed so far, she's willing to ask for details—Kiara almost feels proud.

"That depends on you. On what you want and how badly you want it." Kiara looks into her eyes, holding her gaze. "What is your truth? Tell me, and I'll make it happen for you. You could ask me for a puppy, and it's yours."

Gianna shakes her head without breaking eye contact. "People don't come to you for puppies."

"No. They don't." Kiara looks away, but only for a moment. "Your request can be as sweet as you'd like or as sinister as you can imagine or fall somewhere in between. I make miracles happen. I don't dictate them."

"Oh." Gianna frowns again. "I don't have any money."

"I didn't ask for any." The PRMA gives Kiara enough of it. She donates every single cent she makes from her clients to charities, schools, hospitals, and crowdfunding efforts of all kinds. It'd be nonsensical to take money from Gianna. She continues, "I accept other forms of payment. But. For you…"

The fire in Kiara's heart is raging again—ready to spread like an out-of-control wildfire consuming everything. These moments with Gianna, vulnerable and in need, are when Kiara wants to take her hand and show her what life could be like if she'd give herself a chance. Teach her how to stand tall and believe in her worth. When she tries to envision a scale, it's blurry, refusing to show itself. Probably because it knows she's already biased.

Gianna waits for her to continue, expression open and trusting.

Kiara continues, "For you…no charge."

"You'd help me for free?" Gianna's been tormented too long not to sense a trap. "Why?"

"I didn't say free. I said no charge." Kiara stands up and begins walking down the steps. She needs to clear her head, regain her focus. And she'll never be able to do that sitting so close to Gianna. Everything about her is like a spell weaving its way around Kiara, influencing and enchanting her—and it's not a wholly unwelcome distraction.

"Wait, I don't understand."

"And you won't until you ask for my help." Kiara glances over her shoulder. "Remember what I said about kindness."

The PRMA forces Kiara and Judy to have weekly virtual check-ins with Director Mathers.

But it's not often that Steven joins him. His face looks more mature since Kiara last saw him. His unnaturally white hair would be passable in the buzz cut if his eyebrows and lashes didn't give him away.

"Kiara, you're looking well," Director Mathers says.

She drags her gaze away from Steven's image. "And you're looking...old. And liver-spotted. And wrinkled."

"Kiara, I think that's enough," Judy says.

"I'm just saying." And warning him. Director Mathers' increasingly haggard appearance is courtesy of Steven. They must now know he can siphon life energy—stealing seconds or decades at a time from any being.

Director Mathers says, "I'm going to ignore that."

Kiara shrugs. "It's your early funeral." Steven shoots daggers at the camera, confirming her suspicions.

But Director Mathers ignores that too. "The rumors about you are beginning to reach critical mass. It's imperative we stay ahead of the narrative, and thus we've decided to confirm your existence. You'll begin traveling with Steven as his partner effective immediately."

Kiara says, "No."

Judy picks up the sealed envelope delivered earlier that day, opens it, and scans the pages. "You're planning to say she disappeared after the vortex closed and has had amnesia this whole time? That's the best someone could come up with?"

"It was the easiest to fabricate. Naturally, people will search, and they will find an irrefutable answer. You'll also resume using your real name since your memory has returned."

"I said no. I'm not interested."

"It's not a yes or no request."

"You can't honestly believe you can force me to play good little soldier. Not after everything you've done. You're lucky I haven't ruined your entire life yet."

"Is that a threat?" Director Mathers' authoritative gaze tries and fails to put Kiara in her place.

"More like a challenge. Would you like to play?" Her gaze flicks to Steven. "Because he can't protect you. Not from me." The PRMA believes Steven's limits are Kiara's limits, and she plans to keep it that way for the time being. But she'd make an exception for Director Mathers.

Steven swallows hard. "Sir, if—"

"Be quiet," Director Mathers snaps and turns his attention back to Kiara. "We know what you've been doing."

"Helping people?"

"Trading 'favors' with murderers and petty criminals."

"Oh, it's not just them. I'll help anyone who asks. Anyone. It doesn't matter what they've done or what they need. If I can balance it, I'll do it. I'd even trade with you, of all people. It's just business."

Steven focuses on her, steely-blue gaze sharp as a knife. Even if he figures out her plan, it'll be too late for him to do anything about it. He always came in second for a reason—and he betrayed her trust the moment the opportunity presented itself.

Kiara's phone rings. She holds up a finger while she answers. "Hello?"

"Hi," a tiny voice says. "It's Gianna. I need your help."

"I'll be right there," she says and hangs up. "I'm going to have to cut this meeting short. I have somewhere to be."

"Sit down," Director Mathers orders. "We're not finished."

"You may have placed me here, but don't think for one second you can control me." Kiara pauses at the hallway entrance. "I stay because I choose to. I follow your rules because I choose to. Don't make me change my mind." She gestures to Steven. "Same for him. Keep telling him to be quiet if you want to, but his temper is much shorter than mine."

"Dinner at seven," Judy says, unfazed. "I mean it."

Kiara finds Gianna in an unexpected place—smack-dab between two graves in a cemetery. She's at the top of a small hill, surrounded by other headstones with a tree-lined paved road behind her.

Gianna says, "When I have a bad day, I like to visit my grandparents."

"Ah."

"You can sit. They don't mind," she jokes.

Reluctantly, Kiara sits on the grass in front of Gianna. Places like this make her uncomfortable—full of slowly rotting bodies, bones, and lingering death energy. After saving this world, one of the first things she did was visit her parents' graves. She hasn't gone back since.

"I've been thinking about what you said," Gianna says. Indecision flows around her like mist.

Kiara, not wanting to pressure her, only asks, "And?"

"I have some questions. If that's okay?"

"I'd be concerned if you didn't."

Gianna pulls her legs up to her chest and wraps her arms around them. "Can you make them leave me alone?"

"I can."

Hands up, she hurriedly adds, "I don't want anything bad to happen to them! I just… I would like to be left alone. And I don't want anyone to take my place."

Even when being handed a miracle, Gianna thinks of others. There isn't a selfish bone in the entirety of her body.

Kiara could make use of that. "I understand. From the moment we make the deal, you'll be under my protection, and in exchange, I want you to work for me."

Gianna's exhale of relief leads to a tentative smile. "What would I have to do? Working for you, I mean."

"Tell me about your family first."

This surprises her. "My family? Um, well, it's just me and my parents. My dad is disabled, so he works from home and takes care of the house. He's hilarious." She laughs. "And my mom works at the car factory two towns over and goes to school at night. She's wanted to be a nurse since she was a little kid, and now she's finally doing it. They're great. I love them a lot."

"I can see that," Kiara says quietly. The entire time Gianna spoke, she held her parents in her mind. Their house filled with light and yellow curtains, family outings to beaches with packed lunches, sitting on the couch watching movies together—a real family whole and loving. "Did you know my parents are dead? Opening a rift between realities requires sacrifice. They burned up when The Others pulled me through."

"Oh, no. I knew most of the parents of The Missing 34 died, but they never said why," Gianna says, horrified. "They were with you when it happened?"

"It wouldn't have mattered if they weren't. The sacrifice and whoever goes through the rift must be connected by a bond—love, duty, a favor. The Others believed a guardian bond would ensure the greatest chance of success for chosen one candidates to cross over. So, they used whoever loved us the most."

Gianna freezes, continuing to stare at Kiara, but doesn't say anything.

It took Kiara years to come to terms with that. It helps that her parents' murderer was dead. For the return trip back to this world, the initial summoners agreed to sacrifice themselves to open the rift once more as a penance.

Kiara continues, "They have graves, but they're not there. I can't feel them at all. It's getting hard to remember them now."

"I'm sorry that happened to you," Gianna whispers.

"Me too." Kiara pastes a smile on her face. Thinking about her parents never led to anywhere productive, but she needs Gianna to understand. Each new piece of information connects to a bigger picture forming in her mind. She's catching on much faster than Judy did.

"Was it okay Over There? Did they take care of you?"

"Oh, yeah." Kiara's laugh leads to a genuine smile. "The Others are humanoid, but not human. They think differently, have different values. Everything revolves around balance. I was happy there. Appreciated. Free.

"But there's a reason why only two of us are left. Training was grueling. Brutal." Kiara flinches in remembrance, swallowing the bile that appears like clockwork. "Everyone else burned out one by one. It takes an incredible amount of power and...resolve to become a Savior."

Gianna watches her with a wary expression and asks quietly, "Would you go back?"

"In a heartbeat. First chance I get."

The air shifts between them, and silence takes over until Gianna asks, "Is there going to be another apocalypse?"

Kiara frowned, not following. "Why would you think that?"

"You said you'd protect me and asked about my family, which probably means you want to include them in our deal to make me say yes because something bad is going to happen. Plus, Steven came back and stopped the first one. I figured since you're here now too that—"

"No. We came back together, and I stopped the first one. It was us and Bea, but she died," Kiara says. "The Others from Over There returned us with strict orders. I saved this world because they told me to. For the greater good."

"You came back at the same time? Then why are you here and not doing motivational speeches at the UN?"

"Racism."

"Uh, okay. Um." Gianna bites her lip, looking down. "It's fine if you don't want to tell me. I shouldn't have asked that."

"But that's the answer." Director Mathers' face flashes in

Kiara's mind. "They don't want me there, or at least they didn't."

"Oh." Gianna's pretty face folds in confusion, even as the puzzle pieces click together. "Is that why you make deals with people then? Did they ask you to do that instead?"

"No. This is...my project."

Gianna nods, gaze drifting to the headstone that reads Gregory Thompson, Beloved Husband, Father, and Grandpa. Her breaths are faster now, shallow.

Kiara says, "My plan's been in the works for about a year now. You're right—something big is coming. I need more people that I can trust. People like you who are kind, loyal, and surprisingly perceptive and clever."

"Clever." Gianna's voice lowers to a nervous whisper. "You're going to use them, aren't you? That's what the favors are for. Not an apocalypse—to open the rifts again."

"That's what one favor is for," Kiara says, pleased. "I primarily make deals with criminals, murderers, people who think this world owes them everything. They're the ones who will sacrifice themselves. But people like Mrs. Mac-Donald? I won't use them for the rifts. They have a different role in my plan."

"You made a deal with our teacher?"

"Oh, I've made deals with half the people in this town, and I'm actively working on the rest."

"What about me? Were you going to use me?"

"Gianna." Kiara reaches out, holding her soft hands and giving them a gentle squeeze. "I've been waiting for the perfect moment to recruit you. But it has to be your choice."

That's why clients have to ask for Kiara's help. It must be their choice to make it binding.

They must agree to their own downfall.

"I don't understand." Gianna shakes her head. "How many people do you need to go back? Shouldn't it just be one?"

Kiara smiles softly. "I'm not going alone. I'm taking as many of us as I can. You and your family included. Whoever wants to leave can come with me."

"Over There?" Her eyes widen.

"Yes. The Others will give us the time we need to adjust until we find the perfect fit. Do you really think there's only one parallel reality? There's a home for us out there somewhere. We can start over."

"But what about this world?"

"What happens after we leave isn't my problem. Steven can handle it. He wants this world, and it wants him."

"But—but we'd have to get there by killing people."

"We're not killing them," Kiara insists. "Is it my fault that they don't inquire about the fine print before agreeing?" She scoots closer to Gianna. "Look, if you want to spend the rest of your life being bullied, disrespected, and placed at an automatic disadvantage, more power to you. I literally wasn't raised to tolerate that. I refuse to live here because this world will never see Black people as equal. They'll never give us equity. I saved *everyone*. Then the people in charge of this world turned their back on me without even hesitating. Maybe you can be selfless in the face of that, but I don't have it in me."

There'll be battles ahead—PRMA will figure out what Kiara's been doing. She'll have to go into hiding. Steven will step in as the hero tasked with saving the day and saving the world. PRMA will tell him to stop the rifts from reopening at all costs. He will fight, and he will lose.

And in the end, Kiara will leave this world that never wanted her behind.

"So, do we have a deal? Will you help me?"

★ ★ ★ ★ ★

RENAISSANCE

Emma K. Ohland

EVEN ON THE CLEAREST OF NIGHTS BEFORE the sky disappeared behind dust, when thousands of lights would dazzle down at her from the never-ending blue, Eleni was always Hanna's favorite star. When all the stars eventually disappeared, she'd be the one left shining, the one Hanna would never lose.

Pa taught her a few constellations when she was young, but that wasn't enough. She was outside every night to locate them using the sky map in her book. She practiced naming them, her neck becoming sore from repeatedly looking down at the pages, then craning up to the sky. Eventually, she didn't need the book at all, and her neck only had to strain one way.

The sky was never bigger than it was in the field. It stretched to ten times its size, even more stars peeking up near the prairie horizon. All this space was Hanna's. She didn't have to share anything with her siblings, like she did her bed and her clothes, and she didn't have to hold anything back from her audience.

She told them about her frustrations with her family—how little Peia was always demanding her attention, how infuriating her older brother Eddie's condescending remarks were, and how Simon's angst always ruined fun for the rest of them. The stars never spoke back—she was okay with that. She needed someone to listen.

Everyone could see those shining lights, but no one knew them like she did, and she'd bet the stars didn't know anyone like they knew her.

It wouldn't be long before she'd never see the sky again, and the air would be too dangerous to breathe, when she'd no longer be allowed outside. Until then, she needed to savor every moment and remember each light.

One day, a girl named Eleni appeared like one last gift from the stars. She walked from the trees as if she owned this field. By her clothes, the silk green dress adorned with ribbons, perhaps she did.

"Stargazing?" Eleni asked.

Hanna didn't know why this stranger was here, in *her* field under *her* sky, but as Eleni approached, Hanna didn't feel the need to leave or argue or assert her ownership. Something about her walk was confident, yet precarious, so Hanna needed to know who she was.

Eleni took a seat on the grass, dirtying her clothes without any concern. Hanna still hadn't spoken, not sure how to approach this unexpected interruption.

"Why are you here?" Eleni asked. Not rude, simply curious. She had long brown hair curled into thick ringlets and cheeks powdered with freckles like her own personal constellation map across her nose.

"I come to get away from my family," Hanna said. Only part of the truth, but telling her she talked to the stars was too personal. "I could ask you the same thing."

"It seems we have quite a bit in common already," Eleni said with a single nod. "I go to the boarding school beyond the trees."

"Won't you get in trouble for sneaking out?" Hanna asked, knowing schools like that had expectations beyond any human's reach.

"Haven't you heard? People like me can do whatever we want." It would have been rude had she not said it with sarcasm and a hint of pained anger. Hanna knew what she was referring to.

Their planet was dying. A few years back, the Opportunists had prepared to shift of the planet's orbit closer to the sun. They wanted to harness free solar energy for faster production. That plan had failed, and now the planet was heating too quickly. The oceans were beginning to boil. Eventually, the soil would dry up and the air would fill with dust. The Opportunists weren't at too much of a loss, though. They were building a ship called *GSS Renaissance* to take them to a new planet. If Hanna let herself think about it too long, her blood would boil with the sea.

Hanna breathed in the fresh air to remind herself there was still time. She watched the wind dance with the trees, and she knew there was life remaining.

And when Hanna looked at Eleni, she knew Eleni was one of the lucky ones who'd get to board the ship.

"Why do you want to get away from your family?" Eleni asked.

"We live in a small home. I like my space," Hanna said with a shrug.

"You've got plenty of space here," Eleni agreed.

An entire sky's worth.

"Do you have siblings?" Hanna asked, still curious about who this person sitting beside her was, eager to learn any small detail.

"Three," Eleni answered.

"Same here. Then you get it."

Eleni laughed and nodded. She ran her hands through the grass slowly like the blades were communicating with her. When she smiled, Hanna saw rebellion.

The ship was all anyone could talk about lately, so Hanna was surprised they'd made it this long without it passing their lips.

"Huh," Eleni said, squinting up to the sky even though the sun had long since set. "The last star is missing from Anguis…" Eleni shook her head, returning her glance back to the ground. "Sorry. Thinking out loud."

"You know the constellations?" Hanna asked, her heart fluttering.

Eleni's eyes widened, a grin growing across her face, causing her nose to wrinkle. "Some of them. Do you?"

"Yes!" Hanna exclaimed. "I know all of them. I can even name each star."

Eleni shook her head in disbelief. "I'm not nearly *that* good, but I've learned some of the main ones. Would you teach me the rest?"

They lay back on the grass, and Hanna started naming the stars and the constellations, making sure to point them out with her finger. Eleni nodded along when she knew or grinned when she didn't, and sometimes she struggled to figure out which star Hanna was pointing to, so Hanna would help her by adjusting her arm. It was like Hanna was introducing Eleni to her friends, her secrets, her soul.

Then Hanna remembered what Eleni said before. A star was missing from a constellation. She and Eleni were on a deadline.

She invited Eleni to come back because there was still so much to learn. They made it a weekly lesson. Every time they'd meet, they'd lay on the grass and look up at the stars and name them all. Hanna showed Eleni little tricks to remembering the names and locations. She even brought the book she'd used to learn, so Eleni could study when they weren't together.

After a few months, Eleni knew the constellations as well as Hanna did, but she kept coming, because it was no longer about memorizing patterns and names. Eleni's presence meant Hanna no longer had to talk to lights.

They talked about school, about their big families, about both sleeping and waking dreams. Hanna thought about bringing up the ship. Not talking about it felt like keeping a secret from her, but any time she got close to saying something, she stopped herself.

They already knew what the future held. Eleni was bound for the sky while Hanna was trapped here, waiting for the dust. Even under fading constellations, in this field, they could escape. Hanna didn't want to ruin that. She wanted to never mention it—letting it exist silently between them until the day came. Maybe if they never spoke it into the air, it would never be true.

One time, when Hanna was starting to forget what it was to come to the field alone, Eleni reached into her pocket and grabbed a screen.

Hanna should have known she had one, but seeing it in her hands suddenly made her jealous. Something she didn't want to feel about Eleni because here they were equals. That simple piece of technology shook Hanna out of her fantasy and into reality.

Eleni caught Hanna admiring the gadget.

"Do you have one?" she asked. Hanna loved the way she asked questions. Never judgmental. Only curious.

Hanna shook her head. "Nothing that advanced. And we have a TV and a droid, but they're both refurbished and, like, fifteen years old." She blushed.

Eleni handed the screen to Hanna. Again, Eleni didn't judge. She shared what she had. If everyone did that, maybe their planet wouldn't be dying.

Although Hanna didn't live like Eleni, she still knew all about the Opportunist lifestyle. It was hard to ignore when Pa was constantly watching the news, where the rich flaunted it in their faces. They always had the lightest screens, the fastest vehicles, and the flashiest clothes. They had the technology to shift the planet and the technology to leave it behind. The whole world was dictated by the egos of people like Eleni.

No. People like Eleni's family. Eleni wasn't like that at all.

"Here," Eleni said, leaning in close to Hanna. Hanna felt their shoulders press together, and she caught a gasp. It wasn't the first time they'd ever touched, but it was the first time it felt like this.

Eleni nudged Hanna's hand, raising the screen to take a photo. Their faces were so close, if Hanna turned her head, she could place a kiss on her cheek.

But she didn't. She smiled for the photo, and then Eleni reclaimed the screen to examine the picture. They looked at it together, but Hanna wasn't looking at herself. She had her eyes on Eleni.

They continued to meet every week for months until months turned into over a year. Some weeks, Eleni was home with her family, and all Hanna could do was wait.

She'd still come to the field and count the remaining stars, but when she'd go home, she'd ask their droid, Gerty, about the St. John family.

They replied with information about Roy St. John, Eleni's father. He was an influential investor in the city. Hanna tried to understand the details of his position, but it was complicated. She didn't think it was fair someone could make money simply by having money.

She asked Gerty to find images of the St. John mansion. It was colossal. The building was sleek and angular, adorned with windows for walls, and it wrapped around a courtyard of fountains. It looked more like a place of business than a home. Hanna tried to imagine Eleni existing within those walls, but the Eleni she knew would be so out of place there.

When Hanna wanted to torment herself, she asked Gerty to show her images of the ship in progress. The *GSS Renaissance* was practically the size of a moon. With almost a hundred stories, there were ballrooms, swimming pools, and living quarters twenty times the size of Hanna's home. It even had a level built entirely for animal habitats. These animals would be living more luxuriously than her family.

Imagining Eleni on that ship was even stranger.

When Eleni finally returned from her most recent trip home, meeting at the field felt like the first time all over again. Eleni drew imaginary lines from one star to the next, the gaps between each now far too wide. Hanna wondered which constellations she was tracing back into place.

"Watching the stars is supposed to be romantic," Eleni said.

"Is it not?" Hanna asked, watching her finger glide against the dark blue background.

"Not when they're a clock, counting down the days to the launch."

Hanna bit her lip. She knew deep down they'd have to talk about it eventually.

Eleni sat up, and Hanna braced herself.

"It's not fair," Eleni said, remorse written on her face.

Hanna let out a hollow laugh and shook her head. Of course it wasn't fair, but Hanna had long since accepted that. When she'd first learned of the ship on the news, she'd actually been excited. She was hopeful watching the reporter talk about the design, the plan for its construction, the time line for when they'd be saved.

If only she hadn't let herself feel those things, it wouldn't have been crushing when she learned they wouldn't be passengers because they couldn't pay.

"You should be allowed to come," Eleni said.

"You know," Hanna replied, resting back on the grass.

"I always looked up to the stars in hopes of one day visiting them." It was safe to turn back to the stars.

"You should be able to. Everyone should."

Hanna looked to Eleni, an invitation to join her in her dreams.

Eleni sighed and lay back next to Hanna. "I know they're balls of fire, but I used to imagine holding them." It was safe to dream.

Hanna had that same image in her head. That one day she'd float in the blue and hold a star in her hand. Now when she imagined it, Eleni was there with her. She knew she shouldn't let herself think like that. She knew how it would end.

"I've tried talking to my parents," Eleni started again. "I keep telling them this isn't right. They don't listen." Her face was tense. "I don't know how to grieve like this."

Eleni's guilt wasn't the same thing as Hanna's grief.

"We still have time," Hanna assured her. She wouldn't let herself grieve yet. If she did, she'd be so consumed with it that there'd be no point in what they had left. Why only think about an empty sky when there were still stars left to admire?

Eleni looked to Hanna, her eyes sad and tired, her curls flat from pressing them against the ground. "I hear my father. There isn't much time. Two years at most."

Hanna had heard Pa say the same thing. There were only a few months until the ship was finished, until Eleni and her family took their place on board.

"I hate my family," Eleni said.

"I'm happy that you have a future," Hanna said. As she said it, her heart curdled, wondering whether or not she'd live to see her seventeenth birthday, thinking about her time with

Eleni ending, how little Peia would never grow up, or how Pa would never take her to the stars.

Eleni didn't respond, and Hanna swallowed those thoughts.

As the stars continued to fade, and their meetings started to linger, Eleni and Hanna spent less time looking up and more time looking at each other. Even though they'd finally acknowledged their future, Hanna didn't let it live in every interaction. Eleni wasn't a reminder of how it would end. She was a testament to why it was special to exist here and now.

"I heard you talking to the stars, once," Eleni said.

"When?"

"A few years ago, before we met. I'd been coming to this field, too. To get away from the girls at the boarding school. One day we overlapped, but you got here first. You were talking about how you'd had a fight with your ma. At first, I didn't know who you were talking to, until I realized."

Hanna felt a moment of violation, that Eleni heard secrets she hadn't wanted to share with anyone, but that moment dissipated. She knew her secrets were safe with Eleni.

"I didn't stay to listen. I wanted to share the field. But then every time I came back, you'd somehow be there. Our timing was too good. Too coincidental. I had to meet the girl who talked to the stars."

"Are you glad you did?" Hanna asked, her cheeks hot.

Eleni was hugging her legs, her dress pooling around her, melting into the grass. She nodded. Hanna wondered if that meant she felt the same fluttering in her stomach, the same safety when they locked eyes. She was getting better at reading Eleni's nonverbals, but she wasn't perfect, yet. So she decided to ask.

"Can I kiss you?" Hanna finally said. She'd asked her a million questions since they met, but that was the one she wanted to know the answer to more than any others.

"Yes please," Eleni responded.

Their lips brushed, quick and gentle at first. Then Eleni placed a hand on Hanna's neck and kissed her long and slow, still soft.

They kissed until the sky went dark and their lips chapped. They kissed until even more stars dissolved into the dust.

Hanna couldn't stop smiling the entire way home from the field.

She'd always kept Eleni from her family. Not because they wouldn't understand, but she liked having something all her own. She grew up sharing everything with her siblings, and if they knew about Eleni, she'd suddenly be theirs too. Peia would demand she come to the field, and Ma would invite her to dinner. Eleni, on the other hand, kept Hanna a secret from hers because they wouldn't understand.

"Is it because I'm a girl you like to kiss, or because I'm not like you?" Hanna asked once, their hands clasped by their sides.

Eleni didn't say, but the tightening of her lips told Hanna it was both.

They did a lot less talking and a lot more kissing. It was a welcome distraction. While their lips touched, she could escape the inevitable and disappear into a perfect world. The field itself was a fantasy, but Eleni's lips were a paradise.

Hanna wasn't comfortable with the idea of doing anything more. She didn't completely know why, or what it was about the thought that always made her nervous and hesitant. But she knew she didn't want it right now, if ever. When she told Eleni, she listened. That was what Hanna needed.

She listened better than the stars.

Although she'd seen snippets from newsreels and overheard plenty about the *GSS Renaissance* while Pa watched the TV, Hanna had never sat down to watch. Today, the reporter announced that construction on the ship had finished. They finally had a date for launch. Two weeks from now.

A tightening radiated from Hanna's chest, consuming every muscle in her body. She looked out the window to the stars—her clock—and pictured Eleni floating in them without her. Hanna had meant it when she said she was glad Eleni would have a future. Even though it hurt, she wanted her to soar.

When she met Eleni at the field the next night, the pressure of their remaining time loomed stronger than ever. Hanna thought seeing her would alleviate it, because that's what Eleni was so good at. Instead, each of Eleni's steps across the field was a second ticking away, and each of Hanna's breaths marked another day they'd never have together.

Before either of them could speak, Hanna broke and released her sobs.

Eleni quickly wrapped her arms around her, pulling her close, and they rocked together under the night sky with so few lights to guide them.

"I'll talk to my parents," Eleni whispered into Hanna's ear. "We'll get you on that ship."

Hanna shook her head and wiped her cheeks, leaning away even though she never wanted to let her go. "How? Are they going to pay my way on?"

Eleni gulped, and tears dripped down her face onto her dress. That was answer enough.

"We could sneak you on board," Eleni said, desperate for a solution.

She wasn't joking, but it made Hanna laugh. A momentary relief.

"I could steal the money," Eleni said.

"Eleni." Hanna grabbed her hand, trying to steady her. "Stop. There is nothing we can do. Your family would never pay. If they would, they wouldn't be the kind of people with that much money in the first place."

"But—" Eleni tried to argue, her body shaking. Somehow, Hanna was calm now. Calmer than she'd ever been talking about the *Renaissance.*

"They didn't put a price on it to make money. They put a price on it to exclude us," Hanna said.

Hanna watched as Eleni internalized something Hanna had always known.

"It's not fair," Eleni repeated, her fists clenched.

Hanna blinked tears away for a clearer view of the sky. She remembered how much of an escape it was to name the stars when they first met. Even though they'd known it would always end like this, back then it felt so faraway. Now the last few grains of sand were about to fall.

"You know what? I'm not going," Eleni said.

"You have to go," Hanna scoffed. This shouldn't have been a question.

"Why would I board that ship and spend the rest of my life with the very people I hate most?"

"Because without them you'll have nothing." Hanna needed Eleni to survive.

"I'd have you." Eleni's chest was rising and falling like she was sobbing, but no noise came out.

The tears came back, this time accompanied by rapid breaths. She couldn't fathom how any of this was real.

"If you can't come with me, then I'm staying with you."

Once again, Hanna saw rebellion in Eleni's eyes, and it burned brighter than ever. She wouldn't let Hanna argue any more. Eleni was unfaltering.

They made a plan.

Eleni would make her family believe she was going with them, of course, but the morning of the boarding, she and Hanna would meet in the field, and she'd hide with Hanna's family so hers couldn't find her. The ship would launch, leaving Eleni behind. One missing passenger wouldn't stop the *Renaissance*.

They couldn't plan much beyond that, but whatever happened, they knew they'd be okay if they were together.

Every time Eleni came to the field, she brought belongings and hid them right behind the trees—a few pieces of clothing, her favorite novel, and a leather-bound notebook and calligraphy pen. Each item stored was both a glimpse into Eleni's life beyond the trees and a piece of Hanna's hope building somewhere in her heart.

"Don't you have more things than this?" Hanna asked when the pile wasn't as high as she expected.

"Nothing I'll be needing," Eleni responded.

And when they'd talk of the future, a future that was somehow so much more uncertain yet so much clearer, she began to allow those pieces of hope to eclipse her entire chest. When they kissed, Hanna felt like she was entirely alive, not trapped in liminality. She pictured beyond the next time they'd meet, and that was everything.

"I can't wait to meet your family," Eleni said. "Especially Peia."

"She'll drive you nuts," Hanna warned. "But she's the cleverest kid you'll ever meet. Eddie you'll warm up to. Simon's great. He's just a younger brother, is all. Ma isn't going to be happy, not that I'm with you, that you're a runaway. Pa's going to love it. He's always up for trouble."

"You talk about them with so much love."

Hanna thought for a moment. "You never talked much about your siblings."

"What is there to know about Rufus, Felicia, and Arden St. John? They're rich and cruel."

"You're rich, too," Hanna joked.

"Not for long."

They kissed. They looked up to the stars. They hadn't in a while because they were so focused on their future in spite of them. There were so few left, and almost no complete constellations. Eleni took a shuddering breath when she noticed them, and Hanna knew what it meant. She could read her so easily now.

"You don't have to stay. We both know there's no real future here," Hanna said.

Eleni brought her gaze back to Hanna, back to land. The air was getting dustier, so Eleni was surrounded by a haze, the backdrop of this life-changing—or life-ending—decision.

"There might be a longer future for me there, but it won't be worth anything."

"How do you know that I'm worth it?" Hanna asked.

"Don't take this the wrong way, but it's not just you. If I go, it makes me one of them."

"Are you sure?" Hanna needed to know her decision was unequivocal. Otherwise she couldn't live with herself.

"I'm positive."

When Eleni looked back up to the stars, she exhaled slowly, like she was blowing away the dust.

Hanna held Eleni's hand, their fingers intertwined. They looked up.

"You know this means we'll never hold the stars, right?" Hanna asked.

Eleni didn't say anything. Instead, she squeezed Hanna's hand, and Hanna squeezed back.

The morning of the boarding, Hanna woke before dawn. Her family wasn't awake yet, but she turned on the news, knowing broadcasting had started. The volume was off, but she didn't need it.

They showed shots of the ship, massive and white and glossy, as engineers performed their preflight checks. It waited for the crew to board, the rooms sparkling and the feasts everlasting. It had no idea there would be one fewer person coming.

When it was time to leave, Hanna turned off the television and grabbed a scarf to cover her face. The air was getting less safe to breathe. Even when the sun rose, the days were never as bright as they used to be. She left the house, knowing the next time she'd see it, Eleni would be at her side.

She started toward the field. She could have done it with the scarf wrapped around her eyes because of how many times she'd made this trek. Her heart floated. She'd never been so excited to see Eleni's face, never been so nervous about going to her favorite place.

When she made her way through the trees and into the clearing, she expected Eleni to be waiting for her. It was okay, though. Hanna was early. She took her spot in the grass. The sun was about to rise, but the world wouldn't get much brighter.

She waited. And waited.

Hanna's hands shook without Eleni's there to steady them. Suddenly all the stars were going out before her very eyes.

Hanna stood and checked the horizon to make sure she hadn't missed Eleni. When her sweep came to nothing, she ran. The boarding school wasn't much farther past their field. But when she came across the slick black glass building, she knew it was empty before stepping inside. She threw the doors open just in case, the lobby eerily silent, not a whisper to be heard.

She didn't know where else she could look, so she ran back home. She'd told Eleni where their farm was, so maybe she'd made her way directly there. Yes, that must be it. Hanna ran so fast she swore she reached escape velocity.

When she arrived home, she stepped inside to a familiar sight—her family huddled around the screen. Ma baked bread in the kitchen in hopes of drowning out the noise from the livestream, and Eddie was eating popcorn, some sort of ironic symbolism, Hanna assumed.

Eleni wasn't there.

Hanna started to panic. She fell from her escape velocity and was now burning up on reentry. On the screen, families boarded the *Renaissance*, each of them pulling one or two suitcases behind them. Either those suitcases were for show and all their stuff was already in their rooms, or new things waited for them inside, and a suitcase was all they needed.

They all waved at the camera as they disappeared through the sliding doors, a mockery of those watching from their screens at home. Hanna noticed how the shot wasn't framed to show them inside the ship.

Then, she saw them. A family of six led by a large, hulking man in a suit that she knew to be Mr. St. John. There was a woman on his arm, and they were followed by two boys and a girl—Hanna guessed they were her siblings.

And then, there she was, at the back, trailing along with a suitcase.

Hanna's body shook and her heart shattered into a thousand pieces as she watched Eleni walk up that metal ramp, waving at the camera with her family. Was she mocking Hanna specifically? Was this all some kind of joke?

Hanna wanted to scream. To throw everything at the television and curse the world, but still, she remained hidden from her family. She suffered in silence as Eleni's brown hair and perfect smile and silk dress disappeared behind those glossy walls.

A tear ran down Hanna's cheek, and she wiped it away quickly. She wasn't blinking, her eyes stinging from the pixels and the pain of watching her girlfriend, her best friend, leave for a future without her.

It couldn't be on purpose. Her family must have caught her

and kept her from running. That entire ship was her prison. She'd said so. But she hadn't looked back like she was leaving anything behind.

More families boarded. All their faces began to blur together. Hanna turned from the screen, her gaze now locked on the floor. Her siblings made their own commentary in place of the newscaster's, but she could barely hear any of it over the violent ringing in her ears.

She'd never know what happened. Whether leaving was Eleni's choice or not. She wouldn't know what she'd been thinking when she woke up, or what her life would look like on that ship. She'd never get to hold her hand again or kiss her lips or even see her face. The fusion of Hanna's core threatened to stop. She was collapsing in on herself, preparing to burst. This was her supernova.

Eleni had a photo of them. Hanna had nothing. Only memories that were now clouded by question marks and dust.

It took a few weeks for Hanna to summon the fortitude to return to the field.

It was emptier now. Not because of the missing stars, the fog that kept her from seeing more than a few feet ahead, or a skewed perception that time created. It was because once again, this was only Hanna's field.

She sat for a while, looking up at nothing but cloudy mysteries. She ached for the days where the sky was unreachable because of its grandness, not because it was gone. She felt like any moment, Eleni would appear from the trees, calling her name, ready to wrap her in a hug. She'd sit next to her, and the dust would lift, the lights shining for them. But those feelings were only shadows.

Then, Hanna remembered something.

She left her spot in the grass and headed toward the trees, ready for answers.

There were Eleni's things, tucked behind the tree, right where they'd left them. At first glance, nothing in the pile was anything Hanna hadn't seen before.

She knelt to the ground and reached first for one of the dresses. It was the green one Eleni so often wore, now covered with a layer of dust. Hanna picked up the novel, flipping through it like the words were Eleni's story, like its ending would tell her what their ending meant. Then, she looked through the leather-bound notebook, desperate for a note, but the pages were blank.

A piece of paper fluttered to the ground by her knees. Hanna's breath caught when she saw it. The photo of her and Eleni.

Eleni was exactly as Hanna remembered her. Time couldn't take that.

She looked at it and longed to return to that moment. She checked for writing on it, or something else tucked in the book, but there was nothing. Eleni had the photo on her screen, so why would she need to print it?

All of her unknowns flooded her head. She blinked through the dryness of the air, tears escaping her eyes. If there was nothing else Hanna could know, she would know this—Eleni had her copy, and had made certain Hanna had one, too. No matter what, whether or not Eleni chose to go, Hanna was special to her.

She held the photo close to her chest and held the only truth she had deep inside her heart.

"Get up!"

"It's the middle of the night!" Eddie's voice was still groggy, angry at Pa for disturbing him.

The whispers weren't intended for Hanna, but she hadn't been able to sleep well for months, so even the faintest sound could wake her. She found herself curled around a fast-asleep Peia. They'd been holding each other extra close lately. She stared at the wall, something she'd been doing a lot of since the launch.

Pa laughed, a real laugh, a noise she hadn't heard from him in ages.

"We have a ship," he whispered.

"What?" Eddie said.

Hanna's skin tightened. She almost threw the covers off her and sat up, demanding to be a part of this conversation, too.

"We have a ship. We get to leave," Pa said. His words sounded so familiar to Hanna, yet the reverberation of this version held so much more weight.

"How is that possible? We don't..." Eddie was stumbling through his words the way Hanna was trying to work through the scrambling in her brain.

"I bought an old cargo ship. It needs fixed up. It's lived a long life already. But that's why I need your help. We've got work to do," Pa said.

Eddie clambered to get out of bed, grabbing for his shoes, and Hanna tried to steady her shaking body. Once she was sure they'd left, she untangled herself from Peia and shot up.

She made sure she felt real, that this wasn't a dream, but she felt as certainly real as ever.

She slid her hand inside her pillowcase until she felt the piece of paper she'd kept hidden under her head every night. Whenever she couldn't sleep, she'd stare at the photo and remember.

She looked out her window into the night and brought the photo to her heart. She hadn't been able to see the sky for weeks, but she thought maybe tonight, the dust was a little bit clearer. She wondered where Pa and Eddie were headed, what the ship looked like, and how long it would take until they'd get to board.

The universe was vast, and their small little planet was dying, but a shard of Hanna's heart still shone, a piece of hope alive somewhere inside her. Even if she couldn't see the stars, they were still burning and flourishing beyond the dust, creating a map to guide her. They were waiting for Hanna when she was ready to go find them.

And now she could finally start her own course to the stars.

★ ★ ★ ★ ★

LIKE SUNSHINE, LIKE CONCRETE

Z. R. Ellor

THE RECRUITMENT STATION IN SUNNY PINES

Mall, Albuquerque, has seen better days—but so has the army, and that hasn't stopped them. The parking lot outside the concrete strip mall had been taped off, soldiers posted at the corners of the vast square, more space than we'll need.

Maybe thirty high-schoolers have shown up—Colonel Peterson expected three hundred—and they mill aimlessly around the asphalt, all races and genders and style senses, from the pasty white goths in heavy chain necklaces to the two Black kids in preppy school uniforms waiting on the edge. All they have in common is a darting desperation in their eyes, a desperation I remember.

Now, after a year and a half of military service, I'm just tired. But I'm not allowed to show it. And I'm sure as hell not allowed to want out.

I make my grand entrance from the recruitment station roof. *One. Two. Three.* A quick breath, a neat sprint—my foot pushes off the roof's edge, and I'm airborne. Limbs tucked tight around my torso. Senses shooting rapid-fire as I fall. *Four. Five.* My boots slap down on the asphalt, my knees straightening to catch me.

"I'm privileged to introduce a good friend of mine," Colonel Peterson says at the mic. "Major William James Svenson— who's had a *major* impact on how we recruit."

Applause rings as I jog to Peterson's side. A grin creeps across my face despite itself. It's a cheesy pun, but cheese is my favorite food.

"Did you see my backpack anywhere?" I ask. Without pausing for a reply—Peterson's a crappy actor—I kneel and hook my fingers under the stage. One-handed, holding down a grunt, I lift. The three-hundred-pound platform lifts easily. I fish out the backpack I stashed down there beforehand and pull it on. Scattered cheers and whistles rise from the crowd.

My Kurator injection–infused strength was way more entertaining the first time a video of me went viral, when no one had seen a guy lift a car with his bare hands. But I flash the audience a smile, wink at a green-haired femme in the front row, and fling myself into a standing backflip.

That gets some louder yells, and even one audience member shouting "USA! USA!" like they invented that idea. I'm a walking advertisement, even if the army calls me a recruitment officer, more useful catching eyes than serving in combat.

"Tell them how you joined the army, Major."

What comes out next is a lie, three parts duty and one part a yearning for adventure. This is what really happened.

When the cancer got my mom—pretty common, now

the ozone layer's gone the way of the dodo—and my super-Catholic uncle refused to take me in along with my little brother, enlisting seemed like a smart choice.

I was only sixteen, but recruiters aren't picky about age these days, not if you can forge your parent's signature on a release form. Unfortunately, like plenty of pre-T trans guys, I looked like a better fit for the swing set than the battlefield.

The recruiter saw "19" written on my paperwork and said, "Nice try, son, come back when your balls drop." Before I could counter with "Don't have none, sir," an old guy in the lab coat crooked a finger and said, "Come with me, boy."

Like the sucker I was, I went. Then, I'd have done just about anything for someone to acknowledge I was a boy.

My grandfather had been a solider. When I was a kid, he told me he enlisted to keep America safe from terrorists. He died before I could ask for more details. All I knew was the military was a place even a kid could make a difference. All you needed was bravery and a good heart.

I wish I'd asked him for more information.

Project Achilles, the army called it, after some dead Greek hero who slaughtered hundreds with his bare hands. Frank, that old grandstanding pain in the ass, joked it was ironic—"In the Iliad, he was gay as hell"—because Frank knew things, and I mostly knew how to reach the secret levels in *CombaTopia*.

We'd never been the couple you'd expect to come out of a meat grinder like Project Achilles, and so maybe it was fate we only lasted a few months.

I just wish I knew if he was still breathing.

Focus, I tell myself atop the stage. *Don't mess this up.* Thankfully, I could do this show in my sleep by now, and it comes out seamlessly. A hundred push-ups with an audience volunteer sitting on my shoulders, a yarn about me and the Project Achilles squad breaking all the army records in basic training, and a sparring demo where I knock down a private with his bare chest oiled. When I'm done, six kids stand in line at the table to be matched with a recruiter.

I want to tell them it's a mistake. I've realized pretty quickly the modern army is half owned by big corporations, and mostly fights on their behalf. With the power of Kurator injections in my veins, I make fighting their wars look simple. Easy. Good.

That's anything but true, when war is messy and bloody and no one wins. And I guess how I feel on the inside about it doesn't matter, since it doesn't change anything. I can't tell these kids to run from the offers, not yet. Not until I've fled myself. Not until I've found a way to talk about how worn down this type of *service* makes me feel on the inside. Not when the only thing that keeps me from sprinting off into the sunset is that the army controls the drugs that give me my powers.

"Want to go grab a coffee?" says one of the new recruits, flashing me a friendly grin.

I shake my head. There's no law anymore about being gay or trans in the military. We had a gay president who made sure of that. His one concession to the queer community was giving us the right to die in the desert like straight folks.

"I don't do caffeine," I say, to spare his feelings. Frank liked his coffee black and cheap, rehydrated powder like the kind you got fifty packets of for a buck at the dollar store. He'd drink it from his canteen when he would stay up late and read. Keeping me awake with foot-jitters.

"Oh, sorry. Maybe a burrito or—"

A *crack-crack-boom* pounds over us. My injection-fueled reflexes flare, and I drag him to the pavement as a flower of fire blossoms out the window of a nearby bank. My ears ring with echoing alarms as three men leap through the gap and spring, loaded with heavy suitcases of cash, for a waiting van.

And some part of me goes *thank god, I know how this goes.*

I grab a heavy lighting pole from a stack of stage equipment and sprint across the parking lot. Asphalt thuds under my boots. Sunlight beats down heavy on the back of my neck. The robbers don't look up from the van, and if they did, they wouldn't expect one guy to prove a problem.

Their mistake.

I jam the pole into the ground and lever myself skyward.

My foot slams into one robber's arm, knocking the weapon from his grip. Whipping around as I land, I slam the pole into another's gut. He grunts and drops his gun. *Roll.* I catch it, eject the magazine, and fling it in the bushes.

"Stand down," I tell the men on the pavement, who are groaning and rubbing their bruises. My heart thuds against my lungs, a familiar adrenaline spike. Trouble tends to follow me around. But at least this reminds me I've got more purpose than glossing over the army's ugly truth for teens. "Hands on your heads. No fast movements—"

A hand wraps around my mouth. Firm, neck-snapping force. With a heartbeat to react, I butt my head backwards. It hits plastic, and I feel the impact all the way down in my boots. But at least that gets me free—or free enough to spin around.

He stands tall and mocking, clad in black armor and masked with a silver skull. Behind him, two security guards lie crumpled on the pavement, one clutching an injured ankle, one bleeding freely from a nunchaku blow to the temple—the same weapon resting in this too-familiar man's hands.

"Get back!" I shout as the soldiers rush our way. They're strong, fast, and trained, but Stryker is something else. I recognize the might, recklessness, lightning reflexes in myself, even if I lack the wild destructive fury. The one time I drew his blood, it came out green-tinted in sunlight—another soldier shaped by Kurator injections. Wherever I go, whenever I perform for potential recruits, he's close to follow. Robbing stores. Stealing trucks. Wrecking my whole damn day. "This one is mine."

"You think you can take me?" Scorn carries even through his voice modulator. "Hard to be scared by a man who lost a fight with some mud."

"We *both* tripped the last time we fought. It was *raining*." I lunge for his weapon hand. If I can get the nunchaku away, I've got a fighting chance.

But he slams his thigh up into mine, knocking me skyward. I crash into the bank wall.

"You're the one who landed on his ass. Not that I'd expect better of a glorified cheerleader."

I wince, because that blow lands too. A retort doesn't come to mind either, annoyingly. So instead, I grab a brick from the shattered wall and chuck it at his head. Whoever said *use your words* didn't speak army.

Stryker dodges sideways, but I knew he would, and I'm already there. He slams into my side, and my hands grapple around his thigh. With a practiced flip, I toss him to the pavement. Down he slams. Satisfied, I dust off my hands.

"Freeze!" shouts a voice behind me. Blaring sirens fill the air. I turn to see Peterson rushing over, gun drawn. Can't he see I've disarmed all the robbers?

I slide between him and the downed Stryker. "Easy! They're disarmed—we're clear—"

In a flash of black shadow, Stryker lunges for the van. Peterson's bullet hits the open door as he flings himself into the driver's seat. The engine roars.

I swear and grab the bumper. Dig my heels in. Straining. With my Kurator injection-fueled strength, I can do it easy as a finger snap.

But just because I'm strong doesn't mean the metal is. The bumper fractures in my hand. Creaking, cracking, tearing. A chunk of steel, edges warped and spotted with rust, wrenches off in my fist as the van speeds away.

They drive me back to Air Base Addison once the cops arrive, we're a caravan streaming down the freeway, a moving fortress of tinted glass.

Medical pulls me in for inspection; then, since it's nearly time for my monthly infusion, hooks me up. The Kurator injection goes in my leg, once a month, bubbling green along the big vein there as it runs. Rashes with an oily sheen run down to my knee with spots. Rushing in like a million volts of electric shock.

Those first few months, my head spun constantly with the

energy of changes. My bones, melting and stretching like saltwater taffy. Muscles popping down my arms and torso like plastic from a mold. Brain as fizzy as pressurized soda pop. They had to do a bit of surgery on my chest and other bits, but aside from that you wouldn't know how I was born.

The injection fades after a while, though. You need to keep injecting it, or your body burns through it and throws it away. And only the US Government knows where it comes from.

At first, I thought it was real nice of them, giving this cool free stuff to a bunch of poor trans guys like us. But nothing comes for free. The injection isn't a gift—it's a leash. It means I can't ever walk away.

I hold on to the scrap metal I ripped off the damaged bumper. I should probably share it with the cops, but somehow, irrationally, holding on to it makes me feel like I'm still in that fight, that moment. Where everything made sense down to the blood on my knuckles.

A bumper sticker. Painted over in black, but my eyes can read through the paint. Demeter Lawn and Garden Supply. Blocky, pseudo-Greek font, ringed by succulents in pots with smiling faces. I recognize a cartoon *Aeonium*, an aloe plant, and what must be an *Echeveria*.

Frank would fill his bunk with tiny cactuses and painted pots. It feels like a hundred years have passed since we lay down together, and he taught me the names.

"How'dya learn all this plant stuff?" I'd asked once. "Did your family garden lots?"

He laughed. "My dad did. He quit after my mom left and we had to move to Arizona. I picked it up just because he was putting it down, you know? I like having succulents around."

"They're cute," I said, poking a waxy leaf. It was colder than I expected, even in the shadows.

"They're spiky. They come with their own body armor." He laughed, though it came out sounding cold. "You always see the best in everything, Will."

I learned in, so close I smelled the sweat on his cheek. "Maybe I just see the best in you."

I guess Frank was right. I never see the thorns until they stab me in the back.

Colonel Peterson decided it wasn't worth it, sending the costly Project Achilles boys on secret missions where we'd just get blown up. We made better recruitment tools than soldiers. At least, I would; I was the only one left.

Six boys died in the first six months of experiments. Three, Frank included, disappeared when the army sent them out on their first mission. *Missing in action.* Probably rotting in a ditch no one's bothered to uncover.

Colonel Peterson tells me they're thinking of restarting the project. Of creating a new generation of enhanced soldiers using advanced prosthetics, or cyber-brain implants.

I don't want more people to be sucked into this crappy excuse for a life. I want to get my ass out. Build a life where people don't get hurt around me. Because of me.

"I think I know how we can stop Stryker," I tell Colonel Peterson when he comes in to check on me in the med bay.

He gives me a weird look. "You *did* stop Stryker. Ended the robbery, saved the cash."

"Well, yeah, but he got away. I have a clue about his hideout. Should that go to you, or the police?"

"Look at me, kid." He sighs. "We don't need to arrest Stryker."

"Sir?"

"Your run-ins with him make headlines. You saw those kids back there—it's the best recruiting tool we've got."

"But, sir—" I don't normally argue with officers. It was drilled out of me ages ago. Still. "People could get hurt."

"People always get hurt. What matters is if it's us or them."

The look in his eye says he pities me, that I'm the naive one here. A look that says, don't be a child, go along. Agree.

"Us or them? Sir, aren't we all Americans?"

"I'm not going to answer that question." He stands and walks out the door.

I wish I could do the same. I want to *leave*. I want to run screaming. Maybe that's not what anyone would expect of the perfect American solider, but I'm human and I'm tired and I just want out. If the military didn't control the supply of Kurator—

Stryker.

He has the drug. The one thing I'm sticking around for.

Dr. Kerr says I can't risk myself. Colonel Peterson thinks our run-ins are great for business. But I'm not hunting Stryker out of patriotic duty. That dried up in me long ago. Squeezed out like the juice of an orange. Everything feels squeezed up in me now.

Before I transitioned, I'd sometimes get dysphoric about being too small, about being a massive jock trapped in a five-foot frame. Now I feel that again, only instead of my body not fitting, it's my body fitting too well. For what I want, sure, but really for what they want of me. And that makes my body feel like it's not really mine at all. Like I'm not me—I'm *theirs*.

Stryker holds the key to getting them out of my life, my head. He may be a dangerous asshole, but only he knows how to replace the drugs.

If I can uncover the secret behind his Kurator injections, the Arizona highways will open up for me like a whole world.

Getting off base is the hard part.

Plenty of guys get weekend leave, time to go visit family, check out the local nightlife, socialize. I'm still under medical observation, technically, because of the experiment, and I've never pushed back on that—it's not like I have friends on base to go anywhere with.

The military's not worried about soldiers deserting—the reasons we needed to sign up don't disappear once we realize how different the real army is from what recruiters told us. People vanish for the night, but always come back before they get caught missing morning muster.

For now, a night is all I need.

The clinic is back near the wall, and the cameras have been broken for a dog's age. Easy enough to vault over and walk up to the concrete barricade, join the stream of soldiers catching buses into town. People just assume the clean-cut white guy in the military uniform is going somewhere, or at least he's too tall and buff to bother questioning.

I stop in at a Walmart and buy a pair of sweats, plus a backpack to stuff my uniform in after I change. One more anonymous bus ride, another strip mall, and I'm behind the garden center. They say I'm a hero, but I'm just one more shadow in the night.

I didn't ever tell Frank I loved him. Some nights I wonder if Achilles told Patroclus, or if in Ancient Greece, you just knew.

The garden center is locked. I peer through the chain-link doors with a flashlight. Empty. After jogging around to the back, I vault over the fence. Movement flickers in the greenhouse. I lean in, reaching for the door handle—

A knife pokes into the base of my spine.

"What the hell are you doing here?" Stryker hisses.

"This isn't the dance club?" And before he can answer, I jab my elbows backwards.

They connect—hard, solid muscle. He stumbles back, and I'm already pivoting—foot to instep, second blow. He grunts. His silver death's-head mask shines brighter than the foggy desert stars as he slams up against a wall of fertilizer bags.

"I just want to talk," I say. Keeping my voice open, like I'm talking to a spooked horse.

"I've got nothing to say to you," he says, and flings a handful of dirt in my eyes.

I curse, scratching at my face, and he's on top of me. Shoving me back into the greenhouse wall. Glass erupts in a sparkling shower as we fall. My back hits the ground, and then he's on top of me. Punching.

Blow after blow, like he wants to beat the ghost from me. My hands fumble blindly, reaching for a weapon, a tool—and catch a garden hose. I whip it around, lashing the tight plastic cord about his neck, yanking it tight. Dragging him off me.

"Stop it!" I gasp. My voice peaks. *Real tough, aren't you,*

Will? My fist strikes the side of his jaw, a boulder impact. Stryker flies backwards and hits the wall. Panting, I add, "I just need to know where you get your injections from."

"Of course you do. Everyone wants that shit." He drew a gun out from the small of his back and takes aim at my skull. "You came to rip me off, is that all? Beat me up for applause and steal my drugs?"

I froze. *It's not like that at all.* But it's not like I can blame him for seeing me in the worst possible light. Not when I punch people and lie for a living. The gloss and muscle make for a good show, but it's still not worth the price of admission. A price I've conned so many kids my age into paying. I've got a gun pointed in my face, and I can't say I don't deserve that. If Project Achilles ends here, I can't say it's the worst way to go. At least it's honest. At least I'll see my friends when I go.

"See you on the far side, Frank," I murmur like a prayer.

"What the hell?" Stryker strides forward. The barrel digs into my cheekbone. "Why'd you say that?"

"Captain Frank Marston," I whisper. "I loved him and I'll see him again in heaven or hell. Do your worst, terrorist scum."

"Christ, Will…" He ripped off his mask. Shaggy black hair spilled out. Frank Marston's hazel eyes peered down at me. "You had to make it hard to put a bullet in you."

It's like my heart's stopped. Like time has ripped on open. I see months of darkness and spilled minutes, drifting away, torn away, until I can barely think with the weight of them.

He leans in close. My brain scrambles, years of fear and training and trauma jamming like a rusty gun, until I think he'll kill me and he'll kiss me both at once.

"5831 Bluebonnet Drive," he hisses. Hot, heavy breath in my ear. Physical. Alive. "Come alone. I'll know if you're followed."

I sneak back onto base, leaping over the wall with the dead cam, sliding into my bunk next to the medical bay.

They put me there just in case something happens, to keep eyes on me, and though I miss bunking down with friends, I do as they say. I do as they say so much that the doctor waiting around my door doesn't think to even question when I tell him I took out my own IV to catch the end of a baseball game in the mess hall.

"Good to see you having fun, Will."

I'm not having fun. Fun has always been a luxury for me. I was the oldest daughter in my family—I mean, everyone thought I was an oldest daughter. That meant work. That meant pleasing everyone else first. The army makes sense once you've trained yourself to think that way. Discipline and self-sacrifice become inevitable. That's not compatible with optimism or fun. That's how you beat yourself up and congratulate yourself for bleeding.

All I can think about the next day is the whisper, the promise, the weight. Of another night when clouds covered the moon and the mist rose (Frank had worried his succulents would get moldy in the damp) and we'd been out for a training exercise.

We'd been playing paintball with another group of Project Achilles soldiers when a spring blizzard forced us to bunker down. Paranoid, camping deep in the woods, we'd slept in shifts. I'd woken to the sound of Frank's gun.

Two other boys sprawled in the snow, covered in paint. One held a white flag cut from an undershirt.

"Jesus!" he shouted at Frank. "We were coming to surrender!"

"How could you do that?" I asked him.

"They were armed," Frank said. "Men do dirty things in war."

"It's all a game. You can't know they were going to hurt us."

"We'll never know for sure," he said. "But I know what I need to know. That I can keep you safe no matter the cost."

I wanted to be the center of his attention. But not like that. I wanted to know I could lighten the load he carried behind those serious eyes. I wanted to make him smile.

I'm an optimist. But too many times, optimism has failed me. Colonel Peterson says he's optimistic about the future of our country, even though the cities are flooding and California might secede.

Some things you need to face in the dark.

They send me to perform in a mall the next day, and the recruits are as awkward and unprepared as kittens in a church. I pray through my push-ups and backflips that Stryker—that Frank—won't crash the party. It'd be just like the bastard he's become to expose our rendezvous. But he's a no-show, and twenty new recruits pass on their contact info. Colonel Peterson glows.

"I'm going to grab some Starbucks—can I get you anything?" I say when we finish.

I'm not a spy—the army mostly trained me in muscles—

but sometimes the simplest lies fly swiftest, and Peterson nods and waves me off.

I got lucky on the addresses—5831 Bluebonnet Drive is only two blocks from the mall, an office tower built for some boom of prosperity that never came. The first few stories are occupied by dentist offices and insurance companies, the next few are deserted, and I give a wide berth to the families sheltering up top, since it'd probably scare them to see a massive stranger barging through their shelter.

I know Frank will be on the roof. Back in training, he'd race me up mountains, climb atop bunkers to sit and watch clouds slide across the blue. It makes him feel free. It always left me wondering how it felt to imagine so deeply that your thoughts could only fit beneath heaven.

I climb out atop the service stair. Dry desert air washes down my neck, my throat. The sun rolls in a bleached wave across the concrete.

"Frank?" I whisper. He's got Kurator-infused senses. He should be able to hear me if he's also here. All I hear is the wind.

I stride across the rooftop—check behind a massive HVAC unit, the only place he could hide—and see nothing. Cars honk and squeal below, and I gaze out—expecting, I don't know, that he's pulled back down his silver skull mask to fling a look at me.

Then I realize.

Frank isn't meeting me here. He's across the street, beneath a dying sage tree, reading a book. His eyes don't lift off the paper as a man in a neat suit sets a crate down behind him. A bunch of little glass bottles filled with glowing green liquid.

Frank points at the delivery man's back. Can he see me? Or does he just know in his bones I'd come? That nothing in the universe would keep me from coming for him?

He's trying to tell me something. And when I see it, I'm not shocked. I just know it's the last thing I'd ever want to see:

Colonel Peterson, striding casually away from the problem he's created.

I believed in my country once. And it ripped me open and left a big hole where my heart should be. I believed in Frank, until he tried to put a bullet in my throat. Maybe the only reason I'm going is because I'm chasing ghosts. Ghosts of purpose and feelings and everything that mattered before the world ended.

But I'm the sort of person who needs to chase something. So even if this won't get me out of the army, it'll get me out of my head. It'll give me one small thing I want.

After the year I've had, I at least deserve a distraction. Some answers.

And to punch Frank in the perfect teeth for ditching me.

And to heal his fucking soul.

And to save my own.

Frank would probably want me to play it subtle. He was always good at lurking in the shadows. I guess that's why they chose him to be the bad guy.

I'm just going to get what I want. Not answers—I think I already know them, jumbling about in the back of my head, congealing slowly. Just an acknowledgment, and maybe a place to put all this hurt.

So I slide down the gutters on the building's side, my hands sluicing through muck and grime, palms tearing where they hit loose metal—and with flecks of green-tinged blood dropping to the ground, I block Peterson off from his car.

"So you know," he says. He winces a little, looking down at his shoes—like I've caught him cheating at cards, flirting with someone who's not his wife. Like I've just uncovered an embarrassing wrinkle he can easily smooth away. "Thought it'd still take you a few years."

I fold my arms. "You faked it all. To drive up recruitment."

"People need stories, Will. You fighting Stryker is a good story. We ran out of them a couple wars back."

"What sort of person do you think I am? You think I enlisted to tell your stories?"

"No. I think you're a kid who doesn't know what he's doing."

My jaw drops. Where'd he get the goddamn nerve? Do they teach that in officers' school, along with how to iron your cuffs and pretend your shits don't stink? *Naive kid* described the me I was before they sucked me in. The parts of me they took away until I don't even feel like much of a person.

Frank must notice my face turning purple. He darts across the street, face tucked low against his collar, the way he does when he doesn't want anyone seeing he's upset. "Piss off, Will," Frank says, more pleading than mad. "You know the truth now. I didn't want you to throw your life away for me. Just walk away."

"I can't let this continue," I said. "It wouldn't be ethical. Not after everything you've been through. You didn't choose this. You may be a monster, but they made you one." *And I'm the same sort of monster, but in daylight. I'm the carrot and you're the stick.*

"Always trying to be a hero, Will," Peterson says. "Now get in the car. We're going back." It's the sort of thing that should have a threat behind it, but doesn't.

"Why the hell would I do that?"

"Because you won't find this—" he points at the green bottles "—anywhere else."

The Kurator injections. Yeah. Right. The whole reason I tracked down Stryker to begin with. Not because I cared about him. Just for me.

I thought I was a good person. Maybe I'm just a weak one. Why else would they choose me for the recruitment program's public face and leave Frank for the shadow work?

This isn't strength, what they've given me. There's nothing heroic here at all. It's a façade, a trap for vulnerable kids. It's not right, and I can't keep letting it be my whole identity. That's what gets me—the confident smirk on Peterson's face. How he knows he can leash me.

I've been clinging to the army like an anchor in a storm. But sometimes it's better to be set adrift.

Frank means anger and uncertainty, but also whispered conversations in the darkness. The reminder my hands can do more than work.

And all their stories of dead times and just causes are far behind us.

I spin and pop Peterson on the jaw. He stumbles back and sags. I lean him up against the tree like he's napping, quick, before anyone notices he's knocked out.

"What the hell are you doing?" Frank says.

"Trying to be a hero." Because for all I tell myself I'm pissed about everything the army's done to me, I liked the muscles and applause just fine. I wouldn't have stayed this long if I wasn't trying to cling to that part of it. But half in, half out isn't an option. It's just an excuse.

I need to be strong enough to walk away. Lay down arms. Disengage from this institution that's hurting us both. Peterson never trained me to be this kind of brave. This kind of brave could dismantle everything he's built.

"But I'm done," I continue. "And I hope you're done too. Come with me and stop playing the villain. It's not who you are."

"You don't know who I am. Not anymore. Maybe you never did." He shakes his head. "Because you should have known I wouldn't leave you willingly. You should have looked for me."

I flinch. Spite and consequences brim in his voice. Anger. Frustration. Indictment. *It was out of my control!* I want to yell, but I don't want to yell at him. He's as prickly as his beloved little cactuses. I know that much about him, that he wears his thorns like body armor, and I want to know more.

I clear my throat. "I'm ready to start over. If you give me another chance."

And that's how we wind up blazing out of town in Stryker's van. Arms bleeding under band-aids where we cut out our tracking chips. Bottles of Kurator injections rattling in the back seat.

When it runs out, we'll need to switch to the new high-tech testosterone cocktails, or the black market, depending on the laws of whatever splinter of America we wind up in. Maybe our powers will stick, maybe they won't. But that isn't the sort of power we need. Not when it was the sort of power they were willing to give us.

We'll make something new on the highways. Something like sunlight, with no concrete to block it in.

TRANSLATING
FOR THE
MACHINE

Nita Tyndall

AT THE END, IT CAME DOWN TO EDEN, AND THE
Machine.

The Machine, of course, has existed longer than Eden. It had other names—back before it was The Machine Through Which All Information is Parsed and Sorted, and before that it was Model A12930.778j2, the .778j2 of course being its own identifier in the Model A12930 line.

In its own language, it is 01000001 01101100 01101100.

All.

The names for The Machine have changed over time, of course, but the purpose of The Machine itself has not. The Machine knows all, and therefore dictates all—collecting and aggregating information, using algorithms even Eden doesn't understand to predict future disasters and outcomes, reporting on any current unrest.

And it is this language that Eden knows, this language that they are supposed to parse and report back on. They are, they've been told, the one person who is able to withstand the machine's scrutiny.

There are whispers, rumors, of course, that the reason Eden can withstand The Machine's scrutiny is that The Machine does not know what to do with Eden. The Machine breaks things down into binary, and Eden cannot be broken down into such a way, so they are left alone. Singled out. Special.

(Eden thinks this is bullshit, frankly; but they don't say anything about it, because being singled out as special is what keeps them from working a factory job like everyone else.)

They were chosen to be the Translator for The Machine when they were ten, after the previous Translator died in an accident. (So said The Council. Accidents happen. But Eden's heard the stories (everyone has heard the stories) about the men and women who've translated for The Machine before, who let The Machine go a little too deep into their heads, bodies broken down into binary code until The Machine's systems took them over entirely. The next shift would find them on the floor, skin turned a sickly green and blood pooling from their eye sockets.)

This happened again and again, until The Council found Eden, immune because they didn't fit the binary. The Council came to Eden's door, and even at ten Eden had known to be afraid of them, the way their faceless masks looked at Eden's mothers as if they, too, were simply information to be sorted.

Eden's mother Annette had clutched Eden tightly to her side, her wife, Maureen, fretting the way she always did, hands smoothing Eden's hair over and over, like she couldn't trust herself to stop.

"They're too young," Maureen had said, but no one refused The Council. They took Eden that night, with just their backpack and a stuffed animal they'd claimed to be too old for when Annette had thrust it at them. They clutched it the entire ride to the city center, lights passing beneath the transparent flooring under their feet.

The Council had decided, and that was that. And at seventeen, Eden is no longer afraid of The Council, if only because they've come to regard them as the entity who signs their paychecks, nothing more.

Besides, it's not like they interact often. The Council remains faceless and many-voiced, hidden behind masks, using technology that alters their voices so they all speak in one language, accent- and genderless.

It was not always like this. The Council used to simply be an individual council, made up of members and representatives from every country, every language, as many dialects as possible. But as the world shifted and dialects and languages were lost with each new generation, people rose up against the fact that The Council was largely male, largely white, as many of them said The Council was the cause of their destruction in the first place.

So now, in order to appease, The Council is this—a many-voiced, one-faced thing. It prevented blame or responsibility falling onto any one person or nation.

Eden wonders if people were happy with this shift, this motion, or if it's just an act of cowardice on The Council's part. For all Eden and the rest of them know, The Council is just as white and male as before.

Thankfully Eden only has to report in person to The Council once every quarter. Otherwise, when Eden is done for the day, they upload the most relevant information to a secured file, to allow The Council to decide what's necessary and disperse it to the human translators. Eden often sees them sitting together, little pods of people talking in languages Eden cannot grasp, their conversations fluid and shifting, not the strict order of The Machine's written language.

They wonder, sometimes, how exactly The Council decides which information to give to the human translators and which to keep for itself. They've never told Eden what their exact criteria for dispersal are beyond that the information a) cannot cause panic and b) can have a concrete, measurable effect.

When they were younger, Eden would run to The Council with every scrap of news they thought was interesting, if only to show off their own skill and understanding—today, The Machine predicted there would be a disaster next year; today, it said there would be a great financial crisis in New York next quarter but that we should bounce back with around a seventy-five percent success rate; today—

The Council didn't care. They didn't want vague predictions from The Machine, even if they were mostly accurate. What they wanted was intel. Concrete facts. Even right now, The Machine said there's an uprising happening in Quarter 22.5z and that wouldn't be enough information.

If Eden presented that, The Council would fire back with *Who began it? What are the exact coordinates of the uprising? What percentage of our people are aware of it, and how many of them are sympathizers?*

Eventually Eden stopped bringing information. They compiled reports, uploaded them. Nothing more.

Still. Eden spends their days translating for The Machine,

seven hours a day, six days a week. During their free time, when they get it, they try to spend it doing something, anything analog, where they aren't plugged into a screen or trying to track information. Oftentimes they lie on their couch while Mina rubs their back, talking over reality shows that neither of them will admit outside the four walls of their apartment that they watch.

Mina also works in the city center, as a musician. It was what drew Eden to her the first day they saw her: straight blonde hair pulled back and a look of utter concentration on her pale face as her fingers plucked at a harp. When they'd met, Eden told Mina they thought her music was its own kind of translation, pulling music out of the stark black-and-white notes on the page.

That's when Mina fell for them, she had told them once.

Sometimes Eden wants to ask The Machine about Mina, just to see what it knows about her, about all of them. It would be so simple—just feed it Mina's ID number and translate what comes out.

But Eden won't do that. Some things are best left unknown by The Machine. Eden doesn't want it to have information about Mina because then, inevitably, it would have information about Eden.

The Machine sits in the middle of the room. Eden walks to it, waves to it like it's an old friend, which they suppose it is. They don't talk to it, that would be weird, but they do feel like it needs some acknowledgment.

They sit in the chair they've come to think of as theirs, strap the wrist of their right hand down and place their palm on the sensor. Feel the sharp prick of the needle that means the nano-interface of The Machine is interacting with Eden's own hardware, and close their eyes.

This used to take much longer. When Eden was younger, their interface wasn't as sophisticated, and oftentimes they'd have to transcribe large parts of The Machine's data by hand. They used to translate as they went, too, thinking that was easier. Now they pull all the information at once.

What feels like hours later, they lift their hand from the sensor, stopping the continuous flow of information from The Machine's interface to their own. The process always feels slightly invasive, even after so many years doing it.

Eden knows The Machine can't corrupt them, can't infect them like it did so many men and women in the past, but sometimes in moments of panic the thought still enters their mind like a song they can't stop hearing.

There are days Eden thinks about quitting, but then who would they have to replace them?

It's not like they've met any other people like themselves, not in their city center. (Not like they're even allowed to venture outside their own city center anyway. Too precious a commodity, The Council says.)

They spend the next few hours translating the information before resting their hand back on The Machine. They send a secure message of that day's translations to The Council, closing their eyes as they wait for the upload to finish.

How many hours have they spent in this room? How much of their life has been spent staring at 1s and 0s?

Too much, they think, but it's not like they can do anything about it.

With a sigh, Eden pulls their hand away as the file finishes uploading, jams the hood of their hoodie over their head. Their stomach is growling, and they're tired, and they think tonight they've earned picking up food instead of trying to cook something or asking Mina to.

Takeout tonight? they ask Mina, pulling up their contact interface for her once they're out of the room that houses The Machine.

Where from?

Red Spot, idk.

Sure :) Usual order.

K!

Eden laughs and blinks away the interface before heading into the center proper, their feet taking them toward their favorite takeout spot, already sending their order through the interface so it's ready by the time they arrive. They wave at the person who processes the orders and pick theirs up.

By the time they've made it back to their apartment, they're ravenous. When Mina finally unlocks the door for them, they've already got half of a fry sticking out of their mouth.

"Cute," Mina says as Eden enters and sets the food down on the table.

"I try," Eden says, and Mina kisses them on the cheek as the two of them settle down on the couch.

An hour later they're lying together, Eden's head in Mina's lap while Mina runs her fingers through their hair. Eden closes their eyes at the sensation, at the callused tips of Mina's fingers on their scalp, sighing.

"Hey," Mina says. "Why don't I come to work with you tomorrow?"

Eden freezes, eyes flying open. In the year they've been dating Mina, and the six months they've shared this apartment together, Mina has never asked to come see Eden work.

(Eden's mothers weren't happy about the apartment, but it's not like they could stop Eden. They haven't had any say in their life since Eden was ten, legally handed over to The Council.)

"I'm not sure that's allowed," Eden says. "Besides, you'd just be watching me sit in a chair for like, four hours."

"You like to watch me practice, and that's practically the same thing."

"No, it's not," Eden says. "When you're practicing I can at least—I dunno, hear the music. When it's just me receiving information, you're literally going to watch me sit there."

"Don't you translate by hand, though? You can explain it to me, how it works."

A knot twists in Eden's stomach then. It's not like they don't want Mina with them. They do. And it's not like Eden's ever been told they can't have visitors, not like there's some written code against it. But they've always been superstitious about The Machine, afraid of letting it get too close to anything they care about.

And Mina is someone they care about.

Logically they know The Machine isn't that sentient, that it won't be able to know anything about Mina simply by her being in the same room, but that doesn't do much to loosen the knot.

"You really want to come?" Eden asks, and Mina smiles at them.

"I'll play a song for you," she says. "After. And I'll buy dinner."

And Eden knows that's it, then. There's no arguing with Mina once she's set her mind on something. Eden learned that quickly enough.

"Fine," they say, and Mina smiles and kisses them on the cheek.

How can they say no?

0 1 0 1

The next day Eden takes the train to work, the way they always do. Mina sits next to them, the way she always does in the mornings until her stop comes up. For a second, Eden thinks maybe she'll have forgotten about the whole thing and just get off at her stop like normal and Eden will be able to go on to their job, but when Mina's stop comes, she doesn't make a move to leave, just grins at Eden and squeezes their hand.

Eden keeps looking over their shoulder when the two of them eventually exit the train, like at any moment a Council member is going to step out of the shadows and reprimand them for having unauthorized personnel in the area.

But of course, no such thing happens. The room is the same grey tile it always is, and when Eden holds their palm up to the interface to let themself in, everything proceeds as normal.

"Oh," Mina breathes, and Eden turns to look at her.

Her mouth is open in awe, and Eden realizes that other than them, no one ever really sees The Machine. They try to imagine it through Mina's eyes, the sheer size and scale of it, nearly filling the entire room with wires and screens, but they look at it and all they see is all of the code they'll have to decrypt.

"So I just...hook up to it," Eden says, and Mina watches as they shrug off their jacket and go to sit in the chair. "Sorry there's nowhere for you to sit."

"It's fine," Mina says, and folds herself cross-legged on the floor, looking up at Eden. "So...so what do you do, exactly?"

"I plug myself in," Eden says. "It interfaces through—well, through my interface, really; so I download all the information and then I just...translate it. Not by hand." They point to a smaller machine over against the wall. "Using that."

"There's not like, a dictionary to check or something?"

"I'm the dictionary at this point," Eden says, laughing. "But the download takes the longest. I usually only spend two hours on a translation, then send it off, but—" They swallow. How much should they tell Mina, that they don't send as much information anymore, that they've stopped trusting The Council with it?

"Cool," Mina says. "Well, don't let me distract you. Translate away." She smiles up at Eden, so Eden closes their eyes, and sets their palm on the sensor.

It feels like normal, if a little weird with Mina watching, the rush of information flowing through their system; the automatic sorting of it. There's less and less of it these days. Eden tries not to feel self-conscious but they can't help it. Having the girl they like watching them just download information feels...well, it feels weird.

As if she can sense what they're thinking, Mina says, "Look, don't worry. You've seen all the weird faces I make when I practice."

"That is true," Eden says, and Mina laughs, and Eden lets themselves relax, just for a moment.

And then—

And then.

Their information downloaded, the 100 percent completion bar they never pay attention to shows up at the corner of their vision, yet when they try to swipe it away, it doesn't move.

Huh?

Eden frowns, and quickly flicks through the screen, frowning at the bar that should have left by now.

"What is it?"

"Nothing," Eden says, "just a glitch," but their hands shake as they say it because The Machine doesn't glitch. It just doesn't. In the seven years Eden has been downloading and translating for it, it never just glitches. "Let me pull up the source code."

They navigate through the code, frowning as they do so, the oddness and yet strange familiarity of it like an unknown dialect of a language they're only passingly familiar with. They squint at the screen, unsure of what they're seeing, until at the bottom of the page they find it—

[Error 404-105829. Cannot retrieve information.]

Override, Eden types, but The Machine does not respond.

"What is it?" Mina asks again, now near Eden, now trying to peer at the screen herself. Eden flinches, their instinct to cover the screen, to not let Mina get closer, not let her see, but they can't.

"I'm not sure," they say. "It looks like an error in the code."

"Why don't you ask it?"

"Ask it?" Eden says, staring at her. "I can't—I can't just ask it."

"Why not?"

"Because," Eden says, their mouth dry, "I just—I can't. I've never tried."

"You have access to this machine with all this information and you're the only one who can read it and you don't just…ask?"

"I don't think The Council would like that," Eden says, but their heart beats wilder at the thought.

Why can't they ask it? Human translators do, asking other people who speak their languages for help or guidance when they don't understand something. Why can't Eden just ask The Machine?

Eden puts their hand near The Machine, feels it hum under their fingers. It feels, for the first time, almost impossibly alive.

"I don't understand," they say, and no sooner have they spoken the words than their interface glitches, just for a second, like a pixel out of place. Eden blinks harder and sees something slightly off in the corner of their vision.

"Inspect," they whisper, and nearly gasp when it magnifies. A message. A code, if it could be called that even though it's in the same language The Machine always uses, but Eden supposes it could be a code if they're the only one who can read it.

"What does it say?" Mina asks, and Eden's mouth goes dry as they read the note. Read it again.

It's not right. It's just a glitch. It has to be. Or maybe they've just read it wrong.

But they know they haven't.

"It says things are ending."

Mina frowns. "What is?"

"I can ask," Eden says, and hesitantly their fingers find the ones and zeroes in their own interface, hovering over the final character before they submit their question to The Machine. They've never dared do something like this before, never dared to question anything The Machine has given them, because who are they to question it?

"What's ending?" Eden sends back, and then they hold their breath and wait. The response comes a moment later, only another blip on Eden's interface.

01000001 01101100 01101100

A L L.

Eden jerks back suddenly, removing their palm from the hardware so quickly it's as if they've been burned, now afraid someone is watching, and that someone can see what The Machine has sent them.

No one can, they know, but that doesn't slow the frantic racing of their heart.

"Eden?"

Eden turns, suddenly remembering Mina is there.

"What did you see?"

Eden shivers. "I—I—" They shake their head. "Not here. Home."

Mina frowns but only for a second, and then decisively holds out her hand to Eden. "Home it is."

"Should I tell The Council?" Eden asks that night, socked feet crossed under them as they cup their hands around bowls of broth.

"I don't see why you wouldn't."

"Because what if they brush it off as nothing?"

"Do you think it's nothing?"

"No."

"No, and you know better than they do," Mina says. When Eden frowns, she sighs. "You know that Machine better than anyone. You can communicate with it, understand it. That gives you a power The Council doesn't have."

"I don't think they'll see it that way," Eden says.

"They should," Mina responds, and Eden is about to answer when Mina cuts them off with a kiss. "Just trust me, okay? Go see them tomorrow."

"Okay," Eden sighs, and they let Mina kiss them again before they close their eyes and try to erase the memory of those dreaded numbers. "Can you play something for me to take my mind off it?"

"Of course," Mina says, and Eden curls up on the couch, and tries to sink into the music and tries to forget.

But of course, they can't.

0 1 0 1

They wake before Mina the next morning and steal out of the apartment, taking the train to the outer ring of the city center where The Council conducts all of their work. Normally they'd have paperwork, a pass, but they have no time for red tape this morning. Besides, everyone knows who they are, what they look like. If someone questions what they're doing, well, then that's like questioning The Machine itself.

Still, it doesn't stop Eden's hands from shaking.

They exit the train, and their feet take them through the antechamber, through four sets of double doors locked with a code that has not changed since Eden was small, until they've reached the inner rooms that The Council deems secure enough for their work. They nod to the receptionist, a woman with burnt-umber skin and close-cropped hair, who frowns at Eden as they pass by.

"Does The Council know you're here?"

"They should by now," Eden says, and the woman—Sloane, Eden thinks her name is—sighs. "If they don't, can you inform them?"

"I'm guessing you don't have an appointment."

"It's urgent," Eden says, and something in their face must convince Sloane, because she blinks a few times as if cycling through her own interface, sighing again before finally focusing her attention back on Eden.

"They'll see you. Some of them seem to be in a foul mood. Don't say I didn't warn you."

"Some of them?" Eden echoes. The concept is strange— The Council has always presented itself as one unified entity. Something's wrong, they think, and Sloane's smile slips for just a second before she closes her eyes, shakes her head.

"The Council is in a foul mood," she repeats, pointedly not acknowledging her slipup, and waves Eden through the final set of doors into the inner chamber.

When Eden enters, they're struck as always by how large it is for a room that essentially houses only screens. The Council peers down at them from individual screens, faces distorted so Eden only sees grey; voices enhanced and changed so no information can be discerned. When they speak, they speak as one. Eden's often wondered if they have a script, something telling them all what to say.

"Eden," The Council says. "It's not time for your report yet."

"This is urgent," Eden says, and in so many words they relay what The Machine told them, about everything ending. When they're done, The Council is silent.

"You talked to it?" it finally says, many-voiced and booming. Eden wills themselves not to shrink back.

"Why shouldn't I?" they ask, getting angry because that is a better defense than being scared. "Other translators—they talk to their sources, to each other, they ask questions—"

The Council plays a high-pitched noise that cuts Eden off, brings them to their knees. When they look up, the screens are unmoving, so that they could almost think it's a glitch.

"You're sure you translated correctly?" it asks.

"Yes," Eden says stubbornly, because if they know anything, it's that they are good at their job.

"We'll look into it," The Council says, and the screens flicker as if Eden has been dismissed. They stand there for a long moment, then—

"That's it? I—I come to you with the first useful information in years about things ending and you'll just—you'll look into it? You're just going to take this information and save yourselves, aren't you? All of you," Eden says, gesturing like they can see every individual person that makes up The Council. "I—I'm done. I'm not going to feed you information anymore. I'm not going to be your weapon, and without me—"

The Council smiles as one. It is a terrifying sight, a large mouth looming over Eden.

"Eden," it says. "Eden. We can always find another you."

Eden's palms ball into fists. They want to argue—haven't

they been told, this whole time, that they were singled out for a reason? Singled out, special.

But they're wrong. They know they're wrong, and The Council knows it, and they are smiling like they have the upper hand, and Eden has no words for how wrong all of this makes them feel.

Information is just information, until someone acts on it. Then it becomes treason.

Eden runs.

For a second, when they step into the room that houses The Machine, Eden fears they're too late, that The Council has figured out what they're doing and shut off their access. But The Machine accepts Eden's interface without any sort of protest, and Eden figures they only have so long before someone realizes what's happening.

They should wait for Mina. They need Mina there. Need someone there if this goes wrong. That's why they had messaged her on an encrypted line, from the train.

Meet me at work. Ten minutes.

I have rehearsal.

It's urgent.

They want to wait for Mina, but time is ticking and this has to be done. Eden can only hope that Mina won't come in to find them a crumpled mass on the floor with bloody eye sockets and hands. They begin to type, furiously fast, 1s and 0s and the language they know by now almost as well as their own.

I need to know how to end this.

They wait. And wait, because surely The Machine isn't

going to tell them, surely it's not going to hand over the keys to its own destruction.

God, do they even want to do this? Is this a mercy killing or something selfish?

Finally, The Machine replies, *End?*

A door opens, and then Mina is there. Eden is still interfacing with The Machine, even as Mina hurries over to them and wraps her arms around their back, her head pressed against Eden's shoulder blades.

"What are you doing?" she whispers.

"Ending it," Eden says. "I—I don't want to but I have to. No one should have this information. No one should have this much power, and the Council said it could—it could just find another me, and—and The Machine says it's ending and I don't know what to do—"

They find themselves crying, and they feel so ridiculous, crying over a machine, whatever it is, even if it has come to feel like a friend. Mina pulls back from them, places her hands on their shoulders.

"The Machine says the world is ending," Mina says quietly. "Maybe it just means *its* world. Maybe you're doing it a favor." She presses a kiss to Eden's cheek. "It's just numbers, Eden."

"They're numbers that mean something."

"You mean something," Mina says. "You mean more than that machine, and I'm not going to watch you continue to be used for information, and you're not going to let them do this to someone else. So...so do what you have to," she finishes, and steps back from Eden. Eden wipes at their eyes, places their hand back on the palm interface.

I'm sorry, they think. And then they dive deep into the

Machine's code, into this language that only they can read and only they can understand, and they pull up their own ID number, the thoughts of what makes them *them*, and they start to type it in—but in words, in their own language, not the binary of The Machine. Into concepts The Machine cannot parse, or sort, or understand.

And Eden watches as their own code takes over like a virus and infects the one thing they've been told is sacred, twisting and shaping The Machine's language like it's nothing.

Information is only information, but now Eden has acted on it, and they can call it treason or mercy, but the outcome is the same. Soon there will be no Machine, and no information, and no Eden.

The world is big, after all. And they've never stepped foot outside the city center, never met another person like them, and they think that now it is time they do.

★ ★ ★ ★ ★

RESHADOW

Adam Sass

EVERY LESSON IN LIFE CAN BE LEARNED IN AN escape room—the most important one being "every problem has a solution."

My current problem? My sad little life in this sad little town.

I'm not ashamed to say it: I'm better than this town, which is why I'm escaping it in a matter of months. I've been accepted to Berkeley, so bye-bye, this side of the Mississippi. Everyone—including my parents—finds my drive off-putting. I figure things out before everyone else, I have the answer before everyone else, and I make sure everyone else knows that I know.

A know-it-all. A show-off. Two things nobody likes because it makes them feel small.

So, they try their best to make *me* feel small. On my more vulnerable days, they succeed.

No more.

Well, in two months, two weeks, and four days, no more.

In the meantime, I distract my mind with escape rooms. Very metaphorical, ha ha, I want to escape, so I do these corny puzzle rooms. But actually, I adore escape rooms—even bad ones—but the more challenging, the better. If I have to, I'll drive hours to find a new one to escape. Some new code to break. My best friends, Charlie and Kath, must really care about me because they braved this brutally long trip after school so I could go to yet another one.

Reshadow, it's called.

No other description. No pictures on the website; simply an address and the words "Reshadow: The Last Escape Room You'll Ever Need."

The last one? We'll see about that.

In the middle of a long hallway tinged with a soothing, futuristically violet light, a Reshadow employee hands me and my friends canvas belt straps. The employee is a man in his seventies. A tad shorter than me, but that could be because he looks slightly hunched in his finely tailored suit. A suit! I expected to find a team of twentysomethings in garish T-shirts emblazoned with a Reshadow logo, not some solitary, undertaker-looking dude.

Literally the only definable things in the building are this hallway and that open door. Where does this guy use the bathroom? How does he monitor us while we're inside? Is this grandpa really running this whole operation from a phone? Besides Charlie, Kath, and myself, it seems like this man is the only other soul in the building.

Deeply creepy. Points for that.

I wait my turn while the man demonstrates how to fasten

the straps around our waists. As if we need a demonstration of how to buckle some fancy seat belt. The old man says—in an admirable attempt to be spooky—that the straps carry a tracker in the buckle so we "don't get lost."

Lost...where? I've done a trillion escape rooms, but I can't ever recall needing to be tracked inside a room that wasn't virtual.

Still, my fingertips won't stop tingling. It's been forever since I've been this unsure about what to expect from a room.

I kind of like it. More points for showmanship.

I keep my fidgeting fingers busy with Hooptedoodle, the latest puzzle app to eat up my brain space. Hooptedoodle is like Tetris meets a crossword, and in each level, the words fall faster and faster until they threaten to fill the screen. So far, I'm on level 379. Charlie says it gives him heart palpitations just to watch me play it. Word blocks plummet through my screen in a blur, but my thumb moves twice as fast filling in the answers to make the blocks vanish. The trick is to never hesitate or doubt yourself. Your brain already holds the answers.

Or at least, *my* brain does.

Charlie says I'll be filthy rich someday, inventing something our minds can't even conceive of yet. Charlie says a lot of sweet stuff (that also happens to be true).

"Are my teammates ready?" I ask, shutting the Hooptedoodle app.

Kath fastens a canvas Reshadow strap across her waist and asks, "Could you stop calling us *teammates* and start calling us *friends*?" she asks. "*Teammate* implies that we're serving some purpose here other than to give you a ride home."

Charlie buckles his own strap. "Kath, we do serve a purpose." He smirks. "We're here to witness Evan Franklin's genius."

Genius.

Charlie Meridian thinks I'm a genius.

Even though I know he's making fun of me, Charlie sounds so *soft* and *kind*. How does he do it? I have the opposite problem. I could give someone the best compliment of their life, and their first response would be, "Why are you attacking me?!"

It's not my fault I have a resting asshole face!

Giggling, Kath smacks Charlie's shoulder before being escorted into the next room by Mr. Reshadow. Good. Giggling is good. She's starting to unwind and enjoy herself. I worried she was gonna say "screw this" and take off, but Charlie always knows how to put people at ease.

Except me, of course. He approaches, and I become as brittle as a crunchy little cracker.

"I know you super wanted to do this escape room," he whispers. "Kath didn't want to mention anything, like let you down or something, but her sister just texted her. She forgot she promised to help her with SAT prep tonight. She's gonna have to leave right from here."

Little hairs frizzle on my neck. He's standing close to me. Too close.

"Yeah?" I ask.

He wets his lips. "We'll have to leave with her, too. Unless... I was thinking we could make the best of things, and maybe it would be cool if we just...skipped this. Let Kath do her thing? Then maybe you and me could... I don't know, there's a Denny's nearby. Grab dinner? Catch up before we gotta get home?"

We lock eyes—and yes, that's a bad thing.

Charlie and I have been trapped in this exhausting "will they or won't they?" scenario our entire senior year. Graduation is rapidly approaching—and with it, the end of an era—so the heat has turned up to boiling. Sadly, Charlie seems to have chosen *now* to finally make a move. My lungs scream for air at the possibility of what else "grab dinner, catch up…?" might portend, but…

I can't.

My chest collapses beneath Charlie's massive, metaphorical boot print. It's too late for us. If neither of us made a move at Homecoming—or before the holiday break—or during the Valentine's party…then what is us getting dinner (and maybe, hopefully, please God MORE) going to do for us now?

In a matter of months, he's attending Columbia, and I'm going to Berkeley.

That's it. It's over. We lost.

I'm not hooking up with him tonight—and having all my dreams come true—just to spend my first year at Berkeley emotionally shredded and missing him instead of focusing on my career.

"Um, sorry," I stammer. "I'd like to, but like, we drove all this way here. We already paid…"

"I can get us a refund." Charlie laughs.

"I know, but—"

"I can be very persuasive."

"Oh, believe me, I know."

"So, what do you want to do?"

His impossibly soft, smooth features gaze hopefully up at me. I can't speak. Roiling, nervous acid replaces whatever words I might have coughed up.

It's too late, Charlie. This is all too late!

"Charlie, I kinda wanted to do this," I admit and then watch his sweet face fall.

"Cool," he says in a falsely bright voice.

Then he putters away—*away from me*—towards the room Kath disappeared into, to prepare for our challenge course. A leaden blanket of misery falls on every square inch of my body, only letting up when Mr. Reshadow approaches.

Game time. These challenges are when I shine. The first time I did one of these rooms, I knew they were for me. Here, it's not considered arrogant or embarrassing to be the cleverest one in the room. People at school...in my town...even my parents look at me like I'm an alien.

America hates smart people. They do. It really is an American disease.

But if you turn being smart into a game—like their beloved sports—then you can show off.

Impress them.

In escape rooms, no bad feelings can touch me.

"Welcome to Reshadow," the old man says in a ghoulish monotone. "Your first time with us?"

I smile and tap the strap on my waist. "Yep!"

My stylish new friend sighs, his tired eyelids drooping, as if he's somehow disappointed with my response. Did his lower lip just tremble? He says, "Good attitude, because this is how we do things at Reshadow. No preparation, just walk inside."

"Legit?" I ask. He nods.

Impressive. Normally, these escape rooms will talk you to death before you get started, or tease too much, or both. I practically solve the whole thing before it even starts. Reshadow gets points for mystery.

The room ahead is plain. There's no door. Just an archway.

Yet it's completely dark. I can't even hear Charlie and Kath inside.

"Your friends are already inside," the man says. "You may head in whenever you're ready. If you need—"

I wave him back, politely but firmly. "If I need anything, I'll just yell out for a clue. I know how it works." I laugh with a shrug. "But I never ask for clues."

The man chuckles. "If you say so."

I wiggle my phone in the air. "Do you need to take this?"

"Keep it. Phones don't work inside Reshadow, anyway."

Spoooooooooky.

I nod, hoping I appear more impressed than I really am. It's nice to let folks enjoy their moments of grandiosity. It keeps the fun alive. Like, I'm sure there's just some dead signal area in there that they're drumming up into an ominous "your phone won't help you!" pronouncement.

With that, Mr. Reshadow steps aside, clearing my direct path into the room. A faint prickling crawls up my spine. *Ooh.* I haven't felt that kind of excitement in a while. This has already been worth the trip out of town.

Charlie and Kath have been in there long enough without my help—it's time to face Reshadow.

"Ready or not, here I come," I whisper and march inside.

Dark becomes light.

My stomach lurches with nausea that feels like vertigo, as

if the room is tilting—only it's not tilting. I simply entered this new space so unexpectedly, it's like I missed the last step on a staircase. What happened to the dark tunnel? This room is so brightly lit—and I arrived so instantly—my brain isn't processing the shift quickly enough.

How could I not even see a speck of this light from outside?

The most bizarre detail about the room *isn't* that I don't know where I am. Worse—this room is far too familiar: it's my high school chemistry lab. I'm here a million times a week.

How did they recreate it so exactly, down to the vague rotten egg smell of the beakers?

I'm IN the actual room. This is my high school.

Hot, early summer daylight pushes through the empty classroom's windows. How are they doing this? It was sunset by the time we arrived, but this looks like late morning. Is this virtual reality? If so, HOW? We aren't wearing goggles. The only things Mr. Reshadow gave us were these useless canvas straps.

I pat my waist, and my heart squeezes.

The strap is gone.

I'm wearing my same T-shirt and ripped shorts, but there's no strap.

I exhale deliberately slowly to steady my anxious breathing. "Okay. Not sure how you did this, Gramps, but cool work." I observe my hands. Long and thin fingers—same hands. Real hands, not pixelated, virtual reality hands. My breath pauses again as I reach for the tabletop. A cool, hard, REAL touch meets my fingertips.

It's the same table. This isn't virtual—it can't be. But it also can't be a stage because the sun—the literal capital-S Sun—is right there, hanging in the sky outside the window.

"Don't waste time thinking about the tech," I say. "Just find your teammates."

Escape rooms are designed to overwhelm you with a new environment, full of insignificant, intentionally distracting details so you blow half your time just taking everything in. Somewhere in here is The Challenge. All I need to do is lock on to what the game is, and worry later about how the hell they're making it happen.

The chemistry lab door opens without tricks. No puzzles needed to unlock it; it just opens. It opens into my high school. The real goddamn place. Hallways full of lockers. Other students. Teachers. People I know. HOW are they here?

"Jesus Ch—"

My lips trembling uncontrollably, I turn just in time to collide with a girl with chopped, sandy-colored hair: Kath.

"Ah," she yelps as I leap backwards. She presses a terrified hand to her chest. "You scared me."

"I'm a little freaked out," I say, gasping. "This is…a lot, right?"

"Huh?"

I point at her waist. "Your strap is gone, too. This is wild. How are they doing this?"

"Who's *they*? Dude, what are you talking about?"

"Reshadow." I can't keep the annoyed edge out of my voice. She's been acting "over it" all day, and I don't have time to answer a million questions when I have so many of my own. "How did they build our entire school here? Like, all these people? Everyone we know."

Kath winces. "Reshadow? Eh, Evan, I've been meaning to ask you—do we really have to go to that today? I know you want a buffer person there between you and Charlie, but it would be way more chill if we just got some food or whatever. These escape rooms make me feel like a dummy."

I stiffen with anger. It's the only thing keeping the fear out of my voice. "What are you talking about? We're IN Reshadow right now."

"Huh? In it?"

"Kath. Cut it out."

"Look, I'm sorry, I know these escape rooms are your thing. I don't want to disappoint you, but—"

"We drove here together. We're already here. You just walked in a minute ago…" At last, a clear thought drops onto my brain, battering away the fear that's been eating me ever since I entered the game. I snap my fingers. "You're messing with me. You really had me scared. That was good, Kath. Competitive. Nice."

Kath screws up her face like I'm the most baffling human being she's ever met. She groans. "Fine. We'll go to Reshadow. I was just asking, but I think Charlie would rather skip it, *if you know what I mean.*"

I erupt with another booming laugh. "If it's everybody for themselves, I can play that game."

"I'm gonna…go now. Hope you're okay…"

This is the best acting I've ever seen from Kath. That's genuine concern crossing her face as she joins the flow of students leaving on their way to lunch. While I watch her vanish into the crowd, I realize I'm definitely not imagining Reshadow. Something *is* different after all. This isn't one hundred percent exactly my high school. In my real high school, a traditional wall clock with minute hands hangs above the lockers.

But this is Reshadow, and this clock is digital. Instead of the time, angry red numbers read "43:00." Then "42:59." "42:58."

It's counting down. The game is on. I can't waste any more time.

I'm not sure what the actual challenge is, but whatever it may be, Kath has already locked onto it and is savoring having one up on me. She's reawakened my competitive DNA. No more scared, lost little Evan Franklin. I'm winning this thing. I have to learn what Kath found out about the game, and right now, it seems to be about acting as if we're really in school.

I can do that.

This isn't real.

I have to keep reminding myself of that fact because Reshadow's hyper-realistic facsimile of my school continually threatens to lurch the contents of my stomach.

The double doors at the end of the hallway by the principal's office—so meticulously recreated from real life—open onto a very different sight: a vast, all-consuming star field. I should be looking out onto the faculty parking lot, shrouded in greenery just beginning to bloom for the spring. Instead, there's nothing but deep space. We're hurtling through a soundless, black void dotted with passing stars. I've never seen anything like it.

This is no cheap set. Stars pass beneath my feet.

I hate to admit it...but I'm afraid. Whatever this recreation of my school might be, the boundary of the escape room is the school grounds. I remove a paper clip from my pocket and extend it toward oblivion. My cold, bloodless fingers open. The clip falls.

Falls.

Falls forever into the star field.

Gone.

I don't make a sound. I don't blink. I simply back away. As I gently shut the double doors on literal outer space, I think the word I've never, ever thought, in over a hundred escape rooms: *help.*

"You're wasting time, Evan," says a heavy voice behind me.

I spin around. It's Mr. Reshadow, tall and stooping in his neat, expensive suit. Employees never appear in the actual escape room, but then again, Reshadow is very clearly not like the others. The man blinks and speaks again through clenched jaws: "You have to find Charlie."

"Who are you?" I ask, rebuilding my steely wall of confidence. "What is this shit?"

The man waves me off impatiently. "You know I can't tell you that. What are you doing, standing here, gawping at the boundary for so long? You're running out of time. What is WRONG with you? And you asked for help right away?!"

"I didn't ask for help!"

"You thought it. I can hear you."

My breath slows to such a crawl, it almost becomes impossible to croak out, "Okay, I don't know how you're doing this, but I'm…"

I lose the words. Or rather, I refuse to say them.

"Scared, I know," the man says. "Something is different this round."

"This round?"

He grunts in exasperation. "There's no *time*, Evan. Round. Yes, rounds. Multiple rounds. You have to start getting better at remembering, but all these rounds seem to be doing is weakening you. You're ready to give up right away, and all you can do is stare at the damned boundary!"

"Remember what?!" I take several staggering steps away, my shoes squeaking on the polished floor. "You're saying... I've done Reshadow before?"

Unblinking, the old man advances. "This is your one hundred and twenty-first round. And you're getting worse."

My own jaw locks as I harden my glare. "You're a distraction. You're trying to get me to ask a bunch of irrelevant questions so the clock runs out."

"The clock *is* running out, but I'm not a distraction. You can't leave Reshadow until you win. PLEASE: go find Charlie."

I snort. "Great idea. See ya!"

I'm sprinting as Mr. Reshadow calls: "When you find him, make sure to ask how you got here." He sounds so irritated, he's almost bored. As if he's told me this a hundred times already.

As if he's told me one hundred twenty-one times already...

NO. I remember walking into the game a minute ago. This is my *first time* being here. This old fart is just a trick. Or somehow, he really is giving me a clue to help figure out Reshadow's challenge. Maybe the escape room is about memory. Places you've been before. That's why the school is so realistic and familiar. That's why they cast an actor to follow you around, saying that you're caught in a time loop. Trick or not, it's pretty effective gaslighting to say I've been here hundreds of times before, that I just can't remember.

Impossible to disprove. Guaranteed to trip me up in my head.

Clever. Points for terror.

Turn after turn down a series of near-empty hallways, I follow the sounds of students rushing to their next class. I don't stop. Not even as I spot another digital clock above the lockers: "22:59."

Twenty minutes down the drain. I really am running out of time.

Competition is my fear killer. I sweep every crumb of uncertainty and terror into the corners of my heart. This is just an escape room like any other. There is a task in front of me and a clue, courtesy of my well-dressed friend: find Charlie, and ask him how we got here. I don't know what it means, or how it will help us get out, but it's the next step.

"How we got *where*?" Charlie asks, sipping orange juice through his box's little straw. I'm too frantic to even pretend to eat lunch. This cafeteria is enormous, exactly as it is in real life, and filled with OH MY GOD SUN. How are they creating so much sunlight in here? I sneak one of Charlie's napkins and dab the unacceptable amount of sweat currently flooding down my neck.

How we got where?

Charlie—like Kath—seems to have no memory of walking into Reshadow literally minutes ago.

I'm going to have a massive coronary right here at this very realistic lunch table. I can hear my heart between my ears.

But sweet Charlie just sips OJ so boyishly that I wish I *could* get in a time machine and agree to buzz off to Denny's with him instead of doing this crap. My head is pounding. We have less than twenty minutes to go.

"Reshadow," I repeat wearily. "Do you remember how we got here? HERE."

Charlie wets his lips again. Nervously this time. "Yeah, um, about that. Do you think we could skip the escape room tonight? I was thinking—"

"Yes, I know. I heard this already from Kath! I don't know why you can't remember, but we are currently IN Reshadow. We already drove here. It's nighttime. There's no sun. We're in the game right now, and there's less than twenty minutes left. You already asked me to go to dinner with you and—"

"Oh." Charlie deflates. "Did I already ask? It's cool, then. Never mind."

"Please, Charlie, stop looking at me like I'm nuts. Did you hear what I just said about Reshadow?"

"That we're in it?" I nod vigorously, blinking more sweat into my eyes.

Charlie slowly nods. "I… Okay, well, if I don't remember how we got to Reshadow, can you tell me how we got here?" FINALLY.

At least Charlie is willing to play along and accept that I haven't suddenly, totally, departed from reality. I breathe slowly. Coolly. "We each put on these different colored straps and walked in."

"Right, but before that. The man in the suit you're talking about asked you to ask me how we got to the building, right? So, how did we do that?"

"Well, we…" My smile fades as I remember.

Or rather, try to remember. It's blank. I can't remember walking into the building. I knew we drove because I assumed we did. We drove out of town. But to what town? How long did we drive? What music did we listen to? What did the outside of Reshadow look like? Was it a storefront along the street or a unit inside an office building?

Fear—enormous fear—consumes my thoughts as all breath leaves me.

"I don't remember," I squeak.

The digital clock in the cafeteria counts down past "18:09."

Have I been here already? Is this my hundred twenty-first round? Is Mr. Reshadow right? Can I…not leave?

"Hey Charlene," a handsome boy chuckles villainously as he plunks down beside Charlie. The boy snatches his orange juice and finishes it in a single gulp.

"Anthony!" Charlie whines as he grasps for the little box.

"I was thirsty," Anthony says, rubbing a wide palm along Charlie's back. Intimately. Fire rushes to my temples as I watch this smug asshole from my history class put his greasy rugby paws on Charlie. But Charlie doesn't push him away. In fact, my crush's lips turn ever so slightly into a smile.

They're together. Or at least, flirting.

The image is so unacceptable, I briefly forget that I'm trapped in a hellish virtual world.

I launch to my feet. I don't have time to get sucked into this distracting subplot crap with Charlie and stupid Anthony. I only have a handful of minutes left to figure out what's going on.

"Don't leave just because of me, Devin," Anthony says with a toothy smile.

"Evan," I growl.

"That's what I said." Anthony moves his awful hand up to Charlie's shoulder and turns to him. "You free tonight?"

"Well…" Charlie's enormous, watery eyes flit guiltily up at me, as if asking for permission to bail on our plan to go to Reshadow so he can boink this troll instead of me.

You did go to Reshadow, Evan. You already did. It's happening right now.

"Charlie, it's fine," I say, already jogging away. "You two have fun! I'm just gonna get back to my living nightmare!"

"9:20." "9:19." "9:18."

I've already fallen and banged my knee twice. I don't even know where I'm running. Kath doesn't know what I'm talking about. Charlie doesn't know what I'm talking about—instead, he's about to have some silly, sexy hangout with Anthony.

And I'll still be here.

Heart pounding, sweat-drenched, and miserable.

The only thing I have going for me is my brains—I'm not cute, I'm not funny, I'm not really nice—and I can't even be sure of that anymore. An escape room broke me, of all things. I don't know what the challenge is. I don't know why I'm here. I don't even know how I can leave.

I collapse onto my ass, leaning back against the lockers. At least here I can catch my breath. Maybe I'll run out the clock. Maybe those digital numbers will reach zero, and I'll wake up in the cool, violet hallway of Reshadow, Charlie and Kath standing over me, laughing at how easily they dominated the game compared to me.

Let me be humiliated. I'd just be grateful to go home.

A pair of buffed Italian shoes clip-clop next to me. Mr. Reshadow, once again. From down here, he's imperiously tall. His hangdog face twists in fury. "You let him leave with Anthony."

"I have bigger problems right now, man," I say. "Why do you give a shit?"

"You're a smart guy—"

"Not that smart, apparently—"

"Don't you ever shut up?" He kneels to my level. Nose to nose. "Reshadow isn't like other escape rooms. You don't need to be smart to win, or you would've won by now. You *do* need to be humble. And brave. And not a complete stranger to your feelings. Which is why I don't think you'll ever leave this place. Those numbers will hit zero, and you'll walk into this school all over again. Asking Kath why she doesn't remember. Watching Charlie leave with Anthony. Over and over and over. There will be no escape."

"Who are you?" I ask, almost pleading.

He stands. "If I told you, you'd scream."

"What am I supposed to do?"

"I can't solve it for you, Evan. I can only provide clues."

"THEN GIVE ME A CLUE."

"The game is so easy, but you've never gotten it in all these rounds." He laughs softly. "You're going to do very well in life. A lot of opportunities." His expression hardens. "But you need Charlie."

My blood inflamed, I scramble to my feet and grab the bastard by his pretty little suit collar. My words come out in boiling hot spittle. "What I need is to get out of this game! Let me out!"

The man is fast. Strong. In two swipes, he bats away my arms and snatches my own shirt collar. His rage is fearsome. It leaps off of him like heat. "You think you're some genius, but you're the stupidest boy on the planet! I beat you with a simple puzzle. All I had to do was aim for your weak spot— your heart. You've been asked one question in Reshadow. Only one. You've been asked this question hundreds of times, yet every single time...you answer wrong."

He flings me to the linoleum so hard, I hear my body squeak as it slides across the floor. Pain travels through my neck like a runaway train. This lunatic could've killed me! I have no clue what end is up, but I do know the digital clock just fell past three minutes.

"See you in three minutes, Evan," Mr. Reshadow says as he strides out of view. "You and I are destined to do this forever."

HELL.

I'm in Hell.

I died and this is Hell.

What question have I been asked? I haven't been asked any questions. I've been doing all the asking, but no one has given me a clear, straightforward answer. The only person who even bothered to help is Charlie. Even though he thought I was crazy and making this up, he still sat there, patiently talking it out with me.

You need Charlie.

I know that! I know I brag too much about my grades and test scores. I know I'm constantly telling anyone who will listen about how I'm gonna blow this town and create some phenomenal new tech that's gonna change their small little lives. I hate my town, so I don't feel bad talking like an arrogant bastard to them, but that doesn't change the fact that—yes—I'm a self-centered, rotten piece of stinking driftwood who *does* think he's better than most people.

Charlie is the only normalizing force in my life.

When I'm with him, I don't feel that overwhelming, nagging pressure to prove how smart and amazing I am. Because he *is* better than me. When I'm with him, I can relax, shut up, and listen. I'm a better person with him—but I'm also less ambitious.

None of this even matters anyway. He's going to Columbia, and I'm going to Berkeley, so he's leaving my life no matter what I do to stop him and...

Oh my God.

Once more, I clamber to my feet, but I don't think about the pain in my shoulder or how hot, sweaty, and afraid I am. Clarity washes my mind as clean as a mountain stream.

"The question," I whisper.

I know what Reshadow's challenge is.

I run. My strained hamstring makes me drag my foot down the hall, step after agonizing step, but I refuse to stay here and let that timer reset. The school is darker now. The sunlight is fading. There's no one in the building anymore. No one, except for two other people—and they're getting away.

"0:54." "0:53." "0:52."

Charlie Meridian is about to leave my life forever. Again.

The scrawny, darling boy's laugh carries even from the other end of the hallway. Anthony presses one hand to the small of Charlie's back. His other hand rests on a door handle that, when opened, will fling them into outer space.

"0:44."

Even without my bad leg, I'd never make it to them in time.

"CHARLIE!" I shout. For a moment, no one moves. Did he hear me? Should I yell again?

"0:36."

Anthony opens the door onto the terrifying vacuum outside. No!

"0:31."

"CHARLIE!" I repeat desperately, limping closer. Closer. Finally, Charlie turns to me, as wary as a cat. "Evan?" he asks.

"Charlie, I don't have any time left, so I'm gonna have do something really stupid and scary, but I don't want to stay here and I don't want you to go, so I'm just gonna say it, okay, and if you still want to go with Anthony, that's okay." My tears arrive before my words do. "I should've gone to Denny's with you, or whatever, just hung out with you. It doesn't matter what we do. I should've said yes. I got scared because I know I'm gonna lose you to New York soon, and I'm just... I don't know what I'm going to do without you, Charlie. I really don't."

The digital clock has nine seconds left. Eight. Seven.

Charlie's bright eyes open wider, shimmering in the racing starlight behind him.

Four.

Three.

"You'll never lose me," he says.

One.

Day becomes night.

Two wrinkled hands reach for me through the violet-tinged darkness. The woman's many rings are pleasantly cool on my face as she helps me out of the chair. It doesn't hurt to stand anymore. My hamstring isn't pulled after all, but a phantom sensation prickles down my leg where my wound was a few seconds ago.

"Evan?" she asks. "Oh thank God, his eyes finally opened."

"Ehmmm." I try to speak but can only slur.

Warm light explodes through the room as one lamp after another is switched on. The room is expensive and gaudy as hell: stained-glass Tiffany lamps sit on massive oak desks, their legs hand-carved into animal shapes. Giraffes. Elephants. A series of interlocking monkeys. Mixed in with the inviting, dark green leather sofas are several monitors showing nothing but static interference.

I don't have time to further appreciate the cozy luxury of this room, as dozens of people in suits and Polo shirts rush inside. They race to me, shouting: "Evan!"

"Dr. Franklin?"

"Dad?"

Dad…?

The woman who woke me throws up her arms to shield me from the onslaught of newcomers. She's in her seventies, her grey hair chopped neck-length. Familiar…

"Don't come any closer," she warns. "He's been under for days. He's disoriented." She returns to me and tenderly cups my face. "Evan… What happened in there? What did you see?"

"My…" I moan, but my tongue is as limp and dry as a dead cactus. "My high school?"

"Our high school?" the woman asks.

A sandbag thuds on top of my heart as the old woman's face finally registers: Kath.

My best friend.

Instinctively, knowing exactly what I will find, I turn behind me to the chair Kath pulled me from. The same comfortable dark leather as the other sofas, but in a full recline position. A heavy-looking, electronic headset lays discarded on the top of the seat. Lights across the crown pulse gently with soft purple light. Above the lights, a single word is printed in white: *RESHADOW*.

Above the chair is a grand, gilded mirror. The man in my reflection is painfully familiar.

It's me, Mr. Reshadow. Evan Franklin. One and the same.

I gaze at my hands—long and thin as usual, but wrinkled and spotted. I'm even wearing the man's tailored suit. I always thought he had exquisite taste.

With each second that passes outside of the Reshadow device, the other faces in the room become clearer. Faces etched with worry. Puzzlement. Terror. My secretary, hurrying to get me water. My investors, wondering what the hell they've invested in. My business partner, Kath, who is at once eager to welcome me back to consciousness, and eager to calm the investors.

My children, all grown up.

Their other father, nowhere in the picture anymore.

"Franklin," my investor says. "Jesus Christ, you've been in that thing for five days."

"Evan," Kath says, waving a calming hand at the crowd. "You said you were in high school? Our school?"

Laughter spills over me. Fresh, clean laughter. I feel seventeen again.

For five days—and 121 rounds—I was.

"Yes, it was our school," I say. "I told you all that Reshadow would be a nostalgic mind vacation, but... Something interesting happened. You do go back. You get to live...those moments again. Crucial ones. You can fix mistakes. But you can't leave until you do. I don't even think you get to choose where and when you go. I can't explain it, not yet. I'll need more testing. Honestly, I should probably take an axe to the whole damned thing..."

Kath and the investors look ready to faint, but my daughters, Mary and Dana, laugh with relief.

I laugh too. I have to.

All those rounds, trying to remember that the biggest mistake I ever made was to let Charlie Meridian walk out that door with Anthony Zimm. They married in New York. I didn't attend. Another mistake. I lost Charlie quickly and on purpose, because I couldn't bear to lose him slowly on accident. Anthony passed away twelve years ago, but I refused to reach out.

I thought the window had permanently shut on me and Charlie.

"You'll never lose me," the Charlie in Reshadow said. After hundreds of failed rounds, my mind—powered by Reshadow—led me to the truth. The answers were there the whole time.

I've built so much, but I needed Charlie to keep me grounded.

I became cold. Too cold. That's how I lost Dana and Mary's father.

That's how I lost everything except my work.

Reshadow.

Charlie always said I'd create something nobody had even

conceived of yet. I built the escape room of my childhood dreams, one so flawless I was nearly imprisoned by it. Because Reshadow isn't a puzzle of the mind, but of the heart. I had tucked Charlie away in a small box in my mind, but it was the first box Reshadow chose to open.

I made it out. I beat it. I always do.

But one puzzle remains.

"What's next?" Kath asks, laughing shakily and eyeing the crowd of nervous investors.

"What's next?" I ask. "Get Charlie Meridian on the phone."

★ ★ ★ ★ ★

THE DEPARTMENT OF HOMEGOING AFFAIRS

Kalynn Bayron

I SEE GRANDMA ZORA ACROSS A CROWDED terrace. The confusion is thick and disorienting. I'm new to this place so maybe it's a trick of my subconscious, a misunderstanding of the way this is supposed to work. I am not dead and yet I am in a place that is meant specifically and exclusively for the deceased.

Grandma Zora puts her hand in her pocket and pulls out a ragged piece of paper. It's a ticket. Funny that it takes that form in this place. I never fully understood why, but it doesn't really matter. Grandma Zora studies the paper.

I can't see the words written on it from where I am, but I know it should have her name and instructions for the ticket's use. The directions are clear but still suggestion rather than set in stone.

There is no warning or threat about what could happen if she refuses to board. There is no indication on that little scrap of paper of what she would be refunded should she miss her train accidentally or intentionally. There is only her name and her destination.

Get on the train, Grandma Zora.

Please.

Dee and I sit across from each other on my bed—legs crossed, eyes closed, hands clasped. We're making progress but it's ridiculously slow. Grandma Zora has been gone for almost a year and this is the first time I actually caught a clear glimpse of her in the In-Between. Another distraction is Dee herself. It's hard to get into the right state of mind when she's sitting there, looking like—that. She's gorgeous. She knows it and I hype her up every single time I get the chance. None of that, "Oh, she don't know how gorgeous she is and that's what makes her special." Nah. She's beautiful and she should say it.

As I sit here trying to get my mind right, I can't help but look at her. She's all jet-black coils and brown skin and round belly and long lashes. She's everything. I have to shake my head to clear out thoughts of pulling her close and kissing her. I like that I can get so distracted by her. It lets me know that grief won't always have such a tight hold on me.

I've seen Mama Zora here, in my house at 328 Sycamore Grove, a million times since that awful day a year ago when she went to sleep and didn't wake up. I see her in my room, sitting at my vanity, twisting up her grey hair like she's getting ready for bed. I see her in the kitchen, staring at the stove like she might start cooking. I see her at the end of the upstairs hallway, the light slanting through her transparent figure, a worried look on her face.

I open my eyes and stare at Dee.

"So?" she asks.

I sigh. "She's definitely there."

Dee shakes her head and leans close to me, kissing me gently on the forehead. "I'm sorry, Gia. But like, at least we know she's there, and now maybe we can do something about it."

"Like what?" I ask. "We're not even supposed to be crossing back and forth like that."

"I know, but when you join the Department of Homegoing Affairs, you can do whatever you want."

I tilt my head. "That's not how it works."

"Says who?" She leans forward and rests her elbows on her knees. "The DHA is just a bunch of old dudes who haven't even seen the In-Between with their own two eyes. They really think they can dictate who has access to it?" She rolled her eyes. "Typical."

She's halfway right. It's common knowledge that a lot of senior agents don't really believe in the department's mission, but that doesn't stop them from cashing their checks and spouting the company line.

Dee chews on her bottom lip the way she does when she's worried about something but doesn't want to come right out with it. She doesn't have to speak for me to know what's on her mind.

"I want to join up as soon as we graduate," I say.

Dee stares at me like she doesn't understand. We've talked about it, but I don't think I've ever been as sure as I am now.

"I thought you were gonna wait a little while," she says.

"I was, but I feel like nobody is listening to us." I gently touch the skin poking through the rip in the knee of her jeans.

"My mom requested a consult with the DHA six months ago. They told her it'd be another six months before they even consider putting us on the wait-list, and guess how long that shit is?"

Dee sighs. "A mile and some change?"

"Two years," I say. "My grandma's just supposed to languish in the In-Between for that long? They're supposed to be helping people, but they don't really give a damn about Grandma Zora or anybody else. The sooner I join up, the sooner I can help Grandma Zora get home. I can make a difference at the DHA. I know I can."

Dee readjusts herself and rests her head in my lap. I run my fingers along the side of her face.

"I'm going to Howard in the fall," she says.

I smile at her. She's been wanting to go to Howard since forever, and now she's finally got her start date. "You're gonna be a writer, and if Howard is the move, then do it. I'm with you. But I need to get my foot in the door with the DHA as a junior agent, and the only way I do that is to make a name for myself. Grandma Zora isn't the only one I got roamin' around in here."

Grandma Zora's still here. My favorite grandma. The one who treated me a little better than she treated my badass cousins. The grandma with an endless supply of hard candy in strawberry wrappers in her purse, and an endless supply of advice when I needed it. She called me "Grandma's Baby" and loved me in that way only grandmas can. She's still here, and while I'd like to see her move on, she's family and I love her.

The other thing that walks the halls of my house is something else entirely.

Dee and I have been seeing it since we were kids. It creeps at the edges of our vision, around corners, and in the deepest shadows. I see it sometimes when I'm sitting on my bed, in the doorway just briefly before I raise my gaze to meet it, only to find it has ducked out of sight. The air around it is heavy. It makes me feel like I can't breathe, like my chest is going to cave in. When it comes around, all I want to do it get away from it.

This kind of nameless, faceless entity is the hardest to get rid of. They linger for generations. If I can send it to the In-Between and make sure it doesn't come back, it'll put me on the DHA's radar. It will give me an in with one of the most secretive government agencies in the world.

I run my fingers over the surface of my highly illegal spirit board. Dee and I crafted it out of a piece of plywood and left-over chalkboard paint. We drew on the letters and numbers and made a planchette out of a thick piece of cardboard and the lens from a pair of broken sunglasses. It's not sanctioned. It's not even close to the tech the DHA uses, but it's all we got.

Dee leans away from the board. "We'll be in so much trouble if we get caught with this."

"If we get caught, we'll just say it's a vintage item, a collectable. Did you know they used to sell these things in toy stores?"

"Yeah. What the hell were people thinking?"

"I don't think the average person had any clue what they were actually doing."

"They do now though," Dee says nervously.

I nod and rest my fingertips on the planchette. Dee hesitates, and I reach over and interlace my fingers with hers.

"We're doing the exact same thing DHA does, only we're not stuck behind a bunch of legal bullshit. Besides, some of the agents on the Homegoer teams are sixteen or seventeen, just like us."

Dee narrows her eyes at me. "But they can't work unless they have an official DHA chaperone."

"Dee, for real? You know I don't need a chaperone. This stuff is in my bones. Just wait till they see what I can do."

The door to my room creaks open, and Dee sits bolt upright. The air around us is suddenly thick with the smell of rot. The temperature plummets to the point where I can almost see my own breath. The hairs on the back of my neck stand up, and my teeth chatter. Overwhelming heaviness presses down on me.

Dee grabs my hand. "Pretend like you're a DHA junior agent. Get this thing outta here, Gia." She sets her trembling fingers lightly on the planchette.

I settle in and breath deep. "Speak to us. Tell us who you are. What do you want? Why are you still here?"

"It's haunting you," Dee says. "That's why it's here."

I meet her gaze. "So let's send it on."

I take out a small piece of paper and write the words "board to the left" across the front. I place it in the center of the spirit board and close my eyes.

I know everything there is to know about the Department of Homegoing Affairs. I was the only senior to ace Mr. Wharton's AP History of Homegoing Affairs class, but not because he was making it interesting. Sometimes he fell asleep at his desk while old interviews with the late Dr. Kismet played on a loop in the background. While everybody else took the required notes and tuned out, I was always fascinated by the DHA's genesis.

The Department of Homegoing Affairs was created by the mentees of Dr. Leon L. Kismet. Dr. Kismet was known for his work on the Weight of Souls Project, which proved that the soul, or as Dr. Kismet called it, the "energy core," weighed exactly .0002435 grams, and that it went away at the moment of death, making the human body exactly .0002435 grams lighter. The number never changed. It didn't matter how old a person was or whether they died from illness or injury, natural causes, homicide, or accident. It was always the same.

Dr. Kismet's experiments led him to other questions. If something leaves the body when we die, and if we assume that it is the energy core that powers the human body, where, exactly, does it go at the moment of death? That was the question Dr. Kismet spent his life trying to answer.

And one night, in the winter of 2036, he found what he was looking for—on I-20 between Atlanta and Augusta when an autopiloted semitruck malfunctioned and crossed the median into the driver assisted lane and hit Dr. Kismet head-on. He died.

But then he came back.

What he saw when his heart stopped so deeply affected him that he spent years researching, experimenting—dying—in his quest for answers. He died under medical supervision at least six times that the general public knew of and was able to be resuscitated each time. He catalogued his experiences in the secrecy of his government-funded lab. What he discovered changed the world.

He proved the existence of a place he called the In-Between—
a plane of existence where the energy that powers our bodies—
the soul, the energy core—goes to be redistributed. But some
people refuse to go on. They return to familiar places—a home,
the site of their death, mostly in an attempt to reconnect with
people they loved.

A hundred years ago this kind of thing was called a residual
haunting. Thought to be nothing more than energy left behind, an unintelligent rerun of a life lived, a death suffered.
But the truth was more disturbing, more heartbreaking. Dr.
Kismet proved that ghosts were all that was left of the recently deceased, their essence, and that seeing them meant
they hadn't gone on.

It was out of this research that the DHA was born, so all
hauntings caused by the energy core of recently deceased
human beings are now handled by them. They recruit people
like me on a regular basis, people with a familial memory of
the In-Between, and traditions that are passed down through
the generations that let us access that place and the people in it.

The DHA likes to push the story that Dr. Kismet discovered the In-Between. But how do you discover something
that has always been there? Sounds like some typical colonizer
behavior to me, and that's yet another reason why I feel a pull
to it. The In-Between belonged to me first.

Slipping under the mantle that separates this plane of existence and the other is tricky, and I need a few things to
make the crossing easier. First is a radio. A legit AM/FM
radio with an antenna—not easy to find. The three I own
come from thrift shops and are barely in working order, but

all I need them to do is surf through the stations. The AM frequency is better, less music, less chatter, and an abundance of static. The white noise is like putting on a pair of glasses after you've been squinting at words your whole life. It brings the mantle into focus.

Dee switches on one of the vintage machines and slowly pushes the dial back and forth until she finds me a station that hums with unintelligible sound.

The second thing I need is a clear head. No thoughts of Dee's gorgeous face, no thinking about homework or class. Nothing. It's hard to stay present but I manage to do it, focusing on the task in front of me—get the malevolent entity out of my house for good.

Last, the spirit board. It's a communication device and lifeline if I get stuck and need some help getting back. In the past, people had allowed the ghosts themselves to take control of the board, and that's like giving the car keys to a toddler.

The board is for me to communicate with whoever stays behind, in this case Dee, and for her to communicate with me. In the In-Between, I hear messages from the board like a whisper in my ear, but sending messages back requires a level of concentration that leaves me drained afterward. It's not a game.

With my eyes closed, radio static crackling in the air, and my head as clear as it can possibly be, I allow myself to get lost in the sound, find the edge of the mantle, and slip through to the other side.

A whistle blows in the In-Between. It isn't harsh, just a gentle reminder that the trains that come and go on the hour are pulling in, filling their empty bellies with bodies and ferrying them away to their destinations.

Keeping my head on straight in this place is a chore. The spirit I've ushered out of my house and into the In-Between is solid now, not the nebulous black mass that lurks in the recesses of my home. It's a boy. Eleven, maybe twelve. He has big brown eyes that now hold nothing but fear and confusion. That heavy feeling I mistook for something malevolent isn't that at all—it is the stifling remnant of grief, warped by who knows how many years traversing the mantle. My heart aches for him, and I hate that fear made me wait this long to help.

I approach him slowly and hand him the paper, a makeshift ticket. I don't know where his original one is or if he even had one in the first place. I push it into his hand and close his fingers around it.

"Don't be afraid," I say. My voice sounds far away, muffled, like I'm underwater. "Get on the train. If you forget where you are or what you're supposed to do, just look at your ticket. Board to the left, okay?"

He nods, though I'm not sure he fully understands. As I nudge him to the platform where the trains are arriving, I catch a glimpse of a familiar face. Grandma Zora is shuffling through the crowd in her pink nightgown and tattered house shoes. She looks just the way she did the last time I saw her in the flesh.

My heart nearly stops. The grief is like a thousand-pound weight and feels almost identical to the sadness that had radiated from the young boy. It's magnified here in the In-Between. Dr. Kismet never could fully explain why the emotions were so much more palpable here. But I'm sure it didn't help that I'd kept so much of my sadness inside. I focused on getting into the DHA and helping, thinking I'd deal with how much I miss my grandma some other time. The In-Between wasn't in the business of keeping anything bottled up.

I push through the crowd, though they seem not to notice. They languish at the platform. When the train pulls in, they crowd the car.

"Grandma Zora!" I call.

She doesn't even look up. She boards the train to the right, and before I can reach the door, it slides silently away from the platform, carrying her not onward—but back.

I shut my eyes and breath deep. I go back too, falling into consciousness.

When I open my eyes and my head clears, the tears come in a flood, and Dee wraps me in her arms and holds me together when I all I want to do is fall apart.

I couldn't get to Grandma Zora in time to try and convince her to go on, but I'd managed to clear the boy from my house. When DHA got word, thanks to my dad thinking nobody important had access to his social media posts, the department came calling.

I thought they were going to arrest me at first. Performing an unsanctioned clearing was a no-go with some serious consequences, but it's also a big deal, and that's what I was counting on.

The DHA's mission is to study the disembodied energy core and the In-Between. Investigating hauntings was just a front, a way for them to get in the door. They weren't fully invested in my deceased grandma who couldn't seem to rest.

There were only a handful of agents who could do the work of crossing into the In-Between for anything more than a glimpse of what goes on there. I could do it. And I didn't even have to die in the process. The rumor was that, just like Dr. Kismet, some agents were given a cocktail of medication that would stop their hearts, allowing them quick access to the In-Between before being revived by their colleagues. I don't know if that's true, but it seems like something a shady government agency might do.

I helped give a little boy the homegoing he deserved. That was my only saving grace when the DHA agents came to investigate what I'd done, and it was enough for them to offer me a junior agent position right there in my parents' living room on a gloomy Tuesday morning. They asked me to commit and make it official by signing a contract.

I signed, because of course I did. I did it for Grandma Zora.

As Dee's family mingles with mine in the kitchen downstairs, me and Dee stash our graduation caps and gowns in my closet and pick confetti from each other's hair. I pull her close and kiss her like it's the last time I'm going to see her. It's not true. I'll see her again soon, but this will be the first time we've been apart for this long.

Dee pushes her hands into my back. I miss her so much and I'm not even gone yet.

My sponsor from the DHA is coming in the morning to pick me up and take me to get a physical and fit me for a uniform. They weren't playin' when they said they wanted me to join up with them right after graduation. They meant the very next day, and the time has snuck up on us.

"Training program is like six months long," I say against Dee's ear.

She rests her head on my shoulder. "We'll be okay. You can write to me, and I'll call you every night. You go be the best thing that's ever happened to the Homegoers, and I'm gonna go write a book, and we'll meet back up and get an apartment in Brooklyn like we always talked about." She traces the valleys between my knuckles. We have all these plans, and it all just feels a little too real.

"Let's go dance," I say. "I'll have lots of time to cry later."

And so we do. We dance until our feet hurt, until the sun sinks below the horizon and the shadows in my house angle themselves in that way that makes me uneasy. The other guests clear out by eleven thirty, and Dee and I snuggle into a hammock slung between two trees in the backyard.

As I watch the light fade from the sky, as I feel the rise and fall of Dee's chest against me, I catch a glimpse of something from the corner of my eye:

Grandma Zora, her opaque specter standing in the soft light streaming from the house.

I hold my breath and wait for Dee to notice, but she's lost in her own thoughts. Grandma Zora's mouth is downturned, her eyes misty, a mask of sorrow and sadness.

A sob catches in my throat, and Dee angles her face toward me.

"What's wrong?" she asks as she follows my gaze and sees what I see.

Dee scrambles out of the hammock and I follow her. We

watch as Grandma Zora's figure fades away until there is nothing but the dark.

"Gia," Dee says, breathless. "You gotta go. You gotta find a way to help her. Did you see her face?"

Tears sting my eyes. Grandma Zora is hurting, and she looks worse every time I see her. This can't go on. I glance toward the kitchen widow and see my mom's tearstained face staring at the blank space where Grandma Zora had been.

While Dee goes to the Mecca, to follow in the footsteps of literary giants, I go to the Blue—the training camp for junior DHA agents headquartered just outside of Philadelphia. It's run out of a building made of tinted glass that reflects the sky, hence the nickname. It is there, for the first time, that I step behind the mantle in plain view of anyone besides Dee and my family.

My days are spent in classrooms learning the ins and outs of the Department of Homegoing Affairs. I get to watch the restored footage of Dr. Kismet's experiments. He couldn't slip through the mantle like I could, and so his only way of accessing it was to die. Over and over again.

I don't know what I was expecting. I've heard rumors of the footage for years, but watching it is jarring. In most of the clips, he is lying prone in what looks like a brightly lit operating suite. The tech surrounding him is dated, stuff I've only ever seen in history class.

Monitors beep and alarm as his team lets him lapse into cardiac arrest. The machines keeping track of his pulse and oxygen show flat green lines. As disturbing as those images are, resurrection intrigues me.

Paddles against his chest send a current to his heart, pulling him back from the In-Between with violent shocks. His body lurches on the table until the lines show peaks and valleys at regular intervals. He tries to sit up and has to be restrained as he screams at his staff to bring him his journals.

The rest of my class materials are texts derived directly from Dr. Kismet's research. The Department of Homegoing Affairs was born out of this man's obsession, and as my training progresses, I learn my place in all of this.

As someone who can traverse the mantle between here and the In-Between, I am sectioned off to a group the other trainees call the Troupe. Each of us is assigned a crew and given small assignments; go to the In-Between and observe the people there, obtain samples of the air, swab the platform.

While I aid the senior agents in their research, my beliefs about what their mission is are confirmed—they want only to study the In-Between and don't give a single solitary shit about the people trapped in an endless cycle of hauntings. I take every opportunity to hone my abilities and promise myself that if all of this will bring me one step closer to helping Grandma Zora, then it will be worth it.

Six months come and go. While I was in training, Dee called me every night, and we wrote twice a week. Once a month I was allowed to see her via holographic chat in a clean room. I found myself at the head of my class, with a job offer to start as a junior agent in the fall at the DC field office.

Dee and I have one full week in late October when we're both free, and so we get together at my parents' house on a rainy afternoon under a gathering of billowing slate-grey clouds.

As I meet her gaze through the rain, she smiles in a way that makes me melt. Seeing her face-to-face and not through a screen is like breathing fresh air after being cooped up inside. It's like seeing the sun after being in the dark for too long.

I run to her, and we catch each other midway. I can't pull her close enough, and I'm elated to feel the same urgency in her own touch, in her kiss.

Inside, we sit together on the couch, and my mom and dad sit across from us. I tell them as much as I'm allowed to about my time in the Blue, which is very little. They take what I can give, and I'm reminded of how much I've missed them.

"I'm so proud of you both," my dad says. "We got a lot to be thankful for."

My mom braces her arms across her chest and takes a deep breath. "Gia, baby, I'm so glad you're home, but I have to ask you something."

"I know, Mom," I say gently. I don't want her to feel bad for welcoming me home and then almost immediately pivoting to the elephant in the room, so I bring it up first. "Has it been bad since I've been gone? You see her as often as you did before?"

"Every day now," Mom says.

My heart sinks, and I hold tight to Dee. Every day? Grandma Zora is making the loop back to the world of the living...every day?

"I tried to clear her before, and I just couldn't get to her." I bite the inside of my lip to keep from crying. "I think I can do it now, but I need your help."

My parents exchange glances, and Dee squeezes my hand. A silent agreement passes between us.

"Now?" Dee asks.

I nod. "Now."

Homegoers use an assortment of tools in their work. They include a spirit board, but not the kind made from scraps of wood marked up with permanent marker. DHA boards are digital, intuitive, and equipped to emit a frequency that is almost identical to the energy signal generated by the energy core itself.

There are different models, but during my time at the Blue, I found that my preferred tool was the model-S. It allows me to set the frequency while simultaneously playing an audible track of white noise in the background. There is a planchette, but it doesn't require me or anyone else to touch it. No more broken radios and no more do-it-yourself tools.

I take the board from its case and set it on the coffee table. A pale blue light emanates from it as I switch it on.

"I've never seen one of these up close," my dad says. He edges closer.

"Most people haven't," I say. "It's Dr. Kismet's design, but we had to wait for the tech to catch up to the concept."

My parents sit perched on the edge of the couch while Dee takes up a spot next to me on the floor.

I'd spent the last six months studying every aspect of the DHA's process, their methods and practices, their tightly controlled rules. I'd had to beg them to allow me to take a sanctioned spirit board home with me. The only reason they allowed it was because I promised to document the entire process of my attempt at clearing my grandmother. I'm one of the DHA's rising stars, and I'm learning that they're willing to do what I want if they feel like they're getting something in return.

I place my hands near the board, and it begins to hum as the white noise echoes through the room. I breathe deep.

My chest feels like it's being crushed in a vise when I pass through the mantle. The longer I stay, the more it hurts. The In-Between is not a place for the living, and it makes that truth known every time I go there. This time is no different.

The haze is disorienting, but I've learned to acclimate quickly. I keep Grandma Zora's face in the front of my mind. I need to find her and help her get to the train exiting left. That is simply called "going on," and no one, not even Dr. Kismet, knows what is beyond the platform in that direction.

If there are tens of thousands of deaths every day and if each person has to pass through some version of the In-Between, whatever it is, the odds that she and I will be in the same place at the same time are not in our favor. But I see her now, catching a glimpse of her pink housecoat as she moves against the crowd. It's like we're drawn to each other, and I will not allow this task to be delayed one minute longer.

Grandma Zora suddenly stops, then turns her head. Her dark eyes meet my gaze, and she mouths something I can't quite make out.

I rush forward, but as I approach, she boards the train on the right, and the doors close behind her. I push against them, but they won't budge.

"Get off!" I yell. "Please, you're going the wrong way! You have to go on!"

She shakes her head no. She raises her hand and places it on the glass.

"I miss you, baby."

I hear her voice for the first time in over a year, and my heart shatters into a million pieces. And in that moment, I realize that Grandma Zora isn't stuck. She knows exactly what she's doing. She's choosing to come back.

The train pulls away, taking her with it. I quickly shut my eyes, and when I open them, Mom, Dad, and Dee are staring at me.

"Well?" Mom asks.

I scramble to my feet. "She's coming back. Just wait."

My mom stands up. Dee doesn't move. My dad tents his fingers under his chin.

"When you see her, don't acknowledge her."

"What?" my mom asks. "Gia, I can't—"

"You have to, Mom. Please." If we want her to go on, we have to let her. She has to know that it's okay to do that, which is not gonna happen if my mom can't let her go. Grandma Zora can't become a nameless, faceless thing like the little boy I'd help clear. He'd come back so many times, he'd become nothing more than a manifestation of all his sorrow.

The pressure in the room changes, and Grandma Zora materializes in the doorway. Dad and Dee look away, but my mom can't help herself. It's her mama, and they were so incredibly close. I know what I'm asking her to do. It hurts. I can feel it in my chest.

A knot forms in my throat as the true weight of her loss bears down on me.

I slowly reach toward the spirit board, and the blue light flickers as I turn the white noise all the way up. The specter of my grandmother flickers, and in a blink she's gone. I sit and allow myself to slip past the mantle, into the In-Between.

Grandma Zora is there, racing towards the train, again. I hit the ground running, my chest aching, tears stinging my eyes. I cut her off, blocking her path forward.

"Stop!" I shout.

She stands in front of me, chest heaving, her eyes wild.

"Where is your ticket, Grandma?" I ask through wracking sobs.

She looks confused. She touches the single pocket on the right side of her nightgown. "I miss you, Grandma's Baby."

My throat feels like it's going to close up. The sadness at hearing her call me that almost knocks me off my feet. "I—I miss you more. So much."

"I'll come see you, baby," she says. "Just let me—"

"No," I say firmly, swallowing my pain, my grief. "No, Grandma, you gotta go on. You can't come back. You gotta let go."

Her eyes are lacquered with tears. She reaches out and puts her hand on the side of my face. I can smell her perfume. I can feel her warmth.

"I need you to board the train and exit left," I say, struggling to keep my voice level. "I need you to go on, Grandma. I love you. I miss you. But you can't keep making the trip back. You'll become something you're not, something cold and unfeeling and—and lost."

"I don't want to be lost," she says.

"I don't want that, either." I reach into her pocket, take out her ticket, and hand it to her.

She unfolds the tattered piece of paper and looks at me again.

"I'm here to help with your homegoing, Grandma." The tears spill down my face as the train's whistle cuts through the air.

Grandma Zora watches the train roll into the station. I loop my arm under hers and usher her forward. As the doors slide open, she hesitates at the edge of the platform for a brief moment before stepping over the threshold and turning to face me.

"Tell your mama I love her."

A sob breaks from my chest and my eyes blur as the doors slide shut. She puts her hand on the glass, and I do the same. The whistle sounds one more time, and the train glides away silently.

I watch the train until it disappears. Relief coupled with a sadness breaks over me, and for the first time in a long time, the sadness doesn't feel bottomless.

Grandma Zora finally gets to go on.

I return to the here and now, to Dee's wide, searching eyes. My vision is still blurred by tears. I turn to my mother.

"She said to tell you she loves you."

Mom gasps like a weight has been lifted from her chest. She collapses against my dad, and he cradles the two of us in our sorrow and in our relief.

Dee puts her hand on my shoulder. "You did it. You cleared her."

I nod because I can't seem to do anything else. This is all I wanted, and now that I've done it, I feel a little lost myself. "She touched my face," I say in a state of disbelief. "I could feel her. I could smell her perfume."

"Oh Gia," Dee says softly. "You did the right thing. She'd have kept coming back. She'd never rest."

"No. I know. But, Dee, there were so many people on the train coming back here."

"And that's why you gotta go to work." She takes my face in her hands. "You did all this for someone you love. Now you gotta go do it for other people's loved ones, too."

She's right. For all of the Department of Homegoing Affairs' shortcomings, their selfishness, their shortsightedness, my training at the Blue allowed me to help my own family in a way I hadn't been able to before. Now I can do the same thing for someone else. I'll make the DHA honor their name.

Everyone deserves a homegoing.

★ ★ ★ ★ ★

THE UNDENIABLE
PRICE OF
EVERYTHING

Z Brewer

THE STAIRS SEEMED ENDLESS, AND AT THE foot of them, you could see only darkness. Darkness and a strange orange haze that covered everything below.

It had been that way for most of Pax's life, for as long as they could remember. There was no world outside of this building. At least, not one they wanted to be a part of. That's what the Elders had told them and had been telling them for as long as they could recall.

The Elders had blocked off all exits but the fire escape that Pax was sitting on—a forbidden act that could get Pax in an enormous amount of trouble. They never planned to descend the stairs, but the temptation had been there as long as they could recall—something everyone inside seemed to recognize.

Even now the voice of their own father echoed in their memory. "There is no world beyond those stairs, Pax. For your own safety, don't go down them."

But lately, all that Pax found themself doing when they

weren't occupied with their chores was sitting on the fire escape and staring into forbidden oblivion. Something, they were convinced, must exist beyond those stairs. The world had to be much bigger than this building. They recalled it being so, having moved there when they were no older than five years. It couldn't be as horrible as what the Elders' whispers suggested.

Could it?

"Hey." Finn stepped onto the fire escape, his eyes haunted—the way they always were around sunset.

Maybe it was because he knew that sneaking out here every night didn't exactly qualify as acceptable by the Elders, but maybe also—at least some—because his own mother had disappeared down those stairs three years ago, and Finn hadn't much liked going anywhere near them ever since. But every night, he knew he'd find Pax out there.

Perhaps he blamed them for the uncomfortable ball of tension in his gut from being out there. Pax didn't know. And lately, they found themself caring less and less about Finn's stomach, and more and more about what exactly was waiting at the bottom of the stairs, in the haze that surrounded the house.

It stretched on for miles, as far as Pax could possibly see. There were no trees, no other buildings nearby. Only that strange, burnt-orange haze. It was almost smoke-like and had served as fuel to many of Pax's nightmares.

"Hey, Finn." Pax patted the spot next to them, but as usual, Finn refused to sit down. Ignoring his snub, Pax looked out into the nothingness and sighed. "It never changes. What I would give to see something different out there. Something solid."

Finn flicked his gaze around the balcony, at anything but the haze that surrounded the house. "Why wish for stuff we'll never get?"

Pax sighed again, this time heavily. "Because all we have left is wanting now. Come on, Finn. What about you? What do you miss that the haze took away?"

He shot them a glance then that made Pax sorry they'd phrased it that way. His mother. Of course. He missed his mother. A knot formed inside of Pax, and they sank down, sorrier than Finn would ever know.

Finn looked out over the haze at last, his eyes tearing. A lie left his lips then, that he'd spoken a hundred times before. "Do you remember trees? I can remember climbing them at this park my parents used to take me to. I don't want much, but if I could, I'd bring back trees."

Straining their memory, Pax called a tree to the forefront of their imagination. A large one with a thick, sturdy trunk and broad branches that held thousands of smooth, rounded leaves. Yes. they would like to see trees too. They'd never climbed them, but it sounded like fun.

Finn said, "What about you?"

They looked out over the haze and bit their bottom lip, suppressing the tears that threatened to fall from knowing their wish would never be granted. "I wish Mr. Carl would come back and tell us what's at the bottom of the stairs."

An uneasy silence settled between them then as they watched the sun descend into the darkness.

They'd seen Mr. Carl's face the day he left for the unknown. His chin was determined, his eyes almost grim. As he passed them in the hall, suitcase in hand, heading out with a confident stride, he met their eyes and nodded, his voice deep and hushed.

"Don't let them fool you, Pax. Don't let them tell you that nothing exists for you beyond those stairs. It's a lie. It's all a lie, and no danger exists. When you can, run. Run and be free of this house."

But Pax hadn't run. Not in the two years since Mr. Carl had descended the stairs and disappeared forever. The reason was simple enough. The thought of running was appealing… but not knowing what would happen dredged up more fear in Pax than they had curiosity.

"Do you remember blue skies?"

"Yeah. And clouds. I wonder what happened to them."

Giving in, Finn sat down next to Pax. His hand was next to theirs, and now and again, his pinky would brush against their skin. He liked Pax. More than Pax wanted him to.

"I asked Mr. Carl that once. He told me that one day, people could walk pretty much anywhere. Then the haze came. A lot of people died. Some took shelter in buildings that rose above the haze."

"I remember being able to see nearby buildings, but that was a long time ago. Now there's just us." Slowly, he laid his hand over theirs and squeezed.

Pax pulled away. "You don't know that."

For a moment, Finn sat in silence, his eyes searching Pax's face for any sign of reason. He couldn't understand why they couldn't be together, no matter how many times Pax had tried to explain it. "It's all I'll ever know. I'm not stupid enough to risk knowing for sure."

The truth was, Pax wasn't interested in a romantic entanglement. Not with Finn. Not with anyone. It just seemed so unnecessary—okay for some people, of course, but not for Pax. It was just the way that Pax had always felt. The same way that Finn had always seemed to want something romantic with them. Some things just were.

They sat there in silence for some time: Pax watching the stairs, Finn watching Pax. From inside the house came the usual evening noises. Food being cooked. The table being set. Polite conversation that didn't carry any deep meaning or merit. The moment mirrored the morning routine and would do so again the next day…and the next. Pax shook their head. "Nothing will ever cha—"

There. Just at the bottom of the stairs. A movement. A shifting in the haze. Squinting, Pax sat forward to get a better look. "Do you see that, Finn?"

"See what?"

A shadow. A shape. A…person.

Pax blinked. They had to be seeing things; a figment of their imagination, they were almost positive. But when Finn stood slowly, his eyes locked on the bottom of the stairs, Pax began to wonder if they weren't just imagining things after all.

Gloria's lungs burned as she rounded the corner. She dragged her hand along the wall, as if to brace herself, or maybe to guide herself around the corner and not down the street yet again. She was almost positive she'd been on this street before, in this part of town before, and there was no

way she was going to keep running in circles with him following her. Maybe someone else, but not him.

Her heart pounded in her ears so loudly that for a moment,
she wasn't certain she could still hear him behind her. But
then, between beats, there it was. The sound of his footfalls.
Calm. Slow. His patent leather shoes clicking on the pavement like those of a genteel Southern man simply going for a
stroll on a humid afternoon. So unlike the sound of her own
footfalls—clumsy, hurried, panicked. And she had every right
to panic. If he caught her, she was dead. Or worse.

She couldn't quite figure out how he was closer each time
she stole a glance over her shoulder to get a peek at him, but
he was. She also couldn't deduce how she was pouring sweat
from running in this heat and he appeared cool as cool could
be. At least, the sensible, logical, eat-cereal-for-breakfast side of
her had no theories on that. The scared, running, something-
more-exists-in-the-darkness-than-what-they-say side had its
own thoughts on the matter.

Plus, there was what he'd said to her on the balcony to
consider.

A shiver shook Gloria's spine as she came to a halt, staring disbelieving at the wall that ended the new street in an
alley. Screwed. That's what she was. Royally screwed with
nowhere to turn.

"You can run, but this moment is an eventuality. It will
happen. I've waited too long to do this, Gloria." His comment came out in a slow southern drawl that dripped from
his lips like honeysuckle on the vine.

She scanned the wall quickly. There had to be a way out.
There had to be somewhere to climb, some hole to crawl

through, some door that she'd not yet noticed. But no. There was nothing. Only Gloria, the alley, and the man in the shiny black shoes.

She turned around to face him, at first moving slowly, then spinning, as if she'd hoped to intimidate him in some small way.

Upon facing him, she gasped. But not because his appearance was at all shocking. She gasped at the utter...normalcy that stood before her. He appeared to be a white man in his midforties, slight tan, bleached white teeth, ice-blue eyes.

He stood straight, like his momma must have told him to. His suit was three pieces, white on crisp white, like his tie. His shoes black, like his shirt. In his hand, he held an umbrella, but he used it like a cane. For a moment, Gloria considered looking up to check for clouds, but she had the distinct gut impression that the umbrella wasn't meant to block out the rain. It was part of him, though she couldn't explain exactly how she knew that. The fabric of the umbrella was black, but darker than his shirt and shoes, more...menacing?

Why would that word enter her mind? And its tip and handle were both ornately carved silver—more artfulness than a simple umbrella normally called for. It was difficult to tear her gaze away, but she managed and found his eyes.

"What do you want from me?"

He tilted his head, eyeing her for a moment before he spoke again. "I'm here to take everything from you."

She searched the walls to either side, the ground all around her feet. There had to be something. Something helpful that could aid in her escape. There had to be some way out of this.

Three feet to her left laid a can of ruby-red spray paint, its lid long gone. Mere inches to her right lay a bundle of plaid cloth that might have been a shirt at one time.

Six feet behind and four feet to the left of the man in the crisp white suit was an assortment of old bricks piled against the wall. Nothing helpful at all. She was trapped and feeling more helpless than she ever had before.

She met his eyes again but refused to speak. The right corner of his mouth lifted slightly in a small smile. "I'm going to take it all away, Gloria. And there's nothing you can do to stop me. Everything that you have. Everything that you are."

Everything. He meant it. Which meant that what he'd said to her on the balcony was true.

Pax stood slowly, their eyes locked on the figure in the haze. It looked like a man, but they couldn't be sure. The haze was too thick to tell one way or the other. But when the person took a step up the stairs, the image became clear. A man stood there, looking up at the building.

At Finn.

At Pax.

His crisp white suit stood out against the haze behind him. He wore a kind smile that Pax wasn't positive they could trust, and, in his hand, he held an umbrella. "Good afternoon," he said. "Bit of weather we're having, wouldn't you say?"

Casting a quick glance to the sky, Pax shook their head. It wasn't raintime. Raintime was only once a week, and this week's had come and gone the day before. "Where did you come from?"

The man sighed. "A long time ago."

"I...but..." Pax stumbled over their words. Was this guy

nuts? Or had he just not heard them right? "What do you mean?"

He took a step up. Then another. Pax and Finn both stood, as if they might need to defend themselves at some point. It was silly, Pax thought, but something about the man unnerved them, and they were willing to bet that Finn felt the same way.

The man said, "I'm here to give you everything."

Finn puffed his chest out protectively. "Who are you? What do you want?"

Ignoring Finn, the man took another step, but then stopped. "What do you say, Pax? Why don't we get started?"

Finn stepped in front of Pax, ready to protect them if need be—an action that annoyed Pax immediately. Finn growled at the man, "Leave before I make you leave. They don't want anything to do with you and neither do I."

"Don't make decisions for me, Finn. Or speak for me. I can think for myself." Nudging Finn to the side, Pax met the man's gaze.

They didn't know who he was or where he had come from—and might never know those things—but they were damn sure going to do what they could to understand what it was that he was offering. "What do you mean, you want to give me everything?"

"Want? No. I *must* give you everything. I have no choice." The expression he wore was calm, but the way his fingers tightened on the handle of his umbrella suggested that he was anything but. "Of course, I would be lying if I said that I *didn't* want to give you everything. As much as I am sickened by the idea of putting another soul in this position… I confess, I am anxious to be finished with this task."

From within the building came the sounds of ignorant laughter. Their families, their neighbors, the Elders…they were all clueless to the fact that something had changed. Pax was certain that Finn was wishing that he too was ignorant once more, but Pax wanted to be anything but.

They wanted change. Not in the way that Finn would complain about nothing changing, but then demand that the change undo itself the moment it rendered its head in the form of a stranger. A stranger that shouldn't have been able to survive in the haze. A stranger who had survived and was now offering…what? Everything?

Pax had to force a swallow. Their tongue, mouth, throat felt like sandpaper. "Why should I believe you? Why should I trust you? I don't know you."

The man shook his head, his lips curling into a friendly smile. "You don't have to know me. I'm going to give you everything, whether you trust me or not. Whether you want me to…or not."

When Pax exchanged looks with Finn, he shook his head and reached for their hand, but Pax shook it off. They didn't want or need Finn to protect or love them. They'd just needed support. Friendship.

And Finn couldn't just accept that. He reached out and brushed a lock of hair from Pax's eyes in a manner that reminded Pax too much of the married couples inside. Pax shoved his hand away and shot him a glare.

Finn's eyes welled with tears, but it didn't solve anything for him. Pax loved him, sure. But not in a be-my-hero way. Not in a romantic way. And they wished for the millionth time that he could just accept it.

Finn whispered, "Pax…please…"

They weren't certain which he was pleading with them about—Pax not wanting a relationship or Pax engaging with the strange man carrying an umbrella—but either way, they wished that Finn would just go inside to pout. This was important. Maybe more important than anything had been before.

Turning their attention back to the stranger, Pax said, "I'm confused…and I have questions."

The man took another step up, towards Pax, and said, "I have answers. Just another part of the 'everything' I've been referring to."

"You say you want to give me everything. So tell me what's at the bottom of the stairs." It wasn't until that moment that Pax realized that they'd been clenching their jaw this entire time. Taking a deep breath, they relaxed it.

Finn's voice shook as he said, "Pax—"

If Pax didn't know better, they might have thought he was scared. But then…maybe he was.

"Why don't you come down and find out for yourself? That is…unless you're scared of what you'll find." The man glanced behind him, into the haze, before meeting Pax's eyes again.

"I'm not afraid." Pax's heart rate picked up its pace in protest.

"Funny the lies we tell ourselves, isn't it?" The man shook his head, kind of sinking inside of himself for a moment. Pax finally noticed the bags under his eyes. He looked exhausted. They wondered when he'd last slept.

Finn hissed, "I don't like this, Pax. We don't know this guy. He just appeared from a place that isn't supposed to be safe at all to be in. That haze took my mom. It took Mr. Carl. How the hell did this guy survive in it?"

"Finn. Please. Maybe this is our chance to get some answers."

"You're presuming he'll tell you the truth." A silence filled the air between them, and when Finn seemed to realize that Pax meant to stand their ground, he scoffed and headed inside, his words following him, quieting as he moved. "I can't be here for this. Do what you want."

Pax said to the man, "How did you get here?"

"I suppose you might say I followed you. Through time, incarnations, space, lives. And when I sensed your next incarnation, I knew to come here." A small smile found his lips. "You were an old man the first time we met. With a peculiar scar above your left eye."

Something about what he'd said made their stomach twist and turn. It felt almost familiar, but not quite. "Did you give me everything then too?"

"No. I took everything from you then. And three times after that." A faraway look reached his eyes then—one that sent a chill down Pax's spine. "This is the first time. The first time for giving."

Herbert slammed the cash register drawer closed. It was an old thing and for sure would need replacing soon. *Damn thing*, he thought. *Damn place can't hold out for one more month until I retire for good.*

The bell on the door chimed and without looking up, Herbert grouched, "All outta newspapers, if that's what you're here for."

"You…you must be the first. Yes. You are."

Herbert raised his bushy eyebrows and peered over at the newcomer at last. He was surprised as all get-out to see a young man dressed all in white on this side of town. He smelled like money. Probably some brat kid from the North end, looking for drugs. Drugs or reputation for being badass enough to survive a trip to the South end without getting a bloody lip. Herbert snorted. Damn youngins. Rich youngins, at that.

"First? What are you jawing about, boy?"

The boy paused, as if considering his options. "I'm here to take something from you."

"You ain't taking nothing from me, sonny. I been robbed by far tougher than you, so don't get any ideas or I'm gonna grab my bat and get blood all over your pretty white suit." Herbert glared. He had at least eighty pounds on the guy. The fight would be over before it ever even started. "Now get outta here before I call the cops."

A strange, dreamy expression crossed the young man's face then. "No…not something. Everything. I'm here to take everything from you. The same way she took everything from the others and gave it all to me."

"That's it." Herbert reached under the counter and grabbed his old baseball bat. It still had bloodstains from the last robbery attempt—a reminder of that day. His face held a reminder too. Damn kid had gotten a swing in and cut him above his eye. Mad as hell that punks kept seeing him as just an old man, not a threat at all. Herbert slammed the end of the bat on the counter and shouted, "Get outta here!"

The young man shook his head slowly. When he spoke

again, his tone was softer, sadder. "I can't. Don't you understand that I can't? I have no choice in this. It's the only way to stop the cycle. She said there will be five incarnations. Four to take from and one to give. She said it could take decades, maybe even centuries, and only then can I rest. I've been looking for you for two years, and here you are."

The two locked eyes and for a moment, Herbert could have sworn he saw something familiar glinting in the darkness of the boy's gaze. But that couldn't be. He'd never seen the kid before.

As if making up his mind, the young man stepped inside and locked the door. As he approached Herbert, he said, "I'm sorry. I'm so sorry. But I have to do this."

The man in the suit began his ascent without hesitation, without pause. He was coming up the stairs whether Pax wanted him to or not. "It's time now. Time for me to give you everything."

"I... I don't—" Thoughts raced through Pax's mind, but all they could think to speak was a distracting question. If they could keep the man talking, maybe they could figure out what they should do next. "What did you take from me then? When I was the old man?"

His steps were slow and sure. "I took everything—your breath, your dreams, your life—as you will do to four others. You won't be able to resist. Like gravity, this force is undeniable."

Pax stepped backward but tripped. They hit the metal hard and scrambled back as quickly as they could, but it was futile. Their limbs went numb. They couldn't move. Fear held them frozen in place. "You're insane!"

As he stepped up onto the fire escape landing, he said, "You'll know when you see the ones you must take from, the one you must give to, but I can't explain how. I suspect it's different for everyone."

Pax was frozen in fear. It was becoming difficult to even gulp for air. A panic attack. That's what Finn had called it when they'd felt this way before…the day that Mr. Carl had descended the stairs.

Quietly, the man continued, "When the fifth is revealed, you'll give it all back. And only then can you surrender to oblivion. Only then may you rest."

"Get away from me!" Pax shoved him, but the man barely moved. "Finn! Finn, help me!"

He crouched before Pax and set his umbrella to the side. "I'm sorry. I'm so sorry. I have no choice. I'm so tired. I just want to rest. You'll understand one day, I promise."

Then Pax's world went dark.

"Pax!" It was Finn's voice. He sounded scared. Had they passed out? Had it all been a dream?

Pax willed their eyes to open. They were lying on the fire escape. Finn was crouched beside them, looking relieved that they had woken at last. His eyes were red, like he'd been crying. "Are you okay?"

Pax struggled to sit up. A strange fog was bogging down their memories. "I'm…the man…he…"

"He's gone. He must have run off before I got to you. Are you all right?"

There. Beside them. The black umbrella.

A world of time and travel, of taking and giving, swirled through them until they thought they might burst. Tears choked them for a moment—tears from a realization that they couldn't deny.

They understood the man at last. They understood *everything*.

"Oh Finn…" Their voice cracked as they looked from the umbrella to their dearest friend, the certainty of their task stretching out before them like a slow-moving storm. "I…"

Finn's forehead was creased in concern. "What is it?"

Pax stretched out their arm and took the umbrella in their hand. As their fingers curled tightly around the ornate handle, they looked at Finn and said, "I have to take everything from you."

★ ★ ★ ★ ★

PRESENT: TENSE

Jim McCarthy

THERE IS ABOUT ONE HOUR A DAY WHEN I'M home alone. One hour when my mother's day-shift and my father's night-shift overlap. My sisters are unlikely to drop by without ample warning. I don't have to be at work yet. It's the only hour of the day when I can relax and not have to feel *on*.

So this afternoon, I'm spending the time the best way I know how: wrestling with my dog, Thatch, and letting him give me as many puppy kisses as he pleases.

My phone buzzes.

Miya's on the screen. "Luke, what the fuck is happening? I was talking to my parents, and they *disappeared*."

I reply, "Buh?"

"They were here and then they were gone… I feel like I'm hallucinating," she says, then swings her camera around her empty kitchen.

Listen. Miya is the best person I know. She is hilarious and brilliant and kind and warm. What she is not, however, is a person who under-reacts. She tends to panic first, ask questions later. I'm puzzling out how to respond when another message comes in.

Tak's face pops up, frantic and sweaty. "I'm on Weaver, and it's a ghost town," he says. "I pulled into the parking garage and everything was normal, but I came out and there are cars abandoned in the middle of the road. It's like people just disappeared."

Well, that's fucking weird. Before I can answer, my mother texts.

Are you okay?

It feels like the floor has dropped out from under me. Miya may be a panicker. Maybe something weird is going on with Tak. But my mother doesn't check in while she's at work unless something is *up*. My breath hitches.

I don't have any idea what else to do, so I walk outside. Things look perfectly normal. Cars aren't speeding by, no one's screaming down the sidewalk, the sky is a little cloudy, but not in a stormy way. My car is in the driveway, and the other houses on the block are just as boring as usual.

But then, I notice an abandoned car a little up the road. I head toward it. Maybe it's parked there, or maybe I'm not seeing the driver...

Suddenly, my phone rings in my back pocket. Wait, what? No one *calls* me. I grab it out of my pocket and see it's my mother. I'm a little nervous when I answer. "Mom, what's going on?"

"Oh, thank God," she says. "Tell me you're okay."

"I'm fine. Mom, what happened?"

"Have you heard from your sisters? Or your father?"

"No. Mom, why?"

Mom explains that she was in her office, and her coworker at the next desk vanished. At first, Mom thought she imagined it. She had looked up expecting to see Leanne sitting there, so her brain tricked her for a second, making her think Leanne was there and then gone. But when she went to find her, she ran into one of the doctors in the practice.

"And he said he was in the middle of examining a patient, when he just disappeared!"

Uncomfortable, I laugh. "Mom, that's crazy."

Mom's voice is tense. "Crazy or not, it happened. I don't know what's going on, Lucas, but stay inside. I'm leaving right now and heading home."

I turn away from the abandoned car. I walk toward my house, then start running. Slamming and locking the door behind me, I slide to the floor and lean back. Thatch runs over and crawls into my lap.

"Thatch," I say, "what the fuck is going on?" I grab my phone and start messaging people.

First, I text my three sisters. For a split second, I think about trying to reach my father, but things between us are not good. Really not good. I have a bunch of missed messages from Miya and Tak. They were blowing me up while I was talking to Mom.

Come to my house, I tell them both.

Whatever is happening, they're losing it, and I don't want to be alone. I scroll through everyone else in my phone and decide to text my friend Caleb. If Tak is steady, Caleb is stoic. Nothing shakes him. We work together at the mall, and he once walked over to where I was chatting with our manager, waited for a pause in our conversation and then calmly said, "I think my register might have caught fire." It had. Briefly. A wiring issue. Who knew?

While I wait to hear back from anyone, I get online and feel like I've taken a punch to the gut. People are tossing out words like *Rapture* and *apocalypse*. There are photos of a wildly underpopulated Times Square and near-empty subway cars in Tokyo. The news scrolls so fast, I can barely read it. In Toronto, everyone's been ordered to shelter at home; it looks like a ghost town.

I set my phone on the ground and hug Thatch a little tighter with both arms. He knows something is up. He puts a paw on my hand like he's holding me in place, and nuzzles his head into my neck.

My newsfeed won't stop buzzing. I struggle for a breath and pick my phone back up to see a post that doesn't make any sense.

Has anyone heard from any straight people since this happened?

I have. My mother. And Tak maybe. Maybe? Should I reply? But how weird it is that I don't actually know if my closest friend of ten years is straight? To be fair, he doesn't know I'm gay, but...it's irrelevant. My mother is definitely straight. Therefore, the internet is grasping at straws.

And who fucking cares, anyway?! If what I'm seeing is true, thousands of people have vanished into thin air. Where did they go? Who's next? Is it me? Are planes going to fall from the sky? Are people trapped in elevators and subways and hospitals, alone and stranded?

Thatch whimpers, and I put both of my hands over my eyes. Blocking everything out, I start rocking back and forth, chanting, "What is happening, what is happening, what is happening?"

My lungs feel like they're rejecting air, no matter how much I gasp for it. I can't breathe enough. My pulse races in my neck. It's too loud and too fast. I lean over and put my head on the horrible pink carpet of the hallway. Thatch wriggles beneath me, whining softly.

I try to count my breaths and my pulse, but I get the numbers confused. I can't hold on to anything.

I open my mouth and some horrible keening sounds comes out, and I rock and rock, back and forth on my knees. My heart seems to jerk and double over on itself.

It feels like a heart attack, but it's a panic attack. I *know* it's a panic attack, but I can't stop it. I try to remember anything my therapist has told me about how to get through this. I try, but his advice is slippery and complicated, and keeps sneaking away from me.

That's where I am, doubled over the dog, on the floor, when the door opens. It nearly knocks me over, and my mother gasps.

"Oh, my God, Luke. What's going on? Is it someone in the family?"

I put my arm out to try to wave her off and let her know that I can't speak, but she keeps asking questions, and I'm crying. There isn't air to form words, and she's practically shouting questions at me, and somehow a little burst of anger struggles free, a crack in the glass.

"I'm...panicking," I manage. "Hold...on."

Mom knows I've had panic attacks, but she hasn't seen one. She hovers too close. As I eye her wildly, I swing my arm again, trying to get her to back off. Finally, she slips back, fretting into the empty space between us.

My breathing slows. I remember that I can get enough air in, but I'm not letting enough out before I try to inhale again. Trembling, I push everything out as hard as possible and take a rickety breath back in. Again. Again.

It doesn't end the attack completely, but it feels as though it could be the beginning of the end. I set Thatch free, and move to the landing, gulping as I settle.

"Was that one worse than usual?" Mom asks, pale.

"A little bit, yeah," I tell her.

"I want to talk to you about what's going on, but don't want to set you off again," she says, and I'm irritated because yes, I have panic attacks, but I'm not fragile. I am not a piece of glass.

"Just tell me what you know," I say.

So she does, but it's not much more than I've worked out. People disappeared all over the world. Early estimates are that over half the people in the world were there and then gone. No explanation. But that number is a guess, based on firsthand reports, and people uploading videos as fast as they can take them.

"Mom, are we going to die?" I ask, and it comes out rattling and wheezy.

"I don't know," she answers. "I don't think so. I want to believe we're going to be fine for long enough that people can start to figure this out."

The doorbell rings, and we both jump. Usually, we can hear people coming up to the house, but we must have been distracted by my panic. My mom gestures for me to stay put. She stands, smooths her hair back, then opens the door.

"Takahiro. Hi. What... What are you doing here?"

He answers, "Luke invited me."

I say hey and hug him. I don't want to let go, but I do. Turning to Mom, I say, "I asked Miya to come, too. She said she was talking to her parents and they disappeared."

"Good thinking, Luke," Mom says. Her back straightens, and she looks outside briefly before closing the door. "I'm going to try to call your sisters."

She heads for the kitchen, and Tak and I take over the living room. Right as we go to sit down, a car pulls into the gravel driveway. Pulling back the side of the curtain, I see Miya running towards the front door. She bursts in without ringing the bell. "Dude!" she shouts.

I'm shaking my head back and forth as if trying to deny that this is happening. That the world of...has it only been half an hour? That *that* world is over. Probably. Maybe? Panic rises at the edges of my brain. I need to focus. Miya's already talking.

"My parents decided to ambush me about where I am with my college applications, even though they know where everything is, right? They've seen the application fees on their credit cards! But we're going through all of it, and they're telling me how much is riding on this, and they just disappeared.

"Like, they were there and then they weren't! Not even like mid-thought but mid-syllable. And I'm freaking out because that can't happen, right?" Miya punctuates herself with flying hands. "And I'm thinking that I've just fully lost my mind, and that's when I sent you the snap, and then...well, I'm here now, but what is happening? I can't figure out what is *happening*."

She half laughs, but the end of it is choked off. None of us know what to do.

"It wasn't like that for me," Tak says after a moment. "I pulled into the parking garage next to the library, and I think everything was normal then. But once I walked out of the lot, cars were abandoned in the street, and nobody was around.

"After I texted Luke, I went to get coffee, and there were a couple people, but also something was super wrong. There were bags sitting next to empty tables and drinks splattered on the floor, and the guy behind the bar was screaming at me, asking what was going on outside."

"It was hard to get here," Miya adds. "There were cars all over, but only some of them were moving."

"That was true for me as well," my mom says, stepping into the doorway. She only had to come down the street to get home from the hospital, but it took her more than twice as long as normal. She asks if it's okay to turn the TV on to see if any of the news channels have anything to say.

We all turn towards the television and watch footage of lost-looking people wandering the streets of New York. It's only forty-five minutes away but sometimes feels like a different universe. The biggest city in the country is just a few miles away, but our little town just sits here, boring and unchanging. Well…until now.

The anchor explains that their newsroom is moving as quickly as they can, given their depleted size.

"We probably don't know a lot more than you do," she offers, unhelpfully.

My phone buzzes, and my mother immediately asks if it's one of my sisters. It's not.

Caleb has texted that he's okay. Almost his whole family is accounted for, but no one can find his sister. Still, that feels almost unbelievable given everything that's going on. I don't know if I should be happy for him or jealous.

We all sit in a moment of nervous quiet, and then something from the TV breaks through the shock and concern and confusion.

"We're going to share some footage that has been sent into our station or found on social media," the anchor says. And then we see a shot of a city park that's full of people until suddenly it's not. The change is instantaneous. The girl with the video starts moving frantically.

Everything turns shaky, but you can see some people looking all around them, and there's screaming in the background.

A new video starts. It's somebody's school gym, in the process of being decorated. "We were getting ready for the dance, and all of a sudden all the straight kids disappeared," a voice tells us, the camera landing on someone our age staring off blankly.

There's another clip, but I don't really watch it. My cheeks flush, and I can't look at Mom. She can't know that I'm blushing. Or why.

I lock eyes with Miya, the only person here who knows I'm gay, and I know she's...well, she's not totally sure yet. She's said she may be pansexual. Possibly demi, but on the ace spectrum. She's still working out her words, but she knows she's not straight.

Then, I look to Tak, who is staring out the window, clutching his hands together. I should know whether he's straight or not. We've been best friends since we were seven, but somehow, it's never come up. Maybe it's that we met in Catholic school, that our parents are friends with each other, that we're both scared of God or hell or the afterlife.

But we've always, *always*, avoided talking about anything like attraction or sex, regardless of gender. Instead, we dance a complicated choreography of avoidance, straining at every moment to sidestep talking about bodies, those sinful lumps we're stuck inside.

I've been so scared that he'd tell his mom and then she would tell mine. And ever since everything that went down with my father, I've been even more nervous.

But Tak's here, now. Could that mean…? But wait a minute. That doesn't make any sense, because my mom's here and she's not… I look back to the doorway.

"Mom?" I ask.

Her face is bright red. "I need to try your sisters again," she says and almost dashes out of the room.

Everyone seems to hold their breath for a moment, and we look back and forth at each other. Miya speaks first.

"Luke already knows I'm queer as hell," she tells Tak.

"I…am too, I guess?" Tak looks to me, uneasy.

Holy shit, my heart gallops in my chest. Everything that's going on is TOO MUCH, but Tak… Tak isn't straight! In spite of the epic global event happening, part of me can't help but feel overjoyed. I've never admitted it, not even to Miya, but I've had a crush on Tak for years. How could I not?

We've been having sleepovers since we were in first grade. He taught me how to eat with chopsticks, how to bake the world's best peanut butter cookies, and together, we've watched the best horror movies of all time. I've been in at least a little in love with him ever since we met at Children's Mass.

The first time I went to his house, I was blown away because he lived in an apartment building. I'd never been in an apartment before, and it felt cool and kind of fancy? I've cycled through so many pairs of my own house shoes over there. His mom has been a second mother to me. And Tak was like the brother I never had, but also different.

Somehow, Tak and I muscled through puberty, working overtime to ignore all the changes. They felt embarrassing and maybe shameful. Father Walters reminded us every week that our bodies were vessels of sin, and we needed to fight our urges, our changes. Our bodies were temptation. I figured the best way to avoid that temptation was to pretend it didn't exist.

But it did. When Tak and I went swimming, I noticed that he was stretching out and getting leaner. I felt like a beast who was sprouting hair everywhere at once and started to smell deeply funky, while his cheekbones became more prominent and muscles developed.

By the time he had the ghost of a mustache, I was already shaving my whole face every two days. His was the body I'd seen the most, and dwelled on, comparing myself to him but also yearning for him.

He was the boy I most wanted to kiss, but he was him, and we were us, and I couldn't screw that up. So I never, ever brought it up.

I notice Tak and Miya both looking at me. Acutely aware of my mother in the next room, terrified that she'll come back in at any moment talking about how stupid the theory is, I whisper, "I think I'm gay."

"*Think*?" Miya says incredulously. She's known for years.

"Okay. Yes, I am, but you know *she* doesn't know." I nod my head toward the kitchen. But wait. There's the sticking point. Maybe the three of *us* are queer, but my *mother* isn't. Or...yes? No. That isn't possible. Is it?

Who else is accounted for? Except for Miya, Tak and Mom, my notifications have been quiet. Wait, no. Caleb's family. Caleb is trans. His brother is bisexual. His mother is a lesbian. But his father...is a preacher. And he's still around? Caleb's sister is unaccounted for, but she's the youngest, and everyone kind of assumes she'll be queer based on odds alone.

Caleb's dad is sus. He stayed married to his gay wife for years "for the sake of family togetherness." Would a straight man do that? Would a not-straight man do that? My parents weren't real big on Caleb. They routinely misgendered him in conversation, and even though his dad is a preacher, I can practically feel their condescension. After all, he's *Lutheran*, which to them may as well be atheists or devil worshippers.

"Have either of you heard from anyone that you one hundred percent know is straight?" I ask.

"Uh, no," Miya says, gesturing at the world.

Okay, that sounded stupid. People don't come out as straight. I can't think of a single allocishet person taking the time to explain their identity to anyone. And isn't that part of the damn problem?

So no, I'm thinking about this wrong. We should be trying to reach everyone we know who's *not* straight or cis, and see if we hear back from them. I'm about to suggest it, but Mom comes back into the room, looking ashen.

"None of your sisters are getting back to me. I can't reach your father." She stands still for a moment, contemplating. "Luke, start texting family. Anyone you can think of. Cousins, aunts, uncles. Keep track of who gets back to you. In the meantime, Tak, Miya. I haven't even asked you. Have you seen anyone else? Have you been able to reach your families?"

Miya chokes up a little as she recounts fighting with her parents and then them just disappearing from in front of her and says she hadn't heard from her sister yet. I feel a pang. I hadn't even thought to ask about Emilie. Tak says he's tried him mom a few times, but only gets her voice mail.

"What about your dad?" Mom asks, and he looks down a bit and shakes his head no.

"Okay," she says, "I'm going to add them to my list of people to keep trying. If there's anyone else who you think would feel safer here than wherever they are—" she addresses all of us "—tell them that they can come here. We don't know what's happening, and we don't know what we're facing, but everyone is welcome."

Miya stands up, grabs my arm, and mouths, "Outside."

I follow her through the door, which I have only just closed when she says, "I'm asking your mother if she's queer." Her eyes blaze, and I start to laugh, but...no. She's serious.

"Miya, you can't," I tell her. "Then she would know you... And I... Besides, there's no way. She can't..." My breath gets trapped behind my ribs. She can't really be planning on doing this. I put my hand against the doorway to brace myself. "You can't seriously walk in there and ask my deeply religious mother if she's queer. That's…" I trail off.

"Look, I know you're terrified that she'll disown you like your father did. All I know is that she's in there desperately trying to reach any of our families, and the last thing on her mind right now is whether she's going to banish the one child she actually has at home right now."

She's probably right. But what if she's not? I take a deep breath and hold it for a second. Three months ago, my father discovered I was gay by taking my computer and looking at my search history.

I lied about how someone at school must have used my browser at some point. I could tell he didn't believe me, but he let it slide. Until one afternoon when I came home and found him sitting at the kitchen table with my journals in front of him, staring at me with disgust. I didn't know what to do so I started to run up the stairs, but he chased me.

Everything I remember is in slivers because I sort of blacked out. Most of my memories are flashes of images or sense memories. Dad standing over where I fell at the top of the stairs. A raised fist. Me screaming back at him as he stormed out the front door. And this churning fire rising up my legs, settling in my gut. My knees buckling. I could hear the sound that came out of me—this open-throated moan that hit my ears as though coming from somewhere else. Somewhere beyond the constraints of my body because the hurt and the fear were too big.

I couldn't control them and so I couldn't control me. I was forced out of my body, observing from a distance that felt foreign, but safer... I couldn't breathe inside my own desolation, so I left. In a way. For a moment.

After that, I was convinced Dad was capable of anything. He carried a gun. There were others in the house. I faced a question I could barely even begin to process: Did my father hate me enough to kill me?

I made it through the night but barely. After that, I started avoiding home any time he was there. I'd drive to McDonald's after school if I didn't have work or clubs or play practice. Right there, next to the playplace, I'd sit and eat chicken nuggets, wasting time until I knew he would be gone.

I tried to figure out if he would tell my mother and, if so, what would happen. I knew, or at least suspected they weren't getting along, but they still talked. And if he told her, I didn't know what would happen.

On the one hand, I believed my mother loved me.

On the other, I remembered her handing me books about sin—the difference between venial and mortal sins, and how mortal sins are particularly terrible, especially insulting to God and threatening to your afterlife.

Homosexuality was a mortal sin.

Those were the words she physically put in my head. That was the message. And if she really believed that things were as black and white as that, would she even let me stay at home? Was I so dirty to her that she would force me out? I didn't know.

One night, Dad must have stayed up just to catch me by surprise. I started climbing the stairs to go to bed, and a light went on in the living room.

Beer in hand, shadowed in the darkness of his La-Z-Boy,

he said, "I could have made you a decent man, but I missed my chance. Your mother ruined you." I stared at him. I was so fucking sick of being scared, so all I felt was the hard shell of rage come over me as he said, "You'll never be worth *anything.*"

And as twisted as it sounds, that made me feel hopeful: if he blamed my mother, maybe he wouldn't tell her. And if she didn't know, maybe I'd have a home long enough to graduate and move out.

I'm even more hopeful now. If any of this is true. If this is real. If he's never coming home again.

Now, if what we're thinking could be true, then I don't need to wonder. It will never matter again.

I'll miss my sisters. I'm scared about what happens next. I don't know how anything will look in ten minutes, let alone tomorrow or beyond. But if he is never coming back, then I can breathe.

That realization rushes over me, and I begin to cry. My shoulders shake, and I reach toward Miya. I open my mouth to try to explain to her what I'm thinking and feeling, but it's all too much. I sob—my breath catches, and I can't speak.

Miya puts her hands on my shoulders and her head against my chest, and she holds on.

After a long moment, I step back from Miya's embrace and pull my glasses off. As I wipe my forearm across my face to clear the tears, I make the decision. "You should ask her. Definitely ask her."

With a breath to steel myself, I open the door to go back inside. I hear my mother talking softly and Tak crying. I motion for Miya to be quiet and enter the house. We stand just inside, and take in the sight of my mother sitting on the couch, Tak's head on her shoulder. She has one hand on his back, and one on the side of his face.

"I've never told anyone," he croaks out. "I've been so afraid my parents would find out. That they would be ashamed of me."

My mother looks up to see us standing there and lifts her hand from Tak's back to wave us toward the kitchen. What we're seeing is private. A part of me wants to believe she's intentionally loud enough for me to hear as she tells him, "There is nothing to be ashamed of. I am *so* glad you are still here."

Miya and I walk into the kitchen, and I take my father's seat at the head of the table. Miya sits opposite me. Time slips by or stands still or has stopped existing. I have no idea how long it has been since Miya first texted me. Thirty minutes? Three hours? Nothing makes any sense.

"Are you going to try to reach your sister again?" I ask.

She nods. "You going to try yours?"

We take out our phones, exchanging a few names of people we should reach out to, in case they need somewhere to be or people to be with.

My mother comes in with red eyes and tear tracks on her face. She looks to my phone and then back at me.

"Your sisters?" she asks.

Terribly, I have to answer her, "Nothing yet."

The silence stretches. I look to Miya to see if she's going to ask my mother *that* question. I'm so unbelievably exhausted all of a sudden. Sitting here in the kitchen, phones eerily quiet—it's like every ounce of adrenaline has left my body.

Miya stands, and gestures to the chair. "You should sit, Mrs. O'Connor."

My mother hugs Miya and reminds her that she can invite anyone to our house. Then, she sits.

Miya nods meaningfully at me. "You ask," she mouths.

And unthinkably, I do.

"Mom. I don't even… I'm not sure if it's even okay to… Mom. Mom, are you straight?"

My mother lifts her eyes to me, her gaze somewhere between defeated, confused, and terrified, but she holds it. "Oh, I don't even know what that means anymore," she says.

Still behind Mom, Miya's eyes bug out. I can tell she wants me to prod, but I can think of nothing else to say. I stay quiet, giving Mom time to collect herself. She continues.

"When I was a teenager, growing up in the church, we knew that gay people existed. Of course we knew. But we never spoke about it. The assumption was that this 'affliction' wouldn't even tempt us. We were warriors of God. And I always had crushes on boys, so I didn't have anything to worry about.

"But if you're asking if I ever had a crush on another girl? I did. I had very close girl-friends. But if I had feelings about them that I wasn't supposed to have? I learned to push that down. I found a way to not let it get in the way.

"Besides, I didn't have to worry for too long. I'd met your father by the time I was twenty. And we fit. So I put away everything else, and got to the business of being a wife and a mother."

The sensation in my stomach is too big for me. I don't know how to respond. My heart is shattering for every moment that she had to hide her true self. I want to ask if she was scared of God, whether she thought He would judge her. Or whether He is proud of her for walking the righteous path.

But all I manage, all I can possibly choke out is, "Mom, I'm gay."

I start to cry again. Not out of fear. Not out of sadness. It's relief. It's a journey traveled. I've known for years. Miya has known for years. Now my mother knows. When I pull myself back together a bit, I look across the table and see my Mom smiling at me.

"I sort of figured," she says, sweeping her hands out in the direction of Miya, and Tak, and the world. She half laughs, half chokes, and her face pinches. She looks up at me again. "Do you know if any of your sisters..."

"I don't know, Mom. Not that they've ever told me, but I don't know if they would have."

"I'm so worried for my girls," she says. I walk around the table to stand behind her, put my head down on top of her curly hair and squeeze her tight between my arms.

"I love you," I tell her.

"I know," she says. "And I love you." She rolls her shoulders to shake off my embrace, then turns to face me. "Now shoo. Go be with your friends. I have more calls to make."

Over the next few hours, a couple more people show up. As the hours tick by, everyone seems less terrified and more... shocked, I guess. Or amazed. We call out when we reach people, and we shout anytime something on the news feels important.

Some people did, in fact, get stranded in elevators and subways and other awkward places worldwide, but so far there's no news of any kind of catastrophe. Planes haven't fallen from the sky. The internet is still running. There are stranded people in all kinds of places, but search teams are out finding them.

The possibility of calamity is still out there, but things are going so smoothly, it's as if there was some guiding hand. This isn't the work of the spiteful and judgmental God I was raised to believe in. This feels more like a kindness.

My friend Caleb comes to the house a little after nine. It's been less than five hours since the vanishing. That's what we're calling it, anyway.

"How's your family?" my mother asks when Caleb comes through the front door.

Things have always been tense between them. When he came out as trans, Mom "didn't understand." She said it was "a shame," and she was always wary of me spending as much time with Caleb as I did. But here she is in a new world, a queer woman welcoming a queer trans man into her home.

"I was kind of sick of them and needed to get away," Caleb says.

Everyone goes perfectly still for a moment, knowing that my mother has been a one-woman command center in the kitchen, trying to find any sign that one of my sisters might be out there, that they, too, had been deeply closeted.

I hold my breath to see if she's going to lash out and tell Caleb his ingratitude isn't welcome here. Instead, at the end of the brief pause, my mother laughs.

"How lucky you are." She smiles. "You're welcome here anytime."

A little surprised, I think, Caleb says, "Thanks."

We don't know where everyone who disappeared went. They can't be entirely gone, we don't think. Matter becomes other matter. Thousands (or millions or billions) of people didn't evaporate without a trace. That can't be possible. But then again, none of this makes any sense, and it's already happening.

Here we are, my mom, my best friends. It's hard for Mom to smile. I get that. But Tak? Me? Everything just changed for us on so many levels. I put my arm around him, gingerly. Just around his shoulders.

He looks to me; we smile, and I wonder what the queer future holds.

★ ★ ★ ★ ★

NICK AND BODHI

Naomi Kanakia

"I'M A GENIUS. YOU ARE NOTHING. YOUR IN-
tellects are nothing. I control this world. The president—I've
got him on speed dial. His personal cell. I could kill all of you,
and nobody would care. I'm like Superman, but smarter, and
not as dorky. I have no limits. So screw all of you."

The teacher waited for Nick to stop ranting. Then she said,
"Did you want to take this class?"

This was Mrs. Ferris, one of our oldest teachers, and one
of the few who still tried to teach. Her pinky finger quivered
slightly as she gripped the back of her seat.

"History? Why? It's all lies anyway! You teach this American history BS? I was there. I can travel through time, you
jerks. World War II, let me tell you the real story. Sit down!"

"You're welcome to discuss your insights with me during
the off hours. Or if you want to have a seminar, you're welcome to form a club. But right now, this is my classroom."

Nick's eyes glowed red. Today he was in a new body: this

one was tall, female, blonde, with long eyelashes, long legs—absurdly enough, he was wearing a cheerleader's uniform—our school didn't even have a cheerleading squad! But we knew it was him, because nobody else talked like Nick.

"I'll vaporize you right here," Nick said. "And then I'll go to another time line, drag you back, show you the hole in the ground where you used to be, and ask you to sit down."

"This is my classroom."

Her head melted. There was no blood, just a sort of oozing, liquid mass. The process of bringing in another version of her from another dimension took about five minutes, and then the new Mrs. F sobbed on the ground while Nick cackled.

After he left, most of the kids in the classroom bolted, some of them crawling out of windows. An unofficial rule of our school was that if you'd had one Nick encounter, you didn't need to attend class for the rest of the day.

"Err, it's okay," my friend Numaah said. She patted Mrs. Ferris on the back of the head. "It's okay. Come on, come with us."

We took her to the faculty lounge. Our school was controlled by an AI, designed by Nick, to "optimize" our schooling experience. It was supposed to turn us into what he called "real people" instead of "mindless sheep," but even the AI had calmed down after a while and was okay with us hanging out wherever, so long as we seemed like we were working.

The AI-controlled eyebot said, "Please keep your phones on. I will let you know if class attendance is too low, and we need more bodies. Where will you be?"

"I dunno," Numaah said. "Woods?"

"Not a good day," the eyebot said. "Nick is bored today. If

visible human presence decreases, he will become petulant. Have you seen Nick's new body?"

"I did," I said. "So, is Nick trans now? Is he, like, a girl? What pronouns should we use?"

"DO NOT VOCALIZE THAT THOUGHT IN HIS PRESENCE! NICK TRANSCENDS GENDER. HE IS SUI GENERIS."

"Okay," I said. "Don't go all robotic on us. We'll be hanging near Wall-E, I guess."

We picked up Frida from her meditation class—formerly biology, but Mr. Canto had gone a little wacky over the past year—and convened at the coffee cart, which was also robot-powered (and adorable, with cute flailing arms and humongous eyes, hence its name, Wall-E).

"Mrs. Ferris, really?" Frida said. "Are there any originals left? Besides me and Numaah?"

"A few," Numaah said. "Not many."

"Hey there, arbitrary social constructs."

My neck prickled, and then he was there, Nick in the flesh, changed out of his cheerleader's outfit and into a crop top and miniskirt, along with six-inch heels. He had a handful of some orange gloop in his palm. "Want some? It'll make you stop giving a shit what people think about you."

We kept our heads down even as phones beeped all across the courtyard—the AI sending us instructions. Stalled students hurried forward, messed around at their lockers and more or less acted natural. Most of us had been vaporized and replaced a few times—I originally came from a reality much worse than this one, a total war-torn climate change hell—but Frida and Numaah were originals.

"How about you?" Nick pointed at me. "It's because of you I don't use people's names anymore. See, I know all the names. I memorized them ages ago, because I'm a genius and I don't play trivial power games. But people like you, changing your gender, changing your pronouns, forcing people to participate in your altered reality, acting like some meaningless concept in your brain matters at all, you made me just decide, who gives a crap?"

I'm trans. I didn't always think that way. I'd come to this reality as a boy, but, well, it's a long story. The point is that almost nothing had made Nick as angry as when Numaah had told him my new pronouns.

Then he nodded at Numaah. "Hey, girl," he said. "How's your year going? Want some gloop?"

"No thanks," she said. "And stop fucking with Bodhi. She's faced way worse than you can imagine."

"Whatever. She's not tough. She just got born in a shitty world." Now he looked me up and down, and then he fluttered his long painted nails at me. "You love my body, don't you? Weren't you from a white supremacist, male supremacist world? Isn't that why you turned into a girl? You love this body. You'd love to be pretty, love to be white.

"You want to know where it came from? I bought it, for three galactic credits, at what's basically a gas station convenience store. It came in a little kit, and I grew it. That's how little your hopes and dreams matter, Bodhi. I could give you everything you want, and it wouldn't even matter to me."

I looked at the body, and my heart started thumping. Nick looked just like the daughter of the director of our group home, back in my home universe. She'd been pretty nice, had given us her old books, waved to us from the other side of the gates, where she was having a normal life with her friends. I'd wanted so badly to be her.

"Oh, you're tempted," Nick said. "You're seriously tempted. Well, I can do it, if you have the balls. Your old self, the one I replaced, would've begged for the chance to get on my good side. He loved the shit out of me. I knew him really well, but he never hinted at wanting to be a girl. What makes you so different? I'm curious. I wanna study you."

Frida tugged on my sleeve. "Trust us," she said. "Don't do it."

I turned away, back to the cart.

"Suit yourself, coward." And then we heard the slow click of Nick's high heels as he walked away.

The coffee cart sold cocaine, heroin, and a number of intense alien drugs, but we knew better than to take them. I got a cappuccino, Frida got tea, and Numaah got some interstellar beverage that tasted like dirt and made her mouth numb.

"What?" Numaah said. "It's relaxing. Don't worry, the AI says it's not addictive."

The three of us had more than done our Nick time for the day, so the AI let us hang out in the empty wing—our school doesn't have nearly as many students as it used to.

We sat in some old desks, in an empty classroom, and after a few minutes we were all on our phones. We were minor celebrities because we went to school with Nick, and even more so because he interacted with us a little bit—more than he did with most other students.

"Wow," Numaah said. "The internet is really into that

body offer. But they're all like, try and see if they can give you an Indian one. The internet is totally into using *they* for Nick now, by the way."

"Wow," Frida said. "They really do not know Nick."

Numaah was Black and extremely dark-skinned and kept her hair buzzed down to just a few millimeters. Frida was on testosterone and usually wore a binder, but still used female pronouns. Very outside the gender binary.

They were proud of being the only two survivors of the original Queer Students Association. For some reason, the queer kids really, really made Nick angry. He liked to say: *Jesus, at least the normal kids are just refusing to think for themselves, but you guys are creating a whole new identity for no fucking reason? To feel different? And don't give me that "born this way" crap. I'm proof that people can change anything about themselves that they want.*

"What do you think it's like to be him?" I said.

"Oh, stop this obsession of yours," Frida said. "He's a sociopath."

"No, but seriously," I said. "It must feel incredible. I don't think he's a sociopath. I think we'd all be like him if we had his power."

"No offense, Bodhi, but sometimes you say some pretty dumb shit," Frida said.

On occasion, I felt that I understood Nick more than Frida or Numaah did, on account of I was born a boy. Or assigned male at birth, which is what people in this reality say.

In my reality, boys who were caught dressed in girls' clothes were perverts who got sent to special camps—though that hadn't stopped me from sometimes doing it.

I smoothed my skirt down. I hadn't decided whether to ask

for estrogen yet. My parents in this reality probably wouldn't care. They looked like my real parents, but they weren't them, not really. They let me do whatever.

"Was my original self trans?"

"Uhh…" Frida looked at Numaah.

"What's going on?" Numaah said. "You've never asked about her before."

"Him, you mean. Like, he went by our birth name, Badri, didn't he? Did you know him?"

"Uhh…uhh…"

"I'm not stupid," I said. "I can see his social media accounts. He seemed like he was sort of shallow." His diary had been worse than shallow. It'd been angry and violent. He'd planned on getting close to Nick, becoming one of his foot soldiers, and using him to achieve world domination.

"He was just a guy," Numaah said. "I mean, she was. They were."

"Hey!" Frida said. "I'm a guy! At least sometimes!"

"You know what I mean," Numaah said. "We knew right away you were different."

After coming here six months ago, I'd wandered around the school in sort of a daze. The faculty still welcomed their own, but they left it to students to manage themselves, and most of the kids didn't bother to help orient the newcomers.

I'd been skinny, hungry, and confused. After my first day, the AI had directed me home, and my parents hadn't known what to do—they'd sent their big, strapping son to school, and he'd come back this scrawny wreck. Then they realized "their" Badri was dead, and they lost it, retreating into themselves.

In the group home in my home reality, I used to secretly dress in my sister's clothes. So after coming here, I had snuck into her room—in this reality she was away at college—and I'd done the same thing. After a few months, my parents found me, and they freaked out, called my sister—she sort of explained the whole trans concept to me. I wasn't complaining. It fit me pretty well.

"Has he ever offered you guys anything?"

"He has to Numaah," Frida said.

Now Numaah ticked off on her fingers. "Empress of my own planet. Empress of this planet. Immortality. The power of flight. The power of telepathy."

"A spaceship," Frida said. "Once he offered you a spaceship."

"Oh, I don't count stuff like that," Numaah said.

"And you never took him up on it?"

"It's no big deal. It's not even tempting," Numaah said. "There would be some invisible strings or whatever."

"She says he's only doing it to split us up, and she wouldn't want to leave me behind," Frida said. "He never offers me stuff for some reason. Which is, like, pretty insulting. Or is it? Does he know I'd take it? Because I'd definitely take it."

"No, come on, you wouldn't want to be empress of your own planet," Numaah said.

"Sure I would. I'd just set everybody free and then run for president. No way they wouldn't elect me."

"No, not worth it," Numaah said. "You can't use that kind of power for good. They'd need to take their freedom. Probably by killing you, girl."

"Well, I would've taken the spaceship in a second," Frida

said. "Can you imagine? All of time and space for us to explore?"

I thought for sure I'd outed myself, made them think I was considering the offer. Which I wasn't, really. Or maybe I was. It was May, and I was the oldest of them, the closest to "graduating." The freakiest thing about this twisted reality was that Nick would eventually let you leave.

In June of your senior year, you could just stop coming to school. He wouldn't hunt you down or anything. You could go to college, if any of them would take you, and your parents could move out of this town, if they didn't have any younger kids.

Nick only cared about the school, not the town itself.

The overhead speakers crackled, and Nick's voice rang out: "Attention, attention, attention. I'm speaking to a certain person. My offer expires in exactly one hour. You know who you are."

"Ignore it," Numaah said.

"Yeah, sure."

"Even if you got away with it," Numaah said, "wouldn't you feel sleazy, looking at yourself, knowing you were his fantasy?"

"I don't know. I'd be fine. I think."

"Well, it'd go terribly wrong," Frida said. "Asking him for wishes is like using the monkey's paw."

"What's that?"

They explained the concept, about an object that grants wishes, only to twist and pervert them, and I immediately thought: no, Nick isn't like that. He'd want you to know exactly what you were giving up.

"Has he ever shown up in a girl's body before?" I asked.

Frida looked at Numaah, and something passed between them. "I don't know."

I called out to an eyebot that was passing. "Has he ever used a girl's body before?"

"No," the AI said. "Not in the full two years since his emergence. Not according to my memory."

"Isn't that weird, then?" I asked. "I mean, that's a weird interval. He uses different bodies all the time, right? My first day, he was some sort of giant lizard-alien. But he takes two years to be a human girl? You'd think that'd be, bam, the first thing he'd do."

"Of course you'd think that," Numaah said. "You're trans. He's just a typical masculine bag of dicks; probably was afraid of what'd happen, what it'd make him feel."

"I don't know. I mean, what does it mean to be trans anyway, if you don't have a biological brain? I guess the body swap thing raises a lot of identity questions."

"Booooooo!" Frida threw balled-up paper at me. Then she held up her finger, tore up another piece of notebook paper, and threw that at me too. The eyebot swooped around, picking up the paper, and then it threw the paper at me too!

"Boo as well," the AI said.

"What? You don't even know why she was annoyed!"

"I believe Frida has been triggered by the mention of transhumanist 'identity issues.' Nick, at one time, used to berate the student body for failing to care more about the philosophical implications of his antics."

"All right, fine," I said. "Sue me for thinking the science-fictional wonderland is the slightest bit interesting, compared to, I dunno, a race-segregated group home!"

"Again with the group home," Frida said. After getting a glare from Numaah, Frida said, "Okay, okay, we should respect your trauma. But respect ours too. This…is a nightmare. You're so lucky you're getting out of here soon."

"Yeah…" I said. "It's just…don't you ever think… I mean… with infinite alternate realities, there must be one future where Nick just, like, spontaneously combusts, leaving us free to really play around with all this cool stuff that—"

"BOOOOOOOO." This time the chorus came from all three of them, and I was pelted with balls of flying paper.

Today was obviously one of those days when we were gonna pay no attention to our class schedule. It's not that we had to spend every second of every day together, but it would've been weird to sneak off on my own.

Frida played some song, and Numaah giggled about the video. We were in our own little world, and about as happy as it was possible to be in this situation.

At one point when Frida and Numaah were going over some schoolwork—they wanted to be ready for college!— the AI said to me, "You truly are quite lucky. Most of the students have been made worse. Cheapened by this trauma."

I shrugged. Just outside the window, I could see groups of kids skulking around between the modular buildings, almost like it was some sort of obstacle court. They hid in the alleys between buildings, smoking and drinking, with their arms pulled tight and their heads down. There was no laughter.

"I don't know. I feel sorry for them."

"Of course," the AI said. "But you three are different."

My gut tightened, and I reached up, trying to scratch a spot between my shoulder blades. I deserved the praise. It was fair. No need to feel bad. "Hey," I whispered. "Do you remember when Nick made that announcement, about an hour being left?"

"Ahem…" The AI turned, looked at Numaah.

"Tell her," she said. "It's okay."

"Approximately fifty-one minutes ago."

"And where's Nick now?"

"In the main office, at the entrance to his ship."

"You can't do this," Frida said. "It's not right. You have to—"

"Shh," Numaah said. "Let her go. Just…let her go."

I got up, massaging the lump in my throat, and I looked at the three of them, all staring at me. Then I took off with a swift walk.

They didn't understand. They were from this reality. I was from…someplace else. I'd need to make my way here. And this reality wasn't great to brown people. Was even worse to brown trans girls.

I'd seen what it meant to not belong. If I wore that body, the beautiful one, the cisgender one, the—the—the—yes—the white one, then I'd always have a place.

The principal's chair was turned around, and those high heels were kicked up on the giant metal door, like an old-timey bank vault was set into the back of the office, and that led, we all knew, to the private spaceship Nick used to zip around our universe.

"Five minutes left."

"What's the monkey's paw?"

"Good question!" He swiveled around, and I caught sight of that face, with its green eyes, and framing it, waves of fine hair. My own hair was coarse and curly and dark.

"Take a seat," he said. "I'm suspending the clock, obviously. That'd be a dick move, to run down the clock, making you sweat. Just take a reasonable amount of time to decide, okay?"

"S—sure."

His eyes glowed like embers, then died down. "You won't get laser eyes, of course," he said. "None of my little extra abilities. But otherwise, totally legit, fully functional. You could have kids, bro. And before you ask, those kids would be the genetic offspring of the new body. No brown-skinned babies to out you later on."

"Okay."

"What?" he said. "Not gonna accuse me of being a eugeni-cist? Or a queer-hating piece of shit? Don't you hang around with those two social justice warriors? They haaaaate me. Call me everything in the book. I don't dislike them, you know. I admire them. At least they believe in something…"

He rambled on. I knew not to interrupt him. Instead I focused on the body in front of me, then down at my own.

"What?" he said. "I'm boring to you?"

"Sorry. It's a huge decision."

"I don't see how it's a decision at all," he said. "No mon-key's paw. I'm just doing it because I'm curious. Will your little friends still love you? I'll hold this against them forever, of course. Oh, your friend took my gift, and she graduated, and it was good."

"Forever? You mean…for another year? They're juniors."

"Oh, did I say forever?" he said. "Yeah, I'll need to wipe that from your mind before I leave. Don't worry, I'll let you out of here just fine when the year's over. I don't care about you.

"But those two? Forever. You didn't think it was weird—they're, like, the only survivors from the original school? I created this whole place to fuck with them, basically. It's a hobby."

"That's…crazy."

"Isn't it?" he said. "You know, you ever heard of Faust? That dude made a deal with the Devil, and the Devil was like, I get your soul if you ever get bored. That wouldn't work on me. I never get bored. And don't psychoanalyze me, I know I'm a sick white guy, animated by resentment and a desire for vengeance."

"I don't…"

The words trailed off, but he didn't notice. That was the thing about Nick. He didn't much care what you said. Not unless you were Numaah.

"But… I mean, in some future, they must escape."

As I pushed away from the desk, a corner of my chair caught on the edge of the carpet. The smile grew even wider, and my eyes flicked once again to the vault at the back of the room.

"Sure," he said. "In infinite futures, everything happens. But there are big infinities and small infinities, and the ones where they get free of me? That's a very small infinity."

"So there's a future where I take your offer and a future where I reject it, right? In a way, it doesn't matter what I choose."

"No, that's not how it works. Most human beings are predictable. Whatever you do, it's what you'd always do. It'll be an infinity of you, making that choice in an infinity of time lines.

"An infinity of Numaah gritting her teeth, trying to congratulate you for your new body, hating you inside. Or an infinity of you resenting her, because you didn't get what you wanted.

"I'm the only god here. I'm the only one who gets to reset and re-try, ditch one world, hit another. That's the only way you escape: I get tired of a world and decide, nope, this one is too fucked up for me, I'm gonna cut it off, sever it from the other time lines, and hop over to the next one."

"Oh!"

The thought had come so suddenly that I couldn't help voicing it. That was the key. We weren't the main universe. Nor even the first.

He leaned forward, with his ruby-red lips that encircled perfect white teeth. The skin on his arms was lightly tanned, with soft, nearly invisible hair, and I brushed my elbow, which was rough and stubbled..

"So, what's it gonna be?"

"I asked the AI whether this was the first time you'd used a female body. It said yes."

"The AI doesn't know me."

"Yeah… I thought it was weird. Your nails are done. Your hair's gone through a curling iron. Your heels are high, but you're walking just fine. As if you've had practice."

"Don't try to analyze me. I've got brain mods that can teach me skills in a second. Or this body could have muscle memories—it'd be weird to step into a body that didn't have the skills to function. And of course I want my nails to look nice. All the better to mess with your pitiful human brains."

"Sure," I said. "But I think it's not the first time… I think there've been other ones."

"Who cares what you think?"

"I think every time you come in, people start to talk. They're like, oh…isn't that weird? Nick's a girl now. It's weird. He's being weird."

"Nothing weird about it, bro. You ever seen frat guys on Halloween? They all dress in drag."

But Nick's face was utterly blank, and I saw the madness around the edges of her eyes. Then I caught myself, and I smiled.

"You know," I said, "I was just thinking about you, and I used that pronoun—*her*."

"So what? Is that supposed to rattle me? Do I go, oh no… they all think I'm queer? Well, guess what: I don't care."

"And that's why you've singled out Numaah and Frida. You were like, they rejected me. They thought I was some white guy, but really… I was a girl all along, and they didn't give a shit. They didn't care."

"Well, so what? That's them being stupid, isn't it?" Nick said. "Back before I invented the transdimensional portal and took over, back when I was just another kid, they thought I was just the worst thing in the world. A total piece of trash. A straight white male, the epitome of awfulness.

"If you're right. I was the oppressed one. I was in the wrong body. It doesn't matter, though. Straight, gay, queer, boy, girl,

I don't think in those terms anymore. Gods don't need your petty labels. So now, do you want the body or not?"

"What's the point?" I asked. "You'll just kill me. I've said too much. I mean, there's no way I won't tell Numaah about this conversation. Anyway, I've already speculated to her. The idea'll stick in her head."

"I don't kill people for telling the truth. That's stupid," Nick said. "I don't need to reward them for it, though. So guess what, the offer is rescinded. Take that. Have fun in your gross body."

He got up, and he went to the back door, to the vault that led to his ship. He touched it, and the door unscrewed. Taking a step inside, he turned around, running a finger through his long hair. He put up one foot, taking off the strap of a high-heeled shoe, and then he looked at it, wincing like it was some disgusting animal. He dropped the shoe, and it vaporized before hitting the ground.

As he took off the other shoe, he said, "You look miserable, by the way. You look like a ten-pound sausage in a five-pound casing. People are gonna laugh at you. Do you know what life would've been like in this body? You could've been good, could've been natural. I was giving you that, free and clear, no monkey's paw. Now you've got nothing. Get out of here."

A portal opened behind him, all shimmering yellow and blue and orange. And a voice called out. "Ten. Nine. Eight..."

I got up, and then I turned, my back prickling, my underarms sweating. I put one unsteady foot in front of another. At the moment the countdown hit zero, I closed my eyes tightly, and when nothing happened, I gently closed the office door.

★ ★ ★

Frida and Numaah hugged me tight, crushing me, and Numaah kissed me all along the cheek. Then there was a massive bugle blast, and we all broke apart, terrified, but it was just the AI cavorting and tumbling all around us overhead as it played festive noises.

"You said no?" Numaah said. "Or was it all a mirage? Did the offer vanish? Tell us everything, zero judgment. I want to know the whole story."

"Yeah, I said no. Or I knew I was refusing, which is the same thing. But, no, you're going to think this is insane, but, umm... I think that I...actually beat him."

"What?" Frida held me at arm's length. "What does that mean?"

"I think he's gone. He's severed our reality from the rest of the multiverse. We can't escape, but he can't come back. Or she can't. I don't know. So yeah, he's tormenting other versions of us, in some other, slightly different time line, where he never appeared as a girl today. But, uhh, yeah."

"That's nuts," Numaah said. "There's no way he's gone."

"But..." the AI said. "Bodhi's account is essentially accurate. Isn't that why we were celebrating?"

The two of them turned and looked at the AI. "No, stop it," Numaah said. "Stop it...you're kidding."

All the way to the principal's office, Numaah insisted that I must be lying, or mistaken or brainwashed.

I explained that my theory was that whenever we, the three of us, started to see him as, like, not all-powerful, but just as some pathetic kid, desperate for our approval, he would kick aside our reality and move on to one where we were still in the dark.

"Normally he destroys the entire planet behind him," the AI said. "He's never left it intact before. This is unusual."

"Uhh...okay," I said. "If I'd known that, I wouldn't have pushed him..."

"No," Numaah said. "No..."

We got to the office, and the bank vault was open. The room beyond was flashing red. We went in, and Nick's face—his female face—appeared on all the walls. "You're now stuck in this dimension forever! Have fun not having access to the secret of the multiverse!

"Oh, wait. Also, I forgot to mention—I've cut off the rest of the multiverse, but this universe is still filled with hostile space aliens who're gonna be wondering why their transdimensional portals don't work anymore.

"Sooner or later they're gonna come here, and they're gonna be pissed. If you need me, just hit this button, and beg your hardest and maaaaaaaaaaaaaaaybe I'll come save you."

Numaah and Frida and I looked at each other. "We should deactivate the button, right?" Numaah said.

Suddenly I was tired. I went into the hallway, and I grabbed one of the chairs. Numaah and Frida followed me, and they grabbed two more. Nick's voice kept haranguing us, but I said, "AI, can you turn that off?"

"Certainly."

"And maybe give us a cool map of the cosmos?"

"That is entirely doable."

The room faded to black, and we were standing atop an endless field of stars. I collapsed into a chair. Outside, a student poked their head into the principal's office, but without a word from me, the AI slid the vault door closed.

"This spaceship can no longer travel through the n+4 dimensions, unfortunately," the AI said. "But we can still move anywhere in space and time."

"Well then," I said. "I suppose we should turn in this the ship to the government or something."

The three of them were silent.

"Or...we could not do that..." Numaah said.

"No, yeah, that would be a terrible idea," Frida said.

"Yeah, I was just kidding. So...where should we go first?"

★ ★ ★ ★ ★

CRASH LANDING

Mason Deaver

"YOU'RE SURE THAT YOU'LL BE OKAY BY YOUR-
self?" Mom asks me for probably the fiftieth time since I told
her that I didn't want to go and visit Grandma for the weekend.

"Yeah," I say, sitting firmly on the edge of my bed. "I just
want to be alone."

"Honey, are you okay?" Mom puts the back of her hand
to my forehead like she's checking for a fever. "You've been
acting strange lately."

I pull myself away. "Yes, Mom. I'm fine, I promise."

I just want to be by myself for a few days, to not have to
think about my parents, or school, or my friends.

Or Emily.

"Okay, well... Mrs. Parker is next door if you need her,
and we'll keep our phones close."

"Got it."

"And the number for the front desk is on the fridge, in case we aren't answering for some reason. Not that we wouldn't answer, but you know, just in case. Oh, and we've put some money into your account to order takeout or go to the grocery store if you need to. And you shouldn't have to water my plants—" She's rambling at this point.

"Mom?" I stare at her.

"Yes?"

"It's two days,"

"Technically it's three," she says.

"It's two. I'll be fine."

"I know, I just…been worried about you lately is all." She reaches for me again, this time tucking my hair behind my ears.

That's when Dad pops in through my doorway. "There you are; are we ready?"

"Yeah, just saying goodbye to Sarah."

"Honey, it's two days," Dad says. "Sar-bear, you'll be okay, won't you?"

"I promise that you won't come back to the house burning down."

"We've got insurance." Dad wraps his arms around Mom's waist and pulls her in close. "It's not her first time alone, hon. She'll be fine."

"I know, I know."

"And we're an hour away."

"I know!" Mom rears her head back. She's smiling, but I can tell from the look in her eyes that she's annoyed.

"Okay, come on." Dad takes her by the hand, slowly dragging her towards my door and down the stairs. I follow them out to the driveway, helping Dad fit the bags in the trunk, letting each of them give me a kiss on the forehead before they get into the car.

I wave at them as they back out of the driveway, not daring to go inside until I see them vanish around the street corner. And just like that, I'm finally free. Which is my invitation to myself to go up to my room and dive under my duvet, my comfort spot for the last few days. I get back to watching videos on YouTube, flipping through vlogs from this artist and craft maker I love and videos with titles like *LOONA Moments Every Orbit Should Know.* Try as I might, I still find myself going to my texts, specifically the large block that I have drafted for Emily.

She even has a little purple heart right by her name.

Because she loves purple.

I don't know why I thought that a text message would be the way to go. Maybe it'll be harder to mess up all my thoughts about her that way. Like the softness of her skin, the way her smile lights up a room, that my heart speeds up when she's around, the way she's so dedicated to the online forums of her favorite manga, how she's so passionate about her favorite bands, when she bites her lip when she's nervous or studying really hard.

It's basically an itemized list of everything I love about her, and my feelings. It's ramble-y. Try as I might, I can't bring myself to take anything out because…well, it's about her, and I want to list everything I love about her.

I just…haven't sent it.

Because what dork sends all their private thoughts about a person *to* that person, in a freaking text message? So all it's there, in my drafts. Waiting for me to send or delete. Because I'm a coward.

A coward in love with her best friend.

When I wake a few hours later, it's because my stomach is rumbling. Mom and Dad went grocery shopping before their trip to make sure I'd have enough food for the two days they'd be gone. The kitchen is stacked like they thought I was going to be alone for months.

But the stomach wants what it wants—a burger—and ten minutes later, I've ordered a cheeseburger and the biggest order of fries I can get my hands on. MealDash says it'll be thirty to forty-five minutes, so I've got time to kill. I spend a few minutes flipping through the streaming services we have, and eventually I settle on *Emma*, the 2020 version with Anya Taylor-Joy that is absolutely superior to any other version, and you can't tell me otherwise. Even if I haven't seen any other version.

And no, it's not *just* because of Anya. The sets are beautiful, the colors are amazing, the music is flawless, the acting is hilarious, and even though there's so much about the plot that *should* spike my anxiety, I've watched it enough times to know exactly what's going to happen. Even if the picnic scene towards the end with Emma and Miss Bates will forever give me secondhand embarrassment.

And, okay, yes, Anya Taylor-Joy is perfect. I didn't sit through *Queen's Gambit* just for the chess.

I stare at my texts as the movie begins to play. Emily and I haven't texted in over a week, which isn't even that odd. We have most of the same classes at school, and at home we usually talk on Snapchat for *hours*.

How do you tell your best friend that you're in love with her? That you've been in love with her for forever, and that you want to hold her hand and kiss her, and be her girlfriend? How do you do all that without potentially ruining a decade of friendship? What if it doesn't work out? What if we break up? Or worse, what if she says no to my confession? Screenshots it, spreads it to our friends.

The Emily I know would never do that.

But still…

It's better to live not knowing.

Don't people say ignorance is bliss? Couldn't agree more.

I resist the urge to smash my phone into a billion bits, and instead send a response to Mom's text about them getting to the cabin near Grandma's. I don't even notice the flickering lights until I try to focus on the movie again.

The lamp next to the couch pulses softly at first, but then the change gets harsher right around the time the television begins to act strangely, the colors washing out, and the image wavering.

"The hell?"

I check the lightbulbs, turn on the overhead lights in the living room and kitchen; they're doing the same thing. Is this like a power surge? Am I going to have to go this entire weekend without lights?

About a second after I ask myself that question, all the lights go dark. Then, in an instant, they're all back on, blinding me for a moment. The foundation of the house shakes, like the earth is moving underneath me. It's so quick that I fall to the floor when I try to run towards the kitchen.

An earthquake? But we don't get earthquakes here.

I crawl until I reach the cool tile and get in the fetal position under the dining table. Is this what I'm supposed to do? Are tables safe, or are they dangerous? I feel like I don't have time to think.

Car alarms go off outside, pictures fall from the walls, and lamps turn over. That's when I hear the crash. It's like a *zip*, like a laser in a sci-fi movie. Then a roar, like a jetliner falling out of the sky. Then, everything stops. Silence. The lights glow and the TV picks up where it left off.

Should I call Mom and Dad? The fire department? Mrs. Parker? I know that I shouldn't go outside to see what's going on. That's where teens in horror movies die.

But that was a *loud* crash. What if someone got hurt? I get up and step onto our deck. The back half of our fence has been obliterated, and there's a smoking trail from the impact, a path dug into the dirt that is easy to follow into the forest we live in front of.

The woods used to scare me as a kid. Mom and Dad told me to never go in there. I thought there *must* be monsters that were going to take me, that were staring into my bedroom window. Now, when I look beyond the tree line, there are no monsters past the shattered fence. But there is a bright purple light, pulsating like a heartbeat.

I shouldn't walk closer, I shouldn't go past the edge of the forest, I shouldn't follow the path that leads me to the light. But I do, because I'm curious, because I can't resist not knowing what this is, because it's almost like… I feel it *calling* to me.

As I get closer, the light becomes brighter, and I can see more clearly what lies in front of me. A giant metal object, twisted and broken in some places and smooth in others. Glass crunches underneath my shoes. The wreck almost looks like a plane, or maybe a big drone, but there's something off about it, something about the way it's shaped that tells me it isn't either of those things. It's something right out of *Star Wars*.

It's a *spaceship*.

"Hello?" I call out. "Is someone in there?"

No answer. Then the ship begins to hiss, and I jump back.

"I can call an ambulance or..." What *do* you call for a spaceship crash?

The ship hisses again. I'm way too close to this thing. Something might blow up or attack me. Then that something hits my back, and I scream, falling to the ground, pushing myself away from the thing behind me.

It's only until I've crawled feet away and my vision adjusts that I can make out the shape of someone, a person, bathed in the purple light from the spaceship.

A girl.

"Do you have a name?" I ask as I finish wrapping the wound.

It's probably against my best interests to bring an alien into my house, but when I calm down, I notice the cuts and bruises on her arms, probably from the crash, and well... I can't just leave her there hurt. Dad taught me that his first duty as a doctor is to help people, no matter their situation; I couldn't just leave some bleeding girl out in the forest.

But she hasn't talked once.

I should stop assuming; I don't know this person's gender, or if their species even has gender, or if they're even really an alien. For all I know, they're some military person, testing some super-secret new plane or something. I mean…they *look* human on the outside. Pale white skin, soft black hair with a slight curl to it, this mole under their right eye. They almost—

They almost look like Emily.

There are subtle differences, like the shape of their nose, their lips, and their eyes are a vibrant green instead of a warm brown.

And Emily smiles.

So far, all the alien has done is stare, allowing me to lead them to my kitchen, watching me work. They didn't even wince when I sprayed the disinfectant, just *sat* there.

"Are you from Earth or…somewhere else?"

No answer.

"Do you have a name?"

Nothing.

"Okay, well…um, I guess you can leave now?" Though I'm not sure how they're going to do that, seeing as their ship looks pretty busted. Helping an alien find their way off Earth wasn't exactly in my Friday night plans. I mean, what *could* I do? I'm sixteen, and I don't know anything about repairing spaceships.

The alien stares at me, and stares, and stares, until they hold up their right hand, bandaged in spots from their injuries. I flinch like an idiot, but I don't know what this thing has up its sleeve. I wait for some kind of weapon or laser to blast me, or maybe they're marking me for abduction and I'll never see my family or friends ever again, but nothing happens. They're just holding up their hand, their index finger pointing at me.

"What are you...?" I ask, then I point to my chest. "Me?"

They stare.

"I'm Sarah... Do you have a name?"

More staring, more pointing.

"Am I supposed to..." I reach to touch their finger. "Do you want me to—"

There's a zap, like a jolt of static electricity, and I nearly fall out of my chair pulling away. "What was that? What did you just do?"

"Are all humans so jumpy?"

"Well...not normally, but I do have a strange creature in my house." And then I realize. "Wait. You spoke."

"Yes."

"You've been silent for the last hour."

"I did not know your language," she says. "Now I do."

"Through your finger?"

"Is that odd to you?" she asks me.

"No, not at all." I don't think she gets my sarcasm, so I start packing away the first aid kit. "Great, so can you tell me your name?"

"I believe my name would be difficult for you to say."

"Well then...what can I call you?" I ask.

She looks at the kitchen table, where flowers that Mom picked from her garden—well, her now *destroyed* garden—are sitting in a vase of water.

"What are these?" she asks.

"Flowers. That one's a rose."

The alien thinks for a moment, staring at the ceiling

blankly. "I like this word: *rose*. Is this a typical name for humans?"

"Yeah, yeah. It's fine. Wonderful name. Now, what are you doing here?" My words sound fast even to my own ears.

"I am a part of a group of travelers. We were looking at Earth, and other surrounding planets."

"Why, planning some kind of invasion?"

Rose's brows furrow. "Why would we invade your planet?"

I sit there, suddenly feeling bad that invasion was the first thing I assumed. "Sorry, I just… I'm not sure how to talk to you."

"You can talk to me like any other being you know."

"Yeah, somehow I don't think that's true." I bite the inside of my cheek. "So…how are you going to get back home?"

"With my ship crashing, a message should have been sent to my teammates. They will arrive sometime soon to help me."

"I guess…until then, you can hang out here."

"Hang out."

"Like chill?"

"I am not cold."

"No, you can like, stay here with me, spend time with me until your people get here."

Rose smiles for the first time. "I would like that, Sarah."

The doorbell rings, and we both look towards the living room.

"What was that?"

"My food," I say, standing up quickly. "Just wait here, okay?"

"I shall."

The MealDash driver is standing on the other side of our

front door, looking both impatient and bored at the same time. "I texted you that I was here, but you didn't respond."

"Oh, right, sorry about that. I left my phone in the other room." I grab my food and shut the door. I wouldn't normally be that rude to a service worker, but there's a *whole ass alien* in my kitchen. I make sure to tip them extra to make up for it.

"What is that?" Rose asks as I walk back into the kitchen, setting my food on the counter.

"Dinner," I tell her.

"It smells delicious." And then she touches her stomach. "Hmm, I am hungry as well. Might you share your food?"

"What do you eat on your planet?"

"Meat, vegetables, fruits. What do you eat?"

"The same stuff…" I don't know why I assumed it'd be different. Rose *looks* an awful lot like a human on the outside, so maybe they look a lot like a human on the inside as well? "I'm not sure if you'll like it, but feel free to try some fries."

"And what is this?" She's unwrapped my burger from the foil.

"It's called a burger. It's a meat, or sometimes not meat, between two buns. Sometimes with cheese, sometimes with other vegetables. It just depends," I explain.

"I see."

"Here." I hand Rose some fries and cut off a piece of my burger, plating it for her. "Try it out."

"It seems slimy."

"It's grease, no worries." Or *should* I be worried? What if grease is like, toxic to her species or something? I mean, it's not that healthy for humans, and I can only imagine what it might do to an alien. But around the time I'm thinking of taking the food away from her, she's taking her first bite, her eyes closed. As the flavor hits her tongue, she smiles, chewing slowly.

I watch her closely as she eats, devouring her food in just a few bites, chewing quickly. After less than a minute, she's done eating half a burger, and then she sits there, staring at her now empty plate, glancing towards mine. I ask, "Are you still hungry?"

"No. I would like to clean up now."

"Oh, well…the sink is right there."

Rose stands up quickly, pushing her chair under before she walks over to the counter. She turns on the water, and then she starts to remove her jacket. "This is a small station in which to clean yourself. On my world, most of us have full closets in which to shower."

It only hits me what's going on when she goes to take her pants off.

"Oh my God, no!" I stand up quickly, nearly knocking my chair over. "No, no, no."

"Is this not okay?" she asks me. "I asked to clean up."

"I thought you meant to like wash your hands!" I have to cover my face to stop myself from laughing—or crying. "If you want to shower, I have a place you can do that."

I take her hand and lead her up the stairs to the bathroom.

"Here's where the towels are. That's the soap and shampoo. Just be careful of your bandages."

"I shall."

I close the door between us, only walking away when I hear the sound of the water running. It's when I'm back in the kitchen, grabbing Rose's clothes off the floor, that it hits me that there's an alien *in my home*. Some being from a far-away galaxy crashed in my backyard. And she's showering in my bathroom upstairs.

Maybe bringing her inside was the worst possible thing I could've done. There could be some Area 51 dudes on their way to my house right now to kidnap Rose and dissect her.

That's what always happens in the alien movies.

Am I going to get Rose killed?

Should we run away?

I don't like this. I want to tell someone. I want to tell *Emily*. I want to ask her how wild is it that I have an alien inside my house, using my shower. I want to tell her that there's a space-ship in my backyard, I want to ask her to come over just to be with me. I want to ask her if she's mad at me for ignoring her for the past week, if she can forgive me for ghosting her, if she's even noticed. I want to tell her the truth.

I start cleaning up, my appetite suddenly gone. I fold up my burger in tinfoil and throw everything back into the bag, leaving it all in the fridge for lunch tomorrow. What kind of friend am I? Totally abandoning Emily just because I can't get over my feelings for her.

It's gotten harder and harder with each day, though, having to see her at school, sharing most of our classes, our free periods, the lunch table. It feels so impossible to be around her when she doesn't know the truth. When she doesn't know that every smile, every touch, every note passed, every text sinks into me, filling me with the most euphoric poisoning.

I just want things to be simple.

An alien in my shower certainly isn't simple, but it's the icing on the cake. My life stopped being simple when I came out, when I told Mom and Dad that the name they gave me when I was born didn't belong to me, that I wanted to wear dresses and paint my nails and grow my hair.

When my friends started growing, their bodies changing, I wanted the same things they had, even the things that seem to hurt the worst. Because I wanted to be the best girl that I could be. When I told Mom and Dad, it felt like such a weight off my shoulders, and they supported me through everything. But coming out didn't solve all my problems. Sure, it made things easier, but it made some things harder as well.

I pull out my phone, staring at the text message in my drafts. Waiting, watching, as if I could will it to send itself, and then it wouldn't be my fault. Upstairs, the water stops, so I work to make myself busy. I wipe down the counters, pour myself some water, do the dishes by hand even though we have a dishwasher.

Anything to keep busy.

"I feel much better, thank you." I hear Rose's voice from behind me.

"It's no worries. I'd want a shower too if I'd been through—"

I turn around, and that's when I realize that Rose is bare naked in the middle of my kitchen. I'm so caught off guard that I lose my grip on the plate in my hand and it falls to the floor, exploding into a million little pieces.

Things got a little hectic after the plate broke. I had to push Rose away from the shattered ceramic so she wouldn't cut her feet. I took her to my room, keeping my eyes firmly on the ceiling, which was tricky going up the steps, but we made do.

The entire time, Rose asked why I was acting strangely, which led to a very awkward conversation about being naked in front of strangers and what that meant. She still seemed confused after the explanation, but didn't argue when I gave her a T-shirt and some shorts to wear. While she dressed, I ran downstairs to clean up the broken glass.

"Was your shower okay?" I ask, dumping the pieces of the plate into the garbage.

"Yes, very warm. I enjoyed it." Rose smiles at me, standing awkwardly, like she isn't sure what to do with her hands. "What do we do now?"

"Oh, um." I hadn't exactly thought of Rose being here as company I was expected to entertain. "I don't know. What do you want to do?"

"I have been very curious about that." Rose points to the living room, where the movie is still paused on the TV.

"Oh, that's a television. We use it to watch shows and movies and other stuff."

Rose covers her hand with her mouth and laughs shyly. Honestly, I wonder if Rose knows how adorable she is.

"We have televisions on my world," she says.

"Oh…sorry, I just assumed…" I rub the back of my neck, heat prickling my cheeks.

"I was referring to the picture on the screen. I am interesting in these people. She is very pretty." Rose stares at Anya Taylor-Joy.

"Interested. Do you want to watch it?"

"I would be very interesting, yes."

I walk past Rose, leap over the back of the couch and land softly on the cushions. Rose tries to mimic me, but she ends up moving slowly, her actions looking very calculated. "Your dwelling is very large for a single being."

"I live with my parents," I say, then stop. I'm not exactly sure if I should be telling an alien that I'm going to be completely alone for two whole days. Then again, if she were going to do anything to me, she would've done it by now. And, I've seen Rose's boobs, so are there truly any secrets between us?

"They're out of town," I say. "They go to their cabin every few weeks."

"Cabin."

"Like a secluded house an hour away. They visit my grandma and...stuff."

"I see." The Rose turns her attention to the screen. "What is this movie about?"

"It's based on this really old book all about a girl who gets herself too involved in her friends' love lives, and it comes back to bite her in the butt."

"I have many questions."

I can't help but laugh. "Here, I'll start it from the beginning."

I remember going to see this movie with Emily in the theater and falling in love with how it looked. I think we were both a little too young to understand *everything* going on in the movie. But it's kind of become our go-to. I don't really know why. Maybe because we both liked looking at the scenery and how every shot looked like a painting. Or maybe we just liked staring at Anya Taylor-Joy.

Probably a bit of both if I'm being honest.

But, I mean, the story is sweet, too. We both read the book afterwards, and it wasn't even for school or anything!

There was this one night where Emily fell asleep because we'd watched this one a hundred times before, and she laid there, on the couch, with her head in my lap, snoring softly.

I think that was the moment that I realized my feelings for her were more than platonic, that there was something else there. I'd never really questioned liking girls before. It just felt natural. Of course, that was before my transition. There's nothing weird about someone who looks like a boy having a crush on girls.

But when I came out, when I realized I'm a girl, I had to have the reckoning with myself about what it all meant. I never liked boys the way they did. I never had to requalify my crushes on girls because...well, those were the only kinds of crushes I've ever had.

Rose's eyes never leave the screen as I sit through the first half of the movie all over again. She just sits there, enraptured by every second. Meanwhile I can't seem to stay off my phone. I keep rereading my message to Emily, going to her Instagram to see what she's doing.

The movie ends out of nowhere (I guess I really wasn't paying attention) with Anya Taylor-Joy and Johnny Flynn and awkwardly reading with her dad, and Johnny Flynn proposes and they get married in this adorable ceremony where Anya is wearing this amazing dress. God, the costumes in this movie are so good.

"I enjoyed that," Rose says, her knees tucked close to her chest. "I am confused, though."

"Yeah, I was confused when I saw it the first time too. It's kind of hard to follow what they're saying sometimes, especially with their accents, and how clever everyone tried to be all the time."

"No, it is not that. I am more confused about them putting their lips together in the way they did."

"What do you mean?"

"Like this?" And then Rose leans forward, nearly pressing her lips to mine. She's inches away before I process what's happening.

I lean back, putting my hands up between us. "Whoa, Rose!"

"What is wrong? Are you okay?"

"You can't try to kiss someone randomly like that. You need to have consent. Like, you ask, and the other person says *yes*!"

"Consent. I see. All right, next time I will ask." Then Rose continues. "And that's what they were doing? Kissing?"

"Yeah." I stare at her. "It's a way to show...affection. Attraction. Do you guys not do that?"

"My people have their own way of showing affection, but we do not kiss. Your way seems to be an easy way of spreading disease."

"Well...you're not wrong." I relax back into the couch. "And anyway, it's how *some* people on Earth show affection. There are people who aren't into kissing, or touching," I shrug. "It just depends."

"I see. Are you someone who doesn't like kissing?"

"I...well... I don't know."

"You have never been kissed."

The petty part of me hates that it comes out sounding like a statement and not a question. But it's not her fault. She just doesn't understand what that means on earth. That sometimes people use that as a weapon.

"I almost was, just now!"

"Without consent, I understand." Rose then asks, "*Is* there someone you would wish to kiss?"

I glance at her, wondering how much she knows. "Why would you ask that?"

"You were on this device during the movie." Rose picks up my phone. "On my world, it is considered rude to communicate with others while a film is playing."

Well, glad to know that rule crosses galactic boundaries.

"It's nothing," I say.

"I saw your many communications to someone named Emily. It does not seem like nothing," Rose tells me, staring right at me like she's looking into my soul or something. I don't like the way her eyes seem to cut right through me.

"On my world, it's considered rude to read over somebody's shoulder," I say, my face hot.

"I apologize," Rose says. "But the observation remains the same."

"Just drop it." I stand up, pacing away from the couch.

"I am not holding anything."

"Look," I say. "Do you have someone back home, Rose? Someone that you love?"

"I have someone, yes."

"How did you tell them? How did you tell them that you love them, and that it hurts when you aren't together? That you want nothing more than to kiss them and hold their hand and play with their hair. How did you tell them that?"

"If you feel this way, this explains your many incomplete communications to Emily," Rose says.

I throw my head back, frustrated with Rose, sure. But mostly, frustrated with myself. Of course, she wouldn't get it. Her rules are different, her people are different. With how up-front Rose is, I doubt that she's ever played games with herself or other people. They're probably direct, to the point, no beating around the bush there.

"She's my best friend," I say. "And I want her; I want to be with her."

"You love her," Rose says softly.

I nod, unable to say anything more, not without crying.

"Hmm…" Rose sits there, still at that perfect right angle, as she looks at the television, the preview for the next movie still playing. "I believe that my feelings are not that much different from your own. There is another, on my planet. I am not sure what name they would choose here. But I love them very much."

"You told them?" I can still feel that familiar ache in my jaw, the one that tells me I'm going to start sobbing if I talk too much.

Rose seems to think for a bit. "I did not want to at first. I was very fearful, actually. The sensation for my people, I don't know if it is different from how humans experience it. But there is fear, confusion, a sense of dread almost."

So far, she's pretty accurate.

"But there is also warmth, and comfort."

And that's where she loses me. I sit there in silence for a moment, composing myself. I probably shouldn't be unloading this all onto an alien, someone who will—more than likely—

be gone in just a few hours. When I look into her eyes, I see confusion, yeah, but I also see those feelings of warmth, of kindness, of understanding. It's close to the feeling I get when I look into Emily's eyes.

Not exactly.

But close enough.

"So, Emily," I say. "We've been friends since we were both five."

Rose waits for me to keep talking.

"We've done so much together. We learned how to swim and ride bikes together, we've watched movies together, we've gone shopping. She was the..." I pause, wondering if my next words will be too personal. "She was the first person I came out to. Twice. We laugh at the same jokes, we read the same books, but...it's more than that."

"More?"

"Yeah, like when I'm around her, I feel like I only have to be myself, not someone else. Like even around my parents, sometimes I have to lie. I lied to them about some things for a long time. But with Emily, the world seems different." I feel the smile creeping up on me. "With her, things feel right. They feel perfect."

"To me, it sounds like she is your soul mate."

"Pfft, I don't believe in that stuff."

"Why not?"

"Because the idea of there being *one* person out there for everyone is bullshit, and not everyone is even into romance. It feels pointless."

"Perhaps that is true, though I believe calling it cow excrement is a step too far," Rose says. "But my people believe in soul mates of all kinds. Why can your best friend not be your soul mate? There are best friends who are just as important as romantic partners, sometimes even more so."

"Maybe…"

"And it is natural for people to come in and out, is it not?"

"I guess."

"So then, what is so unlikely about some*one* being perfect for that moment?"

"I…" I'd never looked at it that way.

"So why do you not send your communications to Emily?"

I sigh. "I haven't been brave enough to tell her." I grab my phone, unlocking it and handing it to her with the message to Emily open. "For the love of God, do *not* hit that button." I point at the little arrow next to the texts.

Rose reads my texts, again. Then she says, "You are scared to lose this friend." At first, I think she's asking me a question, and then I realize it's anything but.

I nod slowly. "Yes."

"I believe that it is a normal reaction, yes?"

"Really? Because it doesn't feel normal."

"Fear is a big thing to tackle. But it's keeping you from something that is worth the attempt, is it not? This is what I believe."

"Yeah…" I say, not quite convinced. It sounds like bullshit to me.

"You would rather live in misery, not knowing if your friend likes you."

I feel my face get hot. "What if I ruin the relationship? What if she hates me after I tell her? What if she makes fun of me?"

"What if she loves you back? What if she wants to be your partner? What if you get to spend the rest of your life with her?" Rose stands. "Life is made of what-if's. It does no good to dwell on them the way that you do."

"It's not as easy as you think it is, Rose,"

"I know. It was not easy for me to admit either. But I have learned, Sarah. I have learned in my life. You should be doing what you believe makes you happy. And right now, you are making yourself miserable." Rose holds out my phone to me. "I do not believe you should tell her over these things you call text messages. But I *do* believe you should tell her. If everything you have told me about her is true, she sounds too kind to be cruel."

"She could hate me."

"She will not."

"How do you know?"

"Would it help you to rest easy if I told you my people could see into your future?"

"Can you…" I pause. "Can you really do that?"

Rose giggles. "No, I cannot."

"Oh," I don't want to sound disappointed, but it would've been really cool if she those powers. "Can you at least lie?"

"I have seen into your future, you two will be happy together."

"Thanks." Rose's words do make me feel better, even if I know they're false.

"You are welcome." Rose puts a careful hand on my shoulder. "Though, I must reiterate, please do not send her such a personal message via your communicator. It must come from here." She points to my abdomen, right above my belly button.

"My stomach?"

"Stomach. That is where your species holds their food? That is where my heart is."

That makes me laugh, and I set my phone down, hiding it out of view. "Thank you, Rose. Do you want to watch another movie?"

"I would be excited to do so, yes. I have much to learn."

"Come on, I'll let you pick."

The next thing I know, it's morning.

And Rose isn't on the couch with me.

I made sure to avoid the sci-fi section of Netflix for Rose while I browsed for her. I didn't want there to be any weirdly insensitive movies about aliens that we stumbled upon. But we settled on another romantic comedy, and another after that, and another. I don't remember when I fell asleep, but Rose was still watching attentively when I closed my eyes, her legs crossed, and not blinking.

"Rose?" I listen for the shower at first, but there's nothing, not a noise in the house. I check the kitchen, my bedroom, my parents' room, the bathrooms.

She's not here.

Her people must have come to get her. I knew they would, but… There's this guilty feeling in my stomach. We didn't even say goodbye to each other. But I haven't looked everywhere yet. I slip on my shoes and go out to the backyard to check out the damage to the fence and yard.

Only to find that the fence is still standing. There's no trail either, carved out from where Rose's ship crashed.

I know what I saw! I go through the gate, out into the forest, but there's nothing here. No ship, no wreckage, no evidence.

That's when I run back inside. First, I check the kitchen trash…no broken plate. So I run upstairs to look in my closet. Right there, on the same hanger it was on before I gave the shirt to Rose, is my *Star Wars* shirt. At least, I think this was where I hung it last.

Unless…

No. There's no way it was a dream. It felt too real. Rose was here, in the house. I can picture her so easily.

And yet, at the same time, it doesn't feel quite real. Like when you wake up from a dream, and you instantly forget what happened. But there are parts of last night that linger. That almost kiss, Rose reading my texts to Emily, everything that she told me, it's still there, in my head, her words an echo.

Tell her how you feel.

Maybe it's my brain telling me these things, and maybe there really was some extraterrestrial being from another galaxy giving me relationship advice.

Stranger things have happened.

I find my phone, buried somewhere under the couch for some reason, and I stare at the block of text that I've been threatening to send Emily for the last week. And I hold down the delete button, watching it disappear word by word. Once it's gone, I tap Emily's name, and hit Dial.

It's eight in the morning on a Saturday, so I'd be surprised if she—

"Hello?" Emily's voice is like honey to my ears, even with that tiredness to it.

"Hey, Em." My voice feels quiet.

"Sarah? You okay? It's early."

"Yeah, yeah, I just... I wanted to ask you something."

"Okay?"

"Do you want to go on a date? Tonight. Not like a friend date. A romantic date, with movies and a dinner and stuff."

There's no answer. For a moment, I think I must've ended the call. Or worse, she ended the call, or she's holding back laughter, waiting to give me my rejection.

But she doesn't. She doesn't do any of that.

"I'd love to," she says. I can practically hear the smile in her voice.

"Okay." I can't think of any other word to say right now. Except two. "Love you."

"Love you, too."

★ ★ ★ ★ ★

BEAUTY SLEEP

Alechia Dow

ONCE UPON A TIME, IN A SYSTEM FAR AWAY, riddled by a wicked space fairy with a grudge, there lived two girls who met on Beauty Sleep. And then a whole bunch of drama happened.

Their cheers ring through my ears, and settle heavily within my heart.

The music is soft but sinister. I imagine my tormentors dance to the lurid beat, their bodies writhing in weightless jubilation. My capture is cause for this celebration.

These cold stone walls finally feel warmth for the first time in a century.

The metal clinks at my sides, reminding me that I'm chained to those same stone walls in a castle so very far from home. All because I met a girl in the Briara Rain Forest on Eyvind, cuddled under a starry sky as mechanical parrots cawed and the thick branches of the kapok trees swayed in the wind, and we promised to meet again.

And not in a dream.

Only, when I went back to where we met, and followed the footfalls to her small villa on the edge of the forest, I was ambushed by The Wicked Fairy in black with sparkly tawny skin, and her many mishmash minions, who cooed and cackled and cobwebbed me in itchy rope.

I was dragged onto The Dragon—the small villainous spacecraft known for sucking stars dry of their magical dust— and shepherded across our Triangle realm to the lost castle. The landing was once a hub for trading between Eyvind and Earl; the two sides of the Triangle are now marked by toxic green gas, making it a no-go zone.

No one comes here. No one's been here in a century— well, except me.

All because of a girl.

The girl.

The thought slams to the back of my mind as the lock in the door jingles. It eases open, and the fairy comes inside, her black dress billowing behind her from a cool breeze. Her dark lips twist into something akin to a smile.

"I set my trap for a peasant, and lo! I caught a princess." She clutches her brown hand to her black-swathed chest and laughs. Her onyx staff, with a golden cusp beneath a glittery green orb, thumps against the grey stone, sending reverberations beneath my feet.

The Fairy is powerful and lethal and beautiful. Her words ooze venom…and something else I can't quite decipher.

"I thought it such a pity for you to miss the celebration,

so I've come to cheer you up, Princess Philippa, daughter of the colonizer, King Huberto." She laughs again, and my fists shake at my sides.

My voice rises with confidence, though I feel none. "Let me go."

"Oh, come now, don't be quite so melancholy. Your future shall be glorious, if a bit..." She looks around the room, her gaze falling on dark and dirty crevices even the pests avoid. "Dreary," she finishes. "You will call my home your own, in time."

I try not to jump to my feet. "My father will destroy you and your hovel you call a home."

"He has tried." Her lips round, and her eyelashes flutter in mock surprise. "Though you haven't been told, have you? Oh dear, what an awkward situation." She hovers above me, and the scent of rain fills my nostrils. Both mesmerizing and dangerous. "I hate to be the bearer of bad tidings, but your father went to King Stellan's kingdom, and that peasant you met in Beauty Sleep, well...in a true twist of fate, she's Stellan's daughter, a princess. Cursed."

The Fairy's gaze flashes with delight as I digest the news. She doesn't wait for my response. She lifts her staff, and the orb atop glows. That's when I come to understand, she's connecting to my neural chip, the same one I used to meet and fall in love with username RainyMaven, real name unknown.

"Princess Talia, with nighttime woven through her lustrous curls, lips that shame the most shimmery of pearls, and in her gait, a vibrant autumn unfurls..." The Fairy says.

A picture paints before my very eyes of the girl I met in my dreams and then in the forest. With sparkling red lips, dark brown skin that matched my own, and bouncy curls that fell to her waist. I even remember the way she smelled like spice and fallen leaves.

The picture swirls in front of me...created through our neural connection. Through the damned staff.

"Princess Talia with her gift of song, melodies shall grace her whole life long, her alluring voice brings all us near, to listen and cherish and hold her dear..."

Suddenly, RainyMaven's voice penetrates the evil whirling around me, caressing my thoughts.

Her name is Talia. What a beautiful name.

We first met in Beauty Sleep—a neural app that allows you to dream walk with partners, and then in real life, in the rain forest. We had wanted to see if there was actually something special between us, only I arrived early.

She was singing a sweet tune. I saw her joyful dance with tropical creatures—both real and mechanic. Her frayed dress floated on the air as she twirled and sang and wished. There was magic in her words. I knew her song as clearly as I knew my own name. She would often hum it in dreams. My feet stepped forward of their own volition.

I had to meet her. I had to be in her physical presence. The Fairy was right. Talia was alluring. Even from afar, I felt like she was the other half of my soul I hadn't known I was missing.

My speeder hummed to life as I hopped on its back and jetted over the river and through the heavy thicket of tree branches laden with colorful birds, closing the distance between us.

Then I stood there like a cowardly oaf, sweating profusely,

trying not to be creepy as I watched her dance. She was expecting me, yes, but not this early. What if she didn't like me in real life? What if she would be disappointed?

When she turned and saw me standing there, her lips pinched and her eyes widened, and then she said—

"Princess Talia," The Fairy continues, "and her entire kingdom, as well as your father, have fallen into a deep, unending slumber." She cackles, tapping her staff against the floor once more.

Beyond the door, a crow caws and The Fairy's head swivels, as if she understands what it says.

But when she gazes back at me, her eyes go cold. "Only true love can wake her, and only you can give her that. Her father took my love, and now I shall take hers. Do make yourself comfortable, Majesty. Forever is a long time in chains."

"No," I shout. Her smile stretches across her cheeks as I rise to my feet.

She stands just outside my reach, laughing at my emotions, my uselessness. "I will leave you with these happy thoughts on a most delightful day."

I slouch back down on the sharp, cool bench and glare as she slips through the door and locks it behind her. My head rests in my hands and I think about Talia. Though she hadn't told me her real name. It didn't matter at the time.

"You," Talia said, after the initial shock wore off. "You... you look like you want to laugh."

And because that's the first thing she ever said to me— ever said to me in real life, her brown eyes sparkling in the patch of sunlight that seemed to only beam down upon her, I giggled. I was never one for giggles either. But the way she said it, the way her lips lifted at the ends… She made me feel warm and seen. All of the awkwardness melted away.

"Your voice…" I began, unsure. "It's…you…are, well, very beautiful." I shook my head in mortification, because I'd said that to her before, in a dream, but aloud, it was rather silly. I was wholly embarrassed then, running a hand through my thick braids. My speeder was most likely recording this, and the royal guard would be watching and laughing at my expense. I'd remember later to turn off the wireless connection for privacy.

She giggled back, and for a brief moment, that's what we did.

We stared at one another, me the full-figured girl in wrinkled royal garb, black freckles dotting my cheeks, and a head full of bouncy, bountiful braids, and the girl I now knew as Talia. She seemed to carry the light of the sun within her very smile, and had a shapely, sturdy frame that lingered in my dreams.

After so many nights dreamwalking together, sharing and learning each other's interests—after all that time—we could only laugh.

I knew she wanted to see everything the universe could offer, and I wanted the same. I knew she wanted to sing new songs from different worlds, and I wanted to hear them. I knew a million things about her, but I had no idea how to approach her.

My heart might've burst from my chest if she hadn't crossed the distance and held out her hands toward me. Her voice was strong, and her cheeks were rosy.

"It is you who is very beautiful. I'm very happy we decided to meet. I've wanted this for so very long…"

"I…" When we met in our dreams, we agreed to not share our names, because if she knew I was a princess, then she would have thoughts and ideas and judgments, and she might very well hate me. Most people did.

The royals usually only left their palaces for fun and to seek and steal new resources…as my father had.

Contrary to that dark tradition, I wanted only to escape home and see new places. Help new people. Meet people… like Talia.

"I've wanted this, too," I said finally. "I think, well… I know that I've been waiting my whole life for you."

"Oh…" Her face lit up like a star, and then she reached for my hands. "May I?"

I nodded quickly. Her fingers wove through mine, and then she tugged me into a dance. And that was how we spent our hours together. Singing, dancing, cuddling beneath the leafy trees while listening to birdsong.

We decided there and then that we should never be parted, and though I wanted very much to kiss her, I didn't. Because I was too scared, too nervous. She looked at me, and she asked me if I would kiss her, and I froze. What if I did it wrong? What if I didn't live up to her expectations?

And I couldn't kiss someone whose name I did not know.

"What is your name, so that I may call upon you?" I murmured, as she pressed her head to my cheek and we watched the sun begin to set across the rain forest.

She turned to me then, eyes wide. "No, no I can't. I mustn't!"

"You mustn't?" I reached for her just as she fled my embrace. "Wait, no—"

"I...must go!" Her voice wobbled as she darted back toward to the trees, her heavy footsteps sending whiffs of floral up from the thicket.

"When can I see you again?" I shouted, following after her though I lacked the speed necessary to catch up, nor did I want to chase her lest she reconsider me completely. "In a dream?"

"Never!" She bolted through the trees, and I toward my speeder. "Oh dear, but I can't—" Her voice suddenly trailed off.

"Never?" I repeated aloud, nearly tripping over a branch that would have me crash into a bubbling brook. As it was, my feet submerged anyway.

"Not *never*, just no more dreams. We can't go back to dreams, not when the real thing is better. Tonight?" She turned back then, and though I could only glimpse her through the leaves and creatures, her smile set my skin ablaze. "At the villa. Deep in the heart of the forest. Meet me there? I have a most pressing question to ask."

"A pressing question?" My left shoe filled with water as I struggled to get closer, though not too close.

Her voice floated through the trees. "If you'll...if you'll have me? Be mine?"

I let out a long whoosh of air. Would it be foolish to admit that I had only just met her and yet I was completely taken? Did it even matter?

"I would. My heart is already yours."

Her sweet laughter caused me to bite my lip as I pulled myself up from the muddy muck.

"And mine, yours." And with that, she was gone through the trees, and the rest...became history.

That laughter, those eyes, her voice...they become almost distant in my mind as I sit in a dungeon in The Fairy's castle. Trapped here. Never to be with Talia again. Never to go home again. All my hope sinks to the pit of my stomach, where it's disintegrated by the acid climbing upward. I've made a mess of things, should never have turned off my tracker, should never have...

My fists shake, and I allow myself this moment of self-pity and righteous anger before I sit tall. I am Philippa, Princess of the Earl Kingdom. Before she passed, I was raised by Queen Catherine, a strong woman with steel in her veins, purpose in her limbs, and so much love in her heart. I am my mother's daughter. My people need me.

Talia needs me.

The chains clink by my sides as I push to standing. Right, how am I going to do anything?

I shut my eyes and take a deep breath of the noxious, sour air. The sound of Talia's voice trills through my mind, and I beg to save her from her slumber, to see her again. "If anyone can hear me in this outpost or beyond. Help... Please help."

The call goes unanswered, but I never expected a response. Still, I kick my feet at the dingy stone flooring and the nothingness surrounding me. I yank my chains, tense my muscles, and let out a deep growl as I gnash my teeth.

Which earns me a sudden *shush*.

Two tiny lights emerge from the window bars on the doors, and I jump back, nearly falling onto the bench. I yelp as the little blue light spirals around my head. "Who are you?"

"Your Majesty," the red light whispers. "We are here to rescue you…"

My eyes widen in recognition as I reach out toward one. These two droids are known throughout the Triangle as God-Moth3r. They're do-gooders, kind, compassionate, and always ready to fight. They can hack any system, using their drone forms, nanos and AI capabilities to help those in need. I've always thought them to be a myth; no one had seen or heard from them in years. How can they be here? Why now?

"I—"

"Oh, please be still as we override your chains."

The blue drone circles my right wrist while the red one circles my left. "I'm Merri, and the red drone is Fuchsia," they say joyfully. "Together, we are GodMoth3r."

The red drone shimmers brightly, then the chains thunk to the floor. The nano tech devices they used—little black, indestructible and programmable chips—collapse onto themselves, absorbing the metal.

Fuchsia says, "Come, Your Majesty. If we move with haste, The Fairy will not give chase till—"

And that's when sirens blast through the walls. I drop to my knees, throwing my hands over my ears, yelping. The sound threatens to pull me under. My vision blackens at the edges, and my breath leaves in short pants. I focus on the way Talia's eyes crinkle at the corners as she smiles.

I hold tight to that image until the drones' lights yank at my heavy eyelids. One slithers in between my hand and my ear and shouts, "We only have a few moments. Come."

Reluctantly, I lift my hands and am surprised by the sudden silence. My bruised knees groan as I rise and brace my-self. I need to push through this. Talia needs me.

The once-locked door swings open, and the GodMoth3r wave me along. Using the last vestige of energy in my body, I bolt after them as shouts bounce through the dank walls. In moments, we will be overrun by those sorry creatures that serve The Fairy, with their monstrously pieced-together bod-ies, oversized teeth, and dull yellow claws.

Without a blaster, there's nothing to defend myself with. And despite my brave saviors, I doubt they can protect me until I'm on my speeder. Still I run, cherishing every precious moment we have without the ensuing fight.

The dark hallways are a maze, and if it weren't for the God-Moth3r, I would easily get lost. I pass by doorways leading to nowhere, paintings of decrepit landscapes that must have been there before The Fairy claimed the tower, and splotches of dried blood stark against the black-grey stone.

This castle has been scarred from battles and evil, and I only hope I don't die here. That my spirit won't be trapped among those who lost their lives against her—of which there must have been many.

My body is knocked out of autopilot when a spear, a sur-prisingly shiny armor-piercing one, is leveled at my face, halt-ing my steps.

The creature bearing it reveals itself to be a fairymade monster; it has the body of a boar, ears of a dog, hind legs of a rabbit, and has fuses and wires jutting out where whiskers should be.

We stare at each other then as if time stands still. Its yel-low eyes follow my movements as I feint right, grabbing the spear with my left. The creature nearly tips sideways from the action, and I use that moment to bash it upside the head, knocking it unconscious.

Even if it means to harm me, I can't help but pity the creature. It had no choice in its existence or its allegiance. The Fairy is cruel.

With a jolt, I realize I'm surrounded. They've crowded in behind pillars and chipped stairwells, brandishing dingy spears, lopsided swords, and hobbled blasters. While they all are different forms of animals patched together and powered through dark magic, their yellow eyes are consistently vacant.

I clutch the spear tighter as a tech crow squawks somewhere close and the drones hit the first blocked path. There's a collective yell, and the creatures rush toward me. Although I'm double the size of my opponents, their ambush pushes me off my feet. My body lands with a thud, and I swing the spear around, hitting monster shins as I struggle to gain purchase.

The lights flicker once, and the creatures slump to the ground. I don't quite understand it, but if I had to guess, I'd say my GodMoth3r overrode the palace's atmosphere to deprive these creatures of their essential electricity. If that's the case, I don't have much time before they're back online.

I scramble to my feet, Merri and Fuchsia floating beside me. I toss another look at my fallen assailants. Then I lunge forward.

Outside the castle, the ground is comprised of mud and sharp rocks. The sky is black, and the air is thick and rotten. The Triangle looms in front of me. The rain forest Kingdom of Eyvind, the metropolis of Earl, and the space between.

And here I am, on the last side of the Triangle, shrouded

in darkness. Everything about this place is the exact opposite of sunshiny Talia, and I hate it.

The crow caws while the drones lead me toward my speeder, which sits there on the ledge of the landing—dinged up but bulkier than usual with a droid attending it. I'm about to leap toward it, when the ground gives way. I nearly plummet into a pit of tar when Fuchsia creates a magnetic ledge of nanos for me.

There's barely a moment between my impending dooms. Creatures above drop buckets of hot tar upon us. I throw up my arms, but Fuchsia and Merri send their nanos skittering upward, shielding me. I reach the speeder with only a few bruises and scratches. I'm so grateful I snuck out of my palace wearing pants instead of the dress Father prefers me to wear.

The mech crow circles closer, and Merri follows it. Fuchsia stays with me, nanos leaping out to make repairs to my speeder.

While I slide behind the wheel, I clutch the spear close. Fuchsia attaches to a silver, human-sized mecha and begins tinkering with controls.

Fuchsia and I fend off attacks as Merri flies up and up, chasing the mech crow under arches, around turrets, and along the parapet. Finally, on a pillar just outside the highest tower, Merri captures it with her nanos. In seconds, they deconstruct the mech crow into a million little unsalvageable pieces.

Merri flies back and combines with Fuchsia, now becoming the mech, GodMoth3r.

We start up the speeder, only to hear an ear-splitting shriek from that very same highest tower. The Fairy emerges, her black headdress slightly askew. She raises her staff in the air, and that's my cue to get off this realm before she executes her next plan.

The speeder's shield flies up, and GodMoth3r creates a barrier that keeps the monstrous creatures back, expanding my speeder's built-in system beyond what I thought possible. An exosuit washes over my body, protecting me for the first time in hours. I inhale the offered oxygen greedily, not realizing how much I needed good air until it fills my lungs. My vision becomes almost hazy with relief.

The Fairy's monstrous creatures whimper and throw themselves at my shield, to no avail. It's solid for now, but if we don't hurry, the shield will break. And who knows how long the oxygen in this suit will last?

GodMoth3r takes over my system. I hunker down, preparing to use my speeder to jump to Eyvind. It's not what it's made for, but it'll do the job if I have the droids' help and we make the jump fast. Super-fast before the speeder ices over and we plunge into black nothingness and all the air leaves my body, sending my corpse lingering in space until the end of time.

I can't die like this. Not when both of our kingdoms are in peril, and a girl—*the* girl—awaits me, needs me. My princess.

With a quick look back at the spiraling green gas erupting from The Fairy's staff, we jump off the ledge. GodMoth3r recons the speeder's internal system to boost power. In seconds, we're bursting from the outpost and into the space within the Triangle, where gravity is gone and stardust whirls around us in whimsical flurries. Already, my lungs tighten.

Ice creeps across the speeder *and* my suit. My brain begins to slow, and I just want to sleep. It's so dark. I feel so far from home. My energy is fleeting, and I'm alone. So alone. And then Talia flashes in my mind. No. I'm not alone. Not anymore.

"Wake up, Your Majesty. You aren't done yet." Fuchsia's voice pierces through the haze and yanks me back to consciousness. As my eyes flap open, GodMoth3r steers the speeder for me. I'm not dead yet. And Eyvind is close. We can make it.

"We'll come in hot," Fuchsia tells me. "We can divert the heat, but—" The rest of their statement cuts off as a shadow looms behind us, cast over the surface of Eyvind. The green below blackens as the shadow takes the form of a… I can't believe my eyes. I turn back to see a metal ship, a…a dragon. *The* Dragon.

"The Fairy." Merri's voice holds an edge of awe. "She has The Dragon. She'll destroy the kingdom before she'll ever let it be saved."

"Protect it," I say, though my heart hammers in my chest. This means blocking my way to Eyvind.

As we speed up, the path darkens with nanos, these brown as tree bark. The GodMoth3r forms a barrier between me and Eyvind. They weave together like brambles and vines and thorns. Impenetrable. As far as the eye can see. Let that save Talia.

The Dragon spreads its wings, and there's a moment when I know that I either have to stand and fight, or sit here and let my oxygen run out. I twist the speeder's bar around, turning my back on the kingdom, away from Talia and my father. I may die here.

The Fairy's voice enters my mind, and momentarily, we

are connected again through the neural chip. But I'm prepared this time. Connections go both ways.

"You think you can defeat *me*?"

I take a deep breath, and I push through that connection between our two minds. Visions of her life flash before my eyes as The Dragon swoops closer, shortening the space between us.

I see glimpses of a woman. A stunning woman, who smiles at The Fairy...no, her name is Marella! And the woman is Lyra, with light in her dark brown eyes, with vibrant red hair that tumbles across her shoulders. She's warm like sunshine. And Marella screams as she's taken away from her.

Lyra leaves on a ship and Marella cries, while King Stellan watches. Later, I see a party in a grand palace, and King Stellan—only he is older, begging Marella to rescind her curse on his newborn infant, for the infant should not pay for his mistake. I feel Marella's pain. I feel her loneliness, and loss, so much loss. And rage. So much rage.

My heart breaks for The Fairy, but my resolve hardens.

"Can you hack the ship from here?" I ask Merri and Fuchsia, though I think I know their answer before it comes.

"No, we'll need to be onboard," Merri confirms. "But there's a hatch at the heart of the beast we may open."

I flip a switch on the speeder to start the tracking system, and detach my charged exosuit. There is only one way to save my kingdom and princess, and it is into The Dragon. Into Marella. Into her rage and fury, fire and mech, through the very space that would steal the air from my lungs and warmth from my bones.

I wait for her to fly closer, biding my time for the right moment. When she'll have no choice.

"Open the hatch. We're gonna jump in."

I shake away all my worries as her ship stands between us and the edge of Eyvind. The mech dragon stares us down, and if a mech dragon could smile, it does. We are but a tiny pest, and Marella controls the large foot ready to stamp us.

"Open! We have fifteen seconds!" Merri proclaims.

Which is when I rev the engine, and we fly into danger.

Marella doesn't expect it. She's so close, and I muster all of the energy I have left. We're using breakneck speed to get into her ship, and momentarily she doesn't know why. Either she imagines I'm reckless and desperate, or she realizes I'm not giving up without a fight.

We plunge like a sword, through the opening at the heart of her ship. I stumble off the speeder's back and roll onto the black glossy floor. After a beat to catch my breath, I pick myself up.

"There's nowhere for you to go, Princess." Marella's voice comes through an intercommunication system.

I smile something wicked and stare up at the cams. I know she's watching. "I'm where I want to be."

I pick up my spear and attack control panels, the walls, anything I can reach and destroy, while GodMoth3r wreaks havoc on her systems.

"Stop!" Marella screams through the crackling communication system, and the ship powers down. The entire vessel gets sucked into Eyvind's gravity. The nano brambles clear, allowing passage as we all plummet. Through the edge of space into the planet below.

I may die here, but so will she.

The oxygen is gone, and my exosuit has little left. My brain becomes hazy as my feet rest against the walls.

When we crash into the rain forest, my body's about to hit the ceiling when Merri grabs me tight and holds me. The droids stand as my teeth chitter and my body shakes. I nearly collapse with relief when it's over, but there's no time.

"The Fairy is temporarily incapacitated. We must go, Your Majesty," Fuchsia says as GodMoth3r opens the door to the rest of the ship, and I follow.

We travel through silver hallways glimmering with pilfered stardust, and past unconscious monsters. We stop at the small command center, where The Fairy, Marella, lies on the floor, surrounded by sparking wires and debris. A piece of black shrapnel juts from the side of her stomach.

Purple blood, vibrant and unexpected, leaks from her side as I yank the metal free. Her beautiful face ashens, and I take off my jacket, pressing it to her wound.

"The royal guards should be on their way," I say to God-Moth3r. "Please send a medic droid."

The droid leaves me there, and I crouch beside the Wicked Fairy. I make no sudden moves. I'm aware she could end me, even in her weakened state. I'm aware she holds magic in that staff. And yet, I also know the pain she feels.

"I'm sorry, Marella," I say, causing her to open her eyes and stare up at me in wonder. "I'm sorry for what Stellan did to you. For sending Lyra on a trip to exploit new worlds that killed her. She was the love of your life, the woman of your dreams. You were right to vow revenge upon our kingdoms. You were right to curse us."

She grips her staff tight in her other hand. Still holding my gaze. She must be deciding if she wants to kill me or not.

I press on, even if death looms near. "Talia and I...we are not our parents. I know this is an empty statement. I know..." I gulp. "There is nothing I can do but beg for forgiveness, and dedicate my life to making our worlds better.

"I don't want what my father does; I don't want to colonize and strip away the resources from unknown lands. I want music, and love, and harmony. I want to restore happiness in our kingdoms, in the Triangle."

"I..." she begins. Her voice lacks the edge of anger it once held. She shifts a little, but I shake my head. She's too wounded to move. "He took her from me. Sent her into the unknown and did not care when only a piece of her returned." Her fingers trace the gold cusp beneath the orb of her staff.

"I am sorry." I brush away some of the debris as I sit down on the cool, scratched floor beside her. "You are punishing Talia and me with the same fate, never to be together. I can't bring Lyra back, but I can give you a home. And warmth. You don't belong on that side of the Triangle. You're powerful, smart, and a little bit wicked—" That earns me a smile. "Don't let the King take more from you than he already has. And please, don't take Talia from me."

For a long moment, she stares at me, but finally, she nods.

And then my eyes flick to the guards running towards us wearing my family's sigil. I leap to my feet. "Do not harm her. She is one of our people. We will protect her." I look at her as I speak the words, and the guards slow, taking my commands. She still holds up her staff like a weapon, though the movement is slow. "You have my word. She is no threat."

A medic droid buzzes through to attend her, and I step back. Stellan's kingdom is in cryostasis. Along with my father. And there's nothing anyone can do about it but Marella.

And my two drone friends, GodMoth3r.

I turn to Marella as the medic works upon her side. "Can you just end the curse?"

"No," The Fairy admits. "My magic is not strong enough. A curse can only be broken by true love. Only you."

With a nod, I scurry off to find another speeder, one that's not a heap of pieces, and I find one outside the ship. I slide on, Fuchsia and Merri with me, and we speed toward the palace. I will make this right. I will find a way. I am Princess Philippa, and I am not my father. One day, I may change the universe.

We fly through trees, the breeze nipping at our cheeks, and past fallen, sleeping guards. The sky is still stuck in twilight, as if even the sun sleeps. But it hasn't been that long, has it? Hours since the curse was enacted, hours since I was captured. Only hours since I last saw Talia and fell in love.

She has my heart.

At the bottom of the magnificent castle, a crowd which must've gathered to celebrate or party—who cares?—now lies asleep in piles. I slip off the speeder. GodMoth3r and I jet through the palace and up to the tallest tower to find my princess.

Even the air smells like her, pulling me closer. Like autumnal sunshine. In slumber, she looks just as breathtaking as she did in the forest. Her curls fan across her pillow, her dark brown skin glistening like pearls, and her red, pillowy lips seeming to await a kiss.

A kiss I cannot give her. Not yet.

I lean over her blue tomb of a bed, and thread my fingers through hers.

I shut my eyes and reach for our neural connection through Beauty Sleep. If she's asleep, I should be able to connect to her. Maybe. Possibly. I reach and I reach for her, my grip on her hand growing stronger, nearly ready to give up till her icon flashes on the neural app. My body slumps and I join her in a dream.

Her dream is the same room, only she is trapped in her bed with her eyes open but her mouth shut. When she sees me, there's a smile in her eyes. There's hope for us.

"Talia," I whisper, lifting her hand to my lips to give it a quick kiss. The sensation feels real, even if the action is not. "I am most certainly in love with you. Though we will change with time and grow together and sometimes apart, I know in my heart that you are the one I want to be with.

"You are the one I want to explore every world with, and save the universe with... I love your smile, and your voice, but most of all, I love your soul. It will not be perfect, this love, as no love is, but I can promise that we will always be in this together. And so—" I bend down over her face. "I must ask your permission. May I kiss you?"

Her eyes crinkle at the edges as she gives the strongest of nods she can muster, and I hit the icon, disconnecting from the dream. Once I'm awake in my own body, in the same room, with my beautiful, real Talia, I bend down. Before I can let my nerves sway me any longer, I press a short, delicious kiss to her perfect red lips.

Her eyes flutter open and widen. She smiles, even as her gaze flickers to the mech droid, GodMoth3r.

"It's you," she says finally. Our noses mingle, and she's so soft, so sweet, so perfect. My lips were made for hers. I feel alive as I breathe her in and my chest pounds against hers.

All the pain and battles, the chains and fear of the last day—has it only been a day?—fall away, and it's just the two of us, kissing.

Young and in love. And when we pull apart—because neither of us can kiss the way we want to in front of an audience—we giggle. There I go giggling again. We hold hands, and we decide, again, that we will never be parted.

When the rest of the kingdom awakes, we vow to let Marella stay with us. To give her a home with love, which she scoffs at, but accepts just the same.

After a quick reprieve, lots of talks with our families, apologies, and setting things right, Marella joins us in a very pink borrowed dress from Queen Amara, Talia's mother, which Merri—back in drone form—finds particularly offensive.

"Make it blue!"

Mech nanos swirl around The Fairy, changing the dress from pink to blue in seconds. Fuchsia, in the midst of charting a course for our next great adventure—this time with Marella and Talia tagging along—shakes their drone head. "Make it pink!"

Marella glares at the drones as she says, "Make it black!"

Talia and I laugh, and we stare up at the stars of a million, mostly unknown worlds.

Her cheek presses against mine. "One day, we will have to tell the story of how we met and fell in love. What will we say? Will we tell them about Marella and a curse and—"

"No," I say, my lips lifting into a smile. "We will tell them the truth, which is much better, isn't it?"

"In a dream." She leans in and kisses me quick on the lips. "The most beautiful dream come true."

★ ★ ★ ★ ★

CONCERTO

Abdi Nazemian

THE WHIRR OF OUR AIR PURIFIERS BOUNCES off the walls as I stare out my bedroom window at the toxic air. I'm so delirious that I imagine Amor outside, a gas mask on his face, trying to pry the window open. I stare at the vision of him, tears in my eyes.

Then the vision speaks. "Open up."

I rip off the masking tape that my grandmother stuck to the edge of the window. I open it, and he tumbles into my room. I quickly close the window and put the tape back as best I can.

"What are you doing, going outside?" I ask.

"I'm wearing my mask," he says.

"They're only 97 percent effective," I say. "And I need you to be 100 percent safe."

"And I needed to see you," he says, with a smile.

I rush into his arms so forcefully that I practically tackle him to the floor. I want to hold him so tight that we can never be separated.

"You'll wake your dad up."

"I don't care anymore," I say. "Let him find us naked. Let him open the door when you're inside me. Let him see what our love looks like."

"That sounds like an invitation."

"It is." I pull the zipper of his hoodie down.

We practically inhale each other, our bodies twisting around like they're trying to form one shape. The feel of his skin against mine fills me with a horrible ache, because I know this could be the last time. When we're done, we don't let go. We lie on my floor like a pretzel, legs and arms entwined.

"We're like trees," he whispers.

"Is this some joke about your wood?" I ask, my leg touching his hardness.

"No." He laughs. "It's about how trees—well, they're connected underground. We don't think about that because we're more interested in how they soar to the sky. Human beings have always been more interested in what's above them than what's below. We don't pay attention to what grounds us. Maybe that's been our worst mistake."

"We've made so many mistakes," I say.

"But trees," he continues, his voice full of wonder. "They care for each other through an interconnected underground system of roots. I imagine this is what they look like underneath the ground. Like us. Wrapped around each other. Safe."

"Are we safe?"

He doesn't answer.

"I'm scared."

He tries to say something, but his voice cracks.

"Well, if this is it for us, maybe you'll meet Tchaikovsky in the afterlife, and you can finally prove that he was gay."

"I don't need proof," he says through tears. "The proof is in his music. It's in our concerto. It's a gay concerto. Full of longing and layers and..." His voice trembles. "Shh, listen. Can't you hear it?"

He closes his eyes. I close mine. We both imagine the music filling the room.

We're woken up by the sound of my dad screaming, "WHO ARE YOU?" in the same voice he uses to scream, "CUSTOMER REPRESENTATIVE" and "TAKE ME OFF YOUR LIST" and "TEN PUSH-UPS" and "BOYS DON'T CRY."

I got my wish. I wanted my dad to find us naked and he did. I wanted this moment to haunt my dad forever, but now I know that I'll be the one haunted by the disgust on my dad's face. It brings me back to when I first tried to tell him about Amor, and to every vicious comment he's made about queer people before and since.

"Dad, this is Amor," I say. I leap up and throw some clothes on. "Remember, I told you about him. Or, uh, I tried to tell you about him."

Amor gets dressed quickly, then offers a hand to my dad. "It's nice to meet you," he says. "Strange circumstances, but given the fact that our days are numbered—"

"Get out," my dad says with an unnerving calm. "Now."

"Yes," Amor says. "What I'm hearing is that you want me to leave, but before I do—"

"OUT."

"I do think it's important you know that I love your son very much."

I hear footsteps, and notice my grandmother standing behind my dad. She's clutching her favorite silk robe tight, and giving me a smile that warms me with its love. "Come quick, my son," she says to my dad.

"Not now, Maman. He's my son, and I know what's best for him."

"Come listen to the news," she says. "It's urgent."

We all follow her to the living room, where a newscaster is interviewing both the Governor and the President.

"This is a lot for people to process," the newscaster says. "How do you propose the people in the danger zone approach this decision?"

"What's happened?" my dad asks.

"Shh, listen for once in your life," she says gently.

"I like her," Amor whispers to me. I knew he would.

The President sighs before speaking. "If you are within a seven-hundred-mile radius of any of the nuclear incidences and have not safely made it out, then this is your only option. The technology isn't perfected, and as you now know, it was being developed in secret for reasons of national security."

The Governor steps in. "Given the unprecedented circumstances, I have asked the Federal Government for emergency authorization of the wormholes."

"How safe are these wormholes, and how were they developed?"

"Unfortunately, given the race we find ourselves in, we don't have time to explain all the details of this technology to the public," the President says.

"But you expect people to use the technology without any assurance of its safety?"

The Governor answers this one, her own voice shaky. "If it helps, I will be stepping through one of the wormholes myself."

"Which one?" the newscaster asks.

"I don't know yet," she says. "That is a decision I will need to make with my family. As the people of California know, I chose not to abandon my duty by escaping. But now I have no choice. And my message to you is that you have no choice either. If, like me and my family, you want to remain alive, you may go to our website and sign up for an appointment. For a cost, of course."

"What is the cost?" the newscaster asks.

"All the information is on the website. We need this process to be orderly, so there will be no walk-ins. When you sign up, you will have a choice. One wormhole will take you to the past, and one to the future. The website has further instructions that you should read carefully. You cannot wear jewelry or accessories, including eyeglasses. You must not bring a bag or memento of any kind, and, well, the website has it all there."

"How far into the past? How far into the future?"

"Unfortunately, we don't know," the President says.

"Will families be kept together?"

"Again, we don't know," the President says. "Our hope is that if you step into the wormhole together, you will arrive at your new location together."

"And what about side effects?" the newscaster asks.

The President appears frustrated. "Look, we don't know.

This is an emergency. There is an unprecedented amount of radioactive contamination in the air, and it's traveling fast. Rather than let millions of our citizens die, we are offering them this solution. There may be side effects. There may not. You may land in the seventeenth century. You may land in the twenty-eighth century. What we do know is that you'll end up somewhere on Earth. I think we need to wrap this up now."

"Before we go," the Governor says, "we are looking for volunteers to help at the travel centers we're setting up. The website has all the information. Volunteers will be compensated with travel vouchers."

The President and the Governor disappear, leaving only the shocked and confused newscaster. "And there you have it. Millions of our own citizens might be traveling in time to escape a manmade nuclear disaster. My question is, what might the impact of this new manmade technology be on our well-being? After the break, I'll be speaking with a Biblical scholar who believes that what he calls sexual and gender deviance is the cause of the nuclear—"

My grandmother turns it off at that. There's a long silence in the room, no one sure of what to say.

Finally, Amor speaks. "Of course some idiot is going to blame the queer community for what's happened. Nothing changes. They've already blamed us for floods and earthquakes and rat infestations. Why not blame nuclear disaster on us too?"

"You should go home to your own family," my dad says.

"Your son is my family."

I look into Amor's eyes. I want to go with him. Step into

that wormhole and be together. The past, the future, it doesn't matter to me if we're one.

But then I look at my grandmother, and I know I can't leave her. She sacrificed everything for me. Raised me after my mom died. She could have chased her own dreams. She could've married again. How could I ever desert her?

"I'll walk you out," I whisper to Amor.

"You can't go outside," Amor says. "Even a few seconds could harm you."

"I'll wear a gas mask," I say.

"They're only 97 percent effective," he says with a sad smile. "Three percent is too much risk for me."

"We need to discuss our next steps." Pointedly, my dad adds, "As a family."

There's a strained and thick tension in the room. Thankfully, my grandmother says, "Sia, let's give the boys a chance to say goodbye," and leads my dad out of the room.

I stand as close to Amor as I possibly can, wishing I could bottle his scent and take it with me wherever we go. I'm struck by a sudden fear that I'll forget his smell, his voice, his face.

"I can't leave her," I whisper.

"And I can't leave my sister," he says.

"I know." I feel my throat tighten.

"Which will you choose?" he asks. "The past or the future?"

"Knowing my dad," I say, "the future."

"Yeah."

"And knowing you…"

"The past," he says. "At least it's the devil we know."

"So the past will be your future," I say.

I hold him and let him cry on my shoulder.

"Why did humans convince themselves that the future would always be better?" he asks. "We've always been so obsessed with this idea of progress."

"What other option did we have? Not believing in a better future…it would be losing all hope. It would be…"

"It would be an *opportunity*. To stop looking forward so often, and to spend a little more time looking back. The past has lessons to teach us."

"You're right," I say. "But how can we learn from a past that's hidden from us? My grandmother still won't tell me anything about leaving Iran."

"Yeah, well, my mom won't talk about anything *but* leaving Colombia," he says sadly. "Not sure which is worse. Not knowing anything or knowing too much."

"You see, maybe the future is the right choice."

"No," he says. "When your dad wouldn't meet me, I said, 'Someday things won't be so hard.' When my dad got sick, I said, 'The chemo will work.' When T.J. Lord called us faggots, I said, 'Close your eyes and imagine us a year from now. We'll have graduated. We'll move in together.' Don't you see why I would always choose the past over the future? Every time I believed the future would be better, it let me down."

"We will never be separated," I say.

"Do you believe that?" he asks.

"Of course I do. Because *you* told me that, and you've never let me down. All you have to do is play our concerto and close your eyes. We'll be together again. You'll see."

"Our concerto," he whispers. Then he hums it quietly in my ear.

"I love you," I say.

"And I love you."

The travel center isn't big enough for this. Not just the crowds, but the anxiety. Lines of families clutching tightly to each other. Eyes filled not with the hope of travel, but with the fear of escape. I search the massive space for Amor and his family, but they're nowhere to be found.

"Is this what it was like?" I ask my grandmother.

"What?" she asks.

"Leaving Iran," I say. "During the Revolution."

My grandmother never talks about her life before 1979. Sometimes she tells me it's because she has no memories of her life back then, which makes no sense since she was my age when her family fled. Sometimes she tells me to stop being so nosy. Mostly she just changes the subject. But this time, she says, "Not exactly."

"How so?" I ask.

"Well, for starters…"

"This is ridiculous." My dad cuts her off. "The line hasn't moved an inch. We've been standing in the exact same spot for twenty, no, *twenty-eight* minutes."

"Patience, my boy," she says, and takes a deep breath through her nose, hoping he'll mimic her.

"Did you take a plane?" I ask, trying desperately to get an answer out of her. "When you fled? Or did you take like, I don't know, a truck, or a camel, or…"

"Excuse me?!" my dad screams at absolutely no one. Then, louder, "EXCUSE ME?!"

The young couple standing in front of us glares at my dad. They both have wedding rings on, and I can't help but wonder how long they've been married. I think of Amor. Of how painful our goodbye was.

"Sia, please," my grandmother whispers. "You're drawing attention."

"Your generation of Iranians is so concerned with what other people think," my dad barks. "God forbid I draw attention to the fact that we signed up for an appointment and we haven't even been checked in yet. Didn't the Governor say the whole point was to avoid chaos?"

"I remember one woman," my grandmother says, her eyes wistfully finding their way back to me.

"Yes?" I ask.

"She was begging the authorities to put her on a flight out of Tehran. It was the last day that flights were leaving. She explained that her husband and daughter were already in Vienna. That she had only stayed behind to take care of her sick father, who had just passed away. They were calling off names. Those names that were called were allowed to board planes."

"And those whose names weren't called?" I ask, exhilarated to finally be learning a little piece of my history, even if it's under tremendously difficult circumstances.

"Where are all the volunteers?" my dad asks.

"Sia, you're drawing attention to yourself." My grandmother puts a gentle hand on her son's back.

"What happened to those whose names weren't called?"

I ask, desperate to uncover the lessons of my grandmother's escape before my own.

"They stayed in Iran," she says. "Or they found other ways to get out."

"So you must have been very lucky," I say. "To have your name called."

"No, no," she says. "That woman who begged the authorities was lucky. They took pity on her and gave her one of the last seats on the plane. My father…he had contacts with the airline. We were able to secure a ticket in advance. That's not luck. It's privilege."

"I don't think of fleeing your country as a privilege," I say.

"Yes, you have a point. I never saw any of my uncles or aunts or cousins again. Never saw my grandparents again. Or Paiman…"

"Who is Paiman?" I ask.

A few feet away from us, an overwhelmed woman in a volunteer uniform surveys the chaos around her. My father screams in her direction. "Ma'am!"

She glances his way, then turns her attention to another agitated traveler whispering urgently to her.

"Ma'am!" my dad screams, to no avail.

"Dad, please," I say. "I want to hear what Maman has to say."

"Everything you need to know is in a history book," he snaps. "A bunch of angry people started a revolution almost fifty years ago. People fled. The end."

"If that is your understanding of the Revolution," my grandmother says, "then perhaps I made a mistake not talking to you more about it. I thought I was protecting you from the past, and from my own grief. Perhaps the past shouldn't ever be ignored."

"Maman, is now really the time for this?" my dad asks. "For my entire life, you don't say a word about your life in Iran, and now, as we're fleeing *through time* for our lives—"

"Yes, well…" My grandmother lets out a sigh. "I was never very good at timing."

The woman in uniform walks away from us. "Ma'am!" my dad screams, in hopes he can stop her.

"For starters," my grandmother says, "there would have been no Revolution had there been no coup. The United States and Britain overthrew a democratically elected leader in Iran."

"Why?"

"Because he wanted to nationalize the oil, of course." With a shake of her head, she adds, "We've always chosen greed over love, haven't we? Isn't that why we're in this horrible situation now?"

"Was it hard?" I ask, trying to drown out the anxious chaos all around me. "Moving to the United States after what they did to your country? You must have been so angry."

"I don't know." She shrugs. "I suppose I didn't have the capacity to be angry at a whole country back then. I was too sad to be angry, perhaps. And then, well, within two years of landing here, I got married and gave birth to an American. Your father. I raised an American."

She looks at my dad, who waves his arms in the air, desperate for some attention as he keeps screaming, "Ma'am, ma'am, ma'am," at that one overwhelmed volunteer. Yes, she definitely raised an American.

My dad turns his frustrated stare my way. "Hooman, call that help line they set up. Get someone on the phone."

"Sure, Dad."

I make the call and watch as my dad marches toward the volunteer, speaking so loud that the whole airport can hear him. "Ma'am, we've been standing in line for over two hours now." He is prone to exaggeration, my dad. "We signed up for an appointment online."

"We're delayed," she says flatly.

"Why?" he asks. "Is there a problem? Is this whole experiment not going to work? Because if not, we need to know. We need to be told. Maybe it's not too late to take a plane to...well, anywhere."

"Good luck finding an airplane that can fly with this visibility," she says loudly.

As if on cue, everyone standing in line looks at the large glass doors separating us from the air we're escaping. Smoke and debris and radioactive substances move toward us like a threat, like an embodiment of our greed.

"Get us out of here," he demands.

"I suggest you take your place back in line, sir. Getting angry at me won't get you to the front any faster."

"WHAT WILL?" he barks.

"I'm not sure why you're asking me," she says, a sudden sharpness in her voice. "As I'm sure you know, I volunteered to help *you* escape because I don't have the money to escape yet. So perhaps I should ask you the very same question. What will get *me* to safety, sir?"

"I— Well—" My dad is at a loss for words, so he falls back

on a sentence he uses far too often. "You have no right to speak to me this way."

I know where the conversation is going. There will be a sprinkle of "Who is your manager?" and a dash of "Do you know who I am?" It's all so futile and so humiliating, and it makes me want to disappear.

I turn to my grandmother, who is at her most unpredictable right now. "Who's Paiman?" I ask.

"It doesn't matter anymore."

"You said that when you left Iran, you never saw your uncles and aunts and cousins and grandparents again."

"I didn't see them again," she says. "I left with my mother and father. Just us."

"Then you said you never saw Paiman again."

Her gaze grows wistful. "We were your age, you know. I was seventeen, and Paiman had just turned eighteen. The last time I saw him was his birthday."

"He was your boyfriend," I say brightly.

"We didn't use words like that back then," she says. With a laugh, she adds, "Boyfriend, that's funny."

"Okay, then what was he?"

Without missing a beat, she says, "The love of my life."

"Oh," I say. "Then what was Baba?"

"He was my husband," she says. "He was kind."

I close my eyes, overwhelmed. I imagine myself years from now, in the future we're traveling to, telling my own grandchild that Amor was the love of my life, and that the last time I saw him, we were seventeen years old. And my grandchild will ask, *Why don't you find him?*

"Why didn't you find him?" I ask her. "Paiman."

"I would never betray your grandfather like that."

"Baba is gone," I say. "And he would have wanted you to be happy, wouldn't he?"

She laughs. "Happy, yes. In love with another man, I'm not so sure. Besides, even if I had found Paiman, he would likely have had a wife of his own."

"And if he didn't…"

"Then he'd probably still be in Iran."

"Maybe you'll be reunited with him wherever we're going," I say.

"I never knew what an incurable romantic you are," she says, running a tender hand through my hair.

"I should've told you everything," I say. "About myself. About Amor."

"He's lovely," she says. "I'm glad I met him before—"

"HOOMAN!" my dad screams so loud that it snaps me out of my reverie.

"Yes, Dad?" I ask.

"Have you gotten someone on the phone?"

"No," I say. "I'm still on hold."

He grabs the phone from me and puts it on speaker. The hold music is the very end of a Bach sonata.

"CUSTOMER REPRESENTATIVE," he screams into the phone, drawing the glares of more travelers.

I drown my dad out. It's not hard to do because the hold music changes to *our* concerto. It takes me right back to Amor's bedroom. Sitting next to his record player as he showed me this very piece of music for the first time. *Listen*, he said. *Really listen to what the music is telling you.* And I said, *I don't know what the music is telling me. It has no words.* And he said, *We don't*

349

need words to tell a story. Look into my eyes right now. I looked into his eyes and cried, because I had never loved him more than I did in that moment. And I knew that with every moment that passed, I would keep loving him more and more. *You see*, he said, *you're not saying a word and yet I know exactly the story you're telling me. It's a love story, isn't it?*

"STOP PLAYING THIS TERRIBLE MUSIC AND GET ME A CUSTOMER REPRESENTATIVE."

"It's not terrible music," I say quietly.

But not so quietly that it evades my dad. He chooses to redirect his rage from the phone to me. "What did you say?" he asks.

"It's not terrible music," I whisper, afraid to engage with him and at the same time unable to control myself. Insulting this concerto is like slapping Amor in the face. "It's Tchaikovsky's Violin Concerto in D Major, and it's beautiful."

My dad's eyes narrow, as if he's trying to deduce how I would know this information. My grandmother's eyes dart from her son to her grandson.

"Since when do you know about old concertos?" he asks with a laugh. "Is this what you're wasting your spare time on?"

"There's no such thing as old music," I say. "Art doesn't age. People do."

Art doesn't age, Amor told me as the melodies of the concerto swept over us. This was probably the hundredth time we had laid in each other's arms, listening to the concerto. *People do, but art, it's timeless.* And I said, *I want us to be timeless, to float above time together so that we would never have to be separated.* And he said, *We never will be separated. All you have to do is listen to this piece of music and close your eyes, and we'll be together. This is our melody.* And I closed my eyes and let both him and the music enter my body.

"Tchaikovsky was gay," I suddenly say.

"What?" my dad says.

"He was gay," I say.

"I don't know how you would even know that, and I don't know why you think I would care."

Suddenly, the hold music stops. "They hung up!" my dad says, incredulous.

"Look, the line is moving," my grandmother says.

We shuffle forward, surprisingly fast all of a sudden.

We get closer and closer to the wormhole, watching people leave all their belongings behind and disappear through it. I feel so full all of a sudden. Full of fear and love and gratitude. "Thank you, Maman," I say.

She must hear the ache in my voice, because she says, "Don't say it like that."

"Like what?"

"Like it's the last time you'll ever thank me. I expect you to thank me many more times."

"We don't know where we're going," I say. "We're not even sure we'll be together."

"Of course we will be," she says. "Have faith."

A sudden clarity washes over me. "The reason you never looked for the love of your life is because of me," I say. She gave everything up for me. Her life, her dreams, her love.

"Stop that," she says.

"You had to raise me when Mom died," I continue. "You had to protect me from the world." *And from my father,* I want to add. "If it weren't for me, you could have—"

"Shh," she says. "I've had a happy life."

"Tell me more about Paiman," I say.

"You tell me more about Amor," she whispers.

"Shut up, you two," my dad says. "It's almost our turn."

"He's so beautiful," I say to her.

"I could see that. Tell me what I don't know."

"That faith you want me to have... *He* has it. He believes that art is spiritual, that it connects us through time, that it heals divisions."

"Please stand on the green line so we can scan your retinas," another volunteer says when we get to the front.

My dad scans his eyes first. Then me. Then my grandmother.

"Place your phones and any other belongings in the bin. Make sure your pockets are empty."

We do as we're told.

"Past or future?"

"Future," my dad says.

"That's to the right."

We all hold hands. My father's grip feels like it crushes a part of me, the part that wishes it was Amor's hand I was clutching onto.

Maman turns to me. "You'll tell me more about Amor tomorrow," she says in a conspiratorial hush.

And then we step through the wormhole.

I stare out the hospital window at the drones outside. Flying above us in the grey sky, they transport people to their offices, transport packages to their destinations.

"My love," she whispers, her voice weak.

I turn my attention from the city and to my grandmother. "I'm here. I'm here."

"I can't fight anymore," she whispers.

I feel her leaving her body. Her grip on my hand has no strength to it anymore. She's giving up.

"You're the only thing that's ever mattered to me," she says through tears.

I squeeze her hand tight, trying to will just a little more life into her. "You don't know that," I say. "The wormhole took all our memories from us. For all you know, lots of things mattered to you. You probably had many loves in your life."

"Only you," she says.

"And I've only had you," I say.

She lets out a sad laugh. "You're young. You have love ahead of you."

"I hope so," I say.

"I know so."

Her eyes flutter.

"Don't think about me when I'm gone. You've spent this whole year caring for me."

"You spent too much time caring for me."

"You don't know that," she says.

"I may not remember what happened to me in the first seventeen years of my life," I say. "But one thing I'm sure of is that you cared for me. Where else would I have learned what love is?"

"Love is—" she says, and then she closes her eyes one last time.

She's gone, and I'm gutted. I have nothing left to live for anymore.

A robot nurse descends from above. Her surround-sound voice fills the room. "I'm so sorry for your loss," she says, in her imitation of warmth.

"Please call my father and tell him she's gone," I say.

"I will call John Bradley and tell him that his mother, Sandra, has died," the nurse says.

When I hear the name John Bradley, I can taste my father's rage in my throat. I can hear the way he'll blame her death on me, because he blames everything on me.

"And tell him—" I'm about to stop myself, but then I figure, what the hell. "Tell him there's no need for us to speak again. Tell him she was the only thing left that connected us."

The hot air hits me hard when I step outside. The buzzing of the drones makes my head feel like it's about to explode. People zip past me, the drones completely silent to them.

For those of us who came through the wormholes, the sound of the drones is like shattering glass. Just one of many side effects. Complete memory loss. Insomnia. Infertility. And for the elderly like my grandmother, cancer. They were able to give us new identities, teach us language, but they weren't able to heal her cells from the incurable sickness.

I board a passenger drone up to my favorite restaurant.

"I'll have that crispy rice, Mina," I tell the waitress.

"Coming right up," she says. "You want gheymeh bademjoon with it?"

"Is that the stew with the eggplant and the…"

"Split peas."

"Yes, please," I say.

The dish comes out within seconds, piping hot and delicious. For a few minutes, it makes me feel better. Makes me feel like there's still hope. But there isn't. My hope died with my grandmother. She was all I had in this strange new world. My one source of love and connection.

I can't sleep that night. I can't sleep any night. I think only of her.

I skip school.

It's the last week of my senior year anyway. I have no reason to go anymore. I went for her. To make her feel I was on the right track. But now… Why would I subject myself to those horrible halls where I'm mocked and terrorized for being a wormhole kid? Even the kids who are nice to me view me only as an object of fascination, not as an actual person.

One sleepless night bleeds into another.

One endless day bleeds into another.

Winter is hot. Too hot, the newscasters say. In time, we will all need to flee this part of the world as well. Perhaps north. Or perhaps, if humans are brave enough, we will have a second wave of wormhole kids.

The side effects may still be bad, but at least now they can send you to a specific time and place. Much better than the choice we had, which was no choice.

We stepped through some unknown past and into Manhattan, fifty years into the future, the dawn of a new century. The last place I want to be. But future wormhole families will be able to choose where they go. And if enough volunteers come forward to be a part of the travel trials, they'll be able to keep perfecting the technology.

From the street below, I hear a very old man scream that spring once brought fragrant flowers. He says that trees once clung to each other through an interconnected root system. He sounds mad, but perhaps it's all true. Or perhaps it's not. It's hard to know.

He screams that those in power have destroyed our memories. Burned our books. Silenced our music. Wiped away all evidence of the history of art and beauty. All because they're afraid of people knowing what they've lost. I look out the window, and he seems to sense my gaze. Because he looks right up at me.

"You," he says.

I quickly close the window, fear coursing through my body.

But I can't get the ache in his voice out of my head all night. So the next day, I find him. He's not screaming anymore. Just staring up at the drones in the sky with his haunted eyes.

"Good morning," I say.

"What's good about it?"

"Well, nothing actually."

He laughs. I do too.

"Why aren't you scared of me?" he asks.

"I am." I gulp down hard. "But I want to know more. About trees and flowers and books and music."

"There are places you can go," he says. "Underground. In the old subway system. If they catch you…"

"I don't care," I say. "I have nothing to live for, which means I have nothing to fear."

He leads me underground, into a web of old rail lines where men and women read passages from literature, sketch replicas of destroyed paintings, and blast music thought to be lost forever.

"You see now," he says.

"It's overwhelming," I say, my senses flooded by sound and imagery and texture.

"Of course it is," he says. "Art is meant to overwhelm the soul. If it doesn't, then it's not art."

I close my eyes, letting all the sounds wash over me. When I open them, he's climbing back up to the street.

"Wait," I say. "Where are you going?"

"To lead more people like you to this."

I walk the old rail lines, past dancers and writers and sketch artists. It's both the darkest and the brightest place I've ever been. One track leads me to another. And then to another. I don't sleep anyway, so perhaps the night has come and gone. I wouldn't know.

Then something stops me.

The sound of a violin. Joined by flutes and clarinets and bassoons and trumpets. They're playing a piece of music full of longing and joy. I stand still, letting the music sweep over me. The unthinkable happens. Memories come. Small ones at first. My body intertwined with someone else's. Someone I loved.

"What was that?" I ask the musicians when the piece ends.

"Tchaikovsky," the violinist says. "Concerto—"

Before he can finish, I say, "Concerto in D Major." My hand suddenly covers my mouth, shocked at this knowledge that was hiding somewhere inside me. I remember him. His name. Amor. And then, my name. Hooman.

That's who I am.

"You know it then," he says.

"I do," I say. "But I need to find out more. I need...everything.

Every book ever written about Tchaikovsky. Every performance recorded. Everything."

The violinist stands up and puts an arm around me. "Come with me," he says, as he leads me to a large piano sitting behind the orchestra. He opens the piano bench, and inside I see sheet music, biographies of musicians, and scholarly articles about music. "It's not comprehensive, but it's what I was able to save."

I spend hours poring through it all. The sheet music is a foreign language to me, but the words are not. I read every biography, every article. I know it's morning when the band sets up again."

"You're still here?" the violinist asks.

"Still here," I say.

They play for me as I read, and read, and read.

And then, one morning, I find it. An article published about Tchaikovsky in Buenos Aires in 1947, one hundred and fifty-two years ago. I don't understand the Spanish, but I can read the byline. It's by Amor Garcia.

"Can one of you translate this for me?" I ask.

One of the bassoon players steps forward and skims it. "It's about Tchaikovsky's Concerto in D Major," he says. "It argues that we know from the music that Tchaikovsky loved men. It also argues, somewhat esoterically if you ask me, that art doesn't age and that it has the power to transport us through time. That when one truly hears a work of art in the right way, it guides us to—"

I run as fast as I can.

Up the stairs.

Onto a passenger drone.

Into the offices of the National Travel Agency.

"I'd like to volunteer," I say.

"Are you aware of the risks?"

"I don't care about risks. I just need to go to Buenos Aires in 1947."

"That can be arranged. But the risks are—"

"I've been through once already. And I suspect the side effects are less severe going into the past."

"Why is that?"

Because now I know that Amor never forgot his name. Or his love for Tchaikovsky. Perhaps he suffered different effects, but he remembered the music. And he remembered me. He sent for me when he wrote that piece. He knew that wherever I went, I would find it somehow. And that I would know what to do.

It takes them weeks to prepare me for my trip through the wormhole. They ask me if there's anyone that should be made aware of my departure. I think of my dad. "No," I say. "I have no one here."

The Buenos Aires Philharmonic announces its season in the spring. The scent of flowers fills the air, the wind blowing magic across the city. I attend every performance. Schubert and Ravel and Beethoven and Haydn. With each new performance, I grow a little more confident in my Spanish, a little more ready for October, when the Philharmonic will be performing Tchaikovsky's Concerto in D Major.

I sit down for the performance, scanning the audience.

Just as the piece begins, I see him. He's two rows behind me, just a few feet away, his baby sister on his lap. I want to touch him, kiss him, feel his skin on mine. But I know there will be time for that soon enough, so I let myself revel in the magic of this moment.

I wave to him.

He waves to me.

And then we both close our eyes and allow the music to transport us through the rest of our lives.

★ ★ ★ ★ ★

HOME

K. Ancrum

IT WAS LOUD, AS IT ALWAYS WAS. PASSENGERS pushed past each other, rushing towards the security gates, passports in hand. Their children trailed behind them, tripping over suitcases and groaning at the sight of the long lines.

My father's face was twisted with panic, his grey eyes wide as we made our way across the space station. I didn't need to rush since I knew what was about to happen, but every time I found myself here, I looked at his face warped with urgency and couldn't slow down. I couldn't fail him.

Two hundred seventeen steps away, Mira and his family strode towards the same checkpoint.

These things never change. He was farther than I ever would have noticed the first time I came to this station. But now, as he turned the corner, I could feel him coming closer. The warmth rolling off of his body made me bend towards him.

"Come on, Tovah!" my father said, pushing me towards

the checkpoint. I ached to hear my father's voice saying something else, just once.

This was the twenty-fifth Revolution. We get exactly thirteen hours before everything starts again.

On the first Revolution, everything seemed okay. My father and I were trying to get back home for the winter holidays, just like every other year. My parents had separated ages ago, so I was used to schlepping back and forth from Io to Earth.

Even the time crunches they used on these faraway moons stopped being cool and interesting after my eighth birthday. It was just something that made sense and was convenient. Who has time to wait for flights to connect when you can get a little help from cosmic physics?

My brown eyes met Mira's from one hundred ten steps away, and my heart beat quicker.

We didn't know exactly how this worked, but after the tenth Revolution, Mira and I had a loose conjecture. Neither of us were particularly great at science or math, which was extremely funny, and then later extremely sad. But we were pretty sure our guesstimation was close:

We already knew that during a time crunch, the entire ship shifts space-time a bit. Everyone inside the ship shifts in time along with it. While everyone outside the ship stays locked in linear time progression. Somewhere on the ship, they automatically controlled it to coordinate with incoming flight delays with the same kind of mathematical precision we use to control traffic lights.

After my first time crunch, the only thing I noticed was that my cell phone reception cut out for a second. By the time the Wi-Fi turned back on, two hours had vanished, and a few meters down the hallway, staff started calling people to board their arriving flight.

The space station my dad and I had gone to this year was less extravagant than our usual stopover. It had been a difficult year, and money was tight. Mira's family had never been able to afford any other station. I think it was why Mira had figured out what happened first.

The boarding agent smiled at me brightly, her orange hair as bright and luminous as the first time I saw her.

"Put your shoes, electronics and carry-on luggage in these bins and step through the Filter with your arms up."

I took off my shoes and put them in the bin. Sometimes I didn't. We'd tried that a few times actually. Avoiding the Filter machine, going through with all of our stuff on, trying to go at different times.

But no matter what, at the exact second that we went through, Mira and I would hear a sound like the sky was tearing itself apart. Everyone around us would slow to a stop. Freeze in their tracks. And we would be alone.

So I put my shoes in the bin and took off my coat, belt and metal hair tie. I tossed my phone in the bin, and took my dad's from him as well.

"Thanks, Bumble Bee," he said, and I missed him terribly.

"What are you doing, Mira?" Mira's mom yelled behind us, at the second boarding gate. "Stop staring into nothing and take off your shoes."

I looked over my shoulder, and he was looking at me. Mira grinned and shrugged.

At exactly 7:24:07 Daylight Shuttle Time, we stepped in unison into the Filter.

After the great noise, we both stepped out.

Mira stretched and cracked his neck. He pushed past a large man caught in an argument with a boarding agent—mouth still open, spittle hovering in midair—to make his way to me.

"God, I'm tired this morning for some reason. Ugh. What's the plan for today?" he asked.

Mira was short for his age but terribly handsome. He was a year younger than I was, but we were both sophomores. He had dark brown curls and light brown skin. His eyes were very slender and the whites of them were red, like most of the people who had been born on Fria for the last four generations. That exomoon was bright enough to permanently sunburn the sclera. Humans adapt to stuff like that. Slowly, but they definitely do.

I'm sure he thought I looked bug-eyed in comparison, but he never mentioned it. It was probably terrible to think this, but I'm glad it was him that I got stuck with in this time loop. He's the type of boy who would never have even spoken to me back at school, but here he was.

"Let's get breakfast and just take a day off," I said. "It's almost been a month. We deserve a bit of a break."

Mira sighed hard. "I guess," he whined. "But tomorrow, we have to get back to searching. Who knows how long it's been outside the station?"

"Preaching to the choir," I said with a frown. It's not something either of us could ever quite forget. We tried not to mention it often.

We walked down the main hallway and over to the food

court. Mira picked a french fry off a plate a waitress was holding and popped it into his mouth.

"I still feel weird just, like…eating off people's plates." It's been long enough that the idea everything will buzz back to life doesn't feel realistic anymore.

"Whoever ordered that is going to be so mad when the waitress puts down a plate with no fries. Don't do that to her, man. I'm sure working here sucks anyway," I said, hopping over the counter of a McDonald's outlet. "Leave that alone. I'll make you an Egg McMuffin."

Cooking food in the food court always felt more like borrowing than taking already cooked food. But Mira liked to snag us some snacks from the convenience store. The food replenished itself every day, so that made the time loop a lot less stressful.

We took our meal to the lounge. The lounge had the softest carpets and was the least crowded place in the entire station. It smelled persistently of old lady perfume, because a woman in a fur coat, dripping in jewelry and sitting on one of the couches near the door, had clearly overindulged. But it was the nicest place on the station to spread out on the floor and relax.

Mira finished his McMuffin and turned to lay on his back with his eyes closed.

"I know we said we're not doing work today, but can I talk about it at least?" he asked.

"Sure."

"I wonder if there are other people who are like us, still stuck in the early stages," he said softly. "Like when they were still developing this technology fifty years ago, and there were all sorts of accidents…there hasn't been anything like this since then. But I wonder if there are still people trapped somewhere. Somewhen."

"I wish I'd paid closer attention to history in school." I admitted. "I remember hearing that one of the stations got stuck moving forward, and when they were finally able to break the Faraday cage, everyone in it had died of old age. Oh, and there was that one station that tore apart space-time around it and unmade itself molecularly—which probably wasn't pleasant."

"I'm choosing to believe they didn't feel it, Tovah. That it happened so fast, it was over before they knew it began," Mira said with a wave of his hand.

I hmmed with disbelief, and Mira flung his arm over his eyes. "There was a station closer to Fria where they say time went backwards for a second," he said.

"That's impossible." I huffed. "No one can go back, only forward. It breaks the laws of physics."

"That's why it's creepy." Mira said, peeking at me under the shadow of his arm. "There are like a hundred fifty eye witnesses."

"The government said that maybe it was just like a mass déjà vu event," I insisted.

"What's the difference? If you're perceiving something, and everyone around you is also perceiving the same thing at the same time, then no one is crazy and everyone is living a shared existence." His eyes narrowed, annoyed. "Just because Fria is a small moon with less influence than Io doesn't mean it's a backwater full of superstition and folk legends."

"I didn't mean that, Mira. I just meant that it's… I don't

know, it's scary to think that there's stuff out there that we don't already know about," I admitted. "It's easier to believe the news than to believe people I've never met, saying things that I've been told are impossible."

"Pretty sure we both thought all of this was impossible," he snapped and stood up. "Thanks for breakfast. I'm going for a walk. I'll catch up to you later."

I watched him disappear into the station, his shoulders stiff with irritation. The angles of his silhouette, beautiful.

The anger wasn't new. It had settled from an explosion after we first became this way to a simmering thing that he could control.

His family had been going to pick up his little sister at the gate. She was coming home from University for the winter holidays. His trip was supposed to be simple. Just a quick shuttle to the space station, have a happy moment picking her up, then take the shuttle right back. It shouldn't have been more than a five-hour trip. At this point he'd been in the space station for over five *weeks*.

Anyway, when Mira got like this, he always went off to the hangar to stand by the ships and look out at the stars.

If I went to the customer service desk on the third floor and stood on my tiptoes, I could see him. But it was invasive; I had only done it twice. The first time he caught me watching, he disappeared on me for two whole Revolutions, his anger burning low and steady. The next time, he slept somewhere else. He never slept somewhere else. The warning was enough.

The overhead lights in the station drifted from the yellow-white of morning to a mellow afternoon haze, then a golden hour that reminded me of home. The gold shifted to pink, which faded to red, a sunless sunset. Then blue fluorescent, that kind of lighting where it's bright indoors, but your body still knows it's night outside—like going to Target at 11 p.m.

We had three hours left.

Mira returned to the station lounge. He leaned against the doorway and watched as I used the computer at the boarding podium to read about the station's construction.

"Are you staying up?" he asked warily.

We'd tried that too, ten Revolutions ago. Standing in the same places as when the time loop began, so as not to alarm our families. My vision wavered, unconsciousness hitting softly, like falling asleep during class. Then we both woke up separately and on our way to the space station. Helpless.

"No," I said and turned off the computer.

We went to the back of the lounge and past a discreet door, to a bunkroom. People who had flights that didn't connect with standard schedules went there to sleep. There were only four cots, arranged against the perimeter with two on the longest wall. No privacy.

Mira slept on the left wall and I slept ten feet away, directly across from him.

He pulled off his shirt and settled in for the night.

Before my eyes closed for good, he turned over in his bed loudly. The cheap sheets scraped against each other in the dark.

"I'm scared too," he admitted.

I silently wished our cots were closer.

There was the great and terrible noise, and then the relief of feeling Mira's waffle knit sweater. His arms closed around my shoulders, and I pushed my nose into the side of his neck. He still smelled like the curry his mom had made the previous night, one hundred Revolutions ago.

Every morning, I was taut with the anxiety of getting to see him again. The only boy in the whole world. I didn't care that my dad was talking. I didn't care about the boarding agent or taking off my shoes. I just walked steadily toward Mira until we were together again.

People become strange things, strangers to themselves, in situations like this.

Mira pushed his hands beneath the T-shirt I was wearing and pressed his fingertips into the skin of my back.

"I don't want to wake up here without you," he'd said once. "What if we fall out of sync? What if we're fucking around and somehow manage to knock out of the loop without each other? I can't face this alone. I'm not brave enough for it."

He missed his dad. Once, I saw him standing in the middle of the station, staring at his parents as they walked towards security, his dark eyes even darker with longing.

"Tovah." Mira wound his fingers around mine. "What are we doing today?"

"We're going to have Chinese food, and then we're going to the hangar."

Did you know that most restaurants have instructions plastered all over the place in the back so that new hires can quickly pick up the recipes? We figured that out after ten Revolutions. By that point, it stopped feeling rude to push our way past the workers in the kitchen. We explored, opening drawers and taking out ingredients to snack on, emptying packages and tossing things in the fryer.

After the seventy-seventh Revolution, I'd mastered the easier menus in McDonald's, Subway, Popeyes, The Popcorn Store, Cinnabon and Starbucks and started inching my knowledge base towards the sushi restaurants, the Indian place, Thai and Chinese food.

After Thai we had our first death. Fire and nowhere to run from it. We burned to a crisp, curled in a ball on the floor in front of the doors to the station, so close to freedom and so far from it. We expected to wake up out of the loop, heading towards heaven. But my alarm at home rang the next day, and I was headed right back to the station. My dad sang along to the radio as I sat in the back of the car, trying to get my breathing under control, trying not to cry.

Chinese food was easier. The restaurant was a chain and everything was prepackaged.

Mira and I didn't separate much these days. Even the thought of it made my heart race and my hands start sweating. Who knew what could happen to him while I wasn't looking? Mira laughed, remembering how I used to watch him in the beginning, playing with a rubber band ball he'd made from supplies from the border agents' desks. Back then, I was still intimidated by him and the coolness he had left over from a world that didn't exist for us now.

"You're such a stalker," he'd joked at the time.

He wasn't joking at all anymore. He was quiet as I cooked him wood ear mushrooms with chili sauce, and pork skewers, quiet when we went down to the hangar to eat, quiet as he laid his head in my lap and looked out of the large windows.

"Do you think this will last more than a year?" Mira asked suddenly, looking up at me.

"God, I hope not," I replied with a huff. "If time is moving on the outside of the station, I can't bear thinking about what it would be like if we missed that much of it. Everyone would have moved on by then. I don't even know what my friends from school would be like. They would have already started college, maybe even left Io completely!"

Mira nodded and closed his eyes. "Probably. Anyway, I think that no matter who got stuck in the time loop, they would have wound up like us eventually. Even if it was two old people. Or an old person and a young person, or a couple of kids. People with completely different backgrounds... I think given enough time, you just sort of become friends, and that's it."

"What do you mean?" I threaded my fingers through his curls and watched them spring back.

"I mean, that this is the meaning of humanity. Beyond everything else. At the core, this is what we are. Creatures that need a friend, who need to touch, who can't stand the dark and the cold alone... We don't really have anything in common beyond that, and we really don't need to. That's the secret."

"What, you don't think we could have been friends? If we went to the same school and had the same classes?" I joked, trying to keep him from becoming maudlin again.

"No. I don't," he said firmly. "There would have been all sorts of stupid things that don't matter, that would have ruined it. Pretending that they wouldn't have disrespects what we have now."

I pushed him off my lap, and his head thumped against the linoleum floor.

"What do we have now?"

Mira rubbed the back of his head and scowled at me. "Time. We know that time overrules anything. No one else knows that, Tovah. Maybe sailors or people who get stuck in caves. But no one else normal."

"And why do you think that's disrespectful to 'what we have now'?" I made finger quotes around the words, and Mira's frown got deeper.

"Because," he said, clearly frustrated. "This is a singularity that bypasses anything that happens after this. If we wake up and the loop is over, are you going to forget about this? About what it was like to be alone with me in this horrible station? I'm going to need therapy for the rest of my life and I still won't be able to purge it. I'm traumatized as fuck, aren't you?"

I stood and as I started to speak, but Mira bulldozed over me.

"No matter who else I make friends with, none of them will be like you." He climbed to his feet. "They can't compete, no matter what they do. It won't matter if they like the same sports teams as me, or like the same music, or skateboard with me every day down at the park. It won't matter if they have fun with me for years, or if I fall in love with them, or if they save my life."

I didn't know what to say to that. Mira clasped my biceps with gentle hands and rested his forehead on my shoulder.

"Nothing will ever be like this. No one will ever be like you. No matter who you'd been, or who you are. In here, you're the world."

"I'm...the world..." I repeated, a terror I hadn't felt since the fifth Revolution welling up in my chest.

"And after all of this is over," Mira continued, "for me, you still will be."

★ ★ ★

We didn't kiss until the fourth year. Fifteen hundred Revolutions, no more—no less.

It didn't seem fair, and it was horribly cliché, so we resisted it out of complete embarrassment. Our cots had been pushed together for three years already. I'd stopped paying attention to my dad on the way to the station. His face might as well have been a stranger's.

I knew Mira so well now. I knew the crinkles at the corner of his eyes, the calluses on his palms, the rough heels of his feet that scraped against me at night. From his wrists to his sleeves, from his ankles to his jeans, from his neckline to his face, he was a map of my homeland. Beyond those barriers was a mystery deep as the sea.

He turned toward me, my head already cradled in the curve of his inner elbow.

"Tovah," he said, and it startled me, because he said it like he used to during the first week we met. I opened my eyes. He bit his lip and stared across the inches of darkness.

"I'm not a boy, Tovah. Not really."

"Why are you telling me this now?" I asked, feeling the waves of sleep tugging at my consciousness. My hand was already on his chest, plane flat, unsurprising and unsurprised.

"Because you should know," he replied. "I'm…more… in-between. At home we're called 'The Golden Mean,' built halfway between men and women, a perfect balance between extremes. It's more common on Fria and on Earth than where you're from. Everyone who knew me back home knew. My whole family knew. I wanted you to know."

"You *do* know that it doesn't matter to me," I said. I imagined him sheepishly walking over to me tomorrow morning, expecting an awkwardness that would never come, and it made me want to laugh.

Mira wasn't laughing. "It's important that you know," he said, "so that you know how to touch me. I don't look how you'd probably expect. I need you to be ready and to understand. I want you to know I'm not an alien. I'm normal."

Suddenly, I was wide awake.

"Are you giving up on us ever getting out?" I asked, my voice loud in the darkness. "Is this something that we're doing now because of convenience and hopelessness?"

"No," Mira said, gently. "I'm making a choice."

He tasted like fourteen hundred days.

The stubble that never had time to grow into a beard was rough as it scraped against my chin. He swallowed my strangled gasp like it was his right to swallow my noises. Mira was twenty-one, but his face was seventeen and he was human, every part of him was human.

Mira sank his strong white teeth into the curve of my neck and sucked the salt of my skin with an impatient growl. I batted him away, and sighed.

"Stop bothering me. I think I'm close to figuring out what happened," I huffed, irritated.

He flopped down to my right, grinning up at me from the mess of blankets around him.

"Can we take a day off from this? It's our anniversary. I cleared all the people out of the iHop so we can pretend we're having a regular visit. I know you love that," he said, rubbing his nose against the curve of my knee.

"I do love that, I've loved twenty years of it, but I'm going

to love it a lot more when we can actually *go* to a stupid iHop."
I put down the station manual, tucking my finger into the
page I was reading.

"Tell me your thoughts and then we'll go," Mira insisted.

I pushed down my own annoyance and looked back at his
old eyes trapped in his forever-young face, and my chest ached.

"So, we're pretty clear that the room where the technicians
handle the time crunch didn't have issues with improper maintenance. The badges on all of the employees in there were
over three years old in the system, so no one made any new-
bie mistakes either. We've already taken apart the engine—"

"Not one of my favorite deaths," Mira said contemplatively.

It was an understatement. Death by radiation was incom-
prehensible, and it wasn't something we'd experienced once
or even twice. Four times we'd burned, screaming. I was surprised he even brought it up.

"Yeah, so it's not the engine," I continued. "It has to be something external. The Filters are working fine, and people walk
through them at the same time as the time crunch, all the time."

"Maybe they were broken in a way that they're not right
now," Mira said casually. He got up and stretched, the waffle knit sweater I had grown to love riding up to expose his
hip bones.

"What do you mean?" I asked. "Nothing changes. If they
were broken then, they would still be broken now and we
would know."

"Not if there was like an energy surge, or a solar flare or
something."

"When...when was the first time you thought of that?" I
asked, my blood running cold as my heart sped up.

Mira leaned down to cup my face in his hands. "Three days ago. But today is our anniversary, my dove. Come eat with me." He pressed his forehead against mine and stroked the side of my neck until my pulse slowed beneath his fingertips, until we were breathing in tandem.

I followed him to the food court, his hand in mine as we passed the families with legs outstretched mid-stride.

We knew them all. The girl who dropped her doll in the hallway, eyebrows knotted in anxiety as she leaned down to pick it up. The old man with his wife in a wheelchair, pushing her wearily as she read a magazine. The exhausted married couple with too much luggage, wearing clothes they took out of their bag to avoid a fee. The sports team spending their twenty-fourth year in rugby uniforms, all frozen while talking animatedly. One had his head back and a chip in midair, and his friend's hand stood ready to slap it away from his mouth.

Our table had been set with flowers gathered from many other tables, some of them fresh, some of them fake, a horrible bouquet made by an artistically inept man who I loved so. I watched Mira duck behind the counter to start frying up pancakes and bacon.

His shoulders were loose and happy as he cooked, laughing in triumph as he tossed a pancake and managed to catch it back in the pan. He glanced over his shoulder at me and grinned.

"I could use some applause," Mira said. "It's not easy."

I scoffed. "I'll clap when you can do that with an omelet. We nailed pancake flipping ten years ago, buddy."

Mira groaned theatrically. "Buddy, she calls me," he whined to the fry cook next to him. "The only wife I've ever known calls me buddy."

"He can't commiserate with you," I called back. I could tell Mira was rolling his eyes without even having to see his face. "He can't even hear you."

Plates balanced on each of his arms, he came back to the table. He laid out the dishes like a seasoned waiter—which, at this point, I guess he was.

"You're lucky I like you," he replied, sitting down and unrolling his silverware from the iHop napkin.

"We're a lot of things, but lucky isn't one of them." I laughed.

"Are you sure?" Mira asked, suddenly serious.

I reached across the table and took his hand. Still callused from the baseball bat he used too often when he was a kid, a thousand yesterdays ago. I turned his hand over and brought his knuckles to my lips. Sweet and gentle in the way he liked best.

"No. But it took you three days to tell me about the solar flare, Mira," I murmured into his skin.

"I'm sorry."

"You shouldn't be. Let's just hope this attempt doesn't hurt."

"If you knew that it would," Mira said, brushing his thumb against my cheek, "would you still be willing to try?"

I opened my eyes and touched the tip of my tongue to his finger. His gaze darkened.

"What a great and terrible question," I replied.

"Come on, Tovah!" my father said, pushing me towards the checkpoint.

The boarding agent smiled at me brightly. Her orange hair as crisp and luminous as the first time I saw her.

"Put your shoes, electronics and carry-on luggage in these bins and step through the Filter with your arms up."

I put my shoes in the bin, and took off my coat, belt and metal hair tie. I tossed my phone in the bin and took my dad's from him as well.

"Thanks, Bumble Bee," he said.

"What are you doing, Mira?" Mira's mom yelled behind us, at the second boarding gate. "Stop staring into nothing and take off your shoes."

My heart slammed in my chest as I felt his silhouette move, warm and familiar less than ten paces away. The sound of his sneakers hitting the bin was loud and discordant. I couldn't look at him. I didn't want to see the hope in his eyes. Or worse, the disappointment.

"Tovah," Mira said, and my head turned before I could catch myself. My sunflower body, the bright rays of his face.

"I'll visit you after the holiday. You know how to find me." He grinned. "Wait for me."

The boarding agent nudged my shoulder hard. "Don't hold up the line, miss. We all have places to be."

I stepped into the Filter. I stepped out of the Filter.

My dad pushed through behind me, snatching his laptop bag out of the bin and swinging it over his arm.

"Who's that?" he asked, handing me my shoes.

I watched the back of Mira's neck as he pulled on a coat I had never seen him wear, then put his rough feet back into sneakers he barely ever needed. Traced my eyes across his hair cut sharply across the back of his neck, freshly shorn for years. His mother, irritated, pushed at him from behind, and his shoulders tensed with longing at finally feeling her touch.

He took her carry-on bag and tossed it over his back with his own, jumping a bit to resettle the weight. Then Mira looked over his shoulder at me one last time, dark-eyed and beautiful, before fading into the crowd. It took everything in me not to follow him.

"Do you know him?" my dad insisted.

I put on my coat.

"No. But maybe someday, I will."

★ ★ ★ ★ ★

FRACTAL EYES

Ugochi M. Agoawike

INTERNATIONAL SPACE RESEARCH AGENCY
  SITE-22
  LEVEL 6 CONFIDENTIAL

LOADING...
> **CASE FILE: SUBJECT 0000-A**

SUBJECT 0000-A, ALSO KNOWN AS ESSENCE, IS an entity of unknown origin resembling a human in physical appearance. Subject 0000-A was retrieved from [REDACTED] the same day ISRA launched the Mouria Colony located on Earth's moon, Qamar. Subject 0000-A identifies as "nonhuman" with a preference for the pronouns she/her/hers. The subject does not require liquid or material sustenance. The subject has dark skin that closer examination reveals to contain innumerable stars. The subject is possessed of cosmic-latte hair (see addendum one for more details). The most unusual aspect of the subject is her eyes, the shade of which cannot be pinned down; like the surface of an uncut diamond, they shift with the light to suit the angle from they are viewed. The subject's handlers have come to refer to them as *fractal eyes*.

I look up from the case file to meet the gaze of the security guard. He looks dead tired, deep recesses forming under a pair of glassy eyes as he scans my badge. *Chiamaka "Chi" Oloye—age 18*, the glossy surface reads in thick black print. Right next to my name is an awkward photo of me, braids askew and glasses smudged with a fingerprint in the corner—not my finest work.

Today I begin an internship with Fredericka Klein, on a secret project the good doctor couldn't brief me on.

As the guard returns my badge, I flash him a smile. He merely blinks at me, unimpressed, before waving me along. Cheeks heated, I sling the lanyard over my neck and proceed through the metal detector.

Grey walls meet me on either side as I enter the building proper. Everything inside Site-22 is as nondescript as the outside, concrete fixings and yellow fluorescent lights that shiver as I pass beneath. The walls are bare of decoration save for a few sparse maps and large exit signs, red blaring at me with a demanding hand, gesturing to points of escape.

Readjusting my collar, I round a corner with the words *Director's Office* and *Commissary* written near the top. One or two white-clad scientists occasionally pass me with documents in their hands and worry on their faces. There is a word on everyone's lips: the *visitor*. Murmurs of the thing that fell to Earth on such a monumental day. *A bad omen*, my mother said of the rumours.

When I arrive at the Director's office, she greets me with a stern handshake and leads me into the side room. We enter a command point in a horseshoe shape, with a ceiling-length two-way mirror standing concave at the far side. Sleek consoles line the perimeter, each filled with a screen displaying tiny lines of running code. The two technicians turn to acknowledge me before returning to their work while Dr. Klein waves me over.

"Director Hannon, this is Chi Oloye. They're the best intern at my clinic—quite frankly, they keep my life together. I've chosen them to record and transcribe our sessions," the doctor explains. Looking down, I bite my lip to hide a smile at her compliment—the doctor is far too generous with the affirmations she lavishes on her interns.

Tension leaks from the Director's frame as she nods. "All right then. You've had your briefings. The room's all yours, but keep an eye on the clock. I'll be watching."

"No problem, sir. I'm only here to do my job."

[DATA EXPUNGED] ISRA Audio Log Transcript
Subject: [REDACTED]
Team Lead: Dr. Frederika L. Klein, PhD
Team Members: Chiamaka Oloye, █████████
█████, █████████████
File: Session01_May21xx.mp4

[BEGIN LOG]
[The room is sterile white. Thin blue lines of a cybernetic framework run across every wall, where thousands of micro cameras are watching. Still as a redwood, Subject 0000-A sits on a stool, arms folded, and eyes locked on the doctor. The

subject is clad is a white tunic, grey pants hanging by her feet, a size too large. Moments pass, but she does not blink]

DR. KLEIN: Hello, Essence.

ESSENCE: Hello, Doctor Frederika Klein PhD. Is that what you want to hear?

DR. KLEIN: I was told you were a bit abrasive. Why don't you tell me how your day has been.

ESSENCE: You're the first person to ask me about my "day."

DR. KLEIN: Well, I am a counselor, after all. Whatever you are, it's clear the structure of your brain is similar enough to ours that I can feasibly deduce you must experience humanlike emotions.

ESSENCE: That's what the scans were for. All these handlers just gawk at me and go thinking I can't see what they did and will do. It's not that hard to see and hear through a two-way mirror—isn't that right, Chi?

DR. KLEIN: Please don't address Mx. Oloye. So, your powers. They do exist then: You can, for lack of better term, *see* what happened and may happen?

ESSENCE: Yes. But you already knew that.

DR. KLEIN: How does that make you feel?

ESSENCE: My, my, my. What an open-ended question. I could say anything at all, and you'd write it down. I could straight-up lie, and you wouldn't know—none of you would. As long as it was what you wanted to hear.

DR. KLEIN: And what do you think that is?

ESSENCE: Oh, you know. ISRA chose an interesting spot to begin their project, don't you think? Lucky that I landed so close to [REDACTED].

DR. KLEIN: Interesting. If I were one to jump to conclusions, I'd say that sounds almost like a threat.

ESSENCE: Good thing you're not.

DR. KLEIN: Good thing. Anyway. As for my previous question, you never gave an answer. How does ISRA knowing about your ability make you feel? How does being here, in the facility under observation, make you feel?

ESSENCE: Of course, I feel strange. One moment I'm falling. The next I'm being screened with weapons in my face, and I accidentally blurt out the things that reveal my talents. You'd think a nonhuman would be afforded higher-class treatment. I only fell from the sky; it's not as if I landed in a cruiser and started making demands of the Gaean Federation.

DR. KLEIN: Let's backtrack on that: You meant to keep your ability hidden? To what purpose—did you see something that could potentially impact your future here?

ESSENCE: You could say that. Would you like me to tell you?

DR. KLEIN: No. That's fine. I think that'll be all for today.

ESSENCE: See you next month, Doctor. Chi.

[END LOG]
SESSION DURATION: 01:00:04:84

Standing shock straight, I watch Dr. Klein organize the papers I've handed to her. The room beyond the mirror is darkened. But I know who is behind it—what is behind it.

How did Subject 0000-A know my name? The silly question runs through my mind, though I know the answer. Humanity doesn't know what lies beneath our own moons, and if the subject's true nature were to get out, well. I'm not sure how the public would handle it.

ISRA is a controversial company, often sparking debates over the ethical nature of colonies on Qamar, and the infamous "space rig," a fully manned generation station currently orbiting Mars. Where I stand on the matter is of little concern—the Earth beneath my feet is good enough for me.

A voice interrupts my thoughts. A fleeting warmth touches my cheeks. and Dr. Klein smirks. Then her face turns serious. White light flashes across her glasses, obscuring her eyes.

"I'm sorry, Chi," she apologizes. "She's been known to try and unnerve her handlers by naming them, so don't take it personally."

Pulling a smile to my face, I shake my head. "It's fine, Doctor. I was just surprised to find the rumours true."

The doctor hums. "Indeed. We're still trying to identify the depths of her abilities, but one or two rumours get out." She riffles though the papers with a frown. "I just hope we get what we need before ISRA... Well, I just hope we get it."

I finally pull the session recording into a new folder and fill out the necessary details. When the doctor and I are finished with our work, I hand her the glass slate, and she passes me some documents. I pull it all together and arrange the folders into a formation pleasing to the eye. The sight fills me with satisfaction, despite knowing it'll all be ruined when the Director puts it away.

As we leave the room, I clutch my identification. Glossy beneath my hands, it is a reminder of what we are doing. Of the cosmic secrets within the walls of Site-22.

NOTICE FROM THE SITE-22 BIOLOGICAL HAZARD DEPARTMENT

INCIDENT 12-B: [DATA EXPUNGED]

At approximately 0045 hours, Subject 0000-A was involved in an incident involving ▮▮▮▮▮▮▮▮▮▮▮▮ and McCary, Saoirse. The incident occurred during a routine cleaning of Subject 0000-A's cell while McCary was performing maintenance on a broken camera and ▮▮▮▮ ▮▮▮▮▮▮▮▮ was inserting an IV containing zolpidem and sodium thiopental into the subject. When ████ ████████ was checking the subject's blood pressure, McCary accidentally activated the high-frequency setting on the cameras. In the same manner as ferrofluid, the subject's skin began to shift, small black spikes emerging all over her extremities. Additionally, white growths sprouted from the subject's face in place of eyes.

Presumably as a defense reaction, the subject grew hostile and attacked ████████████████, leaving them with dark burns across their torso and what looks to be a growth forming beneath their nape. McCary managed to alert security, and Subject 0000-A was anesthetized immediately after. It should be noted that the spikes on the subject's skin displayed an adverse reaction to the frequency in the range above 20,000 Hz.

—Askleria Seor, Department Lead, Biohazard

I frown at the incident report as the security guard scans me in. This time, the guard is a woman, with a face almost as youthful as mine. She must be new. I don't catch what she says as I take my badge, too caught up in poring over the files.

Passing through the metal detector is like stepping into an alternate uniform. All the colours in my vision are washed out by grey. There are new signs up on the walls. A few of them contain information I gloss over, but the others detail a mandate.

UPDATED SECURITY PROTOCOLS reads a sign in shocking blue, words practically jumping from the page.

Beneath it are the rules for those with upper-level clearance—*everyone in Site-22, including me.* I smile, thumbing my badge. The smile doesn't last long when I remember the fate of Mc-

Cary's partner. Little news comes out of the biohazard wing, but from what Dr. Klein says: no news is bad news.

The people I pass are all wearing new badges, a red box around their pictures signifying a shift in the facility. The halls are quieter—my breathing, my footsteps, a hammer in this valley of steel and grey.

It's clear the subject's outburst caused a stir that has many of us doubting. What *are* we even doing here? Attempting to communicate with a being that is so alike to us, yet alien in every sense of the word. Those fractal eyes come to mind, chilly fingers crawling up my spine.

Shaking the fractals from my thoughts, I swipe my card into Director Hannon's office and flash her an amiable nod. After weeks of work, daily routines run as smooth as fitted gears—it's just the monthly sessions of which we're wary.

In the side room, Dr. Klein is already a mess, papers strewn across the main console while she taps away on her smudged slate, a pair of pens tucked into her hair. Maybe that's why her hair is so large: it's full of the many office supplies she's stolen and stashed away, only to be forgotten over the years.

"Good morning, Chi." She greets me without looking up.

"It's two in the afternoon, Doctor."

Dr. Klein looks up, brows raised so they disappear in her bangs. Beneath her eyes are dark spots, as if someone dipped their finger in pen ink and painted her face. "Ah, well, time is a slippery bastard in here. Can't always catch it."

Hiding a smile behind my hand, I move to her side and instinctively begin sorting through the heavily redacted files. It's tedious clerical work, a waste of skills that often leaves me wanting more. I want to be a scientist, not just a transcriber, not just an assistant. *Perhaps the doctor could do with another intern—I* banish the thought as it appears. A worm of possessiveness coils itself around my brain. There is a secret within the room beyond the mirror that I don't want anyone else to see. Or maybe, I just don't want to burden anyone else with Ess—the subject.

"You ready?" The doctor pulls on a mask of neutrality as she stares at the mirror. The technicians nod at her.

I sigh, pulling up the recorder on my slate. "As I'll ever be."

[DATA EXPUNGED] ISRA Audio Log Transcript
Subject: [REDACTED]
Team Lead: Dr. Frederika L. Klein, PhD
Team Members: Chiamaka Oloye, ██████████
████████, ██████████
File: Session02_June21xx.mp4

[BEGIN LOG]
[The sterile room is reinforced. Thick cushioned padding covers the squares between the cybernetic framework of the walls with new CCTV fixtures in each corner. Subject 0000-A's body is covered in a full jacket restraint. She appears to be in a haze. The pair remain silent for at least a minute]

ESSENCE: Hello, Doctor Frederika Klein. Do you feel safe?

DR. KLEIN: To be quite honest: no. You frighten me. your ability frightens me. What you did to ████████ ██████ frightens me. Even at that, I'm still here, aren't I?

ESSENCE: That you are. And I assume your intern is, too. How are you today, Chi?

DR. KLEIN: You are not talking to Mx. Oloye; you are talking to me.

ESSENCE: I am talking to whomever I like, you bitch.

DR. KLEIN: I would ask how your day has been, but I see you're still displaying signs of aggression. Let's talk about your recent incident. Could you tell me what the handlers did to make you react as you did?

ESSENCE: They got into my head—we don't like that. We... And I don't like it when I can't think.

DR. KLEIN: You don't like the drugs?

ESSENCE: Try living in a continuous fog and tell me how it feels when you can't feel the rest of yourself.

DR. KLEIN: Let's circle back to that conversation. You mentioned "living," but what does that mean to a non-human? If you'll allow me to bring up the results of your screening... Our medical staff discovered that although you resemble a human on the aesthetic level, your systems are like nothing they'd ever seen before. It makes us wonder—is this your true form?

ESSENCE: Anything I wear is my true form. I am we, no matter what I look like. Bodies are merely a vehicle in which to drive interaction like this useless conversation.

DR. KLEIN: Understandable. But if you would indulge me.

ESSENCE: This form is an amalgamation of several humans with desirable features. I would rather you like looking at me than antagonize me for looking too "alien," as humans say.

DR. KLEIN: So, camouflage? Is this some form of shapeshifting assimilation or a defense mechanism?

ESSENCE: My body is a hex in the whole. I *am* extraordinarily resilient.

DR. KLEIN: You didn't answer my question. If I were to shoot you right now, would your body adapt to defend itself, or are nonhumans typically built for that kind of attack?

ESSENCE: I cannot die. I know what the Gaean Federation is doing. I cannot die at the hand of a human. I will *not* die until—

DR. KLEIN: Slow down, Essence, I'm not trying to kill you. No one here is going to kill you. We simply want to know—

ESSENCE: How to incapacitate me? You'd certainly love to.

[The lights cut out. The muffled blue glow from the walls remains the only source of light. That, coupled with the two glittering dots that are Essence's eyes. Baby blue refracts off their diamond surface and—]

ESSENCE: But there is something else *I'd* much rather be doing.

[DATA CORRUPTED. RECORDING ERROR 505]

In the darkness, I am weightless. It's like sinking into a smooth river until logic pulls me from the depths. My startled heart freezes in my chest, Klaxons blaring panic in each corner of my mind. Fingers tightening on the slate, I turn to feel my way back to the console.

Something stops me. The sensation of hair brushes the back of my hand, smooth and straight, not at all like my usual tight curls. Blood rushes to my ears, heart a beast in the tenuous cage of my wicker chest.

I blink. The lights come back on. And I am no longer in the nameless side room. I sit where the doctor was, yet the doctor is nowhere in sight. Nerves shoot across my body, legs trapped as if hammered into the floor.

A stray braid falls into my face. I turn to meet a pair of fractal eyes where they shouldn't be.

"Oh my god!"

Unable to catch the scream before it escapes, my hands grip the arms of the cushion. The glass slate slips to the ground, bouncing harmlessly off the foam. That doesn't concern me.

What does is the alien face peering at me, skin glowing like distant cosmos and eyes glittering with clinical white light.

Essence is not wearing her typical stoic smile. Instead, her features are flat as she watches me, unmoving, from her stool, where she is no longer restrained.

"I'm no god, but thank you, Chi. Quite the compliment," she says, cocking her head.

Words escape me, throat closing from the tremors across my nervy body. I draw my legs up. Already being small, this should be to my advantage, but the racket in my head makes it difficult to focus on anything besides the nonhuman.

Drawn like a magnet, my eyes rove over stars on her face, and her hair, the colour of the universe. She sits upright, still as death, for she does not breathe. There seems to be something there, something *beyond* Essence, like the afterimage of a greater whole. But as I try to focus on it, the thing flees from my sight, and I am left with chimes in the wind.

As I tremble and shiver, Essence does not move. Shockingly passive, unlike the quickness of her mouth. The corners of her lips rise into an awkward expression halfway between a grin and a grimace. She toys with her white medical bracelet and sighs for my benefit, long and drawn out.

I'm in the clutches of a being no human has ever known, and yet I'm terrified to silence. *What kind of scientist am I?*

Well, still an intern, for one.

"Are, are you okay, E-Essence?" I ask. My stomach flips violently.

More movement as Essence shifts in her seat. "I don't know what's happening to me. We don't—can't feel this."

She kept calling herself that, but Dr. Klein brushed it off

as a quirk—signs of illusions of grandeur. In a human, at least. "We?"

"We is me," she says. "I am apart from the part that is me."

Tilting her head back at an unnatural angle, she makes eye contact. Her face distorts, shocking a screech from me. Covering my mouth, I stare wide-eyed as she slithers off the stool, to her slender bare feet. She slinks to my side with inhuman speed.

Licking my lips, I take a leap. "Are you, um, are you upset?"

Her brows narrow, the most distinct expression she's ever made. "How can I say no? I don't even know what *upset* truly is."

Her frown grows deeper, and I'm moving before I can stop myself. Then, hesitation flickers in my mind before I gently touch her. Her hand beneath mine is what I imagine space feels like: a cool vacuum, forces always drawing things in, leaving me breathless.

There is a cacophony in my head as Essence stills in what looks like shock. She flips her hand over, fingers slipping between mine like a key to a lock. She isn't human and yet I feel closer to her than Earth does to Qamar. I'm unable to look away, entranced at the white misshapen growths. Pale and translucent, they look like blossoms unfurling, fleshy tendrils reaching for my brown skin. Each touch elicits a chill down my spine.

Essence smiles and darts her other hand out.

I flinch as my eyes shut on instinct. Ice like summer cups my cheek, a thumb caressing that spot under my eyelid. It is an effort to crack them open, and I'm stuck in a stupor at the soft look Essence gives me. It is like nothing I've ever seen on her face.

She leans close enough that I'm caught in the moving frac-tals of her eyes.

"Wake up. Wake up before you lose yourself, Chi." Her whisper is a spill of sand, barely there.

The lights snap back on. Lightning cracks in my ear. I re-surface, loosing a gasp as the blurriness fades.

The technicians glance at me, wearing twin looks of dis-pleasure. Warmth spreads across my face, so I refocus on Dr. Klein, blinking the white flecks from my vision. My flush quickly fades when my ears tune back in to the conversation. Essence looks up to the mirror, restrained in white with her hair covering the side of her face. My blood runs cold at her blank smile.

DR. KLEIN: You didn't answer my question. If I were to shoot you right now, would your body adapt to de-fend itself? Or are nonhumans typically built for that kind of attack?

ESSENCE: You've already drugged me—why should I give you anything more with which to harm me? But if you get me out of these restraints, perhaps we might talk. Chi certainly doesn't mind me being free.

DR. KLEIN: I've told you not to address—*wait*... Re-garding your powers: Do they work in a localized area, or on a person-by-person basis?

ESSENCE: Do you want to know your future, Doc-tor? What happens when I get out of here?

DR. KLEIN: You tend to evade my questions with some of your own.

ESSENCE: You're such a good counselor. That's exactly what I'm doing! No wonder they picked you for this role!

DR. KLEIN: I believe that's a good place to stop. I don't think this conversation will be further productive.

ESSENCE: In a month, Doctor?

DR. KLEIN: ... In a month.

[END LOG]
SESSION DURATION: 02:03:45:76

★ ★ ★

INTERNATIONAL SPACE RESEARCH AGENCY: INTERNAL REPORT #17736
Date: 04.21xx
Author: Kendrea Longine-Wen, Secretary, ISRA

1.0 BACKGROUND
A compilation of the long-term investigation regarding ISRA's current projects to evaluate ethical practises and areas of potential expenditure cuts.

2.0 SUBJECT 0000-A: DISSECTION
The subject implies she can change her form based on median qualities from humans within a certain radius. How-

ever, a continued pattern of noncompliance with the subject will hinder progress regarding attempts to harness her internal processes. On recommendation and approval by Director Chai Hannon, plans for dissection of the subject have been moved ahead of schedule.

4.0 RE: MASSIVE RADIATION DETECTION

At approximately 1327 hours, the space rig transmitted record surges in radiation and thermal energy around Pluto akin to solar flare levels (X56 or, 4b, according to the H-alpha classification). The team manning the station (Zaphate, Rae, et al.) deemed the reported numbers to be an anomaly. While indicative of typical values closer to Solis, the sun, the anomaly is of no primary concern. Dr. Rae, however, suggested further study and has submitted an appeal (see addendum four for more details) to Director Hannon and the Prime Minister of Antarctica, Marisse Des Palma, to commandeer the Prospect Rover, currently orbiting Jupiter, to gather data.

5.1 THE JIAMU STATION OUTAGE

As of 1500 hours, ISRA Centralafrica reported loss of contact with Jiamu Station, last reported to be near 4 Vesta (Solis System | 2.36 AU AU, 0.08872, 7.141°, 103.81°, 150.728°, 95.8619°) right before passing the dark side of the asteroid. Launched in 21XX, Jiamu was the one of many generation stations within the asteroid belt mining for materials, a median-class facility ranked in the top 150 for productivity in the last audit. ISRA Centralafrica is still waiting on ping-backs from their transmission to ensure the loss of contact cannot be attributed to unexpected computer malfunctions.

I sigh, closing the internal report as the security guard scans me in. Another new face, elderly this time with eyes that have seen many years and many mistakes. We lock gazes and I try my best to smile, but the weariness wins out. Their comment slips through my ears as I take my badge with a quick thanks.

The report seems to burn my fingers, its contents a searing brand I wish I'd never read.

As I enter Site-22, monotone grey fills my vision. It should be comforting, the routine, all the schedules, but it only ratchets up the anxiety within. It has been a month since the last session, but it feels like a week. All I know is the whisper of Essence's voice in my ear, the feel of her starry skin against mine.

I push my feet forward, shaking unwanted thoughts from my head. It's like walking through molasses.

The building is a ghost town, empty spaces and endless walls where staff should have been. With ISRA's recent shortcomings following the last quarter report, they've had to downsize the less important departments. One would think a facility such as this would require more hands. Unfortunately, those at the top do not think so, least of all the Director, whose name I can't even linger on without a touch of revulsion. No news is bad news, and right now I'm alone in the husk of a plane, a numbers station broadcasting something that will reach no ears.

I pass an obnoxiously large sign with a list of still more new rules, each sentence stamped and bookended by an exclamation mark. *NEW APPEALS PROTOCOL!* is the first, soon followed by *REMEMBER YOU SIGNED AN NDA!*

Snorting, I remember signing my NDA in the good doctor's office; she was meant to be my witness, if witnessing meant sleeping off three coffee pills and several back-to-back sessions before meeting the Director. Filled with hidden threats in judicial jargon, I'd barely given the document more than a cursory glance before signing on the dotted line. What a world of difference that red ink made when the reality was an existential realization of humanity's true place in our own Solis System.

Turning the corner, I pass a slate mounted in the wall. The news crawl displays flashes of information: ISRA issued yet another statement to save their reputation, a prime ministerial scandal, the Seor family donating aid to West-Central Europe, and a whole host of messages I don't have the time to ponder. Speeding up, I briskly slide into Director Hannon's office as she and Dr. Klein are finishing a chat.

We lock gazes, and the Director's lips stretch into a thin smile. She looks haggard, and despite my apprehension, I muster a respect nod.

"Good morning, sir."

"Same to you, Mx. Oloye," she says, massaging the bridge of her nose as the doctor pats her shoulder. She waves us into the next room.

As the door shuts, I catch a glimpse of her face buried in her hands, unravelling as this whole operation is. Soon enough, there will be nothing left but Essence and a white room, staring at the remains of the humans that so arrogantly thought we could control a being we could never dream of becoming.

★ ★ ★

[DATA EXPUNGED] ISRA Audio Log Transcript
Date: July 21XX
Subject: [REDACTED]
Team Lead: Dr. Frederika L. Klein, PhD
Team Members: Chiamaka Oloye, ██████████
███████, ██████████
File: Session02_July21xx.mp4

[BEGIN LOG]
[The sterile room is padded. Metals bands line the walls beneath the blue framework, a distinct metal hum audible through the two-way mirror. Essence sits on a stool wearing a glowing collar. There are dark smears on the hem of her tunic. As the doctor enters, she pulls on a "counselor face" consisting of caring eyes and a nurturing smile. She makes her presence known, but Essence does not react]

DR. KLEIN: Hello, Essence. How are you today?

ESSENCE: Hello, Doctor Frederika Klein. I am well.

DR. KLEIN: We seem to be feeling a little down today.

ESSENCE: I'm sorry I can't be as amusing for you today. I don't have all my mental faculties in order, if you can't tell. Let's see, what was it? Zolpidem, sodium thiopental, and...oxycodone. Wasn't a fan of that last one in particular.

DR. KLEIN: Well, to be fair, you had another incident. 17-C: [DATA EXPUNGED], which put another handler, ██████████, in the biohazard wing. Half their throat is missing. They might never speak again. From what I gleaned in the medical reports, they are displaying [REDACTED] symptoms. Does that sound correct?

ESSENCE: When you put it like that, it sounds like I started it. I don't have many preferences, but ██████ ██ went places they shouldn't have. All I said was the truth.

DR. KLEIN: ██████████████ would speak to the contrary.

ESSENCE: Oh, them. They'll be perfect soon enough.

DR. KLEIN: I'm not here to indulge your cryptic whims, Essence. Let's talk about your goals—

ESSENCE: And here comes counsellor Klein.

DR. KLEIN: Long-term and short-term. It's been three months already, but we've to discuss *what* you want.

ESSENCE: I don't want.

DR. KLEIN: You understand what I mean—I know you do. There is reason you let us take you in. You knew this would happen, so, why?

ESSENCE: I can't really see much right now. A bit out of the loop with this collar.

DR. KLEIN: I'll clue you in then... Recently there was an energy surge that matched the signature retrieved from your scans. My superiors are quite interested in understanding this anomaly.

ESSENCE: *Understanding*? Or controlling?

DR. KLEIN: I cannot speak to what they think. I'm only here to speak to you.

ESSENCE: What would you like to speak about, then?

DR. KLEIN: Essence, you need to understand that you have very few chances left to prove to the Federation that you aren't a threat to Earth.

ESSENCE: Anything that isn't *you* is a threat to Earth.

DR. KLEIN: I apologize. That's not what I meant.

ESSENCE: I thought we weren't going to lie to each other.

DR. KLEIN: Okay... Nonhuman, extra-solar, Subject 0000-A—all these things to us, to humanity, are *alien*. We can't understand why you look, act, and seemingly think like us. It's both terrifying and frustrating. Just when the Mouria Colony is beginning, you fall like a star and destroy everything we know. ISRA's future projects hang in the balance.

ESSENCE: I'm not an alien.

DR. KLEIN: You're not human, ergo: alien.

ESSENCE: You used to call your fellow humans aliens too. Does that make us the same?

DR. KLEIN: It's been 400 years, Essence. We don't do that anymore.

ESSENCE: But you used to. It was all semantics. Smaller and smaller portions until you tore yourselves apart and the All had to save the One.

DR. KLEIN: What?

ESSENCE: Please leave.

DR. KLEIN: Essence, I—

ESSENCE: I'm done here.

[END LOG]
SESSION DURATION: 02:17:33:65

The slate is an anchor in my hands as I stare through the mirror. The room is darkened, a reflection my only company.

But I know she's there; we're divided only by a thin sheet of glass. By routine, I pass my slate to Dr. Klein as she places documents into the coloured folders set out for her. The brightness does little to lighten the weight across my shoulders.

Questions run through my mind, and, much to my shame, they're accompanied by a longing I don't care to press into. Even collared and shackled by unseen fetters within a cage of white walls, Essence is a beast, ravaging through our expectations and concerns.

With a gulp, I force myself away from the technician's console. Standing by the doctor's side, we work silently, but I'm dying to speak. Luckily, Dr. Klein is a saint. But it's not what I want to hear.

"Chi, I don't know what more I can do for her." She sighs, rubbing the heel of her palm to her eye and raising her glasses in the process. Her eyes are red-rimmed. "I don't know if I ever could—ISRA… ISRA was always planning on the dissection. Director Hannon just approved the request."

Gulping, I continue labelling the session recording. Unfeeling hands squeeze my throat, holding the words hostage.

The doctor continues, hands raking through her curly mane as papers scatter across the table. "I am nowhere near equipped to handle any of this, you know. My schedule just happened to be free, and I just— I'm so sorry for putting you this situation, Chi."

Shaky hands clip together a series of papers, the words indecipherable to me. A headache pounds behind my right eye like a hammer to the brain. I look up to see the doctor pull herself together, just barely. She looks almost as much of a mess as the Director. The smile she sends me is weak, mine even more so.

We leave, folders in hand. The room is a gaping maw as we abandon the realities of our monthly work. The Director accepts my file with a nod and turns to Dr. Klein.

I stand in their shadow, eyes squinted from the growing migraine. I clutch my cheek, and my eyes slam shut with a groan. When I open them, the pain steals away my vision, quick as a fox. Then, when my sight returns, I find myself in the dark, and weightless again.

Fear burns me. Finding my balance, I reach out with both hands. It's dim as I spin, looking for the Director, for her office, for Dr. Klein. Instead, I find a pale figure. They stand hunched with their back to me, a statue. A wave of hair falls across a shoulder, skin reflecting the cosmic expanse.

"Essence?" I venture.

The statue moves. Essence raises a shoulder and turns her head to the side, revealing a profile formed of smooth lines. Through her hair, fractal eyes meet mine.

I lean forward, my hands twitching to reach out. "Essence… w-what *are* you?"

She hums, tapping her lip in a jerky-looking movement. "I am the Erote."

That is all she offers, a sliver of the larger picture my mind is too small to understand. Even the name strikes something primitive inside. When she's so close, it's easy to forget that Essence is not like me. *Alien*, my mind supplies. The uncanniness in her form only draws me closer—close enough that she can reach out to touch. Before I know it, I'm there and she's here.

She runs a hand down the side of my face in a familiar gesture. I hold my breath, eyes falling shut as warmth passes over my lips. It's there and it's gone, the hand receding.

Opening my eyes, I find Essence sitting. Not *on* the stool, but rather *in* as if they are both one and the same, a kind of thing formed of ephemeral parts. All I can do is blink. I cannot trust what I see in this place that is not a place, both real and unreal. The image shifts, bursting into many fractal pieces.

Then Essence peers intently with those searching, shifting eyes. She caresses my bottom lip. Her fingers feel like warm plastic, and she smells like sterile gloves. Both sensations I'd run from, but I can't help but lean into her hand, eyes fluttering. A smile forms on her face.

I clutch her wrist as the words spill unbidden. "They're going to kill you, Essence. They're going to dissect you, like an animal."

A strange expression crosses her face. Cocking her head, Essence examines me with eyes like diamond. "All of you will do finely," she says, the flatness of her voice in contrast with the touches over my face.

I don't understand. Somehow, I don't think I need to. Everything evaporates when Essence leans in and presses her lips to mine. Kissing her is like drowning in a winter lake, the entire universe bursting in my mouth. It's both hot and cold, the birth of a star and the death of a galaxy. When it's over, it feels like it never ended, the Essence of a sensation creeping across my skin.

My eyes snap open. Dr. Klein shakes my shoulder, concerned.

"Chi, what's wrong?"

She and the Director stare at me questioningly. Shock and confusion war within me. I hear my name again, but it's distant as if through layers of water.

"Nothing. It's fine," I shrug off her touch. Stars burst along my lips. "I'm fine."

Access ISRA Email? One (1) new message!
  ID: carryon_CarrIon2077
  PASSWORD: ★★★★★★★★★★★★★★

To: ISRA Secretarial Committee [ALL], Site-22 Leadership [Level 6 Clearance], Frederika L. Klein
Bcc: Omnia Enum
From: Chai Hannon
Subject: CASE FILE: Subject 0000-A, Status Update

To whom it may concern,

As many of you know, we've recently added an addendum to Subject 0000-A's case file. The full report will be available within the next week, but, as upper clearance leadership, I wanted to reach out to you with further details, as well as my thoughts on the case going forward.

So, to begin, I have detailed the addendum below in its entirety. Please direct any further questions regarding treatments and precise medical information to ███████ █████, the head handler for Site-22.

> **Addendum Five:** Subject 0000-A has regressed in terms of social interaction. She no longer speaks and does not react to daily IV drips, even with the inhibitor collar (see addendum three). The subject seems to have

dropped all pretence of imitating human sensibilities. According to facility staff, the subject has not moved from the provided stool in three days. Medical staff is on standby in case the above actions can be construed as self-depreciating.

[THE REST OF THIS EMAIL HAS BEEN REDACTED FOR CONFIDENTIALITY PURPOSES! TO ACCESS THE FULL FILE PLEASE CONTACT ▮▮▮▮▮▮▮▮ WITH PERTINENT CLEARANCE]

I swipe up my slate as I pretend to be focused enough to care what information my feed shows me. With my head to the floor and my legs draped across the back of the couch, I feel like a lethargic octopus. Once in a while, my tentacles reach out to the now empty bowl of chips. It's summer break, and as an eternally lonely teenager, I consider these precious hours in the evening to be the highlight of my day.

My mind veers over to the things I'd much rather be doing. Like sleeping. Or working.

Idle fingers run across my lips, brown face heating in a way I never thought it could. *Never mind* I wince, blinking away those wayward thoughts.

Sighing, I return to my endless scrolling sessions, interrupted by occasional laugh—or at least, deeply amused exhale—that someone manages to draw out.

Before my eyes can glaze over, there is a thump as my mother stumbles into the room. I drop my slate as he teeters to the side for a moment, holding a slate up to his ear with eyes so wide I can see some green in the brown. Mother's coiled hair is tied back with a vibrant scarf, and he wears a loose apron with an archaic print on it—something about kissing a cook. But it's vintage, so I'm not too sure.

"Chi?" he says, covering the bottom of the slate. "It's Dr. Klein. She says it's about your next work session. Says it's urgent?" He hands me the phone and folds his arms with a concerned look.

The doctor rarely contacts her interns' homes. Sitting up, I take the phone and wave him off. I *did* sign an NDA. As a semi-broke senior, I'd rather not have ISRA's lawyers breathing down my neck. Although, considering the public sentiment, I might get lucky.

The tilt of my mouth falls as common sense returns—I'm never that lucky. A deeper frown wedges itself on my face as I pick up on what Dr. Klein is saying. I bring the slate closer to my ear as she's speaking so low, almost a whisper.

Her voice is harried, a little rough as if she's been crying—or screaming. "Chi? Chi! If you can hear me, listen very closely. You need to get to the facility *now*. Essence is gone."

"Gone? What does that mean?" It's like I can't think anymore, her words in one ear and out the other.

"Exactly what I said!" I can hear the exasperation, imagining the doctor ripping at her curls. "Gone! Gone as in no longer in her cell. Gone as in, *we can't track her.*"

I'm frozen where I sit. Someone—something is breathing. My ears must be fooling me.

The slate slips slightly in my grasp as I force my body to bend to my will. Turning, I see her before I realize she's here.

Essence kneels across the couch from me. She is bare, the universe glittering across her naked body. Ivory flowers like gemstones cover her modesty, thin vines snaking across her legs and arms, the white stark against her skin. A sheaf of hair hides half her face, tips brushing her bare collarbones.

Our eyes meet, and I'm screaming before I know it. But no noise escapes beneath Essence's hand over my mouth. She moved before I blinked. Or perhaps, she'd always been right there in front of me. Around her, I can't tell whether my mind is melting, or if she changes reality as she moves, twisting perception with a lazy flick of the wrist.

"Put the slate down, Chi."

Her melodious voice commands my whims, and, with a nod, I follow. The distant screams of Dr. Klein reach my ears as she recognizes Essence's voice. Her calls for security are drowned out by rushing blood as Essence trails her hand down my cheek.

Entranced, I see nothing but her. The fractals in her eyes spin, a whirlpool of shimmering facets in my vision.

The cool touch of a single finger lifts my chin. Kneeling at my feet, Essence cocks her head and flashes a crooked smile. So lost, I barely register when she gently guides my hand down. Her lips are parted, constellations across them both. The finger at my chin slides up to my lower lip, tapping it several times until she snatches back my attention from an ephemeral trance with a word.

"Choose."

I blink at her, vision sharpening. "Wait, what?"

"Choose," she insists, gesturing down with her head.

She guides my eyes down to where my hand is wrapped around the handle of crystalline knife. The knife hovers right over her heart. Made of pale geode, the weapon is sharper than a bite. The flowers on the handle curl beneath my hand. Essence's grasp is steadfast around my wrist. She doesn't waver, and neither do I.

"You can kill me and end all this. Or—" her gaze flickers up "—convince ISRA to cease its limitless expansion."

Outside the fractal space between us, I hear muffled speaking and marching feet. Stern voices command with ease alongside a woman's worried cries.

"Choose." Essence whispers into my ear. I can't. My eyes squeeze shut. A sob escapes. Breath seems hard to come by. Even without my sight, her fractal eyes dance in my vision. I shake my head, tremors wracking the rest of me. My fingers fall loose.

"Oh honey," she drawls, imitating human vernacular with a condescending drip to each strangely stressed syllable. In that moment, Essence is the most alien she's ever been. "You *poor* human thing. You're perfect."

Then she kisses me, cool like mint, and I shatter.

The fractals disappear. The door slams open. The cell is empty.

A contingent of security storms in with weapons at the ready. Dr. Klein pushes past them and rushes toward me, looking more out of sorts than she ever has. In a fit, she drops to her knees and shakes me.

"Where is Essence, Chi?" she asks. "Where is she?"

I have no answers for her. Rather, I look to my hands, the doctor's eyes following me.

There in my outstretched palm lies a single white flower. The tendrils reach for something, someone. But she isn't here. Not anymore.

★ ★ ★

BY ORDER OF INTERIM DIRECTOR KENDREA LONGINE-WEN

The following memo is classified. Unauthorized access is forbidden under the Geneva Convention of 20XX.

INTERNATIONAL SPACE RESEARCH AGENCY SITE-22

[DATA EXPUNGED] THE ESSENCE INCIDENT

[1] For more information about the loss of Subject 0000-A, please submit an appeal to ▮▮▮▮▮▮▮▮▮▮▮. Note that Clearance Level 6 is required to access the redacted files.

[2] See INTERNAL REPORT #17741 for updated guidelines regarding extra-solar entities.

[3] See INTERNAL REPORT #17738 for detailed transcriptions of the findings from the Prospect transmission.

I shut the internal report and look up, releasing a lengthy breath. The security guard is familiar, tired eyes scanning my new badge. *Chiamaka "Chi" Oloye—age 19*, the glossy surface reads. Beside it my image stares stoically, lips curved up into a smile that flickers in my eyes.

Today I begin a new internship under Director Longine-Wen as an assistant in the Prospect program. We've been to space many times, but for the first time, humanity is shipping out beyond the asteroid belt, reaching for the edge of the Solis System.

The guard hands me badge and I pass through the metal detector. The facility feels indifferent, grey walls looming on either side as I tread a beaten path through the halls. Around the corner, past glowing exit signs and updated directories.

When I arrive at the Director's office, I pass the wooden door without a look back. I no longer belong in that secret room, its contents a memory I constantly try to press into a void.

My heart jackhammers. Tugging my shirt above my heart, I will my feet through the mud of my mind. All that I am teeters on the edge of collapse. Realization is a cold slap that bears tender intentions.

I liked an alien. One day, I might even admit the truth that lurks deeper: that I may just have loved her.

A heady mist creeps into my head, the sensation akin to drifting on salt water. The whisper of her voice fills me to the brim. *I made a choice.* They are her words, but my thoughts. *Now I must live with that choice.*

Phantom touches caress my shoulders and neck, tender hands that bely a violence, a viciousness. Faint lips press to mine. It's only by the grace of the walls that I don't dissolve into a puddle.

She—or we—speaks again. *Don't worry.* A restless-sounding sigh. *I won't be gone for long, so wait for us. I'll be here for You.*

Cracking my eyes open, I notice an untouched wetness on my cheeks. I uncurl my fist to toy with the medical bracelet that now sits in my grasp. Red stains obscure the name scribbled across the tacky plastic.

Sitting there, memories in hand, I wonder if I ever really had a choice at all.

★ ★ ★ ★ ★

NOBODY CARES WHO WE KISS AT THE END OF THE WORLD

Leah Johnson

I NEVER HAD A FAMILY UNTIL COOP CAME along.

Blood relatives, sure, but blood doesn't make family. Love does. Which is why when everything fell apart, and Coop was all I had left in the world—all that was left in the world, full stop—I couldn't even be mad. Confused as hell, maybe, but I wasn't mad.

We got a paradise, and that paradise was ours. We ruled it with all love and no shame. We were finally in a place where it felt like girls like us could live forever.

"Shit shit shit shit," I whispered, as my life—as cliché as it sounds—flashed behind my eyelids.

The miniature axe whipped past my head and hit the board behind me with a heavy thunk. I felt the brief gust of wind as it soared through the air and narrowly missed my face. I stood with my arms and legs spread wide, more still than I'd ever been in my life. I didn't dare open my eyes until I heard three more axes land their targets: one between my spread knees, another on the other side of my head, and one right above my puff.

"You can open 'em now." I heard the smile in Coop's voice even before I saw her face. Her nose was practically against mine when I finally regained enough fine motor functions to look at her. She was smirking. "I thought you said you weren't afraid of anything."

I pulled back and rolled my eyes. She could be so smug. "Yeah, well, you try having your life on the line, just so your person can get their daily dose of kicks and giggles."

Coop had adopted plenty of talents in the time since we'd been marooned on our island of two. She took up knitting in the sixth month after finding a generous yarn supply and a *Knitting for Dummies* book in what used to be Mrs. Henderson's house.

In month eight, Coop started speed skating when she discovered a pair of neon-green roller blades in what used to be Maddie Aaronson from theater's closet, which had since become our costume room. But the axe throwing? The axe throwing is where I should have drawn the line.

"I don't know why I indulge this stuff. There's no reason for you to become an Olympic-level axe thrower when there is A) no Olympics anymore and B) no one around to even know you can do it."

I marched back into the house, and could hear Coop's heavy tread behind me. I wasn't really mad, but I was jittery in a way I couldn't name (and I had the sudden urge to go

pee, which I would never admit was related to residual fear).
I knew Coop would never do anything to intentionally hurt
me—I mean, I'd put my life in her hands, long before the
day came where her hands were all that were left—but still.
My brain struggled to reconcile what I knew with what I
was feeling.

"Kel, wait." Coop wrapped a hand around my wrist and
tugged me to her. I allowed my head to flop forward against
her shoulder as she wrapped her arms around me. We had the
whole world at our disposal, and there was no place I loved
more than right there. Tucked against her, eyes closed, just
the two of us. I felt her voice rumble through her chest. "You
know I wouldn't have put you up there if I thought there was
even the slightest chance that you'd get hurt. I've been practicing that move for a year."

I nodded. I did know that. I watched her in the backyard
for months on end, practicing with bottles she'd scrounged
from the old recycling plant and teddy bears she lifted from
the neighbors'. I knew that past anything, what she really
wanted was to find a way to loop me into this hobby that had
given her such a thrill—to find a way to make me a part of
it, as opposed to just a spectator. She hadn't even had to beg
me to participate; I'd practically volunteered. I wanted to be
with her as long as she wanted me to be there.

But standing against that wooden board we'd built together last year—laughing and swearing in equal measure as
we battled splinters and my personal ineptness when it comes
to tools—my only thought was about the fragility of it all.
That one slip, one mistake, and this life we were building
together would be over.

Since the day I met Coop, I knew my feelings were too big, almost unmanageable. I'd known since the first time we kissed that my world had shifted on its axis and would never be set to rights, but I didn't quite understand it until an she planted an axe squarely above my head.

I'd dreamed of this, the two of us, tucked away from all the things that could hurt us. But I forgot that we still had the ability to hurt each other. I shook my head and took a step back. "Before, when you said that I wasn't afraid of anything, that wasn't true."

"Yeah?" She placed both hands on my cheeks and cocked her head to the side with a goofy grin. "What are you afraid of?"

"I'm afraid of the way your breath smells in the morning. I'm afraid of Hyper Cooper after she drinks four cans of Red Bull in an hour. I'm afraid of—"

I giggled as she cut me off by tickling me. I was laughing so hard my stomach hurt, doubled over as Coop's hands danced across my ribs. It was sweet. It was simple. And it was so much easier than telling her the truth.

That nothing scared me more than not getting our forever.

Unlike me, Coop was raised by people who deserved her. Her mom and dad were the perfect TV parents: a preschool teacher and an accountant who attended PFLAG meetings after Cooper came out, who marched next to her in Chicago Pride every summer, and invited me over for dinner the day me and Coop decided to make it official. They smiled, and every time they kissed each other, they did it like it might be the last time. We didn't know, of course, that one night it would be.

The morning everything fell apart, I woke up the morning the way I always did. My eyes were red and puffy from crying myself to sleep the night before. My mother had spent most of the evening with a Bible in her hands, reminding me that she thought I was an abomination. That she thought I'd earned the pits of hell if I didn't turn from my wicked ways. Every evening, she spewed the same barrage of righteous rage. And every evening, she'd end it the same way:

"You and that girl deserve whatever comes to you."

The school had contacted her the first time Coop and I were harassed at school. We weren't even together yet. I was halfway through my sophomore year, and Coop halfway through her junior.

We'd been friends for months, but it wasn't until we got too close together in the hallway one day, sharing some stupid inside joke, that the taunts started. The whispers of names I can't repeat even in memory echoed through the halls. Our rural school had never been progressive, but I'd never known it to be that hateful.

We got good at being us only in private. In Coop's bedroom after school, in stolen moments behind school buildings, and in my hand-me-down car around the corner from my house. The two of us, isolated in our little world—protected by our privacy. With Coop, I was safe, but only so long as no one else permeated our bubble.

So when I sat up that morning and was met with silence instead of my mother's voice on the phone with yet another support group for parents of sinful children, or the rush of water from my detached older sister's shower, or the loudness of my younger brother's Saturday morning gaming marathon, I was relieved.

I was grateful that for a moment, I could pretend it was like that all the time. That I lived alone, or maybe that Coop lived with me like we would in college one day, and she was just in the kitchen making breakfast. It wasn't until I heard the frantic knocking on the front door that the illusion fell apart.

Coop stood there, her face red and tear-streaked. She hiccupped out the status of our new world: the neighborhood was empty. Everyone was gone. The phones didn't work, and neither did the electricity or the water. We were the only two left.

She collapsed into my chest, sobbing. I rubbed my hands up and down her back, and tried to pinpoint what that meant for me. I didn't think about the why of it all—about whether or not a God I didn't even believe in had heard my prayers, or if we were the last survivors of the apocalypse. All I thought about was Coop. That I could finally love her outside of the chains of shame and silence that we'd been bound up in for so long.

All I thought about was how goddamn happy we could be.

For the first few weeks, Coop cried more often than not. We moved our stuff out of our houses and into the old Gustafsen bungalow a mile away, since it was big without being cloying, and close to the lake without feeling opportunistic. It was too painful for either of us to be trapped in the shell of where we'd come from. Cooper couldn't stand the ghosts of her mother's perfume and her father's booming laugh that lingered in the air of her family's home. I had never felt much at home in the place I was raised in to begin with. The end of the world was a new beginning for the both of us.

The days she didn't spend grieving, she spent searching. She drove further and further, canvassing nearby neighborhoods and towns and cities in search of somebody, anybody else. She read science fiction literature, spent hours combing the stacks at the university library in the city, trying to find an answer. But every night she'd return home sullen and empty-handed. The silence would be almost suffocating.

Gone was the girl who'd taught me to play paintball and hold chopsticks and how to tie my shoes one-handed. We were all each other had left in the world, and I understood enough to know why that meant something different for me than it did her. Why she'd want to keep looking for answers, and I'd be perfectly content to accept the gift I'd been given.

For six months, I tried to be whatever she needed me to be. Funny when she wanted a pick-me-up, quiet when all she could stand was to be alone. And then one day, after a canvassing mission, she came home and sat down on the couch, so close to me our knees touched. I didn't want to admit what a thrill it was, after having not even hugged since that first morning at the door.

"I think I'm going to quit," she said, rubbing a hand over her knee. "This is it now. Just you and me."

I nodded. I didn't want to say the wrong thing, or scare her away. The same way I was all she had left, she was all I had left, too. And even if all I got to keep of her was a half self, hollowed out by grief, then I'd do my damnedest to do it.

She looked up at me, and it was like we were seeing each other for the first time in months. She tried to smile, but it was still weak. A faint reminder of the bright, goofy girl I'd met in AP Chem what felt like a lifetime ago. She wrapped her hand around mine and squeezed.

"Forever and always?" she asked.

"Forever and always."

"What do you mean, it was written on the walls? There's nobody around to write on the walls but us," I said. I wiped my hands on my dirty gardening jeans and stood up so I could look her directly in the eye. "You're losing it."

I didn't like arguing with Coop. It was the thing I hated the most, actually, after having to boil water over a fire in order to drink it and pooping in a bucket so we could use it for compost now that we grew our own food. There was no adjusting to the idea that I was eating something made possible by my own shit, to be honest.

But these moments were worse than anything else. We shouldn't have been fighting like a married couple at eighteen and nineteen. Coop should have been off at that dreamy little Seven Sisters school on the East Coast she'd wanted to attend so badly, drinking too much and protesting on the weekends. I should have been getting ready to don my CLASS OF 2028 stole at graduation, and biding my time until I could make it out of our hometown forever.

Instead, here we were, going at it again for the fourth time in four days, about something ridiculous. My chest was tight with the tension of it all.

She'd come back so excited, she'd run through the house and into the yard, smiling and waving her hand in my face to emphasize her point. And the second I could make out what she was saying, I knew I couldn't do it. What she was asking of me was too much.

"I'm not losing it, Kel. You're not hearing me. I'm telling you, I walked into the old high school to see if there were any supplies left in the cafeteria we could use, and someone had painted this on the white wall."

She held a hand out with a series of letters and numbers written across her palm, but I couldn't make sense of it. All I could see was that white bulletin board that stretched the length of the far wall in our old cafeteria-cum-gymnasium on the day after Joey Clayton saw me and Coop kissing behind the auditorium. All I could see was the black paint dripping down over the talent show sign-up sheet and the Earth Club callout posters and the prom ticket notices that said: GOD HATES QUEERS.

The way my mother smiled when she found out, gleeful in my misery. The way the principal said there was nothing they could do, that there was no proof. The way everyone looked at us, a mixture of fascination and disgust on their faces, anytime we so much as walked down a sidewalk. My world was so small then, so limited by those people and their hatred.

I didn't want those memories anymore. And I didn't have to keep them. Not here. Not with us. "I told you, I don't like you going back there."

I walked into the house shaking my head. Coop stumbled after me, graceless in her attempt to catch up. She's always so sure until there's unstable ground between us. I didn't know how to tell her that the only thing that mattered to me was this, here, with the two of us. I didn't want us to go back to the high school, or to my mother's church, or any of the places that told us to be ashamed of who we were.

I'd never known a space where it was safe to be in love with another girl. I'd never been around people who didn't recoil at the sight of the two of us together. We were safe here. Now. I didn't need the hovercrafts and the teleportation that I'd been taught the future promised. This was enough for me.

"They're coordinates, don't you get it? Someone was here, in town, and they left a message. There are other people still out there!" Coop ran her hands through her curly brown hair, tugging a bit at the roots. "We have to go after them. We have to find them."

"I don't have to find anybody." I marched into the bedroom. We'd redecorated so much of the house in the past year that I could barely see traces of the Gustafsens anymore. I liked it that way, swiping the paintbrush of us over everything and everybody in this place. "You don't either. After those first few months, don't you remember how much you were hurting? Why would you want to go on a wild goose chase like that again?"

We had built something here that wasn't what either of us had envisioned, but it was a life. We woke up in the mornings and made breakfast together. We read in opposite corners of the room in the afternoons, Coop lazing on the chaise longue under the front window and me curled up in the ottoman against the wall. She foraged for canned goods in the old grocery store, and I made meals with the findings. We danced to songs we made up, and swam in the lake under the moonlight.

It was more than I ever thought we'd have. It wasn't easy, sure. Some days, Coop was withdrawn and quietly angry. Other days, I was indignant and snarky. We argued over what to eat and who should clean and which member of One Direction we'd thought was the best when we were in elementary school. We'd go to our separate corners of the house. We'd pout for a few hours, sometimes days. But we'd always make our way back to each other. Always.

"I know you don't—I know this isn't as important to you as it is to me, okay? I get that. But don't you understand why I need to?"

"No, I really don't." I laughed, even though nothing about this was remotely funny. "What do we need other people for?"

Coop leaned against the wall, her eyes on the carpeted floor. I took the seconds of her silence to really look at her. She was stronger now than she used to be, her wiry arms gone muscular from the heavy lifting of life without modern conveniences. Her hair was a lighter shade of brown, thanks to the summer sun and the amount of time we spent outside. Her skin was brighter from the abundance of greens and the organic sugars we ate.

She was so beautiful it made me want to cry.

"Because this isn't a life, Kel," she whispered. "We're just two kids playing house."

She looked up, her eyes soft and watery.

"And I need more than that."

When she walked out the door, I didn't cry. I wouldn't allow myself the release that tears would bring. I sank down on the bed, which was too big for two people, but would be almost obnoxiously large for one. I thought about the nights that I heard Coop in the bathroom crying, sure she'd left me in bed sleeping. For a long time, I'd wanted so badly to be everything Cooper needed: a friend, a partner, a fan. I wanted to fill all the gaps in her left by our world disappearing.

But as hard as I tried, it was never going to be enough. Not for someone like Cooper. Not for someone who'd dreamed of world travels, and a beautiful future with a big family gathered around a Christmas tree at her parents' house. If I couldn't be that for her, and if I loved her, then I owed her the chance to find out if any of that would be possible.

When she came back a few hours later, I was already in bed. The moon was high in the sky, the most reliable marker of time we had most days since the clocks started dying and we hadn't bothered to replace the batteries. I could hear Coop toe off her shoes by the door, and the thud of her clothes hitting the floor. The drawers opened and shut, and then, the soft swoosh of her putting her pajamas on. I didn't turn to face her as she wrapped an arm around my waist.

"You know I love you," she whispered into the darkness after a moment. "More than I've ever loved anything. But I can't stay here, not if I think there's still civilization out there somewhere."

I swallowed hard around the lump in my throat. "I know. I…" Hate it. Would never do this to you. Will love you with everything I have until there's nothing left. "I understand."

Her breath tickled the back of my neck, warm and familiar. "I'm asking you to come with me, Kel. Please. Don't make me do this alone."

"But you've made up your mind." I felt the tears coming

now, even though I'd known this would be the outcome. Like Coop, I'd made my decision as well. "You promised me. Forever and always. But you're going, with or without me."

The room was silent for too long. She pulled me even tighter against her and kissed the back of my head but didn't answer. She didn't have to.

I knew it was a goodbye.

The next morning, I knew she was gone before I opened my eyes. When I finally worked up the courage to turn over, there was a simple note. Coop had written the coordinates on a piece of the Gustafsens' fancy stationery and left it on her pillow.

Come find me. I'll always be waiting for you.
Forever yours,
Cooper

I didn't leave bed for a week.

There was no getting my life back after Cooper left. Moments of brief reprieve felt unfair, like I was forgetting everything we'd had together. Moments of grief felt self-indulgent, as if I hadn't chosen this path for myself.

Every day, I weighed the consequences of staying against those of finding Cooper. If I stayed here, I would be doomed to a lifetime of loneliness, of emptiness created in the absence of the love of my life. If I chased after her, and found myself back in a community, I would be opening myself up to the same abuse and prejudice I'd known before. The only thing that had ever felt safe to me was being partitioned from the fray, but I'd also always had Cooper right there next to me. Even when I'd felt lonely, I'd never been alone, not really.

In the end, it wasn't much of a decision.

Three months after she left, I pulled out the paper maps we'd stored in the kitchen cabinets. I found a dusty compass in the Myerses' basement a street over. I packed the most important things I owned: a copy of *Emma* that my mother had given me in middle school, before I'd become her greatest shame. The photo strip of Cooper and me at the winter carnival three years prior, the only pictures we'd ever gotten printed of the two of us together. And, the necklace Coop found on one of her scavenging missions, onyx wrapped in gold wire that she said reminded her of me.

I packaged up enough vegetables from the garden to get me through a few days, and some canned goods to get me through when those ran out. I found the keys to the Bradleys' old solar-powered minivan, and stored the reserve power panels in the back seat.

And I went to go find my person.

The trip took days. I misread the latitude and longitude for one of the coordinates, and ended up three hours in the wrong direction. I had to stop to steal the reserve solar panels out of the trunk of an abandoned Kia somewhere in Ohio and shot the entire engine when I connected them incorrectly. One of the tires busted on a bridge in West Virginia, and I had to pull out the manual to learn how to change into a spare.

Too exhausted to drive another hour, I tried to sleep in

a random shotgun house one night, but it felt like ghosts of the former residents were around every corner. So I grabbed my bag and slept in the bedding section of a former Target.

All the while, my gut clenched in anticipation. What if Coop wasn't there at all? What if she no longer wanted me to join her? What if this new place was somehow worse than the community we'd been raised in? What if Coop had found someone else to be for her what I used to be? I feared the truth as much as I yearned for a happy ending.

My destination was somewhere in Pennsylvania, I knew, near what used to be Pittsburgh. I drove through the state, past the dense forests that lined the highways, through the long, unlit mountainside tunnels, dreading what I would find once I arrived, but determined not to turn back.

I reached a tree line before I hit the spot the map told me was my target. The sun was easing its way down the sky, not quite evening but certainly past noon, so I decided to take my chances on foot. I walked through a wooded area for nearly an hour before I could see through to the other side. There, across a surprisingly well-kept field, was a huge ivy-covered building, surrounded by a wrought iron gate.

It looked like a college campus, but smaller. Like a boarding school, maybe. My heart pounded so loud, I could barely hear the voice that crackled from the speaker above me.

"State your name and your business."

I jumped.

Despite how far I'd come to find this place, and how confident Coop had been about the fact that there must have been humanity out there somewhere, up until I heard that voice, I still had my doubts. I nearly gasped at the reality. She and I had never been alone, at least not in the way I'd always thought. The disappearance of everyone we knew wasn't as clean-cut as a wish I'd made in the darkness, terrified and alone, for peace. For a life free from fear.

"I'm Kelendria Anderson. My…friend found these coordinates a few months ago. And um, she came to seek shelter. I'm hoping to find her."

The lies tasted bitter on my tongue.

We had shelter, I thought. We had everything.

I tried to silence the voice in my head that kept clinging to the old way. I tried to remind myself that this was the only way to see Coop again. That us being together in any way was better than to not be together at all.

The speaker crackled again. "Who's your friend?"

It felt strange to search for Cooper's birth name. I hadn't used it in so long.

"Allison Cooper."

The gates clicked open without another word. Then, when I stepped through, they immediately eased shut behind me. It seemed ominous, the depth of the security, along with the long stone walk that led to the building.

I didn't see anyone around, and my instinct was to brace for danger. I thought about how fast I could run if a potential threat rushed me. I tried to remember the two tae kwon do classes I took in the sixth grade, just for good measure.

But none of that was necessary. Because once I got close to the door, I could see her. My love.

Coop wore a pair of overalls that I didn't recognize, and her hair was shorter than when she left: shaved around the back and long on top. But her smile. Her smile was the brightest

I'd seen in years as she ran towards me, with her arms thrown wide. I fell back into the grass from the impact, and didn't even think before tucking my face into the space between her neck and shoulder and crying. I was so happy. So blissfully, unbelievably happy that I almost forgot the concession I'd made coming here.

Someone coughed above us.

"Miss Cooper, I'm sure this isn't the most effective introduction, hmm?"

Coop laughed and scrambled off of me. She held a hand out to help me up, and squeezed harder than necessary when I was back on my feet. Her expression shifted from glee to confusion when I pulled away to put my hand in my pocket. Better not begin this by slipping up any more than we already had, I figured. The last thing I wanted to do was ruin the life Coop had created here by inciting some type of homophobic outrage in my first five minutes.

"Marta, this is Kel." She gestured at me, eyes alight with something close to relief. "She's my—"

"Hi." I extended my hand, cutting off whatever Coop was planning on saying. I didn't want to hear her call me a friend, or worse, just someone she used to know. I tried to remember what manners I had, before I lived apart from other humans for nearly two years. "Thank you for having me."

A bald white man in a black T-shirt emerged and held a hand out, gesturing for my bag. I was so thrown by the sight of another human—two other humans—I didn't even think before handing it over to him.

The woman, Marta, had a severe look about her. Jet-black hair cut into a bob that perfectly framed her jaw. White teeth so straight they seemed sharp. Pale green eyes like something out of a movie. I knew instantly that she was in charge of things around here.

"Any friend of Miss Cooper's is a friend of ours." She shook my hand with a firm grip before turning to walk back towards the building. "I'm Marta Harrison. Please, allow me to show you around."

Coop fell into step beside me and mouthed, *Are you okay?* But I just offered a pinched smile and a nod in return. I was so happy to see her, to be in her presence again, but I wanted to stay vigilant until I had a better lay of the land. Until I knew what kind of people she had fallen into community with.

The hallways of the building looked much warmer than the exterior suggested. It's clear that this was, at one point, the type of elite boarding school that no one from our town could have afforded to attend, but there was a warmth to it. Walls painted in rich oranges and yellows, hardwood floors covered in rugs and textiles. Whoever lived here now had done the work to make it feel like home.

"Miss Cooper tells me you're quite the gardener," Marta said. She pushed open a set of doors to reveal a greenhouse, bigger than anything I could have dreamed up while shoveling shit in our backyard for better leafy greens. "I trust we can find a place for you in our horticultural team."

"Everyone here is on a team," Coop said, smiling. "We all have different jobs to make communal living easier."

"How did you know I gardened?" I was having a hard time processing. "And how many people live here?"

"Well, Miss Cooper had quite a bit to say about you when she first arrived."

I opened my mouth and shut it immediately after. I didn't know what to say to that. I was grateful to hear Coop hadn't forgotten me entirely, but I couldn't fathom what she could have said about me, especially in front of this intense, overly formal woman. The way she spoke reminded me of my mother, a harshness in her tone I couldn't parse through. It made me want to shrink into myself.

"We have about a hundred people in our community, give or take," Marta continued, no mind to my discomfort. She led us back from the greenhouse and down another hallway. "Some people live off campus, for privacy. But we all convene here for meals and work." Marta paused in front of a huge staircase and linked her fingers together in front of herself. "We gain about two or three new residents a month, give or take. You're our first this month."

"I don't understand." I shake my head. There were even more people out there? And they all were somehow finding out about this place? "How did…"

"Miss Cooper will explain everything to you in due time, Miss Anderson. I find it can be a bit overwhelming when you first arrive." She looked at Coop and pursed her lips. "You two should make your way to Miss Anderson's room. Dinner will be served soon."

Marta's dismissal couldn't have been more clear, but Coop didn't seem fazed in the slightest. She just waved me towards the stairs and started in the direction of my room. *My* room. The distinction wasn't lost on me.

Gone were the nights of sharing a bed and giggling under the covers like the schoolgirls we'd never get to be again. There'd be no more of Coop's arms wrapped around me as we slept, holding me close as I fought through another nightmare. We were already setting the terms of this new relationship.

"I have so much to catch you up on, Kel. There's just so much going on here." She turned to me as soon as we were alone in the hallway. It looked like a typical college dorm, without all the sweaty coeds. Coop pressed her forehead against mine and sighed. "I can't believe you came. I wanted you to. Every night I hoped that..." She pulled back and smiled. "I'm just so happy you're here."

She squeezed my hand once, but didn't linger.

"Your bag is already going to be in here because Dennis is like the greatest concierge-slash-security guy you could ever hope to have. And we can go and get your car later. You drove, right? Dennis said you walked up to the gate."

Coop moved so fast it exhausted me just standing near her. I'd never seen her this lively, not even in the before times. Something about this place had changed her, made her lighter.

And then I remembered what was different: I hadn't been with her. For the first time in years, I was looking at a Cooper that hadn't been burdened with the impossible weight of my love. In this community, Coop was surrounded by people who didn't ache for her so desperately the bigness of it felt like it filled every room. When I wasn't around, Coop got to be a different, more buoyant version of herself.

The thought made me sick to my stomach. I barely spoke as Cooper described the bathroom situation, and the day-to-day schedule, and her community duties.

"I'm helping Brewster and Reggie build the stables for the

cattle they're moving on campus." She smiled wide as she added, "I get to use an axe to cut wood and everything. Great use of my talents, huh?"

I forced a smile as she walked us back downstairs to what looked like the dining hall. She grabbed my hand and laced our fingers together. For just a moment, it was like old times.

But I let go of Coop's hand when we reached the door. If this was where Coop wanted to be, if this is what it would take to make her happy, I was willing to do it. I was willing to go back to the days of eyes meeting across a classroom, but ignoring each other in the hallway. The days when I'd put her name in my phone under Robert Cooper, her brother, so my mom wouldn't know I was texting a girl when she came to snoop while I was asleep. The days of dances we couldn't share, and kisses we didn't get, and lonely nights and mornings spent wishing for a way out.

If this is what Cooper wanted, I'd give it to her. Because I loved her.

She looked down at our hands, unlaced and hanging limply at our sides. Her forehead wrinkled in that way it does when she doesn't understand something. "Kel, what—"

"Fresh meat in the building," a booming voice shouted, once the doors opened from the inside.

The security guard Coop mentioned earlier, Dennis, was on the other side, and I took a deep breath. It was probably too late. They'd already seen my fingers, laced together with Coop's, clinging to her like a life raft in a storm. They were going to cast me out before I'd even gotten unpacked.

The entire room buzzed with life—more people than I'd seen in what felt like a lifetime. People of all races, sizes; teenage girls with sweatpants on and grown men in paint-splattered T-shirts; women with hijabs and one man in a yarmulke. All of them, each and every person, paused while getting food from the table with the dishes laid out in Thanksgiving Day fashion to look at us. And then they erupted in claps.

Dennis, the doorman-concierge-security guy, patted me on the back. A woman with purple hair and a black sequined sweater kissed me on the forehead before shoving a roll in my hand. Two little girls, no older than three, wobbled up to me and wrapped their tiny arms around my legs. Person after person came to greet me, to welcome me to the fold. My head swam from the rush of it all, the surprise of such an invitation into their world.

I'd never felt like this before. I'd never been…welcomed instead of cast out, embraced instead of shunned. Not since I'd met Cooper and known without a doubt that she was the person I was meant to spend my life with. I didn't even think it was possible, really, to exist in a world populated by more than just the two of us, and not be made to feel alien in my own body.

Marta was the last person to greet us. Her severe expression from earlier softened somewhat in the face of so much affection. She reached forward and took both of our hands, and then she linked Cooper's fingers with mine. Before raising them to her lips for a soft kiss.

"You don't have to be afraid here, Miss Anderson."

It was such a simple phrase, delivered with such tenderness, I didn't know how to receive it.

"But what about— How did you— We're not even—"

Coop laughed lightly before turning to press our lips together briefly. When she pulled back, just barely, so we were still breathing the same air, I was sure she was speaking only for me to hear. A better promise than always or forever.

"Nobody cares who we kiss at the end of the world."

★ ★ ★ ★ ★

ACKNOWLEDGMENTS

All Out, *Out Now* and *Out There* have been such a special project from the beginning. *All Out* was just a seed of an idea between me and my agent. We joked (didn't dare hope!) that we would get to go to the past, present and future, but look! Here we are! What an extraordinary journey and what an extraordinary gift these anthologies have been.

There are endless people to thank. I have no doubt I'm going to miss someone important, and for that, I apologize profusely.

Thanks first go to my agent, Jim McCarthy. *All Out* was his idea, and he generously let me run with it. It spawned three beautiful queer anthologies, full of action, excitement, romance and joy, and I feel honored to be the one who got to usher them into the world.

I owe so much gratitude to the entire team at Inkyard Press: T.S. Ferguson, Natashya Wilson and Claire Stetzer—three incredibly generous editors who let go of the reins and let me run with my vision for this series. Bess Braswell, the brilliant constant; Laura Gianino and Brittany Mitchell, publicitaire and marketeer extraordinaire; and of course, Connolly Bottum for holding it all together.

So many thanks to Lisel Jane Ashlock, who illustrated these gorgeous covers, and Erin Craig, who designed them. People love to hold and look at these books, and it's all because of your gorgeous work. They're stunning, together and apart; thank you!

Very special thanks to Jayne Walters, a librarian with the Indianapolis Public Library, and an advocate for queer YA fiction—many thanks for her sensitivity reads over all three anthologies. Thanks also to Elliot Wake, who stepped in as an additional sensitivity reader for *All Out*.

Most special thanks to every single author I talked to, whispered to, slipped into their DMs, all the people who said no, and all the people who said yes. Without the contributors, there's no anthology. I want to say, with each story, I asked the authors to do one simple thing: tell the story you wish you had when you were sixteen.

Fifty authors replied with their fantasies, their adventures, their romances, their families—found and kept. Each one answered their own wish, and sent it out into the universe, to find you. To be the story you need right now. The story you want right now. That mirror. That window. That wish granted.

I thank the readers for embracing these granted wishes with their whole hearts. We're the living past, but all of you are our future. More importantly, you're our family. From us, to you…always know that you are valid, you are beautiful, and you are loved.

Thank you for being you.

ABOUT THE EDITOR

Saundra Mitchell (she/they) has been a phone psychic, a car salesperson, a denture deliverer and a layout waxer. She's dodged trains, endured basic training, and hitchhiked from Montana to California. The author of eighteen books for tweens and teens, Mitchell has written work that includes Edgar Award nominee *Shadowed Summer*, The Vespertine series, and Indiana Author Award Winner and Lambda Nominee *All the Things We Do in the Dark*, as well as the Camp Murderface series with Josh Berk. She is the editor of four anthologies: *Defy the Dark*, *All Out*, *Out Now* and *Out There*.

She always picks truth; dares are too easy.

ABOUT THE
AUTHORS

Ugochi M. Agoawike (she/they) is an undergraduate at the University of British Columbia. Born in Nigeria and raised in Canada, she is desperately trying her best. They live in the coldest part of Canada where they spend their days dreaming of writing while studying creative writing. Thanks to a memorable first-grade teacher, she loved reading as a child and has been writing most her life. As a Black queer, most of their stories are about Black queers being messy, soft, and yearning across the genres. Some of their work can be found in *Parallel Magazine* (WCHS) and *Midnight & Indigo*. In addition to watching copious amounts of YouTube, you can find them complaining about writing, life, and books on Twitter. They are also a hobbyist artist.

K. Ancrum (she/her) is the author of the award-winning thriller *The Wicker King*, a lesbian romance, *The Weight of the Stars*, and the upcoming Peter Pan thriller *Darling*. K. is a

Chicago native passionate about diversity and representation in young adult fiction. She currently writes most of her work in the lush gardens of the Chicago Art Institute.

Kalynn Bayron (she/her) is the bestselling author of *Cinderella is Dead*, *This Poison Heart*, and *This Wicked Fate*, and is a classically trained vocalist. When she's not writing, she can be found enjoying musical theater, horror novels, and classical music. She currently lives in Ithaca, New York, with her family.

Z Brewer (they/them) is the *New York Times* bestselling author of The Chronicles of Vladmir Tod series, as well as The Slayer Chronicles series, *Soulbound*, *The Cemetery Boys*, *The Blood Between Us*, *Madness*, *Into the Real*, and more short stories than they can recall, and served as the lead script writer on the upcoming video game *Grim Tranquility* for Poorly Timed Games. When not making readers cry because they killed off a character they loved, Z is an anti-bullying and mental health advocate. Plus, they have awesome hair. Z lives in Saint Louis, Missouri, with a husband person, one child person, and three furry overlords that some people refer to as "cats." You can learn more about Z at zbrewerbooks.com.

Mason Deaver (they/them) is a bestselling and award-winning young adult novelist. Their first book, *I Wish You All the Best*, was an instant bestseller, being nominated for the Goodreads Choice Award and winning Pink News' Best Young Adult Book award, as well as being named one of *Cosmopolitan*'s 100 Best YA Books! Their second novel, *The*

Ghosts We Keep, earned a starred review from *Booklist*, as well as praise from *Publisher's Weekly*. They are a contributor to several anthologies, as well as the author of the horror novella *Another Name For the Devil*. They currently live in North Carolina where they watch too many movies with their cat Rex.

Alechia Dow (she/her) is a former pastry chef and librarian. She's the author of *The Sound of Stars*, *The Kindred* and *Sweet Stakes*. When not writing, you can find her having epic dance parties with her daughter, baking, reading, or taking teeny adventures.

Z. R. Ellor (he/him) is the author of *May the Best Man Win* and the forthcoming adult fantasy *Silk Fire* (written as Zabé Ellor). He holds a BA in English lit and biology from Cornell University. When not writing, he can be found running, playing video games, and hunting the best brunch deals in Washington, DC. Find him online at zrellorbooks.com.

Leah Johnson (she/her) is an editor, educator, and author of books for young adults. Her bestselling debut YA novel, *You Should See Me in a Crown*, was a Stonewall Honor Book and the inaugural Reese's Book Club YA pick, and was named a best book of the year by Amazon, *Kirkus Reviews*, *Marie Claire*, *Publishers Weekly*, and the New York Public Library. Leah's essays and cultural criticism can be found in *Teen Vogue*, *Harper's Bazaar*, and *Cosmopolitan*, among others. Her debut middle grade novel, *Ellie Engle Saves Herself*, is forthcoming from Disney-Hyperion in 2023.

Naomi Kanakia (she/her) is the author of two contemporary young adult novels, *Enter Title Here* (Disney, 2016) and *We Are Totally Normal* (HarperTeen, 2020). Additionally, her stories have appeared or are forthcoming in *Asimov's*, *Clarkesworld*, *F&SF*, *Gulf Coast*, *The Indiana Review*, and *West Branch*, and her poetry has appeared in *Soundings East*, *The American Journal of Poetry*, and *Vallum*. She lives in San Francisco with her wife and daughter. If you want to know more, you can visit her blog at www.thewaronloneliness.com or follow her on Twitter @rahkan.

Claire Kann (she/her) is the author of *Let's Talk About Love*, *If It Makes You Happy*, and *The Marvelous*. She's also an award-winning online storyteller. In her other life she works for a nonprofit you may have heard of where she daydreams like she's paid to do it. She loves cats and is obsessed with horror media (which makes the whole being known for writing contemporary love stories a little weird, tbh).

Alex London (he/him) is the author of over twenty-five books for children, teens, and adults, including the award-winning cyberpunk duology *Proxy* and the epic fantasy trilogy *Black Wings Beating*, which was an *NBC Today Show* Pick, a We Need Diverse Books Must Read, and a 2020 Rainbow List selection. His latest middle grade series, Battle Dragons, is out now from Scholastic. He's been an overseas journalist and human rights researcher, a young adult librarian, and a snorkel salesman. He lives with his husband and daughter in Philadelphia and can be found online at www.calexander-london.com.

Jim McCarthy (he/him) is a VP and agent at Dystel, Goderich & Bourret. He lives in NYC with his husband and their rescue pup, Winston. This is his first publication, and his client, Saundra Mitchell, had wayyyyy too much fun with this.

Abdi Nazemian (he/him) is the author of four novels. His latest is *The Chandler Legacies*. His first, *The Walk-In Closet*, won the Lambda Literary Award for LGBT Debut Fiction. His novel *Like a Love Story* was awarded a Stonewall Honor. His screenwriting credits include the films *The Artist's Wife*, *The Quiet*, and *Menendez: Blood Brothers*, and the television series *Ordinary Joe*, *The Village*, and *Almost Family*. He has been an executive producer and associate producer on numerous films, including *Call Me by Your Name* and *Little Woods*. He lives in Los Angeles with his husband, two children, and their dog, Disco. You can find him on Instagram @abdaddy and at abdinazemian.com.

Emma K. Ohland (she/her) has been telling stories since before she knew how to write them down. She grew up in the middle of a cornfield in Indiana, but her imagination often carried her away to other worlds. When she's not writing, reading, or smelling books, she enjoys traveling, crocheting, and daydreaming in coffee shops. Her first novel, *Funeral Girl*, debuts in 2022. You can find her online at emmakohland.com.

Adam Sass (he/him) began writing books in Sharpie on the backs of Starbucks pastry bags. (He's sorry it distracted him from making your latte.) His award-winning debut, *Surrender*

You Sons, was featured in *Teen Vogue* and *Savage Lovecast* and named a best book of the year by *Kirkus Reviews*. *The 99 Boyfriends of Micah Summers* is his forthcoming novel from Viking. He lives in Los Angeles with his husband and dachshunds.

Mato J. Steger (he/they) is an openly out and proud Trans, Queer, and Anishinaabe and Cherokee (North American Indigenous) fantasy and sci-fi writer. In 2020, Mato had a short story accepted and published by Cloaked Press, LLC, in their Fall into Fantasy 2020 anthology. In 2017, two of his short stories were accepted into a horror anthology by Infinite Darkness that was a bestseller on Amazon in its first week of release. He has had several articles published with *HuffPost*'s Queer Voices on sexuality and toxic masculinity. You can find him online at fantasyandcoffee.com.

Nita Tyndall (they/them) is the author of *Who I Was with Her*, and is a passionate queer advocate and literary translator who writes the kinds of books they needed in high school. Their translations from the German have appeared in *World Literature Today*, and they have previously written for outlets like *Autostraddle* and were part of the Lambda Literary Writer's Retreat in 2017. They live in North Carolina with their partner and a beautifully fluffy cat.